MONIKA CARLESS

THE
RAVEN
&
THE
ASPEN KING

BOOK 2 OF THE DARK POOL TRILOGY

STONE'S THROW
PUBLICATIONS

Copyright © 2017 Monika Carless

ALL RIGHTS RESERVED. No part of this publication may be reproduced, stored in a retrieval system, or transmitted in any form or by any process – electronic, mechanical, photocopying, recording, or otherwise – without the prior written permission of the copyright owners and Piquant Press. The scanning, uploading and distribution of this via the internet or any other means without the permission of the publisher is illegal and punishable by law. Please purchase only authorized electronic editions, and do not participate in or encourage electronic piracy of copyrighted materials. Your support of the author's rights is appreciated.

Cover design by Sue Reynolds, Stone's Throw Publication Services
Cover images: bigstockphoto.com
Interior Layout and Design: James Dewar

ISBN-13: 978-1-987813-16-6 (book)
ISBN-13: 978-1-987813-17-3 (e-book)

Published by Stone's Throw Publications
Port Perry, Ontario, Canada
www.stonesthrowps.ca

1 2 3 4 5 6 7 8 9 10

THE RAVEN AND THE ASPEN KING

"I love you as certain dark things are to be loved,
in secret, between the shadow and the soul."
~ Pablo Neruda

Dedication

For my beloved, Steve.
Your love is the space where my creativity is nourished.

Acknowledgements

On my journey to completing book two of the *Dark Pool Trilogy*, I have met many wondrous souls who have given of their time and love.

Sue and James at Stone's Throw Publications, thank you for your advice and guidance, including the incomprehensible task of self-publishing details that I simply do not have the skill for. Sue, your cover design skills continue to inspire me. I am honored to have your work grace mine.

To my daughters Elizabeth and Jessika - thank you for sharing your island with me. It is home.

To all the readers and brilliant writers I have met along the way, thank you for your love and reviews, this story belongs to you.

Thank you Lois Person, for your expert editing and support of this project. I adore you.

Steve, you have listened, read, edited, held me up in good moments and when I doubted myself. Without your heart at my service, this story could not have emerged.

Lay Yourself Upon My Altar

Lay yourself upon my altar.

Leave your garments and your modesty scattered shamelessly on the floor.

I have made a fire from Oak and Rowan, it will warm you with its glow.

I've prepared my oils and potions, there is nothing for you to fear. Say you're willing, say *I surrender.*

Say the words I've taught you to say.

Let me roam you like a lioness, let me prowl with intent—you, my sun drenched, luxurious savanna...oh my love, I am hungry. I can taste the measure of your soul.

They have told you to be wary, that I'm wicked, that my ways are dark and lead to sin. And yet you stood willing at my doorstep, pride in hand, lust like coal-fire spilling from your raven eyes.

I've allowed you things that I allow no other—to touch my magic, my witch's tools. You've been free to inspect my jars of herbs and roots and dragon's blood. You've heard my chanting, you're danced by my fire; you have watched me consult the moon and the stars. You have kept me safe from the others, and for this, my love, I owe you my life.

So won't you lie here on my altar, watch me comb the braid from my hair, watch me loosen the ties of my bodice, allow me pour you a cup of honey wine.

Don't you worry, you must know this...

I am wicked but I'm kind.
I am solitary but I'm not alone.
I am heaven but I'm hell-fire.
I am flesh and blood and young; but forever is in my bones.

I am nothing that you should play with if you wish to remain unchanged.

For the forest has been my mother.
The sea has been my cradle.
The wolves have been my brothers.
The wind has been my guide.
Venus has been my mistress.
Fire has been my solace.
Magic has been my home.

I've seen peace and I've seen war, I've been run down, I've been burned, I've been saint and mother and whore, and now I'm the goddess who wants her reward.

So while the fire burns brightly, while mid-day turns to dusk, while our supper rises fragrant, let me taste your lips on mine.

Darling you are ever my faithful warrior, the man whose spoken word I trust, the one who never questions the voices that guide my mystic's life. You may not understand my journeys to the Underworld, nor the incantations that fuel my spells, but I'll let you into my most sacred space, because you're a man with a clear and honest heart.

So drink from the well of my intuition. Sip from the chalice that is more precious than gold.

Be the sacrifice to my womanhood, on my altar, by my fire.

Now my hair is spilling wild and my skin is soft with oils, now my breasts are at your fingertips, now my legs are weak with desire.

You, so brutal when you protect me, are now so vulnerable stretched out on my sheets; on my altar, by my fire, muscle and strength, are mine to own.

Touch me with the hands that feed me, touch me anywhere you like, take my screams, my dreams—my longings.

I will be your Jezebel.

Monika Carless

Original Publication
@ http://www.elephantjournal.com/2016/01/lay-yourself-upon-my-altar/

Foreword

Writing the sequel to the first book in The Dark Pool Trilogy, opened me fully to the channeling experience through "Aiden"; a spirit guide who continues to inspire me, act as my muse, and offer insights into a mystical world that I am now very comfortable in.

So many of my readers have come to know and love Aiden's wisdom. My longing to share about the authentic life has evolved into Aiden being available to others. I now channel messages via tarot readings and meditation for a wider audience.

The Dark Pool Trilogy opened a portal into another universe, which I share with joy. Anyone wishing to connect with "Aiden" the channeled energy, can do so by contacting me via my web-site:

https://simplysolitary.wordpress.com/

PROLOGUE

The Dark Pool denied a reflection and showed little of its depths. Dagr sat in contemplation guarding the edges, waiting. He had asked his question, but the divinatory body of water, intrinsically secretive, withheld an audible answer. The reason for its silence lay under a tumbledown tree at its northernmost edge.

Dagr waited until he could wait no more, then stood to his full height.

Tall and powerfully built, he gathered his sword and threw his cloak around his shoulders. It wasn't for him to question the Pool's reluctance. Indeed, he trusted in the wisdom of silence. Turning his face towards the wind, he found his way carefully around the bank.

But what was this? Dagr stopped, hand tightening around his sword and stared at what looked like a pile of dirty garments on the damp forest floor. He nudged the pile gently; breath suspended. A young woman with bloodied and matted hair lay sleeping, curled in against the cold.

Without hesitation, he bent on one knee to collect her, and carried her to a clearing in the Oracle Wood. Once there, he made a roaring fire by the rushing stream and discarded her soiled apparel. His eyes misted at the sight of her bruises. Gently, he washed her. She moaned in her sleep, every part of her seeming to ache.

Dagr's longing stirred as he held her close to offer his body heat. Even in this broken state she was beautiful to his eye, this woman he had thought lost to him for good.

Taking up his cloak, he wrapped her in its warmth and the scent that he hoped she'd find comforting. Dagr whistled softly, calling his horse out of the shadow of the trees. He laid the maiden across the broad back of his steed, and mounting in one swift move, shifted her to lean against the protection of his chest.

He had his answer, of this he was sure. It was the time of the waxing moon, time for him to work magic and rebuild his family.

CHAPTER 1

One day, she remembered
That she was part of the wilderness outside her door
That she was raw and pulsating with life
The huntress who understood the sounds of the forest
And the call of her untamed nature
One day, she let go of what she was supposed to do
And stripped her clothes to run naked and unashamed with the wind
– a Wise Woman embracing her Sacred gifts
And when they asked her – "Who do you think you are?"
She replied, eyes burning bright...
We shall be Witches and Sex Goddesses
We have remembered our Light
And never again will it be wrong to be a Woman
Never again will you throw us into the Fire

"Are you sure we've everything we need?" Sahara checked the shopping basket, trailing alongside Aiden at the food market.

"I'm sure. Except for the champagne."

"Oooh, to celebrate the finish of my book? You'll have to choose, though. I'm no expert."

Aiden laughed. Sahara was all woman; with glimpses of her younger self exposed here and there. It was an intoxicating mix for a man like himself who delighted in her unique brand of sensuality. She let him take care of her when it pleased her. It was a subtle game that they both enjoyed.

He paid and they stepped out into the crisp autumn sunshine to drop the groceries in his truck.

"People are staring at us," Sahara observed, taking his hand.

He squeezed her hand tightly, and gave her a wink. "Have you any idea how much I love you, woman?"

"You're changing the subject. And no," she grinned at him.

"You *are* the subject. I care very much about what you think and very little about what others think. And if you don't know how much I love you, I'd be willing to show you in any number of ways." Aiden's sinful lips curved into a suggestive smile.

"You're no gentleman, Aiden Halloran," Sahara replied, a familiar tingle gathering where his mouth had been just hours before.

1

"That may be true," he countered, lips pressed to her ear. "But no lady does what you did last night on your knees, so throw your stones lightly, my love."

He picked out a case of wine that he said was Holly's favourite at the liquor store, and a bottle of ridiculously expensive Italian champagne. Sahara balked at the total displayed on the cash register.

"Aiden," she began in protest. He ignored her and handed his credit card to the checkout girl.

"Looks like you're celebrating something," the girl surmised. She looked hopefully to the two of them for a clue but neither of them gave one. Aiden handed the champagne to Sahara and picked up the case of wine.

"We'll be just in time to fetch Holly," he said, winking.

Sahara smiled. He was having fun playing the rogue, and it was the furthest she had seen Aiden act out of character. Usually, he would have guarded anything about his private life with a vengeance. He was a fool in love, as was she.

They caught sight of Holly walking towards them, her smile brilliant; golden hair in a messy knot adorned with a length of bead studded ribbon. She wore a loose shift of a dress cut mid-thigh, a woollen sweater tied haphazardly over it; on her feet, a pair of classic high heeled pumps.

"Holy Mother of God! Aiden...I've not seen Holly in heels before. Those legs..."

Aiden growled in response. "I know. I don't think she's aware of the picture she presents. She's completely unaffected. I love that about her."

They met in the middle of the sidewalk, exchanging kisses as if they were standing on a Paris street, a trio of close friends outbound to an adventure. Except that in Riverbend, women didn't kiss each other on the lips.

Aiden gave them a dubious look as they both piled into the back seat of the truck. This was not looking respectable at all. That was it then. They were out of the polyamorous closet with a flourish.

He thought it best, in any case. A clean declaration was easier than trying to hide the fact that he loved them both. And Holly wouldn't have to come out on her own. They were in it together, for better or worse.

CHAPTER 2

Aiden glanced in the rear view mirror as he parked in front of his house and felt his cock stir. They appeared to barely remember that he was there. He'd never seen anything as beautiful as the two of them in an embrace, their kisses sweet but insistent, their soft moans and love words mere whispers to his ears. He hoped to hell that he wouldn't wake up from this most impossible dream, because he could hardly believe that they were his to love and cherish.

"Hey," Holly said, breaking away from Sahara's lips. "What's the surprise you have planned for tomorrow?"

"You're going to have to be cleverer than that to get it out of me. Distracting me with your womanly wiles won't do it either. Tomorrow will tell."

They pouted at him as he held the door open for them. The house would be chilly. He'd light a fire right away.

"Why don't we start supper and then go for a walk?" he suggested. "Do you have anything to change into Holly? I don't think you'll make it through the forest in those shoes, charming as they are."

She leaned in to hug him. "How very naughty of me to wear these…" She slipped his hand along her leg, under her dress.

Sahara bit her lip as Aiden glanced her way. Holly was inexperienced by number of lovers, but she knew how to play temptress very well.

There wasn't any reason for Aiden to not pull Holly in for a kiss. She let him into her mouth with a moan, Aiden tempering his rough lust with a tender nip at her ear. Her hands dug into his arms.

"You'll pay the price if you're going to tease me, little girl," Aiden whispered, and slapped her bottom smartly.

"Ooh, I've missed you Aiden," Holly said, hugging him close.

"I'm all yours." He closed his eyes, hands gripping her hair, her scent soft on his nose. He was already as hard as he could get, and there was no way that she wouldn't be able feel it.

"And Sahara's," Holly reminded, rubbing herself against him like a cat that's missed her master.

"Yes," he agreed. "Although the two of you might kill me with pleasure."

He went out to get more firewood, and to escape the overwhelming feelings that gathered hot in his heart.

"I don't think I can wait any longer," Holly said to Sahara, kicking off her shoes.

"Would it be better if you had the night to yourselves? I truly wouldn't be hurt if you said yes. I've had my time alone with him."

"No! I want the first time to include you." Holly opened her bag and began to change into jeans and a sweater. "I'm still kinda scared; you know how possessed he can look. Having you here will give me courage."

"I don't have the willpower to turn you down Holly, although, you'll see; Aiden is a most considerate lover...unless you give him permission to do otherwise." The memory of herself in Iona's bed with Richard flashed across her face too swiftly for Holly to notice.

"You love me, don't you?" Holly took Sahara in her arms.

"You've no idea. I hope I can be the partner you need me to be. If I ever hurt you..."

"Hey! You could never hurt me. I *know* that. Don't worry, sweetie. Even if you did hurt me, which you won't, I would forgive you straight away. I wouldn't want anything between us."

"Oh Holly." Sahara wiped at her eyes. "You just don't know that. Relationships, especially one like ours, are complicated. It's naïve to think that we won't hit any snags."

"Don't say that Sahara. I know I'm young and that I've only had one other lover, but I'm strong, and I know what I feel. I'd never let anything come between us. And nothing will. You'll see."

Aiden came through the door, arms full of firewood. He looked at Sahara with alarm.

"Tears, my love? What's wrong?" Holly waved her hand at him and smiled reassuringly.

"Nothing to worry about. It's just girl stuff."

He brushed past them pretending to be appeased by Holly's words, giving them each a little kiss on the cheek. But he knew that Sahara's tears were founded on some fear that had surfaced.

"Cheer up, both of you. I've not spent a small fortune on champagne to have it spoiled by tears. We've got a few things to celebrate."

"A few?" Sahara queried.

"I'll tell more at supper. Will there be supper?"

"Ok," Holly laughed. "We'll start supper, you make the fire. But I hope I won't have to work without a glass of wine on offer?"

"I apologize," Aiden put the wood down and went out to the truck to get the wine.

Sahara giggled. "He bought a whole case just for you."

"He won't need that much. I'm pretty much ready for him right now."

<hr />

It was so easy to be light of heart with the forest enveloping them in the late afternoon sun, rich in moist autumn scents. Although Holly was impervious to the company of Pan as he trod alongside of them, she was keenly aware of the presence of tiny wood spirits. They appeared as flashes of phosphorescence, disappearing around bends in the path.

She ran ahead for a while, chasing them, basking in the magic woven by the Aspen King. These were his woods, and he knew a kindred spirit when he saw one. Too bad she wasn't awake to his whispers. But then, he had time.

Aiden and Sahara walked as one; their ability to hear each other's thoughts stronger here.

Sahara, do you think that Holly would be attractive to the fey spirits here?

I'm sure of it. They love folk like her, innocent of heart, sweet natured, open spirited to their pull. She's a natural for magical work.

Aiden looked to Pan, who shook his head at him. *You know that things must fall as they will,* Pan said. *It's her life to make what she wants of it. You can give her tools for dealing with the spirit world, but you can't keep her from living her destiny.*

"You always give me double-edged answers. I'm never sure whether you're on my side or not," Aiden said out loud.

I'm on your side. Always have been, like Dagr. We've been friends for too long for you to doubt me now.

You mention Dagr. Am I ready to walk the path of knowing my previously incarnated self?

"You're ready. Trust in yourself. That's the key to living without fear. Without trust in your own abilities, your truth, your path, you'll make mistakes that will cost you. No doubt you'll need courage. Notice the raven up high; our tenacious companion." Pan pointed up at a dark smudge in the sky. "She is well loved by the Fairy King, and he has granted her powers only given to a disciplined magician. But her love for you is blinding. She cannot always make the wisest decisions.

5

I'm at your side, but can't fight the fight for you. You will find a way to make her love less dark. And when you do, she will be free as well. You'll all be free.

Aiden shuddered. He reached for Sahara. She stood on tiptoe and kissed his lips.

"I have magic too, Aiden. All shall be well. But tonight is not the night to think too deeply. Tonight we celebrate our love." She looked into his eyes, which were scanning the trees for sight of Holly. "If you hang on too tight, she'll disappear. Shall I give you a vision to cheer your heart?"

He nodded, troubled.

Sahara put her hands over his eyes and blew her breath softly under them, sending an image to his third eye. He caught his breath as the picture unfolded before him. His face beamed into a smile. He grasped Sahara's hands and kissed them.

"Truly, Sahara? You wouldn't tease me about this? It would be cruel."

"No my love, I would not. This you shall have, you can be sure. I have seen it enough times to know it for truth."

He picked her up and swung her around, their laughter filling the forest, the wood nymphs dancing in a circle around them.

Aiden meant to call to Holly, he wanted her by his side, but she was already ahead, hand on the door to his house. He laughed as she darted inside, sending a kiss on the wind to them. She felt like spring, as much as Sahara felt like autumn. And he needed them both desperately.

When they reached the house Holly was already changed back into her dress. It hung on her seductively, in a smooth, loose wave; accentuating the round of her breasts, free of an undergarment. Her nipples poked the silky fabric, legs crossed over each other as she sat swinging on a stool next the kitchen island. Aiden's hand tightened over Sahara's. She returned the squeeze. He knew that Sahara was delighted for him. This was a dream that he had harboured patiently and with great resolve. And Holly was making the wait extremely gratifying.

"May I wear my shoes in the house, Aiden, or would you prefer them off?" Holly asked, teasing.

"On," he instructed, his voice betraying his desire.

She offered to pour him some wine.

Sahara took the wine Holly poured for her as well, and opened to a kiss. She was grateful for the pleasure that Aiden would receive at

6

Holly's hand. Sahara loved the man that he was, and she trusted him to Holly with every fibre of her body and soul. There was no jealousy here, no regrets. Only the desire to bring Aiden everything he deserved during this lifetime.

The women worked together in the kitchen, while Aiden arranged the music and lit some candles. The scenario felt very familiar to him, watching them move about. He must have been staring, because Sahara, in tune with his emotions, stopped what she was doing and sent him a message of support.

Breathe.

He smiled as he received her thought. It was true; he had trouble believing that this moment was real. Surely, it was too perfect to last?

"How about some food?" Sahara pointed to the plate of appetizers. "I'm starving after all that fresh air."

Aiden agreed that they should eat. "Shall we save the champagne for later, or shall we celebrate Sahara's book now?"

"Later!" The women said in unison and laughed.

"It's still early. We have lots of time and I'm already half drunk," Sahara admitted.

"You can't be! You've had exactly three sips of wine," Aiden joked.

"I'm telling you, I'm so not good at this," she replied.

"You're good at everything else," Holly proposed. Eyes open, they fell into an easy embrace, glasses of wine in one hand, the other in a caress along each other's back.

"If no one minds, I'm going to shower and change. I won't be long." Aiden added to the already roaring fire. "I have time, don't I, before dinner?"

He needed to be alone. He'd had this house to himself for so long; and now their energy made his pulse race...love was a heady elixir.

"Take all the time you need, my love," Sahara said.

⁎

———————•✿•———————

They sat by the comforting warmth of the fire. Each was lost in her own thoughts; Holly tightly coiled anticipating Aiden's touch and Sahara eager to see the man she adored make love to Holly for the first time. There wouldn't be any secrecy, no accusations about cheating or betrayal. Their love was open and welcome.

Holly slipped off the sofa and knelt before Sahara.

"I want to make certain that you're not going to be angry about what happens between Aiden and I tonight. My heart would break if you didn't want me after this. I just need to know for sure."

Sahara brought Holly's hand to her heart.

"Holly. I want this, and also to know that I can be myself, without fear. It's rare to find two people who love like you and Aiden do. You're both so pure of heart; it is I who hopes the two of you won't tire of me. Whatever happens tonight, it'll be more than I could have hoped for.

Holly laid her head in Sahara's lap. "I feel so safe with the two of you. I'm walking into this with eyes wide open. I want everything that you and Aiden have for me. I just don't want to mess this up. In my wildest dreams, I couldn't have imagined a better love than this."

Sahara ran her fingers through Holly's hair. "There's no love better than this."

"I'm going upstairs," Holly stood. "I want to give Aiden a little tease before dinner."

She lifted her dress a little to reveal the soft pleasure between her legs.

Sahara moaned. "You're teasing *me*." Her fingers trailed lightly along Holly's leg. "Go!"

Aiden stood leaning with his hands against the shower wall, his head under the water, arranging his thoughts. He wanted to be sensitive to them both, to give them everything they needed. He thought about the length of rope he'd bought recently. Sensing a movement behind him, he turned, and drew his breath in; Holly was standing outside the shower door, her face in a coquettish smile. She blew him a kiss.

He sent one back, his fingers to the glass, amused now, aware that she had come to tease him. He found it terribly endearing. He loved the wild side that percolated just underneath the surface of her innocence.

Holly stood in obvious admiration of his appearance. He was a large man, but not overwhelmingly so. Maybe it was because he was so slim of waist, so long muscled, and meticulously groomed, that his size wasn't overpowering. She loved the way his wet hair hugged his shoulders, the sexy curve of his toned arms, the way his cock stood at half mast, waiting for permission to rise for her. The only thing that made her shudder was the look that crossed his face. She was sure that if he wanted to, he could break her.

He stared ravenously at the tips of her breasts poking their way shamelessly through her dress. Holly let her hands travel along her body, pulling her dress with it, exposing her blond mound closely cropped, her tight belly, and over her silken breasts.

His eyes travelled her scenery, cock now standing at attention. Her eyes fell to it, suggesting he take hold of it. His hand moved obediently.

Aiden raised one eyebrow in question, wondering if she would stay, but she turned away, her dress falling languidly over her sumptuous bottom.

If he had had any doubts before this, they were all gone. She wanted it as much as he did, and he couldn't wait to do all the things he had whispered about in her ear.

Holly came downstairs and found Sahara with eyes closed, resting.

"Help me," Holly whispered. She positioned herself on the edge of the sofa, legs spread, graceful fingers draped along her inner thigh. She let her head drop back...anticipation.

Sahara knelt before her, and let her tongue fall softly on Holly's swollen clit, then pursed her lips to grasp it. It took seconds. Sahara knew exactly how to extract the release Holly was craving, resisting the urge to enter her with tongue or fingers. She wanted Aiden to have the first thrust.

By the time Aiden came downstairs, looking devilishly handsome in jeans and a slim cut shirt, they were sitting under the stairs with books in hand.

"I'm opening the champagne. Is there room for me here, or shall we move to the kitchen?"

"We'll make room," Sahara stood and moved over to Holly's chair. "We can share this seat, you sit there."

They heard him pop the cork and fill the champagne flutes. He returned with them slung through his fingers.

"Shall we toast Sahara's book first?" He knelt by their chair. "You must have written days and nights to finish it this quickly. I expected another month or so before you were done."

"It was many a wakeful night, that's for sure, but I do love the process. Once I'm in the groove, it's difficult to *not* write."

They lifted their glasses. Sahara didn't need to explain her passion for writing to them; it was as integral to her as breathing, and they understood.

Aiden turned to Holly, encouraged by the feeling of warmth sweeping over him.

"Sahara and I have something we'd like to offer you, as a token of our love. It comes with absolutely no strings, it's simply to say that we adore you...a selfish offer really."

"What is it Aiden, tell me!"

"We'd like to pay off your operating debt..." He held up his hand. Holly was shaking her head left to right. "As silent partners of course. We'd never dream of interfering with your café. Holly, please stop shaking your head. It's simply so that we can see you more often. You said yourself how tight your budget is."

"No! I don't know when I could pay it back and I'd work even harder to see that I did. No, your kindness is too generous, I won't accept." She stood abruptly, upsetting Sahara from her seat.

Aiden looked to Sahara in frustration. "You explain it!"

Sahara opened her mouth to say something but he jumped back in, voice rough and impatient.

"To pay back? Holly! We don't want it back, it's our way of saying that we're in it together. You've worked so hard."

"But if you get tired of me...then I'll have this thing hanging over my head, and it will spoil everything."

"Tire of you?" Aiden roared. "What do you think I'm playing at here? You're not my latest conquest. I'm planning a lifetime with you. I want you to be able to count on me. The money, however much it is, is not going to make one bit of difference to me, but you...Christ, Holly!"

Holly turned to Sahara, who was glaring at Aiden.

"Sit down Aiden. You're turning into a bear," Sahara ordered.

He sat, and gulped down the rest of his champagne.

"Holly," Sahara began. "Think of it as an investment on our part. In *you*...not the café. We love you, and can see that you're struggling to have any kind of a life outside of your business. If it makes you feel better, you can pay us a dividend at year end."

Aiden's eyes flashed fury. He didn't want a dividend. Sahara waved her hand to keep him from interrupting.

"So you see, we're being selfish really, because we'd like to have you to ourselves more. It can't be that much anyway...how much is it?"

Holly blushed. She looked shyly at Aiden, who was struggling to keep his manners.

"It's thirty thousand dollars." She stared at the floor, her face on fire.

"THIRTY THOUSAND DOLLARS!" Aiden shouted, jumping up.

10

Holly burst into tears.

"Do you mean to tell me that you will thwart my love for a mere thirty thousand dollars?"

Holly fell sobbing into Sahara's arms. Aiden meant to say more but seeing her so thoroughly distraught suddenly brought him back to his senses. Swearing under his breath, he took her to the sofa.

"I'm sorry," he whispered, his mouth searching for hers. "I'm an idiot, Holly. Please forgive me. That was terribly insensitive." He held her tight; she was trembling...hugging into his chest, her lips opening to his kiss.

"You scared me Aiden."

He nodded, remorseful. "I wasn't expecting you to deny our offer. I lost my manners. Will you forgive me?"

"Yes." She kissed his eyes, her face soft with the passing storm. "I'm sorry as well. I don't want to be in debt to the ones I love. It hurts when..." She dropped her eyes and fidgeted with her hands.

"What is it? Tell me."

"It's the occasional call from my mother. She's angry that I moved away, I told you before, remember? She thinks that she's wasted her money on my dreams. And I've never invited her out. It's my own fault I guess."

Aiden held Holly tight; her heart was pounding fast enough for him to feel it. Every ancient instinct screamed that he was her protector, her provider, but he knew that he had to ignore that, and respect her independence.

"Your dream, my love, is a worthwhile endeavor," he finally said. "You're a success; a hardworking, undeniable success. What Sahara and I offered you is a token of our belief in you. The money is not, and never will be, something that will come between us." He looked over to where Sahara was standing by the fire. "It's not the money that we need. It's you."

"We can talk about this another time, Holly," Sahara offered. "It probably wasn't the best evening to bring it up."

"No. It was. I was just taken by surprise. It's a generous, loving offer." Holly stood.

Aiden couldn't help but notice the bounce of her breasts as she moved to the fire to hug Sahara, or that Sahara had noticed it also. His passion began to wake once more.

"I accept!" Holly announced triumphantly. "I accept with much gratitude. Oh God, I need an apprentice to help me, and this will be the only way I can manage hiring one."

Aiden let out a whoop of joy and bounded towards her, calling for more champagne, which Sahara gladly provided. They toasted to the continued success of the café, and all the time they would have to nurture their love.

"By the way, what's the other surprise?" Sahara asked, laughing as Holly's energy warmed to their attention.

"I don't want to say now, considering how badly I messed up the last thing," Aiden confessed.

"I promise I'll be good this time," Holly teased.

"Ok, because it has the potential for a similar reaction."

"No, really, I'll be good. Do tell, Aiden."

Sahara noticed the slight rise of his cock. She laughed out loud at him; Aiden was so easily taunted by Holly's words.

"Ok. Follow me."

Holly looked at Sahara, who shrugged her shoulders.

He led them to the small hallway beside the fireplace. He stood for a moment in hesitation, then swung the door open to a softly lit room.

"I hope you don't mind, I bought you a bed." Aiden took Holly's hand, and pulled her in to reveal an antique four post monster.

Sahara's knees gave in as she recalled Iona's bed, this one almost identical to it. The bruises on her wrists and ankles were gone now, but not her memory of being tied to those massive oak posts.

"A bed! Oh Aiden, what a spectacular bed! Where did you get it?"

"At an antiques store in Denver. It's from France, I had it authenticated."

Sahara tried to figure out when he'd been in Denver. Surely, there hadn't been any time while he'd been on the new house build. She felt weak, and held on to the frame of the door. Aiden kept his back to her, but she saw his hand clench in response to her frantic energy.

"I promised you your own space, and here it is. Look...through the garden doors, you have access to the front porch, and the hammock. We'll bring some of your things so you can make this room just as you like it. Tell me, have I presumed too much?" He took her hands, and kissed them.

Holly shook her head. "It's so very thoughtful of you."

Aiden held his hand out to Sahara.

She came to his side, searching his eyes. But all that she saw there was a deep calm. She could ask him later about the bed and Denver. Such synchronicity begged exploring. "There isn't any champagne left," she observed. "What shall we toast with now?"

"Open more wine, sweet thing."

Aiden was relieved that there weren't any more tears. He was aroused by an image of Holly in the bed, her slender wrists secured tightly to the posts. And he could see that she was having similar thoughts, her hands unconsciously covering her breasts. She blushed deeply as she caught his eye follow her instinct to pull on her nipples. He slipped one hand under her dress. She parted her legs, her head to his chest once more, the need for his fingers making her suddenly shy.

"You'll allow me to make it up to you, Holly? My ill manners?"

"You'll allow me to make up for doubting your generosity? I'll take my punishment if you take yours."

He growled in her ear, pleased with her train of thought.

Sahara called them to dinner, her own clit throbbing when she saw them come to the table, barely able to look at each other.

Aiden pushed his dinner around, eating very little, his hand tight on his glass of wine. Evening had fallen and the house adjusted to the warm laughter of the two women, who, sure that all was now well between them, ate with gusto, hardly noticing the tension settling on their lover's shoulders. He got up a few times to bring them more food, and it wasn't until they asked him if he wasn't hungry that he put down his wine and announced that he had a confession to make.

They turned towards him, Holly picking up her wine, taking a sip for courage.

"There's no way to say this but to just come right out with it. Holly," he took her hand across the table.

She sat silently, watching his struggle to come clean.

"I own the café building. I'm your landlord."

Silence fell between them, covering them like a blanket.

"What? No you're not! Claire told me that it's some guy from somewhere near Boulder."

Aiden watched Holly as she worked out the details in her head. He offered a weak smile.

"I *am* the guy from somewhere near Boulder...originally. I bought the building as an investment, I needed somewhere to put my money, and it was too good a price to pass up. I asked Claire not to tell you, because, well, you can probably figure out why."

"But, so... I've been paying my rent to you all this time? Why didn't you just tell me?"

"Because, Holly, I was crazy about you and thought that if you knew you'd feel weird about dating your landlord. And I just never found an appropriate time to tell you."

Sahara shook her head and got up from the table.

Aiden looked to her for support. She stood behind him and ran her hands through his hair. He relaxed with her touch, feeling the warmth of her hands on his shoulders. Aiden was sure that his need to be honest had ruined the evening for much else. He sighed as he saw Holly exchange glances with Sahara.

Suddenly, Holly was laughing. She stood up and came over to him, her hands on his face, her kisses sweet.

"Can you please tell me what is so damned funny?" Aiden couldn't decide if he should be relieved or irritated.

"Aiden, all this time, when I've been asking Claire to call 'that landlord of mine' to ask him why in heaven's name he wasn't cashing my rent cheques, and sending him frustrated messages telling him that he needed to get his act together and get to the bank because he was messing up my accounting...she was calling you?"

He nodded, a smile beginning to play on his lips.

"I've saved almost all of it. All the rent money, except what it takes to run the building. He paused, sure now that he had lost his mind to continue on in this vein. "I had an idea..."

Sahara and Holly groaned in unison.

"No more ideas, Aiden, for the love of God!" Sahara exclaimed. "I thought you were planning on an evening of debauchery?"

He laughed heartily. "No, no, you'll see, it's good."

"Ok, one last idea, Aiden," Holly conceded. "But that's it!"

"This is the best idea I've had so far, I promise. I thought of renovating Claire's back office into a seating area with comfy chairs and a fireplace to expand the café. We've got lots of rent money to work with." He laughed at the delighted looks on their faces. Finally, something he'd said that didn't end in disaster.

"But what about Claire?" Holly asked, her hands clasped to her chest, eyes sparkling with possibilities.

"I've already spoken to her about moving her office to the antique store. She's all for it." He looked so pleased with himself Holly simply couldn't be angry.

"Oh you have, have you? That's a lot of going behind my back and planning my future. How very bold of you, Mr. Halloran."

He took her in his arms. "Are you very, very mad at me my love?

I know I've taken so many liberties of late. Does my idea for the café make you happy?"

"I suppose you'd have no way of knowing that it was my dream when I first saw the space. I just thought it would take me years to get there. But you'll have to allow me to draft some kind of a business plan with you. I'll be more comfortable that way."

"May I say something?" Sahara interrupted. "Could I please, please help you design the space, Holly?"

"Of course, yes, I'd love that. Maybe a trip to Denver together?" Holly clapped her hands.

Sahara and Aiden dared not look at each other, but both knew what the other was thinking. Holly and Denver could turn out to be a troublesome combination, and they should be careful of the circumstances surrounding a trip there. Still, the word 'Denver' brought with it a certain dark energy that exploded between the two of them.

Danger proved to be a powerful aphrodisiac. Aiden's powerful hands wound themselves around Holly's waist. Her expression changed from surprise to wide eyed pleasure as he lifted her on top of the kitchen island and slowly pushed up the hem of her dress to reveal her stunning, youthful beauty. She gasped as he lowered his face to her inner thigh.

"I'm sorry, Holly, I'm incapable of waiting any longer." He pushed her down and spread her wider, his face grazing closer to her clit, breath hot against her skin.

She moved her hips, giving him permission to please her, eyes locked on Sahara. "Kiss me," she whispered, one hand reaching down to part herself more.

Sahara gave Aiden a slight nod of her head, and their lips met Holly simultaneously.

She cried out, Sahara's kisses deep and forceful, Aiden's tongue as delicate as butterfly's wings on her inner thigh. Holly pushed against Aiden, as he continued to hover over her, his hair teasing along her leg. But no matter how much Holly strained to have him engage his mouth with her clit, he only continued to tease her and speak decidedly wicked words.

He picked her up and carried her up the stairs to his bed. He laid her down in the downy softness of his duvet, and taking a firm hold of his belt, yanked it out of his jeans.

She stared, alarmed. He laughed, and threw the belt to the side.

She could see his cock straining. She reached for it, but he pulled back, and turned her over. He covered her with his body, his kisses soft on her neck, her back, her bottom.

He was drunk on the softness of her skin, his lips etching the road of discovery towards her sex.

"May I?" Aiden asked as he nudged against her. She could only moan her reply. She felt his hands on her, spreading her open, his tongue hot against her, licking from her clit to her bud.

"Damn, Holly, you're delicious," he murmured. Where in God's name had Sahara disappeared to?

He saw her from the corner of his eye, emerging from his closet with the rope he had been meaning to find. He shook his head to clear it; slipping into a memory. He stood up and took the rope from Sahara, pulling it through his hands.

"For you, my love?" His words came softly but his energy leapt from him like a violent storm.

Sahara nodded, trembling, backing up towards the top of his bed. He bound her tightly, and fastened the rope to the headboard. He ripped her jeans off, and slid her shirt up, just over her breasts. How he loved those small upturned beauties, and the impertinent length of her nipples. He opened her, a madman intent on ravaging his conquest, exposing her slick cunt with deft fingers.

Holly observed the insatiable lust between them. She could come just watching their interaction. They were in complete tune with each other's needs, Aiden stunningly possessed. Passion brought out the best in him. She let her hand fall to her clit as Aiden leaned over Sahara and pulled her nipples into his mouth. A moan escaped, as her clit jumped beneath her touch.

He was rough, Sahara cried out and tried to push him away with her legs, but he pinned her down with his knee. His hand slapped smartly at Sahara's dripping slit, her skin in a pink blush.

"Put your fingers in my mouth," Aiden instructed Holly, watching her fingers dip in. "Now!"

She complied. He sucked the scent and wet off her fingers, then, unable to stop himself...he bit down.

Holly took a measured moment, adjusting to the sting of his bite, then, lifting her hand, she slapped his face. Hard.

Aiden sat back, surprise and Holly's hand print on his face. Holly, suddenly frightened shrank back.

Sahara uttered an unexpected "Oh!" She hadn't seen *that* coming.

"I'm afraid you're going to have to pay for that, my sweet," Aiden pulled Holly near, blood coursing hot in his veins. She struggled away,

16

but he tugged her back to the bed, pushing her face down towards Sahara.

"You know what to do, I gather, you've done this before?"

Holly nodded, shaking at the force with which he handled her, stretching her back into a tantalizing curve, her ass spread before him. She lowered her lips to Sahara, who was writhing at her approach.

Aiden watched raptly, his jeans in a heap on the floor, his cock at its fullest. He almost couldn't stand it, the beauty of their love and the moment that hung between them as lips approached lips.

Holly moaned into the sweet tightness of Sahara's pussy.

Aiden's hands were burning. He knelt behind Holly, and gave her one warning.

"Ready, little girl?" His voice washed over her languidly. She nodded; her mouth firmly working on Sahara's pleasure.

He brought his hand down. Holly cried out. He asked if she wanted more. She said yes. He punished her with months of pent up ardour, his hand moving rhythmically, soft kisses breaking up the assault. She was dripping wet and moaning out every strike.

"Aiden," Sahara pleaded. "Please, softer." But he glowered at her so fiercely that she looked away. Holly was rocking on her knees, begging for his cock.

"*Aiden*! I need your cock inside me! Please, please, fuck me."

He reached in the bed side drawer and pulled out a condom.

Holly shook her head. "I trust you, no..."

"We're not discussing this, Holly. Face down, show me your lovely cunt."

She obeyed and placed herself at his mercy, his cock huge even in his own large hands. She looked at Sahara who was crying softly, her love for them bright through her tears.

He slid himself in; gently, slowly, pushing himself to the end, not sparing Holly one inch of his length, savouring every second of pleasure. She shook and clamped down around him, head thrown back, eyes wild, one breast in his hand. He slid out as slowly, enraptured by the vision of seeing himself inside her.

"Ok?" He asked, in a deep groan, wanting very much to collapse from the experience of her tender cunt around him. She nodded, and gripped the sheets with her fists.

"Christ, Holly...I'm going to fuck you so damn hard, open up for me babe...I fucking love you so bad."

He slammed into her, hands on her hips, they rocked back and forth, as she called his name and screamed out her love. She lost focus of where her orgasm started and where it ended. All she could think of was how incredible it felt to be filled with his cock, and to know the ferocity of his love.

Alternating between the tenderest of shallow strokes to the deepest of thrusts, he drew out her pleasure as well as his own. His ears welcomed the sounds of her ecstasy, waiting for her orgasm to wane before he slowed down. She turned her head, seeking his kisses, which he gave freely. She shook helplessly, his arm around her as he brought her closer to meet his lips.

"Aiden, please, some for Sahara."

He nodded, weak. He had thought that she would want him to come for her, but she was, as always, thinking of someone else.

Aiden approached Sahara who was lifting her hips towards him, her pussy wet and swollen. He slipped his condom off. He lifted her legs to his shoulders and gripped the headboard.

Holly watched with renewed lust as he eased himself in, stretching Sahara fully, hips rocking her towards release. Their eyes were locked on each other, Sahara's moans rhythmic. She dropped a kiss on each of their lips. They promised their love to her, lifelong devotion, Aiden's head turned now so he could kiss her properly, as he meted out his punishing lust on Sahara. Holly placed herself where they could see her, and slipped her fingers in.

There was nothing Aiden could do to stop the release he was aching for.

Holly thought she had never seen him as beautiful as he was in that moment, his voice echoing around the room, his body tense with climax, Sahara's pleasure meeting his.

She untied her lover, rubbing the rope marks on Sahara's wrists. Sahara's hands went instantly to Holly's waist, she pushed Holly down to the bed, and straddled her. Aiden lay beside them, satisfied to watch their tender love. Holly gripped Sahara by her hair, turning her over and wrapping her legs around her.

"I need to hold you, Sahara. I want to feel you under my skin."

Sahara sighed contentedly.

Aiden covered them up and snuggled in. The warmth of their bodies was the most intense pleasure he could imagine. If he loved them any more than this he would explode.

"This could possibly be the best birthday present I've ever had,"

Holly mumbled, ever so satisfied with the people she loved by her side.

Aiden sat up slowly. Sahara slid off Holly and sat on her knees beside her.

"Would you be so kind as to tell us when you last celebrated a birthday?" Aiden asked. "Damn it woman, you're especially good at testing me."

She looked at them sheepishly, anticipating their response. "To-day?" she replied, and jumped shrieking from the bed, down the stairs, with Aiden in hot pursuit.

Sahara covered her face with her hands, laughing. Holly was ex-actly what Aiden needed. Sometimes his intensity was too much to bear. And she knew immediately what she was getting Holly for her birthday.

He caught up with her at the bottom of the stairs. His arm wound around her. She was laughing so hard that she could hardly breathe.

"Oh, I know, I should have told you," Holly choked out, "but isn't it bad manners to announce one's own birthday?"

"I made you cry. On your birthday. You should have told me."

Aiden's face was hard once more, angry with himself. He picked her up. Holly's legs wound around his waist, her bottom in his hands. They made their way back up the stairs, Holly whispering in his ear; desperate to wipe that look off his face. He deposited her back in the bed beside Sahara.

"I don't remember crying, Aiden. All I remember is the two of you filling my day with love." She snuggled down under the covers beside Sahara, who was lying on her stomach, satisfactorily watching Aiden dress.

"I'm going down to make coffee or tea or whatever you wenches would like. Which will it be? Are we having dessert?"

"Tea," Holly said. The dessert is in the box in the fridge. "Take it out, Aiden, it needs to come to room temperature. I'll come down and help in a minute."

"No you won't!" Sahara and Aiden said in unison. Sahara got up and dressed.

"I'll help you, Aiden. We'll call you when it's ready. Stay in bed."

They stoked up the fire, and set the table for tea. Sahara opened the box of dessert, and grinned at Aiden.

"What is it?" he asked.

"Birthday cake. She made her own cake."

"What a brat," Aiden laughed. "What do you want to get her for her birthday?" he whispered.

"I've already decided. I'm going to dress the bed you bought her."

Aiden's eyes shot up from the kettle he was pouring to stare at her.

"I'm not ready to talk about that, not today, with Holly here."

She nodded and dropped the subject.

"Why don't you go fetch Holly?" Aiden suggested. "I'll continue on down here."

Sahara came back moments later.

"Well?" Aiden asked.

"She's asleep. What to do?"

"I'll get her."

Holly lay across the bed, almost lost under the generous duvet, her arms stretched out overhead, breathing evenly. Aiden lay down beside her, and slid his hand under the covers. She moaned, turning into him as his fingers traced a line along her side.

"Aiden. Get under the covers. Hold me."

He kissed her eyes. "That's a very interesting proposal, my love, but we have a birthday cake to eat. Why don't you put some clothes on and come down?" He pushed the covers off and let his hands roam her.

She looked up into his eyes. He melted to his very core.

"You've made me fall in love with you, Aiden Halloran."

"Say it again."

"I'm in love with you."

"Again."

"In love with you Aiden. Hopelessly, shamelessly, in love."

CHAPTER 3

"I meant to ask you, are you totally alright with chipping in the half of Holly's debt? It's fine if not." Aiden had just slipped back into bed beside Sahara, Holly safely back to the bakery.

"Aiden, it's pitch black outside. Couldn't we sleep a bit more?"

"No. Wake up. I'm too wired to go back to sleep."

Sahara groaned. "Ok. I can see that you're going to torture me until I do what you say." She turned over to face him. "Yes, I'm more than ok with it."

"So, you have enough to spare this? I mean, you won't need it any time soon, because I'd be happy to cover it."

"Nope. I have more money than God," Sahara giggled.

"Oh you do, do you?" Aiden laughed. "Just how much is that, pretty lady?"

"Couldn't I have some coffee before you check my bank account?"

"No, it's too early for coffee. I'm curious now. Where would you have gotten more money than God?"

Sahara sat up, her perky breasts jutting out at him in the dim light of the room.

"You're impossible. Hasn't anyone told you it's rude to ask a lady about her finances?"

"No, that's her age. Stop stalling." Aiden let the palm of his hand drift across Sahara's nipples.

She gave herself a minute to stare at his powerful build, his muscles rippling as he shifted to lie on his side. He was impossibly gorgeous.

Sahara pulled her knees in. "Ok. I'll give you the edited version. My parents passed away when I was eight. My father's fortune, mainly real estate related, was managed by my uncle, who became my guardian, to be given to me at age twenty five. My uncle's estate, also of considerable value, was left to me when he passed away five years ago. I have no other family, or at least no one that I'm in touch with. My uncle said that my mother's family disowned her when she married my father, and I have no idea who they are or where they are. I suppose I could find out, but really, I haven't any inclination to do so. I legally changed my name when I was first published. And that's it."

Aiden stared at her. She'd said it all as if she were reciting facts about someone else. Was there ever going to be a time when he'd know all of her?

"So... you're not really Sahara Taylor?"

"Of course I am. That's the name I've chosen for myself."

Aiden's heart pounded with increasing frustration. "Any particular reason why?"

"One of the meanings for Sahara from Arabic is 'dawn'. When I began my new career as a writer, it was a new dawn for me. I was tailoring my own destiny, and there you have it."

"I'm sorry that you lost your parents Sahara, it must have been very frightening." Aiden held out his hand. "When you're ready, will you tell me your birth name? I won't press you."

"One day."

He sighed. "So going back to the more money than God thing... shall I assume it's enough to hold you for a while?"

Sahara smiled. "A lifetime...and more."

He pulled her back down under the covers and wrapped his arms around her.

Sahara let her breath out. That had gone much better than she had anticipated. He was silent for a long while, and she allowed herself to slip back into drowsiness.

"Sahara?" She heard his voice through a heavy mist.

"Hmm?"

"I can't wait to give you my surprise."

She could feel the steely hardness of his cock against her back. She shifted and slid herself onto him. When Sahara woke up, the sun was beaming through the bedroom windows, and Aiden, showered and dressed, was placing her cup of coffee on the bedside table.

CHAPTER 4

They stopped in at the café on the way out.

"Remember, you promised to show me the surprise on your way back!" Holly waved them out the door. The place was already buzzing with regulars.

"How long before we're there?" Sahara could tell that Aiden was nervous, for all his words of certainty that she'd love whatever he had picked out.

"An hour there, but I wanted to take you to lunch in Telson. Are you ok with that?"

"Sure. Why not?"

"I've already been there for dinner with Holly," he grinned at her.

"All this wanton love with Holly and me has made you quite emboldened, I see."

"Yes. As long as I can protect Holly from any repercussions of our actions, I can manage any that come my way."

"Oh, so you don't want to protect *me*?" Sahara teased.

"I would, but you're fiercely capable of fighting your own battles." He looked at her. "But say the word, my lady, and I will fight for your honor."

"You didn't call me 'my lady' once around Holly," Sahara observed.

"I thought it would beg some questions. And we had already traversed several dangerous scenarios last night."

"Last night was the best night of my life," Sahara said, suddenly serious.

"I can't even begin to tell you what it meant to me. There are no words for that." Aiden fell silent again, and they rode all the way towards Telson with Sahara's small hand in his firm grasp.

She could tell when his thoughts turned dark by the unbearable clench of his hand.

"Aiden. You're hurting me."

He let go, alarmed.

"I'm sorry, my love. Deep in thought."

She slid her hand along his leg and he jumped.

"Penny for your thoughts?"

Aiden's eyes threw fire.

"When you were with Richard..."

Sahara's heart began to pound.

"I know I said that I was ok with it." Aiden sat up straight. "Will...there be another time?"

Sahara fought hard to still her nerves, the memory of Richard on his knees before her making her increasingly wet.

"Why do you ask? I mean, who knows? I suppose it depends on what kind of encounters we have from now on...where our regressions take us." She shook her head, not sure what else to say. He was leaving it up to her it seemed, which was more than another man would do.

"Aiden?"

He took her hand back. "Tell me what Richard looks like."

Sahara knew that he was leading her into deep waters, but she couldn't resist the pull.

"Much the same as before, dark haired, but it's short this time. His forearms and back are covered with tattoos; he's six one or two, incredibly fit. He kind of looks like a modern day pirate. To say that he's attractive would be a ridiculous understatement. Very charming."

Sahara noticed Aiden's jaw grinding.

"I had a dream about the two of you."

Sahara shuddered involuntarily.

"I woke up with an erection," Aiden shrugged his shoulders.

"Soooo, meaning that you enjoyed watching us in your dream?" Her nipples ached inside her bra, demanding freedom.

He followed her gaze to his rising cock.

"I'd kill to see it, Sahara," Aiden admitted. "I'm damned if I know how I can be half angry with you and this aroused by it at the same time."

Sahara held on to the handle of the truck door. She felt the flutter on her clit as her thoughts raced to an image of Richard, in elegant dress pants, shirtless, his hands unclasping his belt, demanding that she fall down before him, in a humble pose on the floor, to beg him for the pleasure of his cock in her mouth.

"Oh Jesus, Aiden!"

Sahara's hand slipped down her jeans. Aiden's hand went to her hair. He tugged hard.

"You're a whore, Sahara. I love that about you," Aiden's voice rasped out.

She voiced her release as his fingers pushed inside her shirt, tugging her breasts free. He longed to kiss her, but it took all his concentration to not drive off the road.

24

"That's just not fair, Aiden."

He smiled in the decadent way that he had, and adjusted his cock in his jeans.

"I've never known as much freedom to be myself as I have known with you. You're an incredible man and I fucking love you!"

He yanked her into his lap, and holding firmly onto her ass, groaned his kisses into her mouth.

"When I get you home, I'm going to punish you for all your little transgressions. I want to be able to make love to you like a gentleman, but when I'm near you, I want to break you."

His hands went to her throat; she rubbed hard against his erection, both of them oblivious to the occasional passing car.

"I want both, Aiden! You can start out the gentleman and end the rogue. I'll pretend that I need some coaxing and instruction in bed. And if I can't give you what you want, you can take it from me. Is that a game you'd like to play?"

He nodded, his eyes burning through her. "Have I mentioned how much I love you, Sahara Taylor....or whoever you are?"

She flicked her tongue on his ear, holding tight to his shoulders, her heart beating like a hammer.

"I can't imagine what I've been doing without you before this. You're under my skin Aiden. I'm addicted to you. I'll be Sahara or whomever you need me to be, as long as it's authentic to who I am, I can play every game you desire."

Aiden held her so tightly that she pushed back on his chest, but he refused to let go.

"Give me what you have, woman. I want to know every dark bit of you. Before I met you, I thought I knew who I was. Now I'm sure that I don't know myself at all. You've managed to make both yourself and me a discovery. I feel drunk when I'm around you." He put her back in her seat, and checked for oncoming traffic.

"Aiden?"

"Yes, my love?"

"Thank you for my surprise," she reached for his hand once more.

"Thank you for mine."

"Huh? I wasn't aware I'd given you one."

He winked at her. "Holly."

"Holly, yes. She has been a delightful surprise hasn't she? She's been a gift for us both."

He followed a sign down a bumpy road that read simply, 'John

Tennant, Ironworks'.

"Hey!" Sahara exclaimed. "That's the guy who made my bathroom hooks and towel racks. Did you get him to make me something else?"

"You'll see," Aiden laughed. He opened the truck door for her, and helped her down. He was always struck by how tiny she appeared at his side. Taking hold of her hand, he walked her around the back of the house towards a large, wooden workshop.

She commented that she could smell the forge. It was a good smell, she said. It reminded her of horses being shod.

Aiden knocked on the massive sliding door, and waited, smiling down at her until they heard a voice behind them. Sahara turned to see a bear of a man holding an iron rod, rubbing a rather runaway beard with his spare hand.

"Hullo!" the man bellowed, in a thick Yorkshire accent. "I see you have brought your young lady finally."

He stuck out a calloused paw towards her, Sahara's hand disappeared inside his. He smiled expansively.

"Are you ready for your surprise, love? Your man here has picked out the best one."

"Best one what?" Sahara asked, instantly warming to the curious character.

"Why don't we just go inside and see?"

He led them to the back of the building, past the piles of artwork he had created. Sahara stopped dead in front of an old fashioned gate. She pointed to it, wordless.

"Like that? It's a replica of a gate at St. Andrew's churchyard back home. Just a little bit of whimsy." He went back to playing with his beard.

"Is it for sale?" Sahara felt the odd swimmy sensation in her head that overtook her when she was fading into the past. Aiden grabbed her hand, and she slammed back to the present.

"Well yes, we could work out a price, I suppose. It's one of my more expensive pieces," he replied apologetically.

"I wouldn't dream of bargaining with you," Sahara said. "You're an artist, just name your price."

John looked at Aiden. Aiden shrugged his shoulders. "She's her own woman, John. You can work it out with her."

"Well, I'll be... I'll give it some thought, but what are we doing here, talking about an old gate? Shall we go get that surprise?"

Sahara tuned her ear to a whimper in the corner of the room, her feet automatically taking her towards the sound. John and Aiden hung back, both of them grinning from ear to ear. The sound grew louder as Sahara approached. Her steps quickened, her instincts on alert. Something was calling to her, and she desperately needed to reach it. She bent down to look into the box the sound was coming from. Her hands reached out.

"Oh, come here!" She picked up the wiggling bundle of yelping fur into her arms. "Oh come here, little man. Oh! Oh, aren't you adorable?" Sahara turned toward Aiden, whose heart was clearly on his sleeve.

The happiness on her face was the reward he was after. He hadn't been wrong; she *had* been aching for something to call her own.

"Oh darling, is he for me?" She was struggling to hang on to the puppy. He was licking her face, his back feet pumping to climb her small frame. Sahara didn't even bother to keep back the tears.

Aiden closed in on the woman he loved and helped her adjust the weight of the puppy in her arms.

"He's yours if you want him. I recall you telling me once that you were going to get a dog. Remember?"

She did, but knew that she hadn't meant it then. It had just been a jumble of nervous words that had fallen out of her mouth when she'd met him. But now that she was here, she was grateful for his memory and his generosity.

"I want him! I want him! Oh Aiden, thank you! He's perfect."

She stood on tiptoe and kissed him, the puppy delighted to be out of his box. The men watched amused, as she forgot about them altogether and ran to the field outside to play.

"Well," John commented. "I think you've done a good job of surprising her. She's quite something, your lady," he winked.

"I'm a lucky man, John," Aiden said. "Thank you again for keeping him back so long. I couldn't get her here any sooner."

"Not to worry, not to worry. He knows how to ask to go out now. There shouldn't be too many accidents. He's a smart little fellow." He shook Aiden's hand. "I'll keep the gate here for her. Come and get it when you can."

"I think she's forgotten about the gate altogether now."

But Aiden was wrong. Sahara came back, the puppy in tow, her wallet in her hand.

"That's the best puppy in the world, Mr. Tennant. Thank you. Now, about the gate."

"Oh, call me John for heaven's sake. And it's all because of your man here. He insisted I keep him for you...there's been a few that's wanted the little rascal. He's part wolf, you know. He'll be loyal."

"I'll make sure to bring him back sometime, for a visit. The gate John. I have to have it."

Aiden looked at Sahara as she sat with the puppy in a blanket on her lap. She was staring straight ahead, deep in thought. The puppy slept peacefully, one leg jumping now and again as he fell into a dream.

"Sahara?"

She turned her head, eyes misty, love plain as day on her face.

"I know what you've done, Aiden Halloran."

"What have I done, my love?" His hand reached for the puppy, warm from the sun shining through the windshield.

"You've given me the only baby I can have with you."

She couldn't keep from weeping, her tears obscuring Aiden from her sight. But if she could have seen him right then, she would have known that she had speared him through the heart with her astuteness.

Aiden's hands clenched the steering wheel. She had found him out. And he let his own tears fall.

CHAPTER 5

I am always evolving, always shifting. You are like the serpent who bathes on the sunny rock of my being, basking in my warmth, letting your belly find its comfort among my breasts, my hips, my sacred places. I open to you, when you lie in awareness, and test my readiness with your tongue. Because you honor my undulating moods, because you take time to understand my tides, I can give to you like to no other.

Holly peered through the café window. She was on pins and needles waiting to see what Aiden had given Sahara. If she knew the man at all, it would be something that he'd given a lot of thought to. He was like that. Thoughtful...a gentleman.

She thought she'd do better to keep busy, all this waiting made her anxious. It was only when she heard a knock on the window that she looked up again. She wiped her hands on her apron, and opened the front door. A cold gust of wind met her; she adjusted her eyes in the sun. Sahara stood on the sidewalk, smiling broadly. Holly looked down at the shivering pup peeking from behind Sahara's legs. Aiden stood across the street, leaning against his truck door.

"Look what I got!" Sahara bent down to pick up the puppy. "When can you come over to play with him?"

Holly put her hand over her mouth in surprise and looked over at Aiden. She suddenly understood something about their love making the night before. Her heart burst with love for him and she blew him a kiss.

He waved, a grin on his handsome face.

"I can come over tonight. Oh Sahara...did you want a puppy?"

"I didn't know that I did. But Aiden knew. And now that I have him I feel like I'd been waiting for him. Know what I mean, Holly?" Sahara fluffed up the puppy's head.

"I do know. I actually do. Don't we have the best man?" She embraced Sahara warmly, ignoring the gathering pile of customers at the window. "I'll see you later. Gotta go."

It seemed to Sahara that Holly said that a lot. Maybe she could help her this winter. Writing and baking seemed like copacetic activities for long winter days.

"What will you name him?" Holly sat on the carpet by the fire, the puppy exhausted after a thorough romp outside. She ran her hands along his soft belly, and he stretched his legs contentedly.

"I'm thinking 'Ulfred.' It means 'peace'. I feel that he'll bring peace, alongside his strength. He'll be big. What do you think?"

"That's how Aiden feels to me. That same mix of gentleness and power. I like it. Ulfred." "Are you Ulfred?" she asked the pup who had now closed his eyes and was breathing evenly with sleep. Holly lay down beside the dog, beside the fire, stretching into the heat.

Sahara observed the two of them - her lover and her dog - both so relaxed and utterly sure of their place in her heart. Ulfred so naturally, as animals do the instant they feel loved, and Holly, sweet Holly, as innocently as one who trusts like a child. Holly's eyes closed as well. She was tired, Sahara could see it in her every day, the long hours at the bakery taking their toll.

She added to the fire and stepping carefully around them, returned to the kitchen to put the finishing touches on dinner. It would be only her and Holly to eat; Aiden had an evening meeting in town. She longed for his voice, and she sent her energy to him, hoping he would feel her need. Her phone rang as she closed the oven behind the vegetables she was baking.

"I can feel you from further away now," Aiden's voice washed over her.

"You're waking up to your magic. It's going to come faster each day now, Aiden. I miss you, already. I just needed to hear your voice."

There was a short silence on the other end.

"Is Holly there yet? Are you eating soon?"

"She's sleeping on the floor by the fire, with Ulfred," Sahara smiled into the phone.

"Ulfred? Wolf of Peace. I like it darling."

He paused again and Sahara knew that although he wanted to give her and Holly space, he would crave joining them after his meeting.

"Is Holly staying over?" he asked, longing soft in his voice.

"Yes, and I'll go in with her tomorrow. I could use a new distraction and she could use some help baking. I thought I could step in until she finds an apprentice. Aiden?"

"Hmm?"

"I know we're trying to give each other space, but I'm in need of your company. Would you come over later...after your meeting?"

"I'll be there. I need the two of you as well. So much so that I think I might expire from the intensity of my feelings. My senses are so heightened, I barely know how to make it through each day. I've taken to chopping wood every spare moment just to release some of my energy. My brain feels like it's on fire thinking about both of you. Is this real, Sahara, this love of ours?"

Sahara laughed, careful to keep her reply light. She was afraid also, that the circumstances of their love would disappear into the thin air from being so intensely perfect.

"It's real, my love, it's real. But I know how you feel. It's difficult to concentrate on anything but the mystery of how we all found each other."

She sat down on one of the stools that Aiden had fashioned for her from aspen wood. "Until tonight then. Love you."

She hung up, and counted the hours before he would arrive. Then she went to lay down beside Holly, by the fire, by Ulfred. She curled into them, and closed her eyes. This was what she had been looking for her whole life, when she'd felt that gnawing hunger in her belly, that nervous emptiness...this love.

She slept until she felt a wet nose sniffing her face. Ulfred. Holly sat beside them, grinning.

"I'll take him out, you better check on dinner. I'm so hungry Sahara!"

Sahara stretched in that cat-like way that she had, and pulled Holly down on top of her. Ulfred stepped over them, tail wagging. They laughed as he licked their faces, barking at them to get up.

"Is this not the best, Holly? Me, you, Ulfred, fire, food?"

Holly stood and picked up the puppy, her expression soft and serene.

"Yes. Almost perfect. If Aiden was here..."

Sahara smiled. "He'll be here later. He called."

"Oh," Holly sighed the word out. "I'm glad, I love him so bad."

"I know. I've got it bad too. Peace and strength. You're right Holly, it's Aiden's mark."

Aiden parked his truck and looked over his notes regarding the meeting ahead. He reached in the back seat and pulled out the architectural plans. This build was close to home. He'd assemble a crew of skilled local men. Keeping the local economy strong was something he strived towards, and it was well appreciated by the families who gained from it. His mind went back to the conversation with Sahara, about Richard. Only time would tell if he would need to arrange himself around that strange turn of events. He frowned. This wasn't the time to think about it though. Still, it played at the back of his mind.

"Aiden, hello." The man at the door extended his hand and invited him in. "I'm glad we'll have this chance to talk."

Aiden felt it in his gut. It was the smallest tinge of knowing, the slightest hint of intuition. His client had heard something about his love affairs. But it was bound to happen; another's curiosity. He braced himself for the questions, his face a blank slate.

They sat at the kitchen table, the rolls of plans neatly to one side. The man offered a drink. Aiden declined. Thinking it best to just plunge right into their business, Aiden opened his laptop and brought up the plan details.

"Now listen, Aiden..." the man began. Aiden looked him straight in the eye. Waiting.

"I've just heard a little bit of gossip. It's probably all a bunch of bullshit, just between you and me; just woman talk, I suppose."

"If you could speak plainly, Trent."

"Well, you know, it's a little troubling, all this talk of you and the café girl, and then that reclusive writer." Trent took a long drink of his beer, his eyes curious.

"You mean Holly and Sahara," Aiden provided their names. "That has nothing to do with our business here tonight. Unless it's a problem for you, in which case, I can recommend another builder." And that was that. He was shutting Trent down. He had no intention of engaging in a drawn out war of words.

Trent looked quite put out. His hands fidgeted with the bottle of beer, he shuffled it back and forth on the table.

"Now look here, I'm just asking. I have a lot of friends around here, people I work with, a reputation to uphold."

Aiden lowered the lid to the laptop and squared his shoulders.

"I also have a reputation Trent. As a good builder. And that's what I'm here to talk about; my building you a home. My personal life has nothing to do with that."

Trent had the decency to look chagrined. Still he continued. "You have to admit, it's all a bit unconventional. The whole town is talking. Well, don't you care about what everyone is saying?"

Do you wish to discuss your plans or shall I give you the referral?" Aiden stood.

Trent motioned him to sit. "Another man would be happy to share about such things," he muttered.

CHAPTER 6

"Where will Ulfred sleep?" Holly asked.

Sahara laughed. "Not with me! Probably in his bed, by the door. Aiden had all the supplies already purchased before we went yesterday. I haven't had to buy a thing! Anyway, I think his wolf instincts will take over and he'll want to be at the door."

Holly patted the puppy, who was staring up at them as they cleaned up in the kitchen. "He's been following you around as if he knows that he's yours."

"Or that I'm his, more likely."

"What time is it?" Holly looked around for a clock but couldn't see one.

"Almost eight thirty," Sahara checked her phone. "Here, sit in front of me on the sofa, I'll give you a little massage."

"Oh, that sounds heavenly. Those bags of flour aren't light!"

"Is that how you stay in such amazing shape?" Sahara grazed her lips along Holly's neck.

"Sorry, you were saying?" Holly swayed as she felt Sahara touch along her back.

"Sit. I was saying...how did you come to be so fit?"

"Some of it is muscle memory. I ran at school, and took dance for years. Now I just do a lot of lifting of flour bags and kneading of bread, some yoga when I have time. That's it. How about you?" She relaxed into the tender touch of Sahara's fingers through her hair.

"I dunno. Good genes, I suppose, years and years of yoga, digging in the earth, long walks." Sahara took hold of Holly's ears and began to rub the reflex points around them.

"Oooh, that's soo good, Sahara. I can almost forgive you now for calling me Arinn in your sleep."

Holly's words were said in jest, Sahara knew, but she felt the stab at her conscience nonetheless.

Holly looked up, Sahara's words not forthcoming, her touch now softer, hands gliding down her shoulders and arms.

"Sahara? Have I said something wrong?"

"Of course not, darling. I'm just at a loss for words. Actually, if I answer you, it will open up a long discussion that I was hoping we could get into slowly. I'm not sure that I'm ready..."

Holly took hold of Sahara's hands. She kissed them lightly. "Alright. I'll wait. If that's what you need. I love you. It doesn't matter who Arinn is...or was."

It was the complete trust and lack of jealousy that broke Sahara open. Such trust begged honesty, and she was willing to take a step into being forthright. She leaned into Holly's back, her legs a little closer around her, hugging her in.

"Do you know what I do besides writing, sweetness?"

"I think so. You practice magic. Am I right?"

Sahara let out a tightly held breath. "That's right. I practice the Wise Woman Tradition. I'm a witch."

Holly turned around and sat on her knees. She looked up at Sahara, curious.

"A part of what I do, Holly, is work with my friend Iona, from the magic store, to bring a reconnection between the world of Fey and human kind on an energetic level, for the healing of the planet."

Holly nodded.

"It's work we've done before. We're not the only ones doing it. We're part of a large group of energy workers and alchemists."

Sahara sighed. Holly squeezed her hands in reassurance.

"Iona and I have shared another life together, a long time ago. Her name then was Arinn." The last pause was the most pregnant. "We used to be lovers, partners in life."

"Oh," Holly said. "Oh." She looked at the floor.

Sahara slid down to the carpet beside her. They sat facing the fire, staring into the flames, each lost to her own heart's decent into fear.

Finally, Holly spoke. "I want to be strong, but really, I just need to cry. I'm not sure why. It's not that I didn't think you had any other friends, of course, but this is somewhat different, yes?"

Sahara nodded. "Cry, my love. Cry. There's no shame in releasing your tears, ever. Come."

She held out her arms and let Holly fall into them, her fingers tangled in her hair, body on fire. Holly hadn't done anything to deserve punishment, but a thread of heat rose up in her, as she envisioned Holly in a submissive pose before her. Holly's tear stained face pressed closer to hers, her lips searching, testing Sahara's love.

"I'm sorry, Holly. See? I've already hurt you, and you were so confident that I never would." Pain shadowed Sahara's eyes.

"No, you've not hurt me. You've just opened me up to so much more than I expected. But I asked for it, didn't I? I wanted to know." Holly's lips parted as she pressed against Sahara's mouth.

"Iona isn't the love of my life, Holly. You are." Their tongues met.

"But, you do love her?" Holly caught the hint. She licked at Sahara's bottom lip.

"Yes. I won't deny it. We have shared so much, and have this work to do. I do love her."

Sahara locked her teeth in a gentle bite on Holly's neck. Holly groaned and rubbed herself into Sahara's body.

"You've been lovers this time around?"

"Yes. Oh Holly, please; I'm afraid of hurting you more," Sahara whispered.

"Will you teach me about magic, Sahara? I want to learn, to be part of this strange, mystical world you live in. Please?"

Holly lifted her shirt over her head. Sahara's hands went instantly to Holly's bra, slipping it off, blowing softly against Holly's erect nipples.

'But you've been so terribly naughty, Holly, digging into my past, pressing me for secrets, testing my love for you." Sahara's mouth found one and pulled hard.

"Oh, this one too..."

Sahara's mouth moved back to Holly's ear, licking, biting.

"Stand up. Undress. I want to see you naked; I want you on your hands and knees, to pay for your questions, Holly. I'm going to punish your sweet little ass."

Holly's eyes burned with a fevered desire. She undressed in front of Sahara, her hand slipping towards her sex, her clit throbbing.

"No! Take your hand away. I'll touch that."

Holly obeyed and slipped to her hands and knees. She swayed lightly back and forth, anticipating her punishment. Her scent rose to Sahara, the sweet jasmine aroma of the perfume she wore.

"What if Aiden comes, Sahara?" Holly lowered her head to the floor, her bottom spreading prettily.

"I guess you'll have to take his punishment too." Sahara slid her hand along Holly's inner thigh.

"Oh Sweet Jesus!" Holly exclaimed. She pumped her hips back. "But won't he want to know why you're punishing me, what I've done to deserve it?"

Sahara's hand caressed Holly's ass, one finger slipping towards her tightly pursed bud.

"I'll tell. Not to worry, my sweet. He'll know what to do. He's had centuries of experience."

As soon as Sahara said it, she knew that she had let the worst part of her confession out. Holly's long silence was almost unbearable.

"Aiden knows Iona?" Holly pushed her ass towards Sahara. The first strike, drew a soft cry from her lips.

"No, my love, he does not. But he did love Arinn. She was once his beloved." Sahara's hand came down once more, harder this time. Holly moaned.

"Am I new to you and Aiden, Sahara, did I ever know you before?" Her body shook as Sahara caressed her, light kisses and moans on her bottom, spreading her, licking at her sex.

"You're new, darling, to both of us. Except for one thing." She knew that there was no way around this fact...no point in keeping it secret.

"What is it, Sahara? Tell me!"

"You're the spitting image of Arinn. You are a most beautiful reminder of mine and Aiden's past." Sahara pressed her face into Holly's tender cunt, her tongue exacting.

"But you love me for *me,* right Sahara? You and Aiden? For whom *I* am?" Holly's tears fell.

"We love you for the impossibly light being that you are, Holly. For everything you have become as a woman, for the goodness you carry in your heart, for your unique essence. Yes, Holly, there's no-one who could have captured us like you...more pain my love, or will it be pleasure?"

"Your tongue, Sahara. You know where I want it."

"Of course," Sahara whispered, lowering her face to that delightful bottom, now pink where she had let her hand fall. Her tongue circled, danced a light dance towards the place Holly pulled open for her. Lost to each other, they ignored the persistent barking of Ulfred at the door, and the hand that opened it, letting in a blast of cold air.

Aiden placed Ulfred in his bed, in the box by the door. He stood then, one hand on the mantle, waiting. If they wanted him, they would let him in. He would take their lead with pleasure. Holly was face down, her pretty ass spread open, Sahara, still fully clothed, tongue working magic on her tenderness. Aiden licked his lips. He was dying for a taste, the erotic scene before him teasing his cock into a painful fullness. Sahara looked up at him smiling, Holly rocked on her hands and knees, refusing to look at either of them.

"Will it be me or Aiden, Holly? Tell me."

"Aiden," Holly breathed. And with that she looked up at his handsome face - he a little alarmed now that she showed her teary eyes - and knelt before him, stretching her hands to his belt. Sahara stood on tiptoe and dropped a kiss on Aiden's lips, one hand upon his chest.

"Love her well, my lord. Love her well. She needs to know your heart."

Sahara left them to their passion and their heat, Ulfred at her heels as she walked into the moonlit night towards Aiden's. Holly needed him to herself, this she knew, and gladly offered.

"Why the tears, Holly...is it just from the pleasure of Sahara's hand?" Aiden groaned as Holly helped him out of his pants, his shirt already on the floor.

"Sahara told me about Arinn," Holly said, ignoring Aiden's look of alarm. "About you and Iona...well...Arinn. And that I look like her." Her hands swept along his leg, towards his balls, which she cupped in her warm hand.

"Oh, I didn't realize that Sahara was ready to discuss that yet. It's a lot to take in, I know," he said, breathless. "I'm sorry if that hurt you, my love. I'd rather die than hurt you."

She looked up at him, her sweet soul shining.

"You've not hurt me. You can no more help what happened in another life than I can help looking like someone you've loved before." She paused, her lips close to his cock. "I just need to know that you love me for me, not because I look like someone you used to love."

"Holly!" Aiden pulled her up, his lips on hers, his hands a gentle caress on her skin.

"I loved you before I knew anything about that. You took my heart long ago. You were the first woman I've truly loved completely. Shall I show you my love...shall I love you as if you're the only one? Is that what you need, my beautiful girl?"

His fingers searched her tenderness, slipping along her clit, pressing her towards a gathering heat. She melted into his strong, muscular body, soaking up his love.

"Yes, show me. I want your love inside me."

He took her gently at first. He sank into the depths of her passion clouded eyes as he thrust inside her. He took his time and found every place that left her crying out his name. She did not shrink from the

38

fierce look on his face. She had him at her mercy, as he had her at his. When Sahara returned to draw them a bath, and put the kettle on for tea, they were lying spent on the floor.

She kissed them tenderly. "The two of you look so beautiful together...so right in each other's arms."

They drew her in and spoke of love. Could it be that each night got better, that each day ended more satisfactorily than the one before?

Aiden tucked the two of them into Sahara's bed later that night, and then made his way down to the sofa. He lay staring into the fire for a long time. If loving two women was complicated, he didn't care. If this was to be the only heaven he would ever experience, then it was enough. He slept peacefully. It was four in the morning when he felt Holly slip in beside him and he shifted to make room for her. His arm wound around her and pulled her as close as was possible, his mouth warm.

"I've got to go. Sahara will come with me. What will you do today?"

"Chop more wood probably," he laughed. "I'll try to do some work, make arrangements for builds that will start in the spring. I also need to prepare the house for winter somewhat." He turned her towards him. "I can't decide what I crave more, time to myself or time with you? I'm not used to being this out of control with my emotions."

"Shall I stay away? Give you room?"

"Try it and I'll hunt you down," Aiden met her lips. She melted at the warmth of his tongue in her mouth.

Holly searched his eyes. He smiled contentedly at her. God, he was stunning!

"You don't use a condom with Sahara." It was not a question, Holly already knew the reason for it.

"No. I suppose you know why."

She nodded, "I figured it out, when you gave her Ulfred, and Sahara confirmed it. It makes me love you more...your thoughtfulness."

Aiden hugged her closer.

"I want to feel your skin on my skin too - one time...can we?"

His eyes closed, he sorted through all the emotions that peaked in reaction to her question. Arousal because she asked his permission; ego because she put him in the position of deciding for her; love because she needed him like he needed her, hope because she was willing to risk taking his seed.

Holly watched his face, showing so much and so little. It was his complete manhood that she found so attractive.

"I can't think of anything I'd want more, Holly, to feel you slide onto my bare skin." He groaned. "It will be your decision, my love."

"I could go on birth control?"

"No!"

"No? Why not? I don't mind."

"I don't mean 'no' really. Of course it's your choice, but I'd prefer if you didn't take that route."

"Ok." She snuggled in deeper. She didn't even care his reason, although she guessed correctly that he didn't want her to expose herself to an intervention that altered her natural cycles. Somehow it felt nice to take his lead, to relax into his wish. She'd been on her own for so long, she allowed herself this one small indulgence.

"Will you be ready when I am?" she asked him quietly.

It was so very easy to be completely open with him, to ask him these things that she imagined would take months of loving with someone else.

"The second you say the word, I'll be inside you. I'm at your command, my lady."

He spoke the endearment, although he knew that he used it without permission, and that she would know with whom he'd used it before. They lay wrapped up in each other, neither one willing to let go.

Sahara came down the stairs. She laughed as she went past them.

"I see you have the same difficulty as I do, Aiden, keeping your hands off her."

Aiden's hand slipped to Holly's bottom. "Shall we discuss it over dinner in Telson tonight? Who's with me?" Holly moaned her agreement. Sahara made them all tea.

"If you promise to share Holly later, I'm game." Sahara's hand went to Holly's breast, kneading the softness.

Aiden took one look at Holly, eyes closed, mouth open, her legs moving apart.

"One small bit of pleasure before you leave for work, then?"

His fingers slipped inside her, his thumb circling her clit. Holly pushed against him, as Sahara bit her nipple through her nightie. Aiden's and Sahara's eyes met, their love piercing.

"Thank you," Sahara mouthed, Holly's moans rising to the orgasm Aiden's fingers were expertly eliciting.

He leaned in to kiss Sahara, his happiness complete. He saw them off as dark still clung to the early morning, Ulfred barking his protest at Sahara's leaving.

"Come Ulfred!" Aiden turned towards the cabin to tidy up and bank the fire before he went home. "It'll be just us men today. Terrible letting them go, isn't it my friend?"

Ulfred scampered alongside Aiden towards the door, but his eyes searched the lane for Sahara, who already had made a clear mark on his canine heart. She was his.

CHAPTER 7

If Aiden was anything, he was detailed. He checked his list for the day. He would transfer the money Holly needed to her account. Sahara would do the same in the next day or so. Then he would make plans for the renovations needed to the back of the patisserie. He'd have to hire it out, but he knew exactly who he wanted to do the work. He'd already sent a message to the architect for plans to extend his house. He never procrastinated on things that stirred his heart, and his desire to make room for an expanding family life was urgent.

Aiden knew that he had no choice but to accept Holly's business proposal of year end dividends, but he had every intention of saving those dividends in the account he kept separately for her. That thought reminded him of an intention to update his will, and the urgency for hiring an assistant.

He had avoided getting one and office space until now, but things had grown to such proportions that he simply could not maintain the possessively tight grip he kept on his business affairs. He looked over his list of applicants for office help. Out of respect for the women he loved he determined to hire someone that would not give them any reason to suspect his loyalty.

Next on the list was to look over the back rooms tucked behind Holly's apartment. Owning the building certainly made a lot of his plans more convenient. He'd need to upgrade the staircase leading to the top floor, renovate the space to create a reception area and a private office for himself; and add a small bathroom. His chest rumbled thinking of business meetings so close to Holly. Feeling her that near would make for sweet torture, but it was torture he looked forward to. His thoughts turned to the love they had made the night before and his cock rose as instantly as his heart warmed.

Holly had been made bold by the fears that arose after finding out about Arinn. He'd been amused by it at first, watching her hungrily please him with her mouth. But as he'd realized that she was desperate to place her mark on him, his amusement had turned to a dark possessiveness. He had assured her that no previous lifetime could erase what she meant to him, and he had shown her such loving attention that she'd finally relaxed and completely given herself over to his demands. He'd told her that he needed her on his fingers, on his tongue, on his cock, filling her any way possible but one. She had a way of allowing him to possess her completely that he found addictive. She'd asked for his cum on her tits. When he'd agreed, she'd held them in her hands, a devastatingly seductive look on her face, and said such dirty things that he'd exploded in thick, hot spurts all over her fingers. She'd cried out as his heat hit her skin, her clit throbbing to a climax that surprised them both. Once again, Aiden found himself lovingly cleaning her up, his heart split open by her desire to own every bit of him.

"You made me love you, Aiden," she had said. "Now I need to know that you mean it when you say that you love me."

Aiden's eyes had bored into hers.

"Never doubt that, Holly. Never!" He'd gripped her tightly, his teeth on her neck, biting down to mark her. "I'll go insane if you doubt my love, Holly."

Holly had melted into him, her breath soothing on his chest, her arms wound tightly around his waist.

"I don't care what else is going on," Aiden had said, thinking about Sahara and her recent trip to the past. "Nothing changes between you and me. Nothing."

"I'm yours." Holly had said.

"Mine." Aiden had reassured her.

"You're the only man who's had his mouth on my pussy." Holly had said, sucking hard on his nipples, Aiden's hand fisted in her hair.

"I'm the only man that ever will." Aiden's hand had slipped down to cup her sex.

He knew she needed to hear that. Holly and Sahara needed each other deeply, and he accepted that he could never give them what they gave to each other on so many levels, but Holly wanted to know that his love was solid, and he'd make sure that she felt it every single day of her life.

It was impossible to ignore the throbbing erection in his jeans. Aiden reminded himself to make dinner reservations, and, ignoring the roll of plans marked 'Richard Montfort' on his desk, ran up the stairs to the shower. Sahara had once asked him if there was ever a day that he didn't need release. He'd replied that although his sex drive might be considered obsessive by some, he had never given any thought to the consuming desire he felt every day. And then he'd shown her what he meant.

CHAPTER 8

"What will you wear tonight?" Holly asked, guiding Sahara's hands over the dough she was kneading.

"Seriously? How can you think of anything but the fact that we're up before the birds? When will you make me a coffee?"

"Soon. Harder, Sahara! Nothing will come of this if you just play with it."

Sahara shot Holly a smoldering look. Holly groaned and rolled her eyes.

"You're as bad as Aiden. Everything I say is an invitation for taking advantage of me." Holly checked the temperature of the ovens with her hand.

"Why do you stick your hand in there? There *is* a thermostat on that thing." Sahara licked her lips suggestively, calling Holly over with a motion of her head.

Holly sauntered over, smiling from ear to ear.

"I don't trust the thermometer, and I don't trust you. What do you want?"

"I want your tongue in my mouth."

"Over the dough? Are you mad? I'm going to have to fire you on your first day."

"You can't fire me. You need me. As soon as this bread is set to rise, you're going to kiss me."

"Your confidence is overwhelming. What do you think Aiden is doing right now?"

Sahara moaned. "Don't," she replied. "Let's talk about wardrobe instead."

The morning slipped by quickly. Sahara gratefully accepted the steaming cup of coffee Holly prepared for them once the first batch of baking was in. She looked at Holly, in complete charge of her kitchen, moving about with intent; confident, beautiful.

"I can't believe you've done this for all this time with a minimum of help. I couldn't do it. Is there any food?"

"I couldn't write a book. And yes, food is coming. You're so demanding!"

"What about my kiss?"

Holly came over and pulled Sahara into her arms.

"Thank you. I need you here," Holly's tongue slipped languidly over Sahara's.

They kept their eyes open, sinking deep into each other, Sahara ground her body into Holly, her clit tingling and her sex tightening on contact.

"This'll be a good winter," Holly pulled away, dazed.

"*Holly*," Sahara grabbed her hands.

"I love you," Holly purred.

"Are we going to tell our parents?" Holly mused. "Where do *your* parents live? My mother will have a seizure."

Sahara looked away. "I don't have any family, Holly."

She heard Holly's sharp intake of breath. She felt her come up behind her, and slide her arms around her waist.

"That's not true, Sahara. You have me and Aiden. We're your family."

They heard their phones beep, and the moment was broken. It was Aiden, messaging them that he'd pick them up at seven.

"Want to get ready at my place?" Sahara suggested.

"Yes." Holly couldn't wait to see Sahara in a dress. "Have you seen Aiden in a suit yet?"

"No." Sahara had wondered about that, but she'd been inside his closet, and had seen his taste in clothes.

Holly let out a sound that made Sahara's skin jump in excitement.

"God, Sahara. He's stunning. The man knows how to dress. You'll see."

"I can't wait," Sahara admitted, her eyes cast down, reaching for her breakfast croissant. Was there anything more alluring than disrobing a sharply dressed man? She tried to keep the memory down, but once again, she remembered Richard on the night they had met - and the image of him centuries before - opening his chamber door to her knock. She shuddered.

"You ok?" Holly ran her hand lightly along Sahara's arm, stoking a silent fire in her lover.

Sahara leaned in. "I'm dying to make love to you. Get ready, sweetness. Tonight."

CHAPTER 9

"Good morning. Alexander's. Selena speaking."

"Good morning, Selena. It's Aiden Halloran. How are you?"

Selena felt the twinge of recognition at the sound of Aiden's resonant voice on the telephone.

"Hello, Mr. Halloran. I'm well. How can I help you?" Selena imagined helping Aiden in a way that involved her being on her knees.

Aiden smiled into the phone. "I'd like to book a reservation for seven this evening."

"Of course, your usual table?"

"No. A table for three please. Is the one to the right of the fireplace open?"

"Let me check. Yes. It's open. I'll reserve it for you."

"Thank you. Also, I would like a bottle of Krug Clos d'Ambonnay ready at the table."

"Oh! Yes, of course." Shit! Selena's curiosity was beginning to get the best of her, but she knew better than to ask any probing questions. She fell into a series of thoughts as she contemplated what tonight was about for Aiden.

"Selena?"

"I'm sorry. You were saying?"

"Please put me through to the kitchen. I'd like to speak with Alexander."

Selena hesitated. Alexander was in a cantankerous mood, and would not appreciate the interruption.

"Selena, the kitchen please."

She tingled at his forceful tone and put him through.

———⬥———

Reservations made, Aiden took Ulfred outside and headed out for a walk through the aspens. He was well aware of what tonight meant. It would seal them to each other, publicly. It would put him in the position of having to defend his choices, and to protect Holly and Sahara for theirs. As far as opinion was concerned, he didn't care who thought what, as long as his lovers were treated with respect. He knew that there would be gossip, but then he was not new to that. Tonight was a celebration and he intended to make their evening out as special for them as it was to him. In Aiden's heart, this thing was for life. His decision to make it public really stemmed from his desire to quell questions. If they were all seen together, lovers three, the speculation about their arrangement could only be lessened. Or so he hoped.

He knew that Sahara had faced this before. Her lifestyle choice would not be news to the larger community of her fans. But she still had to live with the opinion of Riverbend. As tough as Sahara seemed outwardly, her heart had already been battered over a lifetime of losses and disappointments. Aiden wanted very much to shelter her from any more fallout than was necessary. She was like a small bird, buffeted by the wind on a stormy day. At least, that was how Aiden saw her. As much as she would protest that she was able to stand anything by his side, he was determined to make her life a peaceful journey.

And what of Holly? She not only faced being judged for sharing him with Sahara, but also would come out as bi-sexual, an orientation sometimes understood less than being a lesbian. She'd have to face her parents, her strict upbringing, and out of the three of them, she was most in the public eye on a daily basis, her café exposing her to a direct line of fire. And he wouldn't be there to protect her, should someone decide to make a comment, or simply turn up to gawk at her. It was not easy to be private in a small town. The thought of Holly hurting over their choices made a hard knot in his chest. He walked briskly. Suddenly he realized that Ulfred had stopped a ways back and was sitting on his haunches, tongue flapping.

"Ulfred, my boy! Are you tired? I'm sorry. Let's head back."

Ulfred cocked his head, listening to Aiden's chatter. He turned around and seeing the path towards Sahara's, started to lope along it.

"Hey! Ulfred! Mom's not home. Get back here!"

Ulfred began to run. Aiden laughed and picked up his speed. Sahara turned everyone into an addict.

⁂

He sent her a message.

'We'll be sleeping in my bed tonight.'

He smiled thinking about how amazing it would be to wake up to the two of them in the morning, in his massive bed. It would be the first time they'd all spent the whole night at his house. He made the bed with fresh linens, and aired out his room. He checked his watch. Enough time to chop some wood and rest. His body ached for a workout. Aiden tied Ulfred a safe distance away from the wood pile and picked up the axe. His thoughts turned to Holly in an embrace between himself and Sahara. The axe landed with a solid strike dead center of the log. Aiden growled. He ached for them. Madly.

· ❊ ·

Holly greeted her helper, and gave instructions for the afternoon. Lilith, a pretty girl of nineteen, was fiercely loyal to her boss. Holly had been willing to hire her despite Lilith's obvious limp, leftover from a disastrous skiing injury. When Lilith had said that she was kind of slow on account of her hobbling, Holly had smiled, given her a hug, then offered her an apron to wear. She had never once mentioned anything about the awkward way that Lilith moved. Lilith knew that someone else could perform the job much faster. But Holly wouldn't hear of it.

Lilith gave Sahara a glance. "You dating her?" she asked.

"Yes," Holly answered.

"What about Aiden? You dating him too?"

Holly smiled. "Yes. Him too."

"Do you love them...both?"

"I do. Very much." Holly's eyes misted. It was all that Lilith needed to see.

"Are you ok with it?" Holly asked, sensitive to Lilith's feelings.

"As long as they're good to you. And you know what you're getting into. What do I know? I've never dated anyone."

"That's because the boys in this town are fools," Holly offered.

"I used to have a huge crush on Aiden. He's pretty hot for an old guy," Lilith admitted.

Holly laughed.

"I know. Everyone did...or still does."

"Maybe I should try girls?" Lilith joked.

"You should try believing in yourself, Lilith. You're amazing. Pretty soon someone will realize that, and snap you up."

Lilith noticed that Sahara was watching them.

"I don't think Sahara likes me," she whispered to Holly.

"Sahara is the kindest person I know. She likes you, she's just protective. Aiden probably told her to look out for me."

"What's it like to be loved like that?" Lilith wondered.

"Pretty amazing. You'll know one day. Now let me go. I need to pack an overnight bag."

Lilith rolled her eyes. "I don't even want to know."

48

CHAPTER 10

"When love is without jealousy, without possessiveness, it is divine"
~ *Osho*

Sahara showed Holly Aiden's message about sleeping arrangements. They had a few hours to nap, bathe and get ready for their evening. They were stretched out in Sahara's bed, languishing under the covers, glasses of wine on the nightstand.

"I'm so excited and nervous that I can't think straight," Holly said. "I get a funny feeling in the pit of my stomach when Aiden is being dictatorial. It makes me feel naughty...a little scared."

Sahara nodded, and snuggled into Holly's arms. "Me too. I love that about him, how serious he is about sex, and how he knows exactly what he wants when it comes to us. I love that he's not afraid to play rough. I need it."

"Play rough with me, Sahara," Holly whispered. "Are we saving it all for tonight, or can I have a little bit of you for myself?"

"I want you to myself."

Sahara reached under the bed for her box of toys. She opened it. "You choose."

Holly's nipples perked. "Anything I want?"

"Anything, except for this," Sahara pointed.

"Why not?"

"I'd like to see Aiden use that on you first time."

"Oooh." Holly reached down between her legs. "You're making me wet. What are these?"

"Nipple rings." Sahara bent down to slide her tongue over Holly's nipples. Holly moaned.

"Do you want to try them?"

"Yes."

"What about a bit of melted wax?" Sahara pulled out a candle.

"Will it hurt?" Holly rubbed herself on Sahara's leg, her clit hard and her pussy swelling with anticipation.

"A little...anything else?"

Holly held up two clips attached to some ankle cuffs by leather straps. "What are these?"

Sahara moaned. "To clip to your delicious pussy...open you wider. These bits of leather leading from the ankle cuffs are to tie your legs open....you'll be quite vulnerable. Do you trust me enough for this? The clips will hurt a bit."

Holly laid down, holding her wrists together for Sahara to bind to the headboard. Her eyes shadowed into a lust induced haze.

"*Holly.* You're so fucking hot, surrendering to me like that."

"Please, Sahara. We don't have much time."

⸺✳︎⸺

Aiden dialed Holly's number. No answer. He dialed Sahara. No answer. He knew they were home, because they weren't at the café and it was already five thirty. He reached to a top shelf in his closet and pulled down two small boxes. He opened them both and stared down at the contents. Hopefully, it wasn't too much. He'd wanted to surprise them with a little something that spoke of his love. He placed the boxes on one of the bed pillows, and sent them a message.

"Save some for me. I'm hungry."

He grinned. Having spent some time exploring Holly's desires, he knew that her need for a woman's touch was overwhelming. He doubted that she would ever need him sexually as much as she craved Sahara. And he accepted that. He wouldn't change a thing about her.

A message came back from Sahara's phone. Aiden adjusted himself in the track pants he wore low enough to expose his defined obliques; cock commando, blood humming through his veins. There was nothing that he wore that didn't look better because it graced his spectacular body.

"I hope you're *starving*," Sahara wrote. "I've got Holly ready for what you're touching right now. And I'm dripping wet for you, lover."

Aiden's fingers barely functioned as he typed back.

"Don't play with me Sahara. I'll hold you to those words, and it'll take all night."

Sahara showed Holly the message, sitting on the chair by the tub, watching Holly wash herself.

Holly's eyes closed as she ran the washcloth gently over her breasts and between her legs.

"Sore, sweet thing? I'm sorry."

Holly moaned. "I need him, Sahara. To fill me. Sore? Yes..." She held her hand out.

Sahara took it, kissing Holly's fingers gently. She knew exactly how Holly felt, that rush of deep longing to be submissive to someone you trusted wholeheartedly; how it made you want to serve on your knees, bound, begging for release, and afterward, the sweet calm of knowing that your submissiveness was your dominance. It was a powerful trip, and Sahara knew the dangers and joys of it. But taken with Holly, it was perfection. Holly was all heart, very little ego. She'd submitted so perfectly that Sahara had found release the instant Holly's mouth had latched onto her nipples.

"We've got to get ready." She handed Holly a towel. "What did you bring to wear?"

"You'll see. Something new."

"When did you have time to go shopping? You're a slave to that café."

"Please don't say the word 'slave', Sahara." Holly dried herself and rinsed out the tub. "I ordered it online a while back."

"Is it normal that I want to spread you open again so soon?"

"*Jesus*! Sahara. Stay away from me, or we'll never be ready on time. I could go again right now. How do you do that to me?" She bent over to dry her toes, her sweet ass teasingly close to Sahara's face.

"I'm never going to have enough of you, Holly. Go get ready. Aiden will be angry if we're not on time. This is important to him."

<hr>

Aiden checked his reflection in the full length mirror of his walk-in closet. Pleased with what he saw, he ran his hands through his hair, he'd left it down. He hoped that the black suit he'd chosen would go well with whatever the women would wear. It had an almost imperceptible chocolate pin stripe running through it, slim cut; a perfect fit to his wide shoulders and slim hips. The shirt he wore was white, a fine stripe of blue throughout. His tie was a compliment of chocolate brown with a black and ice blue paisley design. He adjusted his cufflinks and stood tall, squaring his shoulders. Devastating. And he knew it. Aiden looked forward to unleashing all his good looks on Holly and Sahara. Tonight was for them. Ulfred barked as Aiden strode past his box, truck keys in hand.

"I'll take good care of them, Ulfred. Be back before you know it."

He typed a quick message to them. "Leaving the house."

<hr>

They looked at their phones and felt the extreme intensity of his feelings.

51

Holly hoped she would survive the two people who made her legs weak and her heart swell with love.

Sahara put the last touches of make-up on her face. She'd let Aiden greet Holly first.

He came in abruptly. Holly, at the kitchen counter, trembled the moment she saw his ruggedly refined beauty. He stopped, arrested by her appearance. She wore a simple, figure hugging wrap dress, the colour matching her skin so perfectly that she looked bare. Her hair was piled into a classic chignon, her ears adorned by ruby chandelier earrings. They matched her lush lips. She stood tall in nude stilettos. Simple elegance. No necklace, no bracelets, no rings to overpower her natural beauty.

The naked hunger in Aiden's eyes was startling. He gave her a moment to rake him over with her own need, then came over with quick strides. Grabbing a hold of the back of her neck, he pulled her in for a deep kiss, taking her without apology. His tongue worked magic on hers, deep loving strokes that had her gripping his arms. She moaned into his mouth, igniting a fever-pitched desire.

"*Holly.* I'm not sure I can stand you looking like this all night. Goddamn it, woman. You're going to kill me." Aiden stared fiercely into Holly's eyes.

She stammered. "Oh Aiden...I need you."

He wanted to rip her hair down, to make a mess of her dress, to fall to his knees and bury his face between her legs.

"Let me touch you."

She groaned. "No! I'll come right here and now."

"Damn," he muttered. Then, ignoring her plea, spread her legs with his and ran his hand along her leg, fingers soon covering her heat. She throbbed under his touch. They were dangerously close to losing all control.

Sahara watched it all from the loft, hands gripping the railing. "Aiden!"

They looked up, dazed, her voice snapping them out of their lust. Sahara seemingly floated down the stairs, in graceful black stilettos.

"Oh," Holly breathed, Aiden's hands leaving her as his brain registered what Sahara was wearing.

"No!" Aiden muttered. "Are you insane Sahara? I can see your nipples right through."

His blood boiled angry to match the feelings of sexual hunger at her wearing something so provocative. He was surprised at how suddenly possessive he felt over other men seeing what was his.

"*Sahara*," Holly whispered.

Sahara's energy flowed from her in waves of powerful, sensual magic. The bottom part of her black dress was a flowing chiffon skirt skimming her knees, topped by a skimpy halter of pleated chiffon straps, that wrapped themselves rather sinfully around Sahara's upturned breasts, their tips pointing indecently long through the fabric. A silver pentagram pendant hung low on her chest.

Holly, knocked out by Sahara's femininity and pure female allure could only stare.

"Sahara. Please. I'm not ready to share you like that," Aiden said, his intensity filling the room.

Only the two of them knew that he had already shared much more of her than this. The look in his eyes almost made Sahara want to agree, but she needed to play this her way. She faced Aiden's displeasure.

He could see that she had no intention of listening to him. His eyes roamed her breasts, then down to the bottom of her dress. If he could have lifted the hem with his eyes, he would have.

"I need you Sahara," Aiden hand drifted to the growing erection in his Italian slacks.

"Shall I?" Sahara looked down hungrily at his cock.

"We'll be late," Aiden groaned out his need.

"We won't be late. I know how to bend time."

Sahara undid the buckle of Aiden's belt. The way he looked wasn't lost on her, he was fucking hot. His body was built for wearing an expensively tailored suit. She was soaking wet, ready to climax, and knew that she would the minute her lips touched him.

Holly, eyes wild, stood by Aiden, taking his hand, gripping it tight. He looked at her, his love and lust plainly written on his face.

Sahara threw a pillow on the floor and slipped to her knees. Aiden widened his stance to allow her access. Holly watched as Sahara took Aiden's large, beautiful cock in her mouth and heard her groan as her body rocked into orgasm. Her own cunt wet and tight, Holly begged Aiden for a kiss.

He exploded loudly, Sahara swallowing fast to take all of his warm, thick cum. It was all over in a minute. It wasn't how Aiden thought the evening would start. But he wouldn't have, couldn't have; changed a thing. They drove out towards Telson in a shock of emotions and pheromones that fairly dripped off them. Aiden didn't say a word until they arrived there, and was handing them their wraps as they exited the truck.

"I need a drink."

They nodded and taking his lead, followed him into the restaurant, his jaw clenched. His energy dared any man to stare for more than a second. Aiden had never known such intensity of feeling. He'd kill if he had to, but he wasn't going to let anything or anyone come between him and the women he needed more than breath itself. He walked behind them through the dining room, his hands light to the small of their backs, waiting to sit until they were in their chairs. He'd recognized Drew, his foreman, at one of the tables, and a few clients, but thankfully, no Dianne.

The waiter popped the cork on the champagne. Toasting them, Aiden threw back the ridiculously expensive bubbly.

Sahara locked eyes with him. Holly reached for his hand. And he'd thought that it would have been them who would need support on this night.

"I love you," Holly said, her eyes still wild.

"I love you," Sahara whispered. Her heart tearing to see him this overwhelmed.

Lifting up, one hand on his tie, Aiden placed a kiss on each of their mouths, to the deafening silence that enveloped the packed out restaurant. Then he ordered more wine, raking his hands through his hair. He sighed, offering Holly and Sahara a weak smile.

"Sorry," he leaned closer. "It hit me hard...suddenly...how much I love the two of you. I don't know what's happening to me. I'm feeling murderous. I need to know that you're both ok."

Sahara nodded. Holly smiled her most tender smile.

"We're fine Aiden," Sahara said. "I don't care what anyone thinks. Just relax. We've been looking forward to this all day."

She poured him more wine, and said that she'd be happy to be the designated driver. Aiden took his suit jacket off, and eased more comfortably into his chair. His eyes had lost some of that crazed look. But just then, as he found a comfortable position, Sahara stood to use the ladies room. Aiden groaned and stood as well. He knew that every eye would follow her.

She walked away, head high, spreading a wave of heat behind her.

Drew's breath caught as she wove through the tables. She was intoxicating. He looked away, his colour rising, very aware of Aiden's intense stare.

CHAPTER 11

Holly rested her hand on Aiden's leg. She squeezed.

"I know how you feel. She's...well, there's no words for how she looks tonight. She's so confident. She knows herself well. And anyway, at some point she'll go away on book tours and we won't know what she'll be wearing at all."

He nodded. "That's not encouraging at all, my love. But what about how you look tonight? I'm already dreading the moment you leave the table."

She blushed. "Come with me then," she challenged.

"Try and stop me." Aiden refilled her wine glass.

"Planning to make me drunk Aiden?" Holly bit her lip, nipples perking.

He noticed right away.

"You have no idea what I'm planning for you tonight," he rasped out, his hand rising to the back of her neck. She melted to his touch, both of them forgetting where they were, or how many eyes were trained in their direction to see what would happen between them while Sahara was away. But she was back in that moment, and leaning down, found Holly's lips, and dropped a luscious kiss.

"Christ, Sahara," Aiden bit out, grateful for the table cloth in front of him, "you're a brat."

She sat down beside him, hand lightly grazing his shoulder.

"If we're coming out, we're coming out. If people are going to talk, they should talk about facts, not speculations. Now, where in God's name are our menus Aiden? I'm starving! Or are we only to drink champagne worth a month's wage?"

He laughed, realizing that she was right. They'd come to do this, so why was he being so maniacal about it? He motioned to the waiter, who scurried off to the kitchen.

"No menus," he admitted. "I've taken the liberty of ordering for us. Hope you don't mind."

They didn't mind. He was paying a small fortune and delighted in doing so.

The owner of the restaurant came out with the appetizer - a savoury crab cake on a bed of lightly steamed bok choy.

Alexander smiled broadly and spoke with a thick Austrian accent. "Good evening." He took a quick scan of the girls, blatant appreciation evident in his stare. Aiden cleared his throat.

"Alexander, my good friends...Holly and Sahara."

Alexander kissed their hands, if for a second too long.

"Welcome. I'm delighted to have you join us this evening. Aiden has picked out a wonderful menu. He has quite the refined palette." His smile was innocent but they all caught the double entendre.

"We're delighted to be here," Sahara purred. Holly smiled and blushed. Alexander's stare caught on her pulse, lightly visible at the base of her throat. Aiden felt her discomfort. She hated being stared at.

"Thank you, my friend," Aiden's voice, smooth as silk, threw a loud warning to the other man, who was used to charming the panties off the local women.

Alexander gave a low, guttural laugh. He patted Aiden on the shoulder in a show of male solidarity.

"Enjoy your meal."

A bottle of wine later saw Aiden laughing out loud at Holly's attempt to tell a translated joke, which she finally gave up and told in fluid French. Sahara, terribly amused at the look on Aiden's face as Holly spoke with a comedic Parisian slur, suggested Holly begin to drink water instead of wine. Holly announced that she needed the ladies room, and stood abruptly. Aiden lifted the napkin from his lap and stood to accompany her.

"You're going with her?" Sahara looked at him, eyebrow up.

"I need him," Holly grinned and took Aiden's hand. He shrugged and said he wouldn't be long.

Sahara shook her head, amused, as Aiden walked away with Holly's hand in his. He was so lost. She called the waiter over and asked for lemon water for all of them. Whatever stares were directed her way, she met head on. Everyone looked away, except for one woman, who had just been seated two tables over, alone. Sahara recognized her from Aiden's recent description. Dianne. Sahara smiled genuinely, her face soft with understanding.

Dianne smiled back, and her shoulders relaxed. Sahara sent a spell for peace her way. She hoped that she'd never have to feel what Dianne was feeling now.

In the alcove adjoining the rest rooms, Aiden stood leaning against the wall. To anyone observing him, he was the picture of composure, a man of stunning good looks, of powerful stature, the look in his eyes screaming *sex*. When Holly stepped out of the women's side, lips newly stained red and her cheeks flushed, he pinned her purposively to the wall.

"*Aiden!* Someone will see us!"

"I need you naked. Under me. Wet," he growled in her ear, his body pressing against hers.

"Skip dessert?"

"No. I just wanted you to know. You're torturing me."

He moved away, and took her hand. Holly's step faltered. His body against hers felt so damn good. They walked back into the dining room. Aiden stopped at Drew's table, introduced Holly and they moved on. They saw Dianne at the same time. Sahara was sitting beside her. Aiden's hand gripped Holly's so hard that she whimpered. They stopped at her table, Aiden fighting the instinct to wring Sahara's neck.

Sahara stood.

"Aiden. I've just met Dianne. You didn't lie. She's gorgeous."

Aiden's breath left him in a hiss. Holly smiled at Sahara's kindness and Dianne looked up at Aiden with unshed tears.

"Dianne," Aiden bent over her hand. "You're welcome to join us at our table." He didn't mean it, but his manners kicked in by instinct.

Dianne declined. She said that someone was meeting her. Aiden nodded, relieved. He asked if Sahara and Holly would mind giving him a minute alone with Dianne. They agreed and Holly said she hoped that Dianne would stop by the café sometime. She meant it.

Aiden waited until Dianne was seated then joined her, his back blocking the view to the other tables. He leaned towards her, took her hand and whispered.

"Ok?"

She nodded, unable to speak.

"I understand. You needed to see for yourself." He imagined that Alexander's gossiping was to blame for her presence. "I'm sorry, darling. I know that you're hurting." He searched her eyes. "It's not that it wasn't amazing with you, you know that...I want a family, I fell in love. But no more Dianne. We'll have to move on. That's not to say that if you needed anything as a friend you couldn't call me. Holly and Sahara would understand."

58

Dianne agreed that he was right. She'd just needed to see them all together for herself. She looked towards the corner table where Holly and Sahara sat hand in hand, faces close, Sahara playing with a stray lock of Holly's hair. "I can see what you fell in love with. They're beautiful inside and out."

"Thank you."

Dianne felt Aiden's leaving at her core.

CHAPTER 12

"Why did you do that? Oh what am I saying, I know why." Aiden slipped in beside Sahara.

"Because she's hurting. She's lost two men she's loved - her husband, now you. If you left *me,* I'd be grasping at straws like she is to see what made you do it, and punishing myself by keeping you close in any way possible. I have a heart, Aiden."

"And I fucking love you for it."

Aiden teased Sahara with a hungry smile. "I was a little bit angry back there, but I can see that you were only being your incredible self. Still, I'm going to punish your sweet ass for it."

Sahara knew what *that* meant.

"Order us a coffee, Aiden," Holly said. "I'm drunk."

"And I'm planning to take advantage of that," Aiden retorted and signaled the waiter once more.

He'd loosened his tie now, and was looking decidedly rakish, staring them down with downright indecency. He licked his lips as his eyes caressed Sahara's breasts, wanting to sink his mouth over her nipples, to suck them through the thin, transparent material. She felt his desire and they stuck out to tease him, Holly's hand light on her leg, under the table cloth.

Dessert appeared with Alexander. He looked hopeful that he'd be invited to sit, but Aiden scowled at him and he got the hint.

Holly took a bite. A very thin, delicate triangle of sponge soaked in liqueur, topped with fresh raspberries, a dot of double cream and a fine chocolate ribbon dribbled across. Simple. Delicious.

"Like it Aiden?" Holly asked.

"I'd like it more if I was eating it off your naked slice," Aiden whispered to her.

"Aiden!" Holly jumped. She loved his crude words, and that it would mean being delectably abused by his practiced tongue. She'd never seen him this heightened though.

He continued to whisper. "As soon as we get in my truck, you're going to unwrap that excuse for a dress, slip your panties off and offer yourself to me. I want you coming in my mouth seconds later."

Sahara peered at him over her coffee cup. She could feel his energy rising to that place where his hands longed for violence. Her clit throbbed as she thought about witnessing Aiden's tongue assaulting

Holly's pussy. She suddenly wanted to leave this place and to see Aiden half-naked, devouring Holly, his arms locked into hardness as he braced himself between her legs.

Aiden caught her look and told Holly to hurry, they were leaving.

"But what about my coffee?"

"Now Holly, or I'll carry you out of here."

Holly took a last bite of her dessert, and put her fork down.

"I'm ready," her tongue darted along her lower lip.

Aiden's chest rumbled. He stood and motioned them to walk in front of him. There was no doubt as to what Aiden getting when he got home; if not before. He nodded to the host, who had Aiden's credit card on file. They stepped out into the cold and the dark simmering with desire, the air a welcome change to the heat in their veins. Aiden pressed the remote and the truck doors clicked open.

They walked over to the driver's side. Aiden opened the back door and helped Holly in.

"Unwrap your dress."

"It's freezing."

"Do it." He shut the door.

Sahara knew what to do. She knew him and what he'd want, and he knew what she needed. She spread her legs and closed her eyes.

Aiden's hand slipped under her dress, along her inner thigh, and feeling that she was fully wet and swollen, plunged his fingers inside her while his mouth sealed over hers, kissing hard, bruising. Sahara moaned, a thread of ecstasy rushing from her sex to her toes.

"I love you. I'm going to burn that dress." He released her and climbed in after Holly. She was practically naked, shivering and with her legs spread, every bit of her tenderness on display.

Aiden's lips travelled slowly from her heaving belly towards her full breasts, as she writhed helplessly under him, her hands pushing against his shoulders.

"I can't...take it, please darling...stop." He looked up at her. She shook her head. "Don't stop."

Sahara moved the front seat up to reach the gas pedal and giving Aiden room to fit himself inside Holly's legs. He half-knelt, half-squatted in front of her, eyes tight to her pussy, eating her with his eyes. Her hand slipped down.

"That's right, babe, open up for me, show me that delicious bit of cunt. Damn, woman, you're beautiful!"

Sahara moaned in her seat. Aiden, when he was being blunt, was at his most desirable. She tried to look back to see his perfect lips on

Holly's sex. The truck swerved.

"Sahara! Careful."

Sahara's hands gripped the steering wheel.

Holly gasped from the heat of Aiden's breath.

"Please..."

"I like it when you beg for my tongue on your snug cunt, Holly."

She cried out his name.

Aiden's mouth lowered, and his tongue fell wide on her slit. He waited. She waited for the lick. But instead, he plunged deep, tonguing her forcefully. She screamed and tangled her fingers in his hair. His tongue softened to lick inside her cleft, along her lips, then his mouth clasped onto her clit. He pulled rhythmically. He bit it, along the hard ridge, in small, delicate nips.

"Oh, oh!" Holly arched her back and shoved against his face, rubbing herself along it.

"Yes! Rub your pretty little cunt on my face."

He held firm while she rode him, then grabbed her hips and stilled her. He kissed along her inner thigh, circling his tongue along her perineum, close to her tightly pursed bud. She groaned and said yes. He smiled to himself. He wondered if she really would let him. One hand rubbing her clit deftly, Aiden licked a light circle around her bud. He asked her to lift so he could get to her most secret place. She held her breath.

"There's nothing I wouldn't do for you, Holly," Aiden said, feeling how close she was to the edge, as his fingers worked magic on her very erect clit. And then, he slipped his tongue directly over her pink bud.

Holly arched, cried out and descended into a rocking orgasm. He broke her open, every time, made her lose control. Aiden pulled her into his arms, the truck warm now.

Sahara looking back in the rear view. Holly's head leaned against Aiden's shoulder. He was holding her tight, his mouth against her ear, whispering something. She turned around, straddling him, pushing his hair aside so she could whisper back. His hands were under her open dress, caressing her ass. She fit so nicely in his lap.

"I love that you let me in there," Aiden whispered.

"I want you in there...I mean...I..." Even in the dark he knew that she was blushing.

"Trust me. I want in there too." He spread her bottom open, one finger stroking towards her back opening.

"Tonight?"

Aiden groaned. "I don't want to hurt you..."

"Sahara's been teaching me. We've been practicing with her toys."

"You're killing me, that's so hot."

"Home," Sahara announced, and turned the engine off.

Aiden said he'd take Ulfred out and instructed Sahara to throw a match on the fire to light it. "It's all set up. Just light it."

Sahara was doing it before he'd finished the sentence. Holly lit some candles, and pressed the remote of the stereo.

Ulfred came back in with Aiden and ran in circles around the living room, ending at Sahara's feet in a dead stop.

"Hello, Ulfred," Sahara picked him up. "I've missed you."

Ulfred stuffed himself into her neck, and relaxed his wiggling body.

She sat down on the stone hearth by the growing heat of the fire.

Aiden, in the kitchen, rolled up his shirt sleeves and removed his tie. Holly stood behind him, admiring the view of his broad back and tight ass, so perfectly accentuated by his suit slacks. She molded herself to his warmth, running her hands over the rippling mass of muscle that comprised his middle body.

"Mmmm." Aiden moved back towards her.

"I love your hands on me," Aiden's fingers intertwined with hers. Holly's warmth on his back and the sight of Sahara in such a peaceful pose by the fire filled his heart with contentment.

"She's so...I don't know, magical," Holly said as she watched Sahara stand slowly from her place by the fire. "I love her so desperately, Aiden."

"Me too, my love. So much it hurts."

What Sahara did next unfolded in slow motion before them. She reached around to undo her dress, her eyes intent upon them, a smile playing on her lips. She eased the dress up over her head, and stood naked before them but for the black lace panties that curved around her hips. Her hands ran over her breasts, teasing her nipples to their furthest point.

Aiden stood on alert, his body responding with a wicked heat. Holly's hand was already running the length of his hard as steel erection, and pushing herself against his back.

Before they knew what her intention was, Sahara had bunched the dress in her hands, and thrown it into the fire. It was gone in seconds.

63

She faced them, her stare bold and defiant.

"Sahara!" Aiden ripped himself away from Holly and strode over. "What *are* you doing? I didn't mean literally...I'm sorry!" He pulled her close, his face hard; his hands harder.

Sahara shook in his arms and he picked her up to cradle her, her bottom in his hands. She rested against the sound of his pounding heart.

"Why?" Holly choked out. "I loved that dress. It must have cost a fortune."

Sahara held her hand out to her. "It was only for this occasion. Especially for the things we're feeling tonight. I knew that it would make Aiden angry to share me like that in public. But sometimes, I need to push Aiden to those places. It's just something I need from him."

Holly nodded, her emotions raw.

Aiden succumbed to the ancient need to possess a woman completely. Sahara had done it; pushed him to the place of no return, and Holly would be witness to the things he was aching to do.

"Go get it," he instructed, voice raspy. Sahara went obediently upstairs.

Aiden pulled Holly towards the sofa and sat her down. He took her mouth, she yielded immediately. His tongue caressed hers, tender; warm. He loved the way she kissed, every lick, every bite, a precise meeting of emotional and physical hunger.

"Holly, you're going to see a side of me that, well...I hope you'll understand. Sahara and I, we need this from each other. I don't want you to be afraid. I'd never give her more than she can take. You know what I asked her to fetch?"

Holly moaned, "Yes." She continued to kiss him, in that way she had that completely undid him. She was so good with her tongue.

"I'm not afraid."

"Liar."

"I want to know the two of you...every dark place. I'm not afraid."

"You're a charmingly bad liar at that. I can feel it. You're afraid that I'll hurt her."

"Yes," she finally admitted. "But I can't stand not knowing what makes the two of you, you." Holly undid her dress. She took her breasts in her hands, rolling her nipples. "Kiss here. Suck them hard."

Aiden didn't need a second invitation. He buried his face in her breasts, heavy now with arousal.

She found his lips once more, and slid her tongue along the perfect

64

curve of his heartbreaking mouth.

"Shall I pour you a drink?"

He nodded and removed his shirt. He adjusted his cock. Sahara came down, holding a small, feathered whip. He threw back the scotch that Holly handed him, noticing that she was shaking. He could smell the delicate scent of her pussy, wet with anticipation. He asked if she would sit on the edge of the sofa, and spread her legs. Holly obeyed instantly, as was becoming her custom with them.

"God. Holly. That is one beautiful pussy." Aiden's tongue flicked out over his lower lip as he stared at the intricate folds of Holly's sex, swollen by lust.

Sahara knelt in front of her. Holly whimpered as Sahara's breath ran hot along her leg. "You have the most beautiful tits, sweetness. I could spend all night just sucking on those pink nipples of yours." Sahara's lips made contact with the smooth silk of Holly's inner thigh. Holly's hips pumped forward.

Aiden knelt down behind Sahara and lowered his face, his eyes on Holly, dark and smoldering.

"Watch me..." Aiden's mouth made a lazy journey along Sahara's lower back, towards her bottom.

Holly cried out. Desire this intense made her cunt swollen and dripping wet.

It was a pivotal moment. The seconds before tongues met their destination of tight, quivering cunt. Breath held, Sahara waited for that delicious first contact of Aiden's mouth upon her clit. She'd never known a man who loved to taste female sex as much as Aiden did. His breath swept along before his tongue. The first lick landed right over her opening. She tensed.

"Wait," he said, forbidding Sahara a taste of Holly.

He licked with sinful lips along her slit, then bit at the edge of her cunt. He maneuvered a wide tongue towards her clit, then, tender flutters along the ridge of it. Sahara's silence spurred him on. Holly watched, a bead of wet slid down her pussy towards her ass. Aiden licked upward, teasing Sahara's perineum, hands holding her open, then gave one shallow plunge into her depths. He held.

"You're gorgeous, Aiden," Holly licked her lips.

He groaned. "Now!" he instructed Sahara.

Sahara's mouth found Holly's clit in the exact moment that Aiden pressed his tongue to her tightly pursed bud.

"Oh," Sahara moaned against Holly's cunt. Everyone rocked with a surge of passion. Aiden licked and probed, fingers inside Sahara's snug cunt, tongue playing along the seam of her ass.

"You made me angry today," Aiden began the descent to his dark place.

Sahara moaned agreement.

"Say that you're sorry. Tell me that you were naughty to show everyone your beautiful tits. They belong to me."

"I'm sorry, Aiden," Sahara moaned into the panting Holly, whose hands were gripping the blanket Aiden had covered the sofa with.

"You're a whore, Sahara. Say it."

Sahara shook her head. "No."

Holly's breath sucked in. She was new to this game but was sure that Sahara was going to pay for her stubbornness.

"What?" Aiden's fingers began their vigorous pump into Sahara.

"I won't say it."

"*Fuck, woman*! Say it! Say that you're mine!"

Aiden's body, tense, bicep muscles bulging as he finger fucked Sahara, was enough to make Holly's clit throb towards a swollen hardness. His hair hung wild about his shoulders, his stomach a delicious treat, cock thickly veined as it stood to its fullest, reaching his navel.

Aiden slid suddenly inside Sahara, his cock soaked by her passion. He fucked hard. Sahara's mouth left Holly. Holly's hand found her clit.

"I *am* a whore...but I'm not yours Aiden," Sahara defied him, panting.

Aiden exploded into fury. Those were not the words he wanted to hear. He picked up the whip, and using every bit of control, he sashayed it across Sahara's ass, tender strokes the calm before the storm.

Holly's eyes widened. She slipped her fingers inside herself.

Aiden shook his head, eyes hard, voice deceptively soft. "I'll do that, my love."

Holly nodded, truly afraid of him now. She took her hand away.

Sahara pushed against Holly, her tongue now beginning to work her folds, urgent, hungry; crazed with anticipation of the first strike.

Holly stared at Aiden's cock standing at throbbing, wet attention as he caressed Sahara's ass tenderly with his hands, spreading her cheeks and sliding his finger along the seam. She could tell that he wanted more than anything to lick her.

"I love you," Aiden said softly to Sahara.

It was a dangerous time when Aiden whispered with a whip in his hands.

66

The whip came down and Sahara cried out. Holly tensed and pulled Sahara by her hair, urging her to suck on her clit. She could only stand this if she kept Sahara distracted. She opened herself further with her fingers.

"Eat me, Sahara. Please. Fuck me with your tongue."

Aiden roared. He whipped Sahara without mercy, yet asked for her safe word. He hated hurting her as much as he needed to do it. She said it quicker than he was used to, and he was sure that it had everything to do with Holly.

He returned to pounding Sahara's soft flesh, his cock hitting her cervix hard. She was stretched as far as she could go, and the pressure on that deep place swept her into a seldom accessed orgasm. She came in a rush, wetting him thoroughly while he kept up the merciless thrusts. She turned on him, and taking the whip, she pushed him towards Holly, who was staring at them with tears in her eyes.

"No!" Holly said, as Aiden presented his back to Sahara, and slid on a condom. He spit on his hand and, although it was not needed, made sure that Holly was wet enough to accept him. His cock slid effortlessly into her swollen pussy. He started to pump, Holly melting into ecstasy, as his fingers caressed her clit, eyes hard on her face, watching for her cues.

She heard the first strike. Aiden winced. Sahara wasn't holding back. Holly's breath came faster, concerned.

"I'm alright," Aiden said to her, but his eyes closed on the next strike. "I need you to come for me, sweet thing," he whispered. "The way you did before...the first time, remember? God, that looks so hot, your cunt stretched around my cock."

He shifted Holly's hips and began a hard assault on her magic spot. She wanted to shield him from the whip, but try as she might; she couldn't get to that part of him with her hands, and still concentrate on the sensations inside her body.

"No fucking way, Holly. Stay away from that whip," Aiden growled. He pumped harder, he pulled up on the hood of her clit, exposing it. He spat directly onto it.

"You're going to come for me Holly. Sahara's going to keep that up until you do."

"Oh!" Holly cried out. Her body responded with a loud orgasm that gushed out in frenzied spurts. Holly's hand went out to Sahara. "Stop! Please stop!"

Sahara slid over, her mouth on Holly's in an instant, face covered in tears. Aiden slipped the condom off, and came in hot spurts all over the women he loved. They watched fascinated as his muscled hands pumped his beautiful cock and he groaned out his orgasm.

He leaned his hands against the sofa, drained. It was the best and longest orgasm he had ever experienced. Holly and Sahara lay covered with every drop of cum that he'd had to give them. He looked at them, lying beside each other, their stomachs and breasts an abstract design of his seed. Aiden began to laugh. They stared at him.

"What the hell is so funny?" Sahara asked, her hand tight in Holly's.

"What a mess. What a big, fucking, beautiful mess." Aiden smiled down at them. "I've never seen anything more enticing in my life." His kisses were tender, all that heightened energy spent, speaking soft words of love.

He turned to go upstairs and warm the shower for them. It was then that Holly saw that his back was bleeding, and covered in welts. She burst into tears, hiding her face in her hands.

Aiden froze. He took Holly's hand and pulled her to her feet. He then lifted her into his arms. Sahara met his gaze, neither of them sorry that they had given in to their needs, but in silent acknowledgement of Holly's distress.

Wordlessly, he carried her upstairs, her body wet, pressed against his. She sobbed her tears into his chest. He stepped into the shower and turned the water on. When it ran warm, he brought Holly in. He wet her hair, and lathered it with his shampoo. She relaxed as soon as she smelled his familiar scent. Caressing gently, he spread his seed around her breasts, on her taut belly, before he rinsed it off. She gasped, unfamiliar with the erotic habits of a man as confident as Aiden.

"I can't wait to fill you with this one day. To pump you so full of my cum that it drips out of your pussy because you can't take anymore." Holly felt suddenly weak and leaned into Aiden's hard body.

He lathered his hands and washed her gently, his hands roaming her familiarly, until he reached her bottom. He winced as water hit his back, and turned abruptly. But Holly's sadness over his back cut him deeper than the whip itself.

"Could I ask you to put some salve on my back when we get out?" He pulled her close once more, his fingers running towards her tightly puckered bud.

"Yes. Anything. I can't stand it...to see you hurt." She stood on tiptoe and kissed him softly, her breath catching as his soapy fingers slid over that most tender place.

68

Eyes dark, Aiden slipped his tongue over her lips, soft strokes that turned into delicious plunges inside her mouth. She moaned, his finger now close to the mark.

"Doesn't it hurt you to hurt Sahara like that, or for her to hurt you?"

"Yes. But it builds our trust for each other as well. The pain is a reminder of our total surrender, of knowing that we can leave our life in the other's hands. But more than that, it has things to do with our last life together."

Holly moaned as Aiden gripped her nipples and pulled hard.

"Did that hurt sweet thing?"

"Yes. Oh God, Aiden, do it again."

He did, then licked them tenderly to soothe the pain.

"Remember what you asked me for earlier?"

"Yes," Holly groaned and spread her legs as if on command.

"Are you afraid that it'll hurt?"

"Yes."

"Shall we try anyway? Only if you're sure you're ready."

"Yes." Holly gripped the towel bar, she bent over slightly, and spread her legs wider.

Aiden growled and fisted her hair in his hands, burying his mouth close to her ear.

"*Holly*. Such sweet surrender....you have no idea what it's doing to me."

"Do it, Aiden. I want...oh God, I want you inside me."

"I'm afraid to hurt you. It's not going to be like with Sahara, her sex toy has give; but my cock doesn't."

Holly turned to look him in the eye. "Aiden *please*."

He reached for a small bottle of oil, and poured a little in her hands. His cock stood rock solid between them. He moaned quietly as her hands slid in perfect, smooth strokes over it.

"Turn around," he said, voice rough. "Trust me?"

She nodded, and turned.

Sahara entered the shower as Aiden's fingers oiled the seam of Holly's ass. Holly pulled Sahara between herself and the shower wall, her mouth opening to Sahara's tongue, as Aiden pushed carefully against her slick, tight bud.

"More, sweet thing?"

"More." Holly leaned into his touch. Her tongue caressed Sahara's, anxious.

"Best day of my life," Aiden said in a whisper.

"Finger my ass, Aiden," Holly groaned out her request.

His finger slid in, easily. Holly pushed back and begged him to fuck harder.

"*Beautiful*, Holly!" Aiden was now kneeling on the hard shower floor, paying close attention to her responses, high on seeing every erotic plunge that his finger took.

He slipped it out when he thought her ready.

She complained, but all her words were lost to his ardent kisses.

"Did that hurt, babe?"

Holly shook her head. Her colour rose. He smiled.

"You're devastating. I love you. How you can beg for a cock in your ass and still look so innocent?"

"More, Aiden."

Aiden caught Sahara's eye. He sent a telepathic message. *Help her*

She nodded.

He instructed Holly to take hold of the towel bar once more. Sahara stood at Holly's side, close enough to kiss her, or to find the cleft of her sex. She offered her mouth, and kissed her as Aiden ran another bead of oil down Holly's bottom.

He pressed against her, his cock teasing between her legs, his lips hot on her neck, biting, urging her passion on.

"Mmmm, Aiden please... fuck my tight little ass." She thrust her hips back.

His finger entered once more, then two, without a whimper from her. He had the edge that he wanted. His cock, to his concern, had swollen to monstrous proportions. He guided it slowly, with gentle thrusts, against her slightly open ring. Sahara found Holly's clit, and began a slow, rhythmic massage. Holly groaned into Sahara's mouth.

"You're so beautiful like this, Holly," Sahara whispered. "It's such a turn on to see you give yourself to him."

Holly kissed harder, her tongue in hard thrusts through Sahara's lips.

"Open a little more for me, sweet thing. Yes, like that, let me into your pretty ass." Aiden's voice caressed along her back, his need palpable. He massaged her neck, rubbed her scalp and ears. He took his time, waiting for her complete readiness. More oil, more love, more dirty words in indecent layers. He rolled a condom on.

She relaxed. He pushed the head of his cock in, Sahara's fingers keeping their steady pressure on her clit. Holly bit down on Sahara's lip. "OH!"

70

"Christ!" Aiden bit out. "Tell me to stop, Holly, and I will."

"Please Aiden, more...oh..."

He bit along her shoulder, while Sahara rubbed her clit. Holly cried out as it began to throb towards orgasm, lost in a haze of sensations. Aiden slid further, and began to thrust. Soft, tender movements that made Holly scream out her release, taking his rigid cock no further than halfway way in, but opening so prettily that he was caught staring at the way she received him.

Holly kissed Sahara viciously now, Sahara's mouth absorbing Holly's rapid moans.

Sahara's eyes closed as Holly ravaged her mouth, and Aiden, undone by their combined pleasure, came in hot, thick spurts, his groans meeting theirs.

Her lover's muscular body caressed by rivulets of water, an exquisite expression of male prowess, was where Holly focused her attention. She was incapable of words or even thoughts. Nothing could have prepared her for the intensity of what they had just done. He had said that it was about trust. But more than that, it was about complete surrender. And for Holly, this was the first time she had ever let herself be entirely possessed, relinquishing all control.

For the next few minutes, Holly felt nothing but Aiden's tender caress. It was intimate, raw. She wondered at how well he understood the female form, and exactly what she needed him to do. She couldn't keep from blushing, letting this powerful, self-assured man tend to her. And yet, it was wonderful to be in his hands, to know that it pleased him greatly when she allowed him her submission.

Aiden lay on the bed as Holly tended to his welts. An hour of peaceful rest had mellowed their emotions. Next, Holly applied salve to Sahara's bruised bottom.

"I love the smell of this salve. Where'd you get it?"

"Sahara made it," Aiden mumbled, holding Sahara's hand.

"You made it?" Holly said to Sahara. "How does one make salve?"

"We'll make some together in the spring," Sahara replied, sleepy.

"What's in the boxes?"

"Later, my love. I need rest," Aiden closed his eyes, and fell back asleep.

Holly lay down. She stared into Sahara's eyes.

Sahara nodded...she knew.

"I'm sorry. I know you're angry with me. Did Aiden explain it?"

"Yes. But I still hate to see him hurt. But I think I understand your bond better now. It's deep, isn't it, Sahara?

"Deep, yes. It hurt Aiden to see you cry over him," Sahara mumbled sleepily.

"Perhaps we could file tears shed during lovemaking under tears of passion, and then forget them." Holly felt a pang of guilt.

"Aiden can't be objective about your tears, Holly. Ever. You're the one person on earth that makes him lose perspective on reality. You're essential to him." Sahara fell asleep.

Holly stared at Sahara's pretty, compact body, the way her face had already slipped into a sleep induced peace, her lips curved into a content smile. This woman loved her and Aiden to distraction and had a deep understanding of how unfettered, unconditional love functioned. She took Aiden's complicated love for the two of them at his word - unselfish, devoid of jealousy. It was the purest love Holly had ever experienced.

She covered them carefully, taking a lingering and appreciative look at the tight curve of Aiden's ass, and how his large frame looked so powerfully inviting sprawled along his bed. She slipped in-between them. Turning towards Aiden she traced a finger along his arm pit and inner arm, down his side towards the rise of his buttocks. All muscle. He stirred, and moaned as Holly's hand made its way back along the same trajectory.

Aiden rolled onto his side, eyes dark with sleep.

"Turn over," he said. "All right, my love?"

She pushed back against him. "I used to think you were a gentleman," she whispered, not wanting to wake Sahara.

"Oh? And now?" Aiden sank his teeth into her shoulder.

Holly's hand reached back. "A gentleman would hardly press a weapon of that magnitude into a lady's back without an apology."

Aiden laughed softly under his breath. "No chance. I'm not apologising for that. Wake up with me every day, Holly? Promise."

She felt the rumble that rose in his chest when his emotions ran high.

"After I get my apprentice...it'll be easier then," she said, her body a tangle of nerves as he awoke her need again.

He growled into her ear. "When the hell will that be? How long will you make me wait?"

"Maybe next month? I sent a few inquiries a while back, just exploring my options..."

Aiden turned her around. "He?"

It was Holly's turn to laugh. "Jealous?"

"What do you think?"

"You once told me that you don't get jealous."

"I lied," his mouth lowered to hers. "Is it too late to cancel his arrival?"

"He's coming from France." Holly giggled and hid her face in his chest. Aiden's hand fisted in her hair.

"How old is he? Damn it Holly."

"Mid-twenties? I'm sure he's not my type."

"He better not be," Aiden bit her lip.

"I don't like boys, remember?" Holly slipped her tongue out to lick the spot he'd bitten.

"Remember what we did in the shower?" Aiden asked.

Holly blushed and nodded.

"You can't say you don't like boys anymore. You were begging for cock."

"*Your* cock, Aiden, to be fair."

Aiden directed her hand to grasp his erection. "You call this fair, little girl?"

She laughed. "Sleep!"

"Ok. But in the morning, your sweet cunt is mine." He caressed along her mound, his fingers pulling at the small tuft of blond hair. "I love this little bit you've left here. It's sweet, seeing your tight blond curls, and then the smooth skin below, how your clit is exposed."

"Keep your hand there," Holly purred. "Would you want me to change anything, take it all off?"

"No," Aiden hugged her tight. "It's perfect. And mine." He stroked one knee, his hand pulling her legs apart. She shifted to let him. "I think about it all the time. How you look when you're lying with your legs open, using your hands to spread wider for me, blushing, bold and shy at the same time." His hand slipped to her clit. "I think about how fucking great you taste, your lips pink and swollen. I hope you don't mind, I want to taste you every single day of my life. I need it. I love every sexy, perfect bit of you."

"*Aiden.* You're the one who's perfect. *Magnifique. Tres Delicieux.* There's no other man like you. No other man could have stolen my heart and made me want to be as un-inhibited as you do. I want you between my legs as much as you want to be there."

"I want to be between your legs, pretty lady," Sahara purred. She slid over. "Hold her open for me, darling?"

He obeyed, overwhelmed with love for Sahara who understood his obsessive need for Holly; without being intimidated. He sat up and held Holly in his arms, against his virile, muscular core, his hands on her breasts, pulling her nipples deftly.

"Oh, sweetie!" Holly breathed. "Yes, please. Lick me there. Here...let me open wider for you. I love you Sahara."

Aiden's one hand went to Holly's hair, caressing and teasing her senses. She melted into him, his sensual touch relaxing her into renewed passion. His tongue flicked along his lips, almost tasting what Sahara was tasting, his cock hard against Holly's back.

"I want to see her clit in your mouth, Sahara. Make her beg."

"I love you, little girl," Aiden whispered in Holly's ear, her hands firmly in his. "You look so damn amazing."

"Oh!" Holy cried out as Sahara's mouth found her throbbing clit. "Oh! Sahara, please!"

Aiden watched as Sahara licked, kissed, spanked and finger fucked Holly's pussy, taking her time to exquisitely raise her energy, and allow for her whole body to respond. Holly asked for Aiden's fingers in her mouth, he obliged and she sucked hard. His head hurt from lack of sleep and the deep need to spill himself once more.

"You have any toys here?" Sahara sat up, to Holly's protests.

Aiden smiled. "Actually, I do..."

"Where? Can I get them?

"In my closet, look in the left drawer closest to the sweaters. They're new, you should wash them."

"I know what to do," Sahara grinned.

"Apparently," he kissed Holly's upturned face. "Oh, that one!" he exclaimed when Sahara came back.

Sahara ran the toy along Holly's slit, whose hips pumped forward in anticipation. She placed it on Holly's lips. Aiden almost came seeing how well they interacted, Holly licking the vibrator with a seductive tongue, Sahara urging her on before she took it in her own mouth, wetting it thoroughly. Sahara turned around to give him a peek at her loveliness.

"Fuck. *Sahara.*" Aiden groaned out. His hand went to her sex. It was hot, wet; greedy for his hand.

"Watch me," Sahara begged. "I want you to see me fuck her, darling.

74

She's mine too."

"Of course...I know how much you love her." He grasped his rock hard prick, elegantly sliding his hand along it, eyelids heavy with passion.

Sahara slid the toy inside Holly, stretching her fully.

"*Holly*, you're so stunning. Your greedy little cunt looks so good filled like this." Sahara said under her breath.

"Harder, Sahara," Holly moaned.

Sahara pumped harder, teasing the man she loved with every move she made. He could smell her - cunt dripping her desire, open for him to see as she bent over Holly.

"You're so wet, darling. So very fucking wet," he observed.

"Get inside me. Now, Aiden!"

He slid in easily, not sparing an inch, balls deep.

"Fuck me hard! I need it hard." Aiden slammed into her, hands spreading her open.

Sahara pulled the vibrator, and clamped her mouth onto Holly's clit. She sucked hard, her orgasm voiced into Holly's flesh, Aiden roaring his own into the night, as Holly erupted into wave after wave of release.

They lay tangled and spent, the fierceness of their love expressed.

"Fuck, Aiden," Sahara said. "Just how much sperm can you possibly manufacture in one night?"

Aiden laughed and slid his finger inside her. "From the feel of it, quite a bit...looks like tomorrow is laundry day. You girls are messy."

They both punched him in the ribs.

And finally, they slept, the women curled up like kittens, their man a powerful, loving presence at their side.

CHAPTER 13

The smell of coffee and warming pastries woke Holly and Sahara up. Both regretted having to leave the warmth of the bed, but the comforting scent of a fresh fire downstairs made it easier to slip into some clothes.

"What do you think happened to those little blue boxes?" Holly asked Sahara in the mirror as they brushed their teeth.

"Dunno," Sahara replied, spitting into the sink. "Maybe he's rescinded them for services not rendered."

Holly laughed. "I doubt *that*. That man got more than the legal dose of pussy for one day."

They kissed, and ran down the stairs.

Aiden sat in the alcove under the stairs, dressed, coffee in hand, a book in his lap; Ulfred at his feet. His face lit up when he saw them.

"Good morning," he greeted them, accepting a kiss from each, an amused look on his face. "May I get you some coffee?"

"Three questions," Holly said. "One, you planned this alcove all wrong, there is only room for two chairs. Two, how do you look so fresh after being up half the night, and three, what happened to those little blue boxes?" She moved his book and sat in his lap.

Aiden put his cup down, and slid his arms around her. Sahara rolled her eyes, and said she'd get the coffee. Ulfred padded along behind her.

"Kiss me first, and I'll answer, although, technically, that was only two questions."

Holly planted a warm kiss on his cheek. Aiden scowled. "That's not what I meant. I mean, *kiss* me." She did.

"Mmmm. That's better."

Sahara returned with a tray of coffee. "Did I miss anything?"

"No," Holly said.

"You missed one of Holly's kisses," Aiden smiled.

"I've had mine, for the record," Sahara retorted.

Aiden thanked Sahara for his refill. "You're wrong, Holly. I planned this alcove all right. With only two chairs, one of you will always be sitting in my lap. Two, I have no answer for how I look 'fresh' as you say, and three, I have your little blue boxes right here."

He reached down beside his chair and held the boxes in his hand. He grinned. "I thought you might have forgotten about them in all the excitement of last night."

"Women don't forget little blue boxes, Aiden," Holly laughed.

Aiden held the boxes out. "Ready?"

"Which one is which?" Holly asked.

"Just pick one."

"Are they the same?"

"No. This is just something small, a token of my commitment, a promise towards the future. Pick."

They took a box each and by silent consent opened then simultaneously. Aiden no longer looked amused. He sat silently, pensive, as they pulled silver bracelets out of their cases.

"Oooh, Aiden!" Holly exclaimed. Hers was a delicate chain of infinity symbols, while Sahara's, quite similar, a weave of interconnecting circles.

"Darling," Sahara slipped to her knees beside Aiden. He leaned down for her kiss, his heart on his sleeve.

"I hope I've not made a fool of myself. I'm not trying to mark you..." Sahara covered his mouth with hers once more.

"You're so very generous, my love. It's perfect." She asked him to put it on for her. He looked so very serious, and she knew that this was a big moment for him, try as he might to play it down.

He looked at Holly, who also held out her wrist. "Too much, too little? I'll learn about what moves you, just give me time."

"I love your heart." Holly placed her hand over his chest, and fluttered a kiss on his lips.

Sahara felt from Aiden the deep longing that he had to make everything perfect in Holly's life.

"I have some work things to attend to today," Aiden began. "We should probably eat soon. I'm starving anyway." He got up, and made his way to the kitchen.

Sahara and Holly exchanged glances. He was so very sensitive underneath his commanding presence; it was easy for them to tell that he needed a few minutes of space after making his hopes for the future plain with his gift. They waited until he called them in to breakfast. He had boiled eggs, baked breakfast sausages, heated croissants to a perfect crispness, and put out an assortment of preserves. He pulled out their chairs, handed them their napkins and sat.

"Wow!" Holly exclaimed. "This is wonderful Aiden. I had no idea you were this domesticated."

"So you'll keep me?" Aiden asked, his voice deceptively light, his startling blue eyes cast down.

"*Aiden*," Holly admonished.

He got up from his chair, all six feet three inches of sinuous male animal, and slid to his knees before Holly, placing his head in her lap and wrapping his arms around her waist.

Holly, stricken with emotion, placed her hand on his head, and welcomed Sahara as she wrapped herself around Aiden's back. He stayed silent, breathing in their love, absorbing their body heat.

"Aiden." Sahara's breath washed over his broad back. "We know that last night was much more than an expensive dinner and a sensational night of sex. You were telling us that we're a family. And we *are* a family. We're not giving you back! Back to what? To our lives before you made everything grey turn to a rainbow of colour? Back to not knowing the gentle parts of your soul, or the wicked heat of your love? Yes, my love, we're keeping you. For as long as you'll have us."

"Forever, then." He looked up, his face stained with tears, his hands in a tight grip on Holly's hips. Sensitivity ran deep within Aiden's soul, as deep as his convictions to steer to the right and the good, as deep as his distinct masculinity.

Holly placed her hands over his. He relaxed.

"I know the odds are stacked against us," he said. "All relationships are hard at times, but we're in uncharted waters here." His voice broke. "I need this to work. I need both of you to make it through each day."

"We'll make it work," Holly stood and took him with her. "Kiss me."

He covered her mouth with his, taking her with skill, then let her kiss him back, her tongue sweeping his in sweet strokes. He pushed against her, cock hard.

"See, you're hard for me, sweetie. And I'm wet for you. The second we touch each other, our bodies are in sync." Holly felt his heat. He groaned into her mouth. "Look at Sahara. See those nipples; that look on her face? She can't do without you either...without us. We're one in body and heart. Our bodies instinctively speak of what our hearts feel. There's nothing to worry about."

But Aiden, who had grown into his intuition since meeting Sahara and Pan, could not shake a feeling of foreboding.

They all jumped as the phone rang and snapped them out of the moment. Aiden said he'd leave it. They said it might be important, a client perhaps. He left them to finish eating and picked up the phone.

That moment transformed a vulnerable Aiden into the self-assured, confident man who ran his business with a great degree of control. He stood with his back to them, his voice firm as he discussed plans with a client who was doing his best to get Aiden's hackles up. He ended the conversation with a curt farewell, and swore under his breath as he made notes in a thick journal.

"Any food left?" There was no sign of the Aiden who had just spilled his heart to them.

Sahara brought a plate of food she'd kept warm in the oven.

"Oh. Thank you." He dove in.

"All good?" Sahara queried.

"I think so. I hate changes mid-build. They hardly ever remain the brilliant plan the client thought up while sunning in the Bahamas. We'll see." He looked up and offered a crooked smile. "So, what's on the agenda for today, girls?"

Sahara said she needed to go home and see to Willow. She had a conference call at one o'clock and some other things to attend to. Holly was going to stay with Aiden until noon then head back to the café.

"What about you, lover?" Sahara asked.

He ran his hands through his hair. Phone calls, go over some drawings, and prepare for a week away. He'd leave tomorrow.

"Did I tell you about my plans for an office in town?" he asked suddenly. No, they had no idea.

"Holly, you know the empty space behind your apartment? I'm building a new staircase and renovating the rooms for a receptionist's area and an office for me. I thought I'd furnish with a pull-out sofa in my private office in case you ever needed to stay over, and a full bathroom."

Holly stared at him. Sahara smiled. *Here we go,* she thought.

"Why wouldn't I sleep in my own apartment?" Holly wondered, trying to restrain a decidedly annoyed tone.

"Because your new French boy will be renting it, and you'll be sleeping in my bed," Aiden said, not seeing the problem with his having planned Holly's life once again without her consent.

"Oh. When am I moving?" Holly looked at him, eyes flashing.

"Soon...what's the problem? I thought it all made perfect sense. French boy will have a place to stay, you'll be here...like we talked about, right?"

"Who's the French boy?" Sahara asked, trying to lighten the mood.

They both glared at her, and snapped, "The new apprentice!"

"Oh! Listen, I'm going home. You guys can work this out. Come Ulfred!"

She left them, saying she'd see Holly later at the café. She laughed out loud when she got outside, not caring if they heard. They had that electric way of solving their issues, and Sahara was sure that it would be Holly putting Aiden in his place, not the other way around. The air was brisk. She welcomed the wind on her face and raced Ulfred home.

Holly looked at Aiden, who was clearing the table and avoiding her stare. Both of them were aroused by the friction between them, but neither would admit it.

"Aiden, look at me."

He did, unhappy, angry with himself for spoiling their time together.

"Come here." Holly took the hair brush from her purse. "Let's sit down for a few."

She led the way to the sofa. He followed, body tense, muscles bristling.

She sat on the floor and settled in-between his legs, handing him the brush. The touch of his legs around her perked her nipples, sending a surge of energy to her clit. She closed her eyes. They could talk this out.

Aiden began to brush, in smooth, even strokes, the moving meditation bringing them back together to a softer place. He sighed.

"I fucked up, didn't I?" he whispered.

"Yes. It's not that I don't love your plans…it's that you don't discuss things. You're used to functioning like this on your own, but so am I. I need to know that I'm included in your decisions. I'm happy to move into my fabulous new room, to share your bed, your home, everything. Aiden…I ache for you! It will be thrilling to know that you'll be so close to me while I work, but I still need to be able to make my own decisions. You're confusing taking care of me, which I thoroughly appreciate, with taking over my autonomy. I can't play like that, Aiden."

He listened silently, as his hands worked rhythmically. Holly's hair shone a brilliant gold, and it broke his heart, it was so beautiful. Instinctively, because he had done it so many times for his sister, Aiden began to braid. Holly smiled. He was so endearing when he did things so unlike a man as rugged as himself.

"I'll learn, my love. You'll see. I'll learn not to be such a brute. Forgive me?"

"You're forgiven." Holly felt her hair. He'd made a surprisingly intricate braid. She ran her hands over his long legs, and leaned into him, her heart at ease now that she'd told him how she felt. "Actually, I think your plans are perfect. Except if you're hiring an office manager, maybe I should screen the applicants," she joked. "But then again, I didn't ask you to approve the 'French boy', as you call him." Aiden remained silent, his hands away from her now. "Sweetie?"

Holly turned, eager to kiss and make up, smell his scent...but all she could do was scream. Aiden sat blank faced, his eyes rolled back in his head, breath shallow, and his hands in fists.

CHAPTER 14

Holly ran for her phone. She dialed Sahara's number with trembling fingers, cold suddenly and with a sick feeling in the pit of her stomach. Aiden was non-responsive.

The hair on the back of Sahara's neck rose as the phone rang. Her heart plummeted as intuition surfaced. Aiden!

"Holly! What is it?"

"Oh Sahara, come back! It's Aiden. I don't know what's wrong. Come now!" Holly heard an alien sound escape from Sahara's lips and then the phone went dead. She crumpled to the floor at Aiden's feet, she was afraid to touch him, and afraid not to.

Sahara called to Iona, a deep, agonized wail that caught the witch sharply in her heart. Alert, Iona consulted her guides and swiftly shifted forms, arriving at Sahara's side as she ran full speed across the plain towards Aiden's. Sweeping past her, Iona cast her spell and they flew together to the man they loved. Arriving at Aiden's door, Iona lifted the spell. She entered his home, keenly aware of a ban placed upon her so long ago. The sound of Iona's soothing voice reached Holly, who sat up with shock on her face, not comprehending the woman before her.

Iona held out her hand, and on contact, Holly was swept by a comforting peace.

"Iona? Can you...please, help Aiden."

"Can you tell me what happened? Quickly!"

"He was brushing my hair, and then this."

"Oh God!" Sahara cried. "Iona, hurry!"

"Don't be afraid," Iona cautioned them both. "I will return. I'll bring Aiden back, if it's the last thing I do." And she swept out the door. The sharp cry of a raven pierced the air.

Sahara wept. She turned to Holly, who was still sitting at Aiden's feet.

"Holly, hold me. I'm so cold."

Holly opened her arms. She held Sahara tightly, crooning quietly, rocking her. They stayed like this, not looking at Aiden. Waiting.

"I don't understand what is happening," Holly finally whispered, beginning to shake once more. "Tell me what's happening. I need him back. How did Iona get here? Tell me he'll be alright, Sahara!"

Sahara looked at her with such pain in her eyes that Holly pulled her back in, light kisses in her hair to soothe her.

"Tell me sweetie, tell me. I love you. Nothing can change that."

Sahara nodded weakly. Her mouth searched for Holly's; needing the reassurance of her touch, her tears hot on Holly's face.

They kissed out of a need for Aiden, each touch of their lips a reminder that they couldn't touch the man they loved, sprawled out on the sofa, but so far away in spirit.

"Oh Holly! He's gone back in time, he's time travelling, it's dangerous. I think that when he brushed your hair, it triggered him. But he wouldn't have had any way of knowing his triggers; there's not been enough time for us to explore our past life together. Oh Holly, this is all my fault! He must have had a habit of brushing Arinn's hair back then, and that's the portal for going back."

Holly stared at her, horrified. Sahara shook her, intuition prickling.

"What, Holly, what?"

"It happened once before, almost."

"What? What happened before?"

"Once before, when you were away seeing your agent, I was here and Aiden brushed my hair, you know how he loves to do that...anyway, I thought he hadn't eaten enough, he looked so spacey, kind of out of it."

Sahara groaned, pain wracking her heart. When she'd been away, fucking Iona and Richard, Aiden had been on the brink of disappearing. And Holly had not known any of the dangers. There was so much to explain. She knew that she would lose Holly's trust, her love. She felt her world slipping away from her. She wanted Aiden. She wanted to go after him too. Her eyes began to roll back, then close.

"Sahara! Open your eyes! God damn it, Sahara. No!" Holly slapped Sahara so hard that a welt appeared instantly on Sahara's face. Her eyes flew open. Her hand went to her face.

"Holly!" Tears sprang to Sahara's eyes.

"Listen!" Holly held her tight. "I don't care what there is to explain. I don't give a fuck what you've not told me, or what has gone on. I FUCKING LOVE YOU! Do you understand me? I love you and Aiden and I'm not giving up on us. No matter how fucked up this gets, I'm hanging on. So get your shit together, Sahara. I NEED YOU! Aiden needs you. Please!"

Sahara sat up, dazed. She took one look at Aiden and swallowed down nausea.

"I'll make coffee," Holly offered. "You add to the fire."

They moved about like robots, Aiden's still body a terrifying reminder that their life would be suspended until he came back, and that they had no clue how long that could take. It was like a premonition of his death, and how empty their existence would be without him. He had filled so much of their hearts.

Holly called Lilith, her voice strong and sure as she did her best to sound normal, and they went over plans for the next day.

It was an almost normal scene - Sahara facing the fire, sitting cross legged on the floor - as long as Holly didn't glance at the sofa where Aiden lay like a shallowly breathing corpse. Holly had never felt so afraid or confused in her life.

Sahara sent a quick message to Kathryn, asking for a change in date for the call. The publicist could wait. She turned and held her hand out to Holly, who came immediately, and sidestepping the sleeping Aiden, slid to the floor beside her.

"I wonder how long...hey! Do you smell that? That forest scent? I've smelt it before, that night Aiden almost slipped away." Holly sniffed the air.

Sahara stiffened. Pan appeared to her left. The alarm in her eyes was enough to signal him to send her a telepathic message.

"She can't see me. I'm with Aiden. He's stubborn, Sahara. He's following a path I can only guide him on."

"Help him! Please. Keep him safe," Sahara replied silently.

Pan smiled knowingly, the smile of one who understands the quirks of intra-dimensional travel, and that life is so much more than the linear path it appears to be.

"Sleep, Sahara. I will return."

Sahara nodded, her hand clasped firmly in Holly's who was already sliding into a slumber meant to soothe their fragile nerves.

CHAPTER 15

"Touch has a memory" ~ John Keats

"Where are you going? Aiden! Here, connect with me."

Pan swept along beside Aiden as they slipped quickly through time and space.

Aiden cast a determined look in Pan's direction. "I need this. I need to know."

"I'll meet you there. Don't run from me. I'll be your armor if you'll let me."

Aiden slammed into the Oracle Wood.

It was night. He looked around him. His nose picked up a familiar scent. Horse. His horse. He stepped closer and laid his hand upon the side of the great beast, who snorted softly in his direction. He pressed his face close, feeling the flutter of muscle that moved under his touch.

A sound to his right made him jump. He had to recall quickly. He called to Pan who lifted the veil from his third eye, and the transition was complete. At home, Aiden's form disappeared from sight.

Dagr lifted from the crouching position that he was in. Hand on his sword, he crept on silent feet towards the sleeping woman by the cautiously small fire. She stirred, her moans soft. Dagr's heart broke all over again. Her hair was tangled into a matted mess of knots and dried blood. She looked frail and vulnerable curled into a fetal position. He would kill whomever did this to her. Fury rose within Dagr's breast. Richard! But even as the name came to him Dagr shrank from the possibility. He was about to turn to throw more wood on the fire when she opened her eyes.

Shaking from shock, Brigida tried lifting her arms, but she was too weak.

He was at her side in an instant, and the sound that she made as Dagr lifted her, cut him deeply. Like a wounded animal, she voiced the only sound she could make, adrenalin filling her tissues as he held her to his heart.

"Brigida!" Dagr's voice washed over her in waves of relief, love...gratitude. "My love, my love. Forgive me, my love."

The forest bore witness to their tears - to the loud sobs that neither of them could hold back. They clung to each other with a desperation known only to those who have loved and lost and found love once more. Dagr sent his love through waves of telepathic channels, filling her internally, calling to his allies in the underworld. She needed healing, strength. He laid himself beside her, and cradling her, poured himself into her heart. Brigida could only stare at him, her eyes wide. She touched his face, forcing herself to believe that he was real.

Dagr's mouth reached for hers. She turned her head, embarrassed. She had been travelling for days on end. There had been no way to keep herself clean.

He understood. He always understood.

"You are safe now. I give you my word," Dagr's eyes pierced hers.

She knew that his promise came with a pledge to die before he broke it. She opened her mouth to tell him that she knew he had fought for her...before. But all that came out was that strange wail. Eyes registering panic, Brigida's hand went to her mouth. She shook her head.

"Shhh," Dagr's fingers rested on her lips. He caressed them with a light touch, his tears falling again. Brigida's eyes began to close once more, exhausted from this very small bit of expended energy. She struggled to keep focused on Dagr's face, so different from the dark countenance that she had grown to love over the last two years. Her heart broke at the realization of her disloyalty. She fell asleep once more.

Dagr kicked dirt into the fire, and satisfied that the flames were dead, wrapped Brigida in his cloak once more and lifted her onto his horse. The ride home would take most of the day. Daybreak was just ahead. One strong muscular arm held Brigida close to his chest. Her scent filled his nose. He could discern oils in her hair. Expensive oils. Even though she was covered in dirt from her travels, her skin looked well cared for...like the skin of a well-loved concubine. Bile rose to Dagr's throat. Enough time had passed for Richard to have worked his charms on Brigida. He would forgive her for the transgressions he was sure she had committed. Richard was skilled at seduction, and Brigida had been at his mercy. And that Dagr accepted as his own fault. But he would not forgive the man who had once held his heart like a brother. Dagr rode with determination. He had so many questions, ones that might never be answered if Brigida didn't find her voice. He had seen this before. Soldiers, clubbed on the head in battle, had returned home mute, the injury to their skull too deep to comprehend.

He looked down at Brigida's once pretty face now grown into

deep beauty, and thought of the days ahead. When he had bathed her, he had noticed that her arms were well toned, her muscles used to some kind of work. She was brown...all over. But the bruises on her back and legs spoke of something that Dagr's mind hoped was not the kind of love play Richard had often enjoyed...enjoyed with Dagr at his side.

Guilt as ripe as a summer cherry bloomed in his heart. The sun rose and warmed, and had dipped again when Dagr's horse slipped silently into the section of the Oracle Wood that would bring them home. The wind picked up - Arinn's welcome. She could feel his closeness. A hint of a smile touched Dagr's lips as he thought of Arinn's joy upon seeing Brigida once more. It had been so long. Despite himself, Dagr felt a pang of longing to see the two women naked in his bed, and the love that they would make. Still, there was no peace in his heart as he rode into the small clearing where the hut stood, door open, the smell of a cooked meal on the air.

He should have felt nothing but joy when the slender figure of Arinn filled the doorway, and he heard her strangled cry upon seeing the woman in his arms. Instead, there was a strange dread. Suddenly, his memory cleared, and he remembered what he was dreading. The child. Where was his child? Dagr slipped down, and fell to his knees, Brigida waking and struggling to her feet. He heard the sounds of their greeting, the tears, and once more that strange wail coming from Brigida's lips. But he could not move as he heaved onto the ground beneath him. Arinn lifted him to his feet after a long while, her eyes swollen from weeping.

"My lord, thank you." She kissed his hands, and pushed some dirt with the toe of her shoe to cover his vomit. "You are tired from your journey. Allow me to care for you."

She pulled him towards the hut, and motioned to the tub of hot water by the outdoor fire. "Get in there," she commanded.

Dagr obeyed. Stripping naked, he got in, the water soothing his aching muscles. Arinn came with soap. She knelt beside him and offered him water to drink. When he looked with worry towards the hut, she waved her hand to calm him.

"She is asleep, my lord...my lord!" Arinn broke into fresh tears. "Thank you. You have found her. I am grateful." And she lowered her head before the man she respected and adored.

Dagr laid his hand upon her. His heart cheered a little to see her so fulfilled. When he did not speak she lifted her head and stared deep into his eyes.

"All shall be well now, my lord. You will see. We are together once more."

He nodded, not sure that she remembered. His eyes, so very blue, now dulled with pain as he made his worst fears known.

"Do you remember, my lady," Dagr's voice broke, "do you remember the child?" They had never spoken of it. Perhaps Arinn had chosen to forget.

Arinn's face twisted in horror, then cleared as she willed herself to be strong. Strong for him, for Brigida, for all of them.

"I do, my lord. But you will give her another, when the time is right. And we will mourn the first when the time is right. But today, my lord, and for many days henceforth, we will show her nothing but love and joy. Until she is strong again."

Dagr looked at her gratefully. She was wise. He would do as she said. He melted to her touch, as she washed his hair and eased the tension in his shoulders.

"Your meal is ready, my lord. It would please me to see you eat," Arinn whispered in Dagr's ear, unable to help the deep longing she felt for his hands on her skin. He caught her wrist roughly as she stood to leave him.

"I will lie down with Brigida for a while. I need her against me. Will you brew us some herbs, my lord?"

"I am at your service, my lady," he kissed her hands and felt his own fire rising. It had been so long since he had served them both.

CHAPTER 16

Dagr barely left the hut save to bring in more wood to keep the fire burning. Brigida slept. Arinn lay beside her, eyes roving the room, following Dagr's every move. He brewed some herbs for their tea, and added to the soup simmering on the hearth. Tomorrow he would hunt. The thought of leaving his women even for a moment pierced Dagr's heart like a well- honed knife.

Aside from an occasional faint moan, Brigida lay silent and still. Dagr exchanged looks with Arinn when dark fell and Brigida showed no sign of waking. He would have to make his bed on the floor. The alcove was simply too small for the three of them. He would fashion another cot another day.

A cold blast of wind greeted Arinn as she stepped outside to relieve herself. She had left Dagr in her place beside Brigida, to offer warmth and because he yearned to wrap himself around their long lost love. Arinn had called upon her guides and asked for healing to seep through her fingertips as she laid her hands upon the blood encrusted scalp of the woman she loved with every fibre of her body and soul. Now, the cold air felt good on her cheeks. She sat on the porch muttering incantations half to herself, half to the spirit world. She needed help. She had never encountered an injury of the head before. What if...but no, she would not allow herself think that way.

Arinn stood, and wrapping her cloak tight around herself, peered through the window at a strange image that brought her heart to a wild thumping. Dagr stood over Brigida where she sat at the edge of their bed, hunting knife in one hand, a pile of Brigida's hair in the other. Before she knew it, Arinn's voice broke into a scream, shrill and poignant. Dagr turned slowly towards the sound. Brigida did not move.

"My lord! What do you plan to do with that knife?"

"I would cut her hair," Dagr looked miserably towards Arinn. "Our lady has requested her hair shorn."

"No! We could wash it, work on the knots, I can do it!" Arinn knelt before Brigida, taking her hands and shocked by their cold, blew warm breath onto Brigida's fingers.

"Do you truly want this, my love?" Arinn looked into Brigida's eyes.

Brigida nodded, oddly calm. She touched her head and made a

face where it hurt. She pointed to her eyes and touched Arinn's heart with frantic fingers.

"What does our lady say?" Dagr struggled to understand Brigida's signing.

"She wants me to look at her head, to look for the wound; to see with my heart what is wrong."

Dagr knelt. "You are certain that I would do this?"

Brigida nodded once more, a hint of tears glimmering in the corners of her eyes. Her heart was strangled with emotions. She had longed for months to see this man's handsome face once more. To her shame and overwhelming sadness, she had forgotten some of the nuances of Dagr's countenance. Richard's face had replaced her memory of the man who had taken her virginity. Now as she stared into the beauty of Dagr's soul, burning within the stunning blue of his eyes, she remembered something Richard had once said. Suddenly his words became clear.

"Dagr's beauty shines from the inside out," Richard had muttered, as he had laid his head to her breast and wept. Brigida had not understood the tears then. She thought them perhaps the sadness of a friend lost, a warrior sadly missed. Dagr's encouraging smile as he kissed her hands shone the truth on Richard's words. Brigida wondered if she would ever know the details of Richard's and Dagr's friendship now. He stood and gripped her hair once more; taking up his knife, face hard, lips thinning with determination.

Brigida fixed her stare on Dagr's legs as he towered over her, and that place in his leathers that had so often caught her imagination in years past. The heat of Brigida's stare stirred Dagr's lust. His legs tensed as he contemplated the closeness of her face to his manhood. Then, with Arinn's eyes boring into him, willing him to action, he cut through the thick waves of black hair, and let it fall to the floor, along with Brigida's tears. The complexity of emotions in that moment left them all longing for air, and Dagr left the door open to the cold wind when he left the cabin to gather himself.

Upon returning, he saw that water had been heated and that Arinn had washed the choppy mop of hair left on Brigida's head. The long tresses had been swept up off the hut floor and sat in a basket to be offered to the birds for nest making. The two women sat huddled by the fire, Brigida wrapped in Arinn's arms. She'd been scrubbed clean, and wore a shift of Arinn's, one that had been dropped off by Richard in a pile of supplies. Dagr stood arrested at the door, the sight of them heating his blood. How long had he dreamt of this, and hoped that the right circumstances would lead to Richard's release of her?

"My lord," Arinn stood and greeted Dagr.

"Is it better now? Can you see the wound?" Dagr came swiftly and pulled Brigida towards him, warrior arms engulfing her slight frame.

The contact forced a deep shaking in Brigida's legs, and if not for Dagr's tight grip around her waist, she would have fallen. She lifted her eyes to his. He had that fierce, determined look that she adored. Brigida looked to Arinn for help, their ability to communicate tele-pathically strong.

"I can see the wound, but come morning you will have to take up your knife once more. The rest of the hair must be shaved clean. I need better access."

"As you wish, my lady." Dagr felt Brigida calm as Arinn's voice washed over them.

"Will there be anything else tonight, my lady. Anything that Brig-ida desires that I can provide?"

"You may take her to your bed, my lord," Arinn faced Dagr's stare. "I will find rest by the fire. You need not worry."

He stripped his clothes off, and doing the same for Brigida, lifted her into the bed, then covering them with furs, he sought to warm her enough to end her trembling. He had a right to her. He wanted her. He wanted her to forget what lying in Richard's arms had felt like.

And he could tell that she knew his suspicions about what must have happened, by the way her fingers gripped fearfully at his arms.

She smelled like the rich soaps Richard had left them. Her body felt much tighter than before, her arms muscular, her legs hard...as one who had walked a great distance. She felt like a woman. Dagr tried to banish all thoughts of her infidelity. She had been lonely, cut off from his love, afraid. These were all things that could drive one into the arms of a new lover; the seeking of comfort, of solace. His manhood strained against her back. Brigida lay still now as Arinn sat beside them, reciting a story of old, something that they must have been told as children, because Brigida was nodding and smiling, re-laxing under the soothing warmth of Arinn's voice.

And soon they heard Brigida's breath soft and even, as sleep found her once more. Although their bodies ached for contact, and their eyes spoke of their need, Dagr stayed beside Brigida throughout the night while Arinn slept curled up by the fire on top of Dagr's cloak and wrapped in a fur.

As the sun rose so did Dagr. He woke Arinn, urging her to take his place in the bed. He built up the fire then rode out with his bow and arrow on his back.

Dagr scoured the woods for rabbits and peace of mind. The rabbits were in endless supply. He'd ridden out with several intentions: to give his women the space they needed to ease back into each other's arms, to make sense of his riotous emotions and to provide them with a supply of meat. His thoughts played upon his face. He rode without a conscious decision to leave the shelter of the woods or to find his way to the ocean-side cave of his childhood. But when the icy cold wind of the open plain hit him, Dagr realized that it had been his mission to find Richard and face him. As synchronicity would have it, they would meet.

Richard saw Dagr first. His heart pounded with anxiety, with lust, with love. From a distance, Dagr's silhouette was the same broad, intimidating sight that had brought fear into many a man's heart when facing him on the battle field. His long, fair hair whipped in the wild wind. His horse, the towering black stallion, was equally fearsome and dangerous, his loyalty to his rider unwavering. When Richard sensed that Dagr had seen him, he stopped. He waited. He wasn't sure if he was more afraid of having to fight Dagr or of hearing that Brigida was not with him. Either way, this meeting could only be difficult.

When Dagr saw Richard, his legs pressed into his mount and his heart exploded with rage. The great beast that he rode upon sensed his angst and threw himself into speed of hoof. And as the distance between the two men decreased, it was Richard who paled when he saw the flash of Dagr's sword as it left its sheath. Yet he stood firm, and kept his hand away from his weapon.

Dagr's horse braced for battle. He knew the signs: Dagr's energy rising; his knees pressed tight around him, the smell of his master's anger. His eyes rolled back, revealing white.

Richard's horse, who had safely delivered his master from many a fierce battle, reared high on his hind legs. He had only known Dagr's horse as an ally. This feeling was new, and terrifying. Equally terrifying was his masters' command to stand still. Why were they not facing the approaching threat as a united force? He wanted to burst into speed yet his master commanded stillness. He obeyed.

Dagr approached, his hand tight around his sword, his heart aching. At first sight, Richard had not changed, his face the same hard etched profile, strong and proud, his excellent physique arresting. Only his eyes seemed older. And something else...tortured. Dagr rode a mad circle around the only man he had once been sure would never evoke murderous feelings from him. But now, Dagr saw red, and wished for Richard's blood on his sword.

"Get off your horse, coward!" Dagr's voice fought the wind.

Richard got off and stood in dangerous striking distance of the stallion's hooves. He knew that given the signal, the great beast would trample him though he knew Richard as friend.

Dagr leapt to the ground.

"Before I kill you I want to know what you did to her. *Everything you did to her*! She is covered in bruises. By God Richard, I hate the very sight of you!" Dagr's voice broke and his tears welled up. "How could you hurt such a beautiful and helpless creature? Speak!"

Richard's face contorted into rage. He threw himself at Dagr and faced the furious strikes that Dagr meted out. Neither man flinched from the pounding of fists.

"Hurt her?" Richard gasped out. "Hurt her? Hurt the only woman I have ever loved?" He groaned as his ribs cracked under Dagr's brutal boot.

"God damn you! I asked you to protect her. Not to love her, abuse her, beat her!"

Richard's fist landed square into Dagr's jaw. "Beat her? What the hell are you talking about? Stop, my lord! Let me speak!"

Dagr paused. He searched Richard's eyes.

"She is with you then?" The part of Richard that rejoiced over Brigida's safety overrode the part of him that mourned her loss, for the moment at least. Richard knew that his time with Brigida was over.

"What do you mean 'found her way back to me'? She ran away from you, you beat her and she ran."

"I repeat, I have not harmed her. I am guilty of loving her. How could one not?" Richard hung his head. "I left for court and as usual, left her in the care of Hannah. You remember Hannah?"

Dagr nodded, a bit of relief flooding his brain. Hannah was one of the kindest women he knew.

"When I returned, Hannah told me that one of my men had... dear God, I have already speared him! Hannah confided that Brigida had run off. I have only just returned and rode out in search of her. My hope was that somehow, she had found her way back to you. She must have been journeying for at least a fortnight...my lord!" Richard fell to his knees before Dagr. "She lives! Dear God, she lives." Richard broke into sobs.

Dagr shook where he stood, waves of emotions buffeting his aching heart. Richard could very well be speaking the truth, but how was he to know? Brigida could hardly tell him her version of the events that led to him finding her at the Dark Pool.

"You did not beat her? Use her in the way...Richard? I need the truth."

Richard stood up, pulling his cloak around him, the cold penetrating.

"I have never beat her, not in anger, not in the way most men feel is their right... although she is outspoken for a woman. She does not hold her tongue. But if you want to know whether she and I found certain pleasures, then yes, I confess, we did engage in that kind of play."

"You mean that you taught her. You trained her to like it. She was never that way with me."

"Yes. You speak the truth, and so shall I. I taught her to love me the way I like to be loved, and she taught me that she was brave and willing."

Dagr's blow to Richard's face left them both weak and nauseous.

"Did she taste sweet to you, Richard? I know you like a woman who is sweet and compliant yet brave. Did you like the spark in her eye as she bent her will to you? Tell me, was her cunt as delicious as any you have tasted?"

So it was pain that Dagr sought, to Richard's surprise. This was a game that Richard excelled at.

"As for her taste, my lord," Richard growled out, "You know well that she is worthy of hours on one's knees. As for her ability in bed...there is neither more trainable nor skilled."

"Do you wish for my sword through your gut?" Dagr roared. "You anger me beyond belief Richard!"

"Shall I grovel at your feet and apologize for loving her? For falling under her spell? You threw her at me and I caught her. She opened up for me out of her longing for you, you idiot! I was her only way back to you. And she my only way back to you. Yes, I took her, corrupted her view of tender lovemaking - of the kind I am sure *you* taught her. But if it is honesty you seek, then hear this, my lord. She wanted to love only you, but she needed a sensual touch as much as she needed breath, and I took advantage of that. Her scent and her taste drove me to madness and when she uttered your name while she rode me, it only made me love her more. You are still my first love, the first face I imagined when I took myself in hand while we were lads. Kill me if you want. My life is worthless without the two of you in it."

"Stand up Richard. I will take you to her. She can choose."

Richard recoiled with horror at Dagr's words.

"Make her choose?" Richard whispered. "Are you completely mad? Do not do this, my lord, I implore you! It can only cause her pain. No. I will step away." The thought of seeing Brigida again brought sharp pain to Richard's heart, and more...hope. But the thought of her having to choose brought an agony that he could not fathom.

Dagr almost fell down with relief. The purity of Richard's love for Brigida overwhelmed him. In that instant he loved Richard more than he had ever done. His sense of fairness and gratitude overtook all else and he held out his hand to the man before him. And there it was...that undeniable pull between them that Dagr had long suppressed.

"May I?" Richard's voice caught in his throat. Dagr nodded and Richard lifted Dagr's hand to his lips.

"Come with me, Richard. It is only fair that she can say farewell to you. I am not that hard of heart that I would deny either one of you that moment."

"My lord." Richard pulled Dagr in. "I cannot promise composure. I love her so."

Dagr moved his face through Richard's hair, and the scent of wind and sea. He felt Richard arms stiffen into hard honed muscle, and embraced him earnestly.

"I have never loved you more, Richard. Thank you for loving her, for giving her what I could not when she needed it. I am in your favour, my lord."

They rode in silence to the wood, and into an uncertain future. But Dagr had one more question that begged an answer.

"Richard. The child?"

"It was lost. The night of the battle. Hannah saw to her healing." Guilt rose in Richard's eyes.

"And she has never..."

"We were not blessed. I suppose it is fitting. Still, I would have welcomed her child."

"She has lost her voice, Richard. She cannot utter a word."

Dagr was quick to notice the pain on Richard's face, the guilt of having left her to be abused by another man.

"Arinn, my handfast - I have told her about you and what happened between us."

Richard winced. "And what did your lady have to say?" He'd have to face the woman whose lord he had taken in his mouth.

"Arinn understands love better than anyone. There is no resentment in her heart towards you."

Richard sighed. There were no words left to say.

It was well after the noon hour when the two men stopped their horses short of the clearing, hidden by the trees. Arinn and Brigida stood by the fire, over the pot that simmered rabbit bones and roots. Arinn's hair shone golden in the setting sun, she was laughing, teasing Brigida's kirtle open at her breast, feeling for the soft of her lovers skin. Brigida was leaning into Arinn's touch.

"Do you still yearn for my touch?" Arinn asked.

Brigida nodded then looked up sharply, tugging her garments close.

"What is it? Do you hear something?"

Brigida pointed to Arinn's heart and her own.

"Dagr? He is close. I know."

Dagr looked at Richard who for the life of him could not control his emotions. The sight of Brigida, and the knowledge that it might be his last, broke him. The image of Arinn, golden, resplendent in her beauty, took his breath away.

"My lord! She is like the sun, and Brigida like the moon." And Dagr knew that Richard coveted them both.

The women looked to the dark of the woods. Dagr rode out, with Richard behind him.

That strange sound escaped Brigida's lips once more at the sight of her lover. She stood trembling, rooted to the ground. Dagr slipped off his horse. She would not know what to do, and his heart ached for how much this would hurt her.

"My love," he held her tight, whispering in her ear. "You must be strong. Richard has come to bid you farewell." He looked at Arinn standing behind Brigida, his eyes beseeching her to understand. There was much to explain. Again.

Arinn turned towards Richard and curtsied before him.

"My lord, welcome to our humble home."

Richard barely dared to look at her, her beauty and utter femininity overpowering.

"My lady," Richard bowed.

"Will you share our meal?"

He noticed that she did not apologize for the obvious meagreness of the soup.

He turned, and pulling a sack from his horse, handed it to Arinn.

"You will find provisions in here, my lady. They are yours."

Arinn took the sack and taking Dagr by the hand, led the way to the hut, leaving Richard and Brigida to face the rawness of the situation - the sharp pain of their love.

"My lady," Dagr held Arinn close. "I have much to tell you. Please understand that this will be very difficult for Richard and Brigida. It had been so long. They had no power over the love that took hold of them."

"The love they felt for you was at the heart of it, I am certain of this my lord," Arinn offered.

Dagr looked gratefully at the woman who had lost so much but who loved so easily still.

"I learn from you each day, my lady."

"Let us prepare our meal." Arinn unpacked mead, roasted boar, sour berry preserves, and sweetmeats. "Earl Dumont is most kind. We shall eat well tonight."

"And what is your opinion of my friend, sweet lady?" Dagr braced for the worst, and Arinn delivered it.

"He is frightening...most beautiful - his hair's like the raven's feather, weaving dark magic. I imagine him to be most ardent in bed. Dagr, you must allow Brigida to feel his passion one last time."

"Why must I my lady?"

"Brigida told me how he protected her, how he allowed her to speak of you day after day without ceasing, how he took her to his bed when she ached unbearably for your touch. A man servant whom Richard trusted tried to take her while Richard was away. She ran from the castle, and fell from a precipice wandering around in the dark. That is how she hurt herself, Dagr. Richard has never hurt her. He loves her though she does not belong to him. You will forgive him. And her. They had no other way."

"She told you all this, my lady? But how?"

"She drew pictures in the dirt. The rest she told me with her eyes and heart. I can hear her thoughts at times."

So Richard's words had been true. Arinn touched Dagr's face where it showed signs of swelling.

"Do men always fight when they have no answers to their questions?"

"Most men do, my love. Perhaps one day I will find a more peaceful path."

They laid out their meal and found privacy in the alcove to embrace, Dagr taking Arinn's mouth hungrily, his mind racing with thoughts of how to arrange Richard and Brigida's farewell. The images of what might be fueled a mad desire between them.

Outside, Brigida and Richard stood at arm's length. He, dark and brooding, let his eyes do the talking. His love and desperation found their way out in tears that welled and clouded his sight. She, shaking and covering her shorn hair, thinking that he would hate it, abandoned herself to the complexity of their love. There was no way forward or out of what she felt. She would have to gather her strength, for she knew that letting go of Richard in Dagr's presence would be painful.

Richard fell to his knees before her. He begged forgiveness for leaving her alone, for leaving her in danger. Brigida's hand on his head tore a shock of passion through his loins, and he stood to kiss her, openly, voraciously, his hands gripping her cropped hair, growling as she moaned her protest.

"Do you think, my lady, that I despise your hair this way? How could I despise anything about you? You are my treasure, one that I must give up. But how can I give you up? How will I wander the rest of my days without you at my side? My lady, I think that I cannot!"

Richard gripped her at her bodice, his hands demanding as he sought the soft of her flesh, Brigida's breath coming quick, her eyes rolling back, falling into the rhythm of their pattern; Richard rough, she compliant, acquiescing to his commands, taking what she needed from him when he gave her the signal to make him the slave.

"Richard!" Dagr called out, voice gruff. "Come in! For the love of God, would you take her in the cold and the mud?"

Richard whisked Brigida into his arms, and holding her tight, strode into the warmth of the dwelling. He greeted Arinn's gaze boldly but respectfully.

"My lady," he bowed his head. Her smile told him that she was sharing Brigida without hesitation.

"We are bound by strange circumstance this day, my lord," Arinn's voice washed tenderly over them all.

Richard held Brigida by the fire, her trembling now concerning.

"Warm her, Richard, she is not strong yet, the journey was difficult. Sit on this bench, and wrap her in this fur."

Richard did as he was told, and held Brigida on his knee,

wrapped tight in the fur. Dagr knelt before them.

"My lady. One day, when you have found your voice, we can sit and find meaning in this. For today, we will live and love like friends and keepers of each other's hearts. We will not hold anything that happens against each other; indeed, we will grow stronger in our love. Arinn and I have spoken, and there is nothing that we would not do for you. There is nothing that Richard and I would not do for you. We are bound by blood, Richard and I, to provide to yours and Arinn's comfort. Do not shake so, we will eat, we will drink, and we will find peace in what must be. I need only one nod of your head to show me that it is indeed your desire to make your farewell to Richard. Out of my love for you, I would stand aside if you chose it."

Dagr shook his hand at both Richard and Arinn, who faced him furiously. "She deserves to make her heart known. We cannot take this from her. You and I Richard, are the ones who have brought this pain upon her."

Brigida beat her fist against her heart. She made gestures at Arinn, her tears streaming like a river.

"What does she say, my lady?" Richard asked of Arinn.

"She cannot choose. She does not know how to divide her heart, cannot love only one of you now. She will, however, take your passion with your farewell my lord Dumont, for she will not leave me again."

Dagr let his breath out in a hiss, and turned away as Richards' face registered grief mixed with some kind of wild hope that Brigida's love, if not her physical presence in his life, could sustain him. Richard kissed Brigida's neck, his arms a vice around her.

Dagr touched him gently on his back. "We will eat now, Richard. And drink the mead you have provided. She is too weak for what I know you desire. There is no hurry."

Richard bowed and sat at the table. Arinn stood to serve.

"We will need more fuel, my lord," Arinn instructed Dagr, pointing to the door. He realized that she knew him better than he knew himself. His energy was ripping at the three of them like lightning bolts. He stepped outside and took hold of his axe.

Somewhere in the thick of the trees, a shadow moved and caught Dagr's eye. Instantly alert, Dagr made his way stealthily past the dwelling and into the dark woods. Adrenaline coursed his veins as the shadow led him deeper. He called out, axe firmly in hand, ready for action.

"Who goes there? Show yourself!"

Pan formed before his eyes, the shadow becoming solid.

99

"Why, it is you!" Dagr's intuition told him that there was a purpose to being led away from the hut.

"Dagr," Pan spoke, and as he did, another form came into the visible beside him. It was a woman, tall, slender, with hair the colour of flames, tucked behind delicate elfin ears. Dagr stood transfixed at her luminescent beauty. The strange sensation of lifting away from his body seemed somehow connected to his staring in her direction. He struggled to understand.

She spoke. Her whispering tone rang musically and lulled him into submission. "You will come with me now."

Dagr was sure that she meant it.

"You have seen enough. It is time for you to return to the future. The others are waiting for you there."

"I cannot leave. Brigida, Richard...Arinn needs me."

"Do not fret, everything will unfold as it should. I promise to bring you back."

"Who are you? I have not met you before in my Fey travels."

The woman's laughter rang in silvery tones, and cast Dagr further under her spell.

"We will meet again. But you must forget that we met here. Your present self must go back to the life you are learning from. And when we finish our travel, you will remember that I am familiar to you, a friend."

Pan stomped his cloven hoof and the woman's form waned somewhat.

"There is no time left, Dagr! Go back to your life. You must let go of what is here and come with me. *Holly is waiting.*"

Holly is waiting. The portal opened and Dagr felt a strange sensation, as if a weight was lifting from his shoulders. He wondered if he was indeed losing his mind when he stood at the door of the hut with a pile of fuel for the fire in his arms with no memory of having gathered it. He shook his head. Strange day from start to finish. Except that it was not finished. There was still the matter of Brigida and Richard.

CHAPTER 17

Aiden opened his eyes slowly, trying to remember where he was. The room was cool. His skin adjusted temperature as his consciousness recalibrated to his surroundings. Sitting up, he was shocked to see Sahara and Holly lying in a tangle on the living room floor, seemingly hanging on to each other for comfort, or maybe it was for warmth. It took a few moments, but recollection after recollection filled his memory bank. The sight of Holly's sweet face and cascade of blond hair pulled up a sharp vision from the forest hut he had only just returned from. A deep groan escaped his throat, as he beheld the past and the present in such close proximity. Aiden knelt beside his lovers and laid a gentle hand upon them, his voice soothing and warm.

"Sahara. Holly. Wake up! Wake up!" He shook them ever so slightly.

They stirred, confused, and then greeted him joyfully.

"Aiden!" They fell upon him and wept tears of relief.

He held them tight, kissing their foreheads.

"You scared us," Holly accused, but her eyes spoke only of love.

"I am so very, very sorry, my love. I don't know what happened exactly. I'm sorry."

"You must be hungry and tired." Sahara offered to prepare a meal. The day had turned to night. The room was only dimly lit by a small lamp near the kitchen, the fire almost out.

"Wait," Aiden pulled her back down beside him. "I need to hold the two of you."

They sat on the sofa with him between them. They felt his keen eyes on them, as he tried to make sense of what was real, what was in the past.

"Don't try to understand it all right now, Aiden," Sahara read his mind. "You should have a bath, rest, eat something to ground yourself. I promise you can hold us all night. But right now, you need to gather strength. A journey through time is...well, dangerous at best."

He immediately recognised the dark haired maiden who had begged to have her hair shorn. He touched Sahara's head, his fingers running through her short pixie cut.

"You are not much changed my lady. The same strength, the same power of the moon emanating from your soul." He kissed her hands, his heart breaking with the realization that Sahara's past life wounds had followed her to this reality, her sterile womb an unhealed nod to that dark time.

"After you have rested, Aiden. There is time for us to discuss it all." Sahara took his pain and folded it neatly into her heart. She would take this from him if it killed her. He deserved only joy.

Holly swept the tear that rolled down his cheek with her fingertips. Placing a kiss on his lips, she knelt at his feet, putting her head in his lap. Aiden's fingers gripped her hair. How she made him melt, and he could not help feeling a little bit mixed up as to who he was really looking at.

"Will you run a bath for me, Holly...if that's not too strange a request?"

"Of course, darling. Anything you need. That's not strange."

"Everything seems a bit strange right now." Aiden had come very close to calling her Arinn; so soon after being led into a bath by his lady love in the forest.

Sahara interrupted them to say that she would take Aiden's truck and drive home to fetch Ulfred. "He's been alone all day, and Willow probably hates me."

"I'll go Sahara. I can use some fresh air." Aiden stood and stretched. "I'll have my bath when I return, and then we can eat."

The three of them set to their assigned chores. Their busyness kept their minds from running wild with the questions that needed answering, and the answers that needed questioning. By the time Aiden returned with a well-run Ulfred, Sahara and Holly had built a roaring fire, laid out a simple meal and agreed to let Aiden take the lead with the conversation. But Aiden was quiet and brooding; through the bath where Holly sat by him and burned with lust as she played with his hair and ravished his muscular body with her eyes; through dinner while Sahara touched his hand often to reassure him of their presence; and finally through coffee and dessert, while they sat by the fire and stared into the flames.

"Can you stay, Holly?" Aiden finally asked, grateful that they had given him room to breathe.

"I can. You couldn't get rid of me if you tried," Holly offered a playful smile.

Aiden, undone, leaned in to kiss her, Sahara watching his handsome features as he took Holly's mouth. She never got tired of how utterly beautiful that looked.

"I'm so exhausted," Aiden said. "I saw so much, felt so much, and have come back not entirely as I was before. I can never have the same perspective on our relationship again, and that scares me. I don't want to lose anything we had, but then again, my new knowledge makes me love you both more."

"Did you see Iona, Aiden?" Holly blurted out, not from jealousy or any kind of concern, but in her own innocent way, wondering if Aiden had been brought back by the kind interception of the red-haired woman.

"Iona? No!" Aiden looked at Sahara with alarm. Of course he had no way of knowing what conversation had been had between his lovers, how much Sahara had revealed. But it was obvious to him now that Holly could no longer be kept in the dark, and oh God...Richard. His heart twisted with the memory of how Richard had looked at Arinn.

"Iona came to your rescue, Aiden." Sahara offered. "I was frightened, and called Iona for help. She agreed to time travel to you. Surely you met up with her along the way?"

"I don't know. I'm not sure." Aiden shook his head. "Yes, I did meet a woman I assumed was Fey, a guide, but in retrospect..."

"She promised to bring you back to us," Holly said, "And she did. She's so beautiful!" Holly's voice trailed off as she remembered her shock at seeing the wildly attractive Iona in Aiden's home.

"I must find a way to thank her," Aiden offered, his hand tight in Sahara's.

"We will invite her to dinner, Aiden," Holly said, voice firm. In her heart, Holly felt fierce gratitude to Iona and was determined to thank her properly for shielding Aiden from harm.

"As you wish," Aiden conceded. He could barely imagine how he would manage an evening with three women who were all determined to hold his heart. A sigh escaped his lips, and Sahara suggested bed.

"Soon, Sahara. I thought I would journal. Perhaps I could have a few moments to myself."

"Of course, we'll go up ahead of you - warm the bed."

"Thank you."

Aiden very much wanted to hang on to what they had had before all this, the innocent love Holly felt for him; but knew that those days were over. He also knew that Sahara would blame herself for the dark places they must trod, and determined to show her that he held no blame in his own heart. They could not have avoided this. He saw that now. The best they could do was to love Holly so completely that she would never doubt her place in their lives.

Tomorrow morning would see him leave for work. As much as he wished to lay in his lovers arms until the end of time, he understood that space to think and absorb his journey was what they all needed. Sahara was right. There was time to sort it all out. Aside from the secrets that Holly would become privy to, he looked forward to evenings of discussions and learning from each other. It was, after all, the lifestyle he had longed for.

He jotted down his memories of his time travel in point form. He decided to expand on it all while he was away, perhaps with the aid of Pan. Tonight, he wanted to hold them close and reassure them that no matter what he had seen or discovered, he was still very much theirs. He couldn't deny that the shadowy memory of Iona was something he was ultimately curious about. He heard Sahara and Holly talking softly to each other upstairs and smiled. How had he lived here alone for so long? Their presence was everything he had ever dreamt of.

He rolled three small joints and grabbed the matches from the mantle, then headed up the stairs to his bedroom.

Sahara was just getting out of the shower when she heard Aiden's voice. Her senses were heightened, her head spinning with questions.

Aiden was sitting in the chair by the window by his sinful bed. The lights were out and he had lit some candles. The room had taken on a soft and comforting light, and Aiden was smoking, staring at Holly who sat naked on the bed, arms wrapped around her knees, hair spilling over her shoulders and down her back. Sahara sighed. It was just what they needed, an evening to relax and just be.

Aiden offered them a joint each. "I know you don't usually smoke, Holly, but would you, tonight, with me?" He stood and lit Holly's as she nodded her head.

"I'll share hers," Sahara said. She never needed much herb to get where she wanted to go.

"Ok," Aiden sat back down and looked Sahara up and down. "Getting dressed again?"

"Ummm, not if you don't want me to?"

"I don't." He took a long drag and stood up again.

"Where you going?" Sahara asked.

"To get us a pitcher of water." And he slipped down the stairs, his energy electric and intense.

"It's pretty up here just with the candles and the moonlight." Holly stretched out on the bed, and held her hand out to Sahara. "I

104

have to be out of here by three thirty. It's going to be hard to leave the two of you. Again. All I do is leave."

"I'm coming with you...here give me a drag," Sahara slipped into bed with Holly.

Holly passed the joint and curled up in Sahara's lap as she now sat against the headboard. Sahara's free hand automatically went to play with Holly's hair.

Holly's tone was vehement. "I want you to stay here with Aiden. Please. I need some time to myself and besides, you can get Aiden to drop you off on his way out. I think he needs you, you know. There must be things he can tell only you about that time."

"I would argue with you but you're right. We do need to do that. But Aiden will disagree on keeping anything away from you. You know how he is."

"I do, and I love that about him. But I also know that the two of you have something I cannot be fully part of...just like he and I have something you're not part of...so let's agree on giving each other the space each relationship deserves. K?" Holly reached back for the joint, but Sahara shifted so she could kiss Holly and blew the smoke into her mouth.

They were vaguely aware of Aiden as he set down the tray with the pitcher of water and poured their drinks. When they untangled, he was sitting down again, watching them with that deeply handsome expression that they loved so much.

"If I could have a minute of your time, ladies," he smiled, all charm, having decided to leave the day's events behind them for now. "What's the plan for tomorrow? And mind you don't burn down my bed."

"I'm going to work before four. I have an order to prepare for the Monfort gallery in Denver. I have a full day's baking ahead," Holly replied, eyes closed while Sahara rubbed her shoulders. "You'll bring Sahara in when you head out to work."

She didn't see the wild look of alarm exchanged between Aiden and Sahara. Sahara's touch didn't waver.

"The Montfort gallery? Is this a regular thing...baking for them?" Aiden observed Sahara's face as it navigated emotions. "Do you know the owner?"

"No. Oh, Sahara, keep doing that, yes, right there! I've never met him, Richard Montfort...so many Richards!" She gave a small laugh. "Anyway, I always speak to his secretary. She's, to put it diplomatically, a bit uptight. But the gallery pays a good price for my baking, and

I'm happy to do it. I'll just run over to your place pick up my car in the morning."

"Not by yourself you're not," Aiden said. "I'll walk you over."

"It'll be dark, and there's bears!" Holly feigned fear.

"There's a full moon. And I know these woods by heart."

Really, neither Aiden nor Sahara were all that surprised at the dark and twisted path woven by circumstance. The thread of connections joined them all with a wicked humor. Sahara drank in the feel of Aiden's love as he poured himself towards her telepathically. She would need his arms around her, and he hers. There was solace in their combined angst.

Holly and Sahara curled up together, facing Aiden's intense expression. They waited. They could have just laid there all night staring at him.

He knew they wanted to hear the details of his journey. Sahara suggested telepathically that he spare Holly some details, but she knew that he would keep as much to the truth as he dared, and the stern look in his eyes confirmed her thoughts.

"Sooo, I met Richard, the Earl I was knight to," Aiden began. Sahara groaned internally. She trusted him to not spill anything that was hers to tell. Aiden nodded as if to silently acknowledge her fear. Holly pulled Sahara closer, wide-eyed and curious.

"Is that the same one you talked about in your sleep that night, Sahara?" Holly's voice rang deceptively calm.

But neither Sahara nor Aiden were fooled. She was about to get dragged into a world that would shape her life with them. And she was scared.

CHAPTER 18

The phone rang once, then again ten minutes later. Iona ignored it. She knew that it was Richard, checking in before he boarded the plane from Europe. Lying curled up in a hot bath, face stained with tears, Iona had nothing left to give to anyone. Not even the man who commanded her heart.

Time travel. It had been some time since she had actually shifted from one century to another. Regressions to the past were an entirely different experience. And it had been centuries since she had seen Dagr in the flesh. She broke down into fresh tears. Oh how her heart ached for a touch, a kiss, an embrace from the first man she had ever loved. Seeing him again, and at such a vulnerable moment in his life, awoke a fierce longing within her.

The only way to experience the beauty of Dagr once more was to leave her life here and retreat to that medieval time or to connect with Aiden...the modern day sorcerer. But that man belonged to Sahara. Sahara, and now, Holly. They had the pleasure of Aiden's love and embrace. He would never be hers to explore. And how that hurt deep into her tortured soul. She should be satisfied with Richard, who by all counts, was truly the man for her. He suited her to perfection; his style, his mind, and his proclivities. And she did love him above all. Still, the essence of Dagr haunted her and always would. Seeing Aiden when she did, at his home today and before - when she had swooped her raven wings above him, opened a wound and a need that begged to be assuaged. She needed forgiveness for something she was sure Sahara and Aiden were not aware of yet. She needed, and wanted, to relive some choices she had made, and to feel the complete bliss she had once experienced with Dagr and Arinn.

Seeing Holly had brought her in painful touch with that lifetime. Holly, the innocent. She would be hurt in the end, Iona had no doubt. Sad. But the clever Universe had placed her in front of Aiden, and there was no escaping from the All Knowing.

Her body ached to be held. She cried out to Sahara. She knew that Sahara could hear her, and would come if she could, but shape shifting was not something she had mastered as yet and anyway, she had Aiden and Holly to attend to.

Once more, she called to Sahara. A plaintive cry that seared through space to where Sahara lay in bed, waiting for Aiden to return from walking Holly to her car, through the moonlit forest of the Aspen King.

Aiden Halloran ✶ Custom Homes
Riverbend, Colorado

Dear Mr. Montfort,

It is my understanding that my portfolio has been recommended to you by the architectural firm of Grant and First.

I have looked over the plans drawn for you by Stephen Grant, our mutual colleague.

You had a question as to whether the scale and style of your building project would suit my schedule and my passion in house design.

Having had time to go over the details, I can confirm, that indeed, I would be pleased to accept your offer to discuss project plans.

Please contact me at your earliest convenience, I am often in Aspen and can arrange a dinner meeting at the Mountain View Hotel.

Kind Regards,
Aiden Halloran.

Richard read the message and sighed, sipping a scotch in the first class lounge at Heathrow Airport.

It had been a longer trip than Richard had anticipated. First of all, he had had no intention of staying so long in Northern England, but once there, he had been swept into a dizzying amount of dreams that left him wandering the ocean coast without direction.

When he'd left for Europe, his memories had been fresh from his meeting with Sahara. No matter how many times he tried, he could not rid himself of her essence or the intense emotions he had felt during the regression facilitated by Iona.

His mind had been completely taken away from his house building plans, and now as he read the letter from Aiden Halloran, he was overwhelmed by the immensity of the project. He would rather devote himself to exploring his past life instead.

108

But plans would move forward, because Richard was self-disciplined if he was anything at all, and because he had promised Iona a place to escape to where they could build a life all of their own, away from the city and where she could practice the witchcraft she loved so much.

Thoughts of Iona relaxed him somewhat, but now it was difficult to imagine her without her diminutive lover at her side, and the recollections of a young girl named Brigida whom Richard now felt like a searing brand on his heart.

He hoped that the architect had not overstated when he had said that this Halloran fellow was 'the best around, because Richard could not work with incompetence, and indeed, needed a builder who would be sensitive to the design. It was complicated and required attention to detail. Oh well, he would know when he met him. Richard had a keen sense for accomplishment.

The tattoo on his arm caught his attention as it often did, and he ran his fingers over it, a chill along his spine. Since the regression, Richard had awoken to feelings emanating from the artwork, and he meant to ask Iona for another regression, so he could meet the man represented by the ink. Strange, he was not usually attuned to other men, save for his sharp sense of character or lack thereof, but he was curious about the medieval warrior and what their connection was.

Richard was frustrated that Iona was ignoring his calls, and he was sure that it was that, because she did things as they suited her. If she was deep in some magical ritual, she would have her phone turned off. Or maybe Sahara had returned?

Damn! Richard crossed his legs and returned the smile of a woman traveller. He checked his watch...a long stretch of time between now and when he could hold Iona once more. Sahara's naked body draped over his knees, his hand caressing her delightful bottom appeared as a memory. He had taken his time to worship her ass, Sahara moaning her delight as he had switched from caressing to light spanking, every so often opening her to Iona's tongue. It was all he could do to keep from groaning out loud as memories of that evening swept in one after the other, and he adjusted himself in his chair.

The woman traveller in the lounge chair opposite his sensed Richard's heightened energy and leaned in, raising her glass. Richard gave a polite nod of his head, but his look remained discouraging.

In his heart, Richard pondered his increasing love for a woman who would never be faithful to him, in thought or deed. But he supposed that he was no different, except that he had long ago stopped needing the chase. Iona satisfied in every sense. And Sahara had been her idea. He shifted again, wishing he was outdoors, breathing salty ocean air. Now seemed as good a time as any to confirm his meeting with Halloran, since leaving the airport was out of the question. He opened his tablet and smiled at the screen saver. It was his favorite picture of Iona, in the dress he had met her in, looking over her shoulder at him, laughing. He adored this side of her. A fairy queen - that's what she looked like.

CHAPTER 19

Holly drove away, having kissed Aiden a thousand times.

"I hate feeling this vulnerable," she'd said to him.

"I need vulnerable," Aiden had answered. "It's the only way for us to know each other completely. Broken open, raw, wounded, real."

"But I've not ever had to rely on my heart for anything before. I was safe, my own island. This feels so dangerous, allowing so much love in that I feel like I might die."

"I love this pain. I do, Holly! I love being ripped open even though I need so much more physical activity now to maintain my sanity. You've got to go. I promise that I'll stop in on my way out." Aiden had shoved Holly towards her open car door. This was indeed dangerous, this feeling of no self-control.

"That's how this whole thing started, Aiden, with you stopping in on your way out that time...remember?"

"I couldn't possibly forget. I play that over in my mind all the time. Our first kiss. My first real touch of you. It was a pivotal moment in time. Magic."

He watched her taillights until she rounded the bend in the road. That bend was something Sahara loved, it was the first glimpse of her cabin as she rounded it on her way home. Aiden now understood what portals were, and that certain places opened a surge of energy that left one on the brink of discovery. It could be a different discovery every time - one of emotion, of other times, or intuition, but each portal was a dip into conscious awareness.

Stopping at the Elder tree, Aiden looked up at the night sky, festooned with stars, except where dark clouds were rolling in.

He had been right, this tree was new. And he had seen another, near his home, Rowan, Sorbus Aucuparia, for protection and inspiration, to be used in ritual. The word ritual created a rush of heat through his veins.

Aiden approached his house with renewed interest. It seemed to have taken on a new energy, it was protected, not only by Rowan, but also by the Fey. It must always have been, but he hadn't noticed to this degree. All was dark, Sahara has stayed in bed. He stood for a long moment breathing in the moisture of the early morning, acclimatizing to his emotions and making calculated decisions about what would happen when he went in.

A week away. A long time and yet not long enough. He was a new man. He felt it in every fibre of his body. And this was a new day.

———————

Sahara felt the rough rip of bedclothes as they left her body. "Hey! I'm still sleeping!"

"Come to the edge of the bed. Lie on your belly."

Sahara's eyes flew open...she recognized *that* tone.

"Now, Sahara. Face towards the edge."

She could hardly make him out in the dim light, but she could feel him.

"What if I need to use the washroom?"

"Do you? If you need something, ask for it. Don't play this game with me."

She understood. He was in his role, and he expected her to be in hers. Playing games would cost her.

Aiden lowered to his knees and slowly left a red hot trail of kisses along her back, from her toes to her tight bottom, where he lingered, spoke under his breath, his hands never touching her, just breath and lips. He continued to her neck. There he left tiny bites and made love to her ears. Every time she squirmed he warned her that he was counting every mistake she made. So far, four.

"Kiss my mouth, Aiden, please."

"Five."

"Aiden, I need your tongue in my mouth."

He didn't answer nor did he kiss her, just left for his closet. Sahara felt the rush of expectation on her skin, rising into goose bumps. She moaned quietly.

Aiden returned with rope. Methodically, he began to tie her, knots at her feet, arms tied behind her back, feet and hands looped together. He placed a pillow under her chest, to ease the curve in her spine and so she could rest her head.

"Comfy?"

"Where did you learn to tie knots so well?"

"Boy Scouts," Aiden's voice rumbled out, a caress of lust and love.

"Boy Scouts? Is there a badge for this sort of thing?"

"Well, actually, I already knew how to do it. Back then I didn't understand why. But now, things are a little clearer. No more questions."

112

He sat down in his chair and stared at her.

"I love you, Sahara. Very much."

She stayed silent, contemplating what six or seven lashes would feel like at the hand of a madman.

"It won't be lashes," Aiden said. "You forget that I'm getting better at telepathy."

"You haven't forgotten that one of my favorite things is being made to wait...I'm getting so wet, Aiden."

"You're stunning. I'm so fucking lost in you. I wish I wasn't, I know that you're going to hurt me, but I need you more than ever."

She nodded, tears on the brink. Aiden's love was complete and overwhelming. His willingness to experience it all with her made her heart break in the most beautiful way.

"There's something about that girl I met, Brigida. She had a strength and a softness, like you. She was beat up and broken when I saw her in the time travel, but I could see that she was vast. You're vast."

Sahara looked him in the eye and he saw the Universe shining back.

He stood and very gently passed his fingers over her pussy, feeling her wetness. He knelt before her and put his fingers in her mouth.

"You're dripping. I think I'll have you wait some more. You may put your head down on the pillow. Rest."

She did as she was told.

He came back with a vibrator and lifting her a little, pressed it to her clit. "You don't have my permission to come."

Sahara groaned and accepted the terms. Putting the vibrator down, Aiden kissed the bottom of her feet, and gently began to suck on one of her pretty toes, carefully observing the moment when Sahara could no longer take any more stimulation, then, giving her a moment to relax, moved on to the next one.

Sahara's writhing body and forced surrender drove him into a wicked heat. His lips ached for more and with a great hunger, Aiden lifted Sahara at her hips and placed his mouth on her dripping cunt.

She cried out as his tongue found all her secrets.

"May I please come, my lord?"

The question was moot as she rocked against his face and climaxed while his unshaved jaw rubbed rough against her tender skin.

"Ah, Sahara! You're a very bad girl, you'll take your punishment. But you don't really mind, do you?"

He came around to kiss her. She had that look on her face, the one that drove him to wanting to fuck her like a demon, but that would have to wait.

"Please Aiden," she said obediently, as he faced her with his erect cock, his skin scented, the forest never far from his being.

She opened her mouth, and Aiden moaned.

He gave her the tip first, let her drop soft kisses, tender licks, taking only the head of it in her mouth. Sahara purred her delight.

"Look up at me. That's it..." He slid himself further in her mouth. Her lips tightened. She had very little room to move. He would have to control how deep she took him. She wanted more and grunted in frustration, but he kept himself at a certain distance, allowing her tongue to work its way along his length.

"May I ask for more, please?"

"How much more?"

"All of it my lord."

Aiden growled and slid in slowly, then began to move his hips.

"Suck it like a whore, Sahara."

Sahara's lips tightened and her cheeks hollowed. She moaned loudly, hungry, starving for his pleasure, aching for him inside her, sucking his deliciousness with every ounce of talent that she possessed. Aiden's hips kept up their swaying, he filled her mouth completely. She expected his cock to gag her at every thrust, and she would have welcomed anything that he did, but he, acutely aware of her point of gag reflex, kept himself from giving her what she wanted.

She looked up at him, eyes begging.

"No, Sahara, this is your punishment. I won't give you that, no matter how much you beg. Next time, listen when I give you instructions."

She nodded, tears rolling down, understanding that he was once again, teaching her about the sacred dance of trust. She wanted his cum, on her tongue, down her throat - but she didn't dare ask.

She could tell that he was close, that he too wanted release, but she knew him well enough by now to expect the unexpected. And so she continued to suck him vigorously, while his love poured onto her, in waves of unexpressed words. Their connection was soul deep.

"I know that you want me to drip hot in your mouth, my love, but I have need of your tight little cunt." He slipped out of her mouth, cock slick with her saliva, a thickly veined monster ready to devour its lover.

Quickly, he untied her, allowing her time to stretch.

"Show me."

114

Aiden's eyes burned Sahara's skin. His decadent smile made her shy. This man was a total delight. His body, in its exquisite hardness, towered over her as she rolled over and spread her legs.

"Mmm. Yes, my love. Delicious and sinful," Aiden licked his lips.

She couldn't help herself. She had to ask. "Please punish me with the rod, Aiden...please. I know you have one!"

He growled and lunged at her. "No. Not today."

Sahara looked so desperate that Aiden almost gave in.

"But why?" She continued to spread herself, his face close, his breath a maddening tease.

"I told you at the beginning, no whippings today. I'd like nothing better, but today, your lesson is in waiting. Being happy with what is. Staying in the moment." He placed his hands on her inner thighs, thumbs stroking her outer lips, pulling her open. She shoved her hips up towards him.

He complied. In one swift move her clit was in his mouth and he sucked gently. Sahara came while his tongue swiped hot over her opening, so close to entering her.

Satisfied that he had served her well, Aiden turned Sahara around and to the sound of her pleasure, slid his aching cock inside her, moaning along with her as she came in spurts, fucking hard against her cervix, unloading spurt after spurt of hot cum inside her.

CHAPTER 20

They don't know you
You, who are ancient
With memories written upon your bones
Sacred, older than the hills
Your light kept hidden under your witch's robes
They can't hear you
Your whispered words
They can't see you, wandering the woods
Because you're the forgotten, the sinful, the willful
The one they erased with their sacrosanct swords
But you won't be extinguished – mystic's child
Your footsteps will haunt us and awaken our tribe

It was difficult to make out anything but shadows in the dim light of Iona's apartment.

Richard shut the door quietly behind himself, and put down his overnight bag.

She was home. He could feel her electric energy. Incense burned in the little brass container on the kitchen table. One tiny candle flickered on the shelf where Iona kept her sacred pyramid container of herb. A joint lay rolled and ready for him.

He loosened his tie, and wondered why he had taken so long to come see her. She had continued to avoid his calls. He had gone straight to the gallery after his flight, and after showering and changing, had held a meeting of his staff. But his mind had never strayed from his anticipation to reunite with Iona.

He lit the joint and poured himself a scotch. The tie came off. He rolled up his sleeves and walked into the living room. He loved this space. A well-established fire threw shadows on the tall walls.

Richard smoked sitting in his favorite chair, chiselled face serene, but his heart raced and his thoughts kept pace.

Something had happened. He had no way of knowing what but when Iona waited for him in their chamber it was always because she was fighting her own demons. Although he had been quiet coming in, she would know that he was there. He was deliberately making her wait. And who knew how long she had already been in there. When Iona hurt, she created her own punishments.

Music drifted in from the chamber. Richard recognized the strains of early music, a signal of the play they would engage in. Theirs was a complicated dance, Iona dictating her needs, Richard seeking her surrender, the lines blurred between who was dominating whom, but this dance was well rehearsed and they each knew other's sexual desires well.

How he loved Iona's tenderness, the quiet that overcame her when she hurt, all her defences down, begging for his strength. He almost didn't have the courage to give her what she wanted but in the end, his true nature surfaced, and he, riding the wave of her rising power, would always please her.

The joint done, Richard refilled his glass and washed his hands. Finding a bottle of red wine in Iona's cupboard, he grabbed a crystal goblet and made his way to the room where all sins lay waiting to be explored.

Iona reclined on the table in the center of the room on a luxurious faux fur blanket. Her gown, a white transparent chiffon, lay opened to the waist, her breasts spilling out; hair in a wild tangle around her. Her eyes glowed green, catching the fire of the candles in the sconces on the walls.

Richard absorbed the coursing energy of the witch in her seduction dress. He clenched his fists as his lust grew hot and violent. He carefully observed the implements of play that Iona had laid out - a bowl of small wooden clothes pins, metal nipple clips, a rod, a Hitachi wand, a bundle of feathers, candles, rope, electric prods. His cock rose and he adjusted himself, while his mouth ached to kiss the red lips of a woman who knew no boundaries.

"Darling, what has happened?" Richard asked silently. Although Iona knew his thoughts, she didn't offer an answer. But he wanted so very much to know what it was...to hold her; shield her. He wanted to kiss her tenderly, to wipe the tears that gathered at the corner of her eyes and spilled down her cheeks.

But she wouldn't want that. Later, yes, she would soak up his love and fall asleep in his arms. Most likely she would not tell him which demons she had fought. Sometimes he just wanted her to let him fight for her. For Richard, the battleground was familiar territory.

"I've missed you," he said, pouring Iona a goblet of wine, and offering his hand, lifting her to a sitting position. Iona's breasts, heavy with desire, fell pleasingly out of her dress. Richard caressed one with a tender touch, his fingers toying with a tightly pursed nipple.

Iona obediently took a sip of wine, while her eyes devoured the tight fit of Richard's dress shirt, and the strength of his forearms.

She lifted her mouth to his, red lips searing.

Richard savored the moments of intimacy, the delicious taste of Iona's kiss, how her tongue sent a rush of blood through his veins.

"I'm going to use you, in whatever way pleases me," he growled at her, biting her neck as Iona's head dropped back.

"I'm here for you pleasure, my lord." Iona slipped down to the table, closing her eyes.

Richard placed the blindfold over her eyes. Before he tied her he wanted to spend to a few moments unveiling her beauty. His hands slid into her dress, at her waist, then over her breasts, caressing.

His mouth lowered, tongue slipping over her areola, then sucked on the tips that teased his taste buds. He nipped at her ear, whispered her name, and quickly climbing onto the table, he allowed her the pleasure of his weight, cock hard against her mound.

Iona cried out, legs spreading, grinding herself onto him. Richard could feel the cleft of her sex, and imagined the first thrust...but that would be some time from now. Climbing down, Richard took a gentle hold of Iona's feet, and rubbing their soles, pulled on each toe individually. Adept at massage, Richard knew the value of fully relaxing Iona before he subjected her to an evening of tortuous pleasures. Besides, he loved touching her languidly. It created the tension he needed.

He had incredibly soft hands, muscular as they were. Iona's legs begged spreading, and gently, Richard slid along one of her inner thighs towards his goal.

"What a wicked slut you've turned out to be, my love," Richard noted, his mouth aching to taste her.

"Richard!" Iona reached down to touch his hand. She lifted her gown, and all of her came in to view.

He didn't touch her yet, not there, although he could tell that she craved his fingers, or tongue, or the heat of his breath. Before she had a chance to protest, Richard ripped Iona's dress in half, his hunger peaking.

He spread her legs wider, and pulled her roughly towards the edge of the table. Her folds opened sinfully. She was wet, glistening in the candle light. Richard's tongue slipped out over his lips...this was torture!

Picking up the rope, he tied her legs, calves to thighs, ropes fastened tightly to the rings at the edge of the table so she wouldn't be able to lower them. Next, he bound her hands and tied them up over her head to another ring. Giving the rope a tug, Richard made sure that Iona had little opportunity for movement. Once more he kissed her, tender, loving. Iona lay open, vulnerable, incapable of seeing his next move nor or defending herself should he prove too rough. Her chest heaved as she breathed into the panic that always befell her when they began their play.

Richard wet Iona's nipples with his tongue before he placed the clamps on them. His fingers in her mouth allowed her something to bite on as she adjusted to the pain. She loved this, he knew. For her, pain was integral to pleasure.

Pulling up a chair to the edge of the table, Richard sat himself down before Iona's delicate pussy, and took a drink of Scotch.

He approached her with care, breath first, then a sensuous mouth on her inner thighs. The music enveloped them. Their energy rose, both of them anticipating the meeting of mouth and tender cunt. Iona's clit stood erect, a bare morsel of deliciousness.

Richard would circle her clit until she begged for contact. He would lick at her opening without penetrating. He would wait until her clit was fully engorged before he would take it in his mouth and suck it expertly while she begged for permission to release. And he would give it, long moments later, to watch her squirt her first orgasm in complete abandon.

She made him thirsty. For this and for her love. He could do this all night.

The clothes pins were next, four on each outer lip, exposing Iona's cunt as far as it could be exposed. This was one of Iona's favorite things - to be opened like a flower in full bloom, and Richard loved seeing her spread like this.

"I've never known a more delicious woman than you, Iona." Richard slipped the clamps off and immediately pulled her nipples into his mouth, one after the other, ignoring Iona's pleas for mercy. While wet, they jumped to the electric implement that Richard applied next.

Tears sprang up. Iona moaned. Richard was so good at timing, teasing her breasts, inner thighs and feet with the prod. Squirming as much as the ropes allowed, Iona fell into the pain of the electricity on her skin, each shock a reminder of how much she needed to release her internal battle.

He ceased, kissed her mouth gently, and then stroked her whole body with the bundle of feathers. How lovely she looked as she relaxed under his touch and his love. And indeed, Richard's heart was full.

Loving Iona was a gift that he appreciated in every form.

"Are you ready for more?" Richard kissed Iona's open palms and teased her fingers into his mouth.

"Water, please, my lord."

He allowed her the drink, kissing her after each sip.

"I'm scared, Richard."

"Can you tell me why?" Richard threw his shirt to the floor and allowed her to touch his lean core, an addiction of hers.

"I've been travelling..."

Richard turned his back to her, and gathered the tools he needed. He'd been sure that she wouldn't share what pained her. His heart opened to receive her.

"Have you been somewhere that I would be displeased with?" He knew that Iona, drunk on the symmetry of his frame, the tattoos that she loved to trace with her tongue, would say whatever it took to anger him so that he would torture her longer, fuck her deeper, demand her slavedom. But he hoped for truth nonetheless.

"I went back in time. To Dagr and Brigida."

Richard gently caressed Iona's very pleasingly exposed bottom, his fingers insistent, then softly licked her perineum, three deliberate strokes. Iona responded with loud moans.

"That's a good little whore, who likes her ass licked. You once promised me that you would let me know in advance if you were to time travel. What if you hadn't returned?"

Richard slid an electric prod inside Iona's tight ass. She shook with delight and cried out in pain. Sucking her clit into his mouth, Richard enticed Iona closer to another orgasm, then released her. Several teasingly light swipes of the flogger across her belly and breasts prepared Iona for what was coming. Lighting a candle, he created a trail of hot wax settling onto her nipples and tender belly.

"Richard, please take the blindfold off, I need to see you."

"I don't think so, my love."

"I have something to tell you..."

"Tell me."

Richard applied the Hitachi wand to Iona's clit. "Don't you dare cum, Iona. Take it...take it. Yes. Christ, you're hot!" He turned up the intensity of the electric prod. Iona's body thrashed, she struggled against the ropes.

"I need to see you when I tell you."

"No, darling. Not what you need. What I need."

"Richard, finger me..."

"Stop asking me for what you want. I know what you want. There's no need to school me!"

And with that, Richard untied Iona, released her pussy from the clothes pins and slid out the electric prod, watching with interest as Iona transitioned into the pleasure of being pain free. Out of an intense need to touch her, Richard oiled his hand and massaged Iona's pussy, a merciful touch that elicited more moans.

"Sit up!" He kissed her, rough. "Your mouth tastes like it's hungry, my sweet little whore. Are you hungry Iona?"

She nodded. Blindfolded, she had to rely on her other senses. She could smell Richard's cologne, the intoxicating scent of his lust.

Richard guided her from the table onto her knees on the floor. Watching her carefully, Richard gauged the level of her discomfort. She had always hated cold, hard floors. They reminded her of that other century when he had been a crueller master. He ached to provide her with a pillow, a drink of wine, to serve her on bended knee, to worship her beauty. But none of that would help her. He picked up the cane she had laid out. Out of all the whips and floggers they had bought together, this one was the cruelest on Iona's tender skin. Richard winced even as he held it.

"Palms flat on the floor, Iona." His voice, so terse now, could only excite her more. Richard was dedicated to her pleasure; every nuance created the delicate balance they needed to find freedom in their roles.

She did as she was told, the round of her ass in the air. The air between them moved in smooth waves as he approached her from behind. The delicacy of her sex exposed thus, Richard was moved to drop to his knees and lick her, wetness dripping along her thighs; his elegant face artwork against her skin.

Iona rocked as he pleased her, the skill of his mouth always an erotic reminder that this man understood women well.

But at the other end of that thought was the realization that soon he would turn cruel and that she could do nothing about it. She had to trust. Trust that he knew the moment when pain was no longer necessary. He was a faithful master.

"Richard...Richard!"

He took that as his cue. The cane left one mark, then two, then three. Richard's cock reached its fullness as the thin, red stripes appeared on Iona's bottom.

She dripped freely from her cunt to the floor, aroused by the pain and Richard's resolve.

"Count with me, darling. Four, five, six...louder, keep your palms flat!" He decided on ten.

Tenderly picking her up by her chin, Richard, now naked, pulled her towards him, still on her knees. "Open your mouth. Look up at me."

Iona licked her lips, Richard's cock stood thick and velvety, balls shaved perfectly clean. Her hair in a tight grip, Richard stood rigid as she took her first swipe of his cock. A deep moan escaped him. Iona licked with a very wet mouth and took him deep into her throat, without one gag or watering of her eyes, because he insisted on manners, even when swallowing his delicious length.

"Christ, Iona...suck harder! God your mouth is wet. Use your hand..." Richard gripped harder on her hair, and moved his hips.

"Say, please fuck my mouth."

"Oooohh, please fuck my mouth, Richard!"

"I own you, Iona. You're mine to use, to fuck, to cum on. Understand?"

"Yes," she answered, words muffled by his cock.

"Tell me what you did. Tell me where you went."

"Now?" She looked up at him, alarmed.

"Now, with my cock in your mouth."

"I...I can't. It'll take too long."

"I'd like you to, Iona." Richard's voice softened. Iona shook her head and sucked harder.

"I can't." She shut her eyes, anticipating his next move. But even though she always thought he would strike her for disobeying, he never did, and never would.

Reaching for her arms, Richard pulled Iona to her feet. He dragged her to the leather bound bench and bent her over it.

"Spread your legs!" Iona's pussy was engorged and ready for penetration, and Richard could see that she was trembling as she lay there, awaiting his assault. At this moment he needed to be inside her, to feel her dripping her cum all over him. His hand came across her ass, hard and rhythmic, her cries falling on deaf ears. Then, suddenly, he was inside her, a roaring, angry lover because he was truly afraid that one day she would disappear and maybe if he owned her, she wouldn't dare leave. Once, she had had to obey him, but now, he had no right to her. He fucked her hard until she squirted her release and he allowed himself his own pleasure.

"Turn around." He lifted her, and placed her before him once more.

"Lick that up."

She serviced him, a teary mess, a grateful mess, licking her cum from his balls, and sucking the last drops of sperm from his cock.

"Goddammit, Iona, I love you. I fucking love you."

Iona collapsed to the floor.

Richard took her aching body to her bed, where he lay as close to her as he could get, warming her under the thick duvet. She lay silent for a long time, listening to his heartbeat, and his murmured love words.

He would wait patiently to hear why she had disobeyed him and left to search for another man. He would wait until after she had had a bath, after some food and drink, after his tender care, after he had gathered his unravelled wits.

In a startling turn of events, Richard had slipped into Iona's mind while he was fucking her within an inch of her life. He did not think that he had the ability to read minds, so she must have worked some magic. But he had caught a glimpse of a man, towering and blond, a rough warrior with startling blue eyes, and the image had caught his heart in a dull, twisting ache.

Was he so jealous? This man was not a threat. What then, was this feeling of emptiness and longing? He hugged Iona tighter. She was clever, this witch that he loved beyond all reason.

No words that Iona could have said to him would have made a bigger impression than that image had.

CHAPTER 21

Morning light filtered through the trees alongside the outbound road.

Aiden drove away from Riverbend in a turmoil of emotions. For the last few years, the drive from home to a work site had been meditative in nature. He enjoyed the last bit of night, the promise of sunrise after the hours of darkness. He unfolded as the day did before him, easing into the anticipation of working with his hands and the creativity it afforded him.

Today, he noticed for the first time that leaving home also came with an ache in his heart for whom he was leaving behind. Perhaps this was what parents spoke of when they said that leaving home was forever a reminder of their offspring's vulnerability. He himself felt vulnerable leaving his lovers behind.

His lips were still warm from a kiss he had stolen from Holly and Sahara at the patisserie. Their laughter and warm bodies had added an amusement to his eyes that they said they loved...that mix of his manliness and slip into tender emotion. He had groaned when they pulled away, reminding him that he must be on his way.

Aiden was in no way fooled by their light mood. There hadn't been enough time for the discussions that they all needed, nor for any of them to process the events of the last day. But they loved him and would not have sent him away with any of their worries evident.

And so Aiden didn't mention that he intended to meet with Richard while away or that he had no idea where his emotions would take him when he did. Holly, of course knew nothing about what had transpired between Sahara and Richard when they'd met. There was still that.

His life, once so ordered and within his control, now showed no signs of turning away from the madness it was careening towards. The intensity of what might be created a vortex of energy that he had to expend, and he looked forward to a few days of hard work. Sahara had said that when he came home from work, he always looked bigger, more ripped; and that she couldn't wait to worship at his altar once more.

He smiled. Giving her what she craved was a major turn-on and motivated him to take great care of his health and conditioning. Holly adored his physique without a doubt, but their connection was centered in some ways more on his mind first, body second. Still, that made him all the more intent on winning that flash of admiration in her eyes.

These thoughts soothed him somewhat. They were frivolous and by the time the sun had fully risen, Aiden was in a better frame of mind.

He dropped his bags at the hotel, in his usual room. He instructed the desk to light the fireplace by eight. Aiden had every intention of using his time wisely. He'd packed his journal and tonight he would begin recording his thoughts on the time travel and making sense of his future.

His meeting with Richard was two days away. Enough time to relax into his intentions.

"So now? What plans for the week?" Iona made herself comfy in Richard's arms. He was feeding her ice cream, drizzled with Bailey's Irish Cream. He had that dark, wild look in his eyes again, the one that made her want to keep him forever.

"So now, I'm going to dedicate some time to our house project. Remember that?" Richard deposited Iona onto the sofa and went to add to the fire.

"Yes, I remember. I thought maybe you were going to wait awhile, with all that's going on at the gallery and...you know."

"You mean this thing you've told me nothing about? I'm still not sure how your time travel is going to change much for us, except that I forbid you to do it again."

They smiled at the ridiculousness of his command. "This man, Dagr, whom I now know to be a vivid part of my past, is he going to materialize for me to have to fend off?" Richard laughed.

The look in Iona's eyes stopped him cold. "Iona, I'm not in the mood for mystery right now. If there's something I need to know, please, for the love of God, just out with it." Richard sat in his chair, separating himself from Iona's gift of touch. It made all things blurry for him and he needed to stay sharp.

Iona understood. He would wait patiently until she had at least satisfied his need to feel safe in their love once more.

"If you can't tell me where you went and why, just tell me the parts I need to make sense of us. Wait, I'll get us a drink. What would you like?"

"I don't want anything."

"Ok. Start talking then." Richard smiled but his eyes were cool. He left for the kitchen.

"It was not that big a deal, Richard!" Iona called after him. "Tell me about your trip...I didn't really mean to go back, it was quite accidental. The thing that startled me was how vivid the experience was and seeing Dagr and of course the other version of you...surreal."

By the time Richard had returned with his drink, Iona had rearranged her intentions for honesty and composed her face into something trustworthy and impenetrable.

Richard knelt in front of her. He took her chin in his hand.

"Darling. You're lying. I've already beat your sweet ass for the truth, and can do so again. You let me into your scheming mind and I saw Dagr as clear as day. Are you in love with him still? Because if you are, I can deal with a man who's been dead for six hundred years or so. What are you so fucking afraid of?"

Iona tried to wrench herself away from his tight grip and penetrating look. This is what she was addicted to in him - his strength. She fed for a moment on her attraction to him.

"It's not Dagr you need to be worried about, Richard!" she spat out. "It's who Dagr is reincarnated into now." She pulled away. Richard sat back on his heels, his hand tight around his glass. Too tight.

"You know him?" He got up and went to his chair. Sitting down heavily, he let out a sigh. "I swear, Iona, you're pushing me into a dangerous mood." He thought for a moment. "You know what? I'm going to give you some time to gather your courage and myself time to prepare for your confession. I'm meeting with the builder, and when I get back, you and I are going to get to the bottom of this."

"What builder?" Iona asked, her chest a knot of anxiety and fear.

"The builder of the house that I want us to live in!" Richard barked. "Aiden Halloran! Really, Iona, I could wring your neck sometimes. You're so exasperating!" He threw the wine down his throat and left for the shower.

Iona, pale and frightened, called to the Aspen King. And he, delighted to entertain her long gone, vulnerable spirit, left his throne and enveloped her with a blanket of his essence. And that is how Richard found her, asleep on the sofa with a tear on her cheek.

He picked her up tenderly and brought her to bed. Oh well, how bad could it be? Their love was strong. He'd deal with this mystery man who had Iona turned around in his usual manner. Directly and without mercy.

126

CHAPTER 22

He arrived at the restaurant early, tablet it hand, and sat down at the bar, facing the door.

Aiden had no desire to be the one walking in second. He liked being prepared emotionally. He knew what Richard looked like, the gallery and the society pages had plenty of images to check out. Sahara had perhaps understated Richard's looks. Aiden, appreciative of art and form, thought Richard one of the most attractive men he'd ever seen, even with that calculating expression in his eyes.

He had to be honest with himself, he had not much idea as to how he would broach the subject of Sahara. He knew that he must or give up the project. He swirled the Scotch in his glass, looking pensively into its depths.

They hadn't talked about it, but Sahara knew intuitively what Aiden faced and had left him a note in his coat. She had no advice to offer, save to say that she would respect whatever he decided to do.

And even though Aiden thought that he was aware of his surroundings, he was caught by surprise when Richard stood beside him, elegance personified. Aiden stared as he remembered his time travel and the man who had once been his friend. Richard couldn't have missed his look of surprise.

He stood. Richard held out his hand - impeccably groomed, tan and self-assured. Aiden picked up on the details quickly: expensive watch, shirt starkly white - probably custom tailored; lean and muscular.

"Richard Montfort - Aiden?"

They shook, a puzzled look on Richard's face.

"Have we met before? Perhaps at a charity function?"

Aiden, taller, broader, felt the immensity of Richard's energy.

"We haven't," Aiden said, not immune to the irony of the question, and the piercing intuition of Richard's eyes.

He gestured towards the stool beside him. "Please, join me in a drink." He summoned the barkeep, and asked Richard what he preferred.

"I'll have what you're having...the Isle of Jura. I can't believe they stock that here."

"They don't, I do. I can't believe you can tell what it is by looking at it."

"I can smell Isle of Jura from a mile away. It's my favorite. What do you mean, *you* stock it?"

"I had some imported. They kindly keep it for me here. I'm here quite a bit." Already, something else in common, Aiden realized wryly.

Richard smiled, a genuine expression of his warming feeling towards Aiden.

The little bit of silence between them didn't bother either man. They drank in communal appreciation of the whiskey.

Richard pointed to the tablet. "I'm assuming you have the plans in there, but I would prefer if we left that until after dinner. I've never enjoyed eating and discussing business. Do you mind?"

"Not at all," Aiden replied knowing full well that they might never get to the plans anyway. "That sounds much more civilized. They're going to call us in any minute, I asked for the table in the corner, there by the fire."

Richard laughed. "That's fine. I'm used to sitting in corners. My partner, Iona, prefers anywhere there's a fire and with her back to the wall."

In that split second of an opportunity, Aiden, true to his character and his ancient warrior heart, delivered the crippling reply with meticulous timing. He looked directly into Richard's eyes. In a calm yet dangerous voice he observed, "Yes, something in common with my partner, Sahara. Probably not a coincidence."

Richard reeled inwardly, and tried to get his senses around what was happening. It was like having his life flash before his eyes! Images of making love to Sahara, remembered snippets of conversation, regressions, and what Iona had said the other night...*It's not Dagr. It's who he's reincarnated into this lifetime* cruelly invaded his mind. The intense, and by all counts, riveting man before him and he were connected by their shared past, by lovers, by a long ago friendship. How could this be, this trick of synchronicity?

To his credit, Richard didn't try to pretend that he had nothing to make right with Aiden. But his heart ached as he realized that Iona couldn't be blamed for wanting a man this extraordinary. Richard, even in this critical moment, was impressed with Aiden's composure and dedication to acting like a gentleman.

The hostess interrupted their reverie, and led them to their table.

Richard sat first. Aiden ordered more drinks. Each took a few moments to compose themselves.

"I don't need you to explain anything, Richard. And I'm sorry for the ambush. There was no comfortable way to begin this. I don't expect us to work together at this point. But I do expect us to talk about our unusual, to say the least, connection."

Richard shook his head. "Iona didn't prepare me in the least. I realize now that she knew what I'd be walking into." He looked at Aiden, and suddenly that twisting pain in his heart returned. An ache he could not make any sense of, but one that Iona had allowed him to access when he'd glimpsed Dagr. For once in his life, Richard was lost for words.

Their drinks arrived and so did the menus.

"I'm just going to order, Richard. The lamb for both of us. Drink, for God's sake." Richard, eyebrow raised, agreed. He wasn't used to not being in charge, but deciding on dinner seemed irrelevant now.

"You know, if you were simply a man who'd had an affair with my lover, I would have handled this differently. But since we are caught in something far bigger than us, I suggest that we take our time and untangle this mess."

Aiden himself couldn't believe the compassion he felt towards a man who although knowing that Sahara was taken, had still fucked her every which way from Sunday. But, looking at Richard, he understood why she had wanted the roguish art dealer. Even in this vulnerable position, or perhaps because of it, Richard was a desirable presence. Anyone could see that.

Richard faced the inevitable. "There's nothing I can say that will change what happened between Sahara and me, Aiden. I do apologise. There is no excuse, really." Aiden's piercing stare was met unflinchingly.

Aiden imagined Sahara at Richard's mercy. It was easier this way, and he had already admitted to Sahara that he had been aroused by images of her being taken by another man. The worst of it was not that he was having dinner with that man, but that after all things had been discussed and revisited, someone would have to let Holly in on this twisted tale. And that made Aiden bristle.

"Sahara will do as she pleases and our relationship allows for that. I mean, I'm not without ego. I was angry at the time, and another day, we'll hash this out." He shot the pirate a look of intent. "Just not today. We have much deeper mysteries to face."

"I'm at a loss as to where to start. I don't know what you know, and I'm assuming, vise versa. Neither of us are in love with a conventional woman, which is a colossal understatement. Hi, I'm Richard. My partner is a witch, and she's in love with you." Richard smiled at Aiden sardonically. "So what's new since I saw you last, six hundred years ago?"

Aiden, despite himself, burst into laughter. Richard laughed along, noticing every detail of Aiden's charm; the way his hands raked his hair, the width of his shoulders, the light in his blue eyes. His thoughts returned to Iona, and the struggle she admitted to. Just as he desired Sahara, and had had many fantasies of revisiting their connection both past and present, he was sure that Iona wanted those same things with Aiden. But could he be so generous as to share Iona with such an exquisite threat? In the end, he knew that he couldn't control her whims.

"Have you met Iona?" The question further opened Richard's vulnerability. "I never did get that far with her, and anyway she can be quite evasive."

"Not yet," Aiden replied. "But my Holly is planning to have her over for dinner, to thank her for a certain time travel incident we were part of. That should be interesting."

Richard's brow furrowed. "Do you...remember her? I mean...do you...?"

Aiden interrupted. "Do I think that I love Iona the way she thinks she still loves me?"

Richard looked up from his plate, his darkness making its way back from wherever it had shrunk to.

"No, Richard. I don't. I have two women whom I'm totally committed to. I have no intention of falling in love with a third...one that's yours, especially."

Richard was quick to understand Aiden's meaning. But neither of them ate with any confidence that things would be that simple.

CHAPTER 23

Conversation waxed and waned, sometimes they talked of work - what their lives revolved around, sometimes they talked of their shared past and what discoveries had been made. Aiden, never having craved the friendship of men, found Richard to be intelligent and engaging.

Richard also enjoyed Aiden's forthrightness.

"I'd kill for a good strong coffee," Richard said. "Is it any good here?"

"No," Aiden replied. "It's not what I'm used to."

Richard scowled. "That's too bad. I won't bother then."

"I can get you a good cup, if you're ready to leave? I am."

"Sure, why not? I'll get the check. Hang on." Richard moved to get the attention of the waitress.

"It's taken care of. Relax." Aiden shifted his large frame and the waitress was at his side with the bill.

"Where are we going? Is it far? Because I can call for my car."

Aiden laughed. "Your car? Still the Earl, Richard?"

Richard shrugged his shoulders. "Well, where is it that we're going?"

"My suite." Aiden got up and retrieved his credit card. "I've got some of Holly's coffee there from the Patisserie. You'll recognize it, I think. She caters to your gallery."

Richard groaned under his breath. "You're a master of calculated play, Aiden. You're not planning on having me drugged and killed in your suite are you?" Richard attempted a joke, out of his own need to release the sudden tension.

"I'm capable of anything where Holly's concerned, but the last time I poisoned a man the laws were a bit different," Aiden shot back, lips curled into a pleasant smile and eyes as cold as ice.

"Make yourself comfortable. I'll get the coffee. Don't worry, I know what I'm doing...you're looking skeptical." Aiden filled the bodum, watching Richard remove his jacket and roll up his shirt sleeves. *A man of style, is what could be said about Richard,* he thought to himself. *Stealthy, and too fucking attractive to let anywhere near any women one treasured.* Even through his shirt, Aiden could see the definition of Richard's arms.

"I drink from a bodum at home," Richard said absent mindedly as he looked out the French doors to the balcony. "This is an incredible view. Now I know that you're a good builder, otherwise you wouldn't be able to afford this," he quipped.

"We don't have to side step around that, Richard. I don't expect to build your home. I won't lie, I'm disappointed. It's rare to find a project that truly inspires me...but that's water under the bridge now."

Richard turned and walked over to the fire, warming himself against the chill in his heart. "I was hoping to revisit that, Aiden. In no way am I making light of the situation we're in, but I'm willing to separate business from personal issues, and still talk about hiring you on."

Aiden sighed. "Do you see the irony of all this? I used to be for hire by you, as your knight. My life depended on your whims. I'm not interested in that again. Perhaps we should just let it go."

"You're probably right, but my house needs someone who understands the design and you already said that you would have loved the opportunity."

"You're used to getting what you want."

Richard smiled. "I am. But I'm also trying to be practical."

"Let's give it a few weeks and see how things unfold. Here's your coffee. Sit down."

Richard sat by the fire and took his coffee from Aiden, who removed his suit vest and tie. That odd ache returned. A quick flash of Dagr in battle garb shadowed his mind's eye. He watched silently as Aiden opened a small box and took out rolling papers and herb. He rolled two joints and laid them on the lid. Finding a seat across from Richard, he offered one to him and picked up his lighter.

"How do you know I smoke?" Richard picked it up and leaned in to take the lighter from Aiden.

"Sahara."

"Sahara..." Richard mused, forgetting himself.

"Careful," Aiden growled.

"This is the oddest night of my life, and I've had some," Richard rasped out, savoring the quality of the herb.

"It's about to get more odd," Aiden replied as Pan appeared out of nowhere in the middle of the room, a looming figure festooned in ivy and moss upon his horns.

132

"Jesus Fucking Christ!" Richard stood abruptly. "I forgot about your sorcery."

And in that instant, they found themselves in a dim, stone chamber, the scent of a woman perfuming the air.

CHAPTER 24

Maybe it was the way she lay between them - soft breath on her pillow, one leg curled over Dagr's body - that made her seem so fragile.

They were hesitant to touch her, for fear of waking her out of her hard won slumber.

Dawn streamed through the castle windows, throwing tendrils of sunlight against the smoke of the room and catching the dust in the air. A great log burned on the hearth. The candles in their sconces sputtered as they came to the end of their life.

Richard reached carefully to smooth a wisp of hair from the girl's face. She moaned in her sleep, her small fingers gripping Dagr's great hand. A tumbling riot of golden hair dressed her breasts.

She was neither of theirs, but that hardly mattered because they had shared her many a time - young men with lust in their veins - a maiden from the village with the heart of an angel and the courage of a wolverine.

Dagr frowned. "Leave her be, Richard." But his eyes lingered over the curve of her hips where it dipped to softer flesh.

Richard stared hungrily at the way the pink tips of their lover's breasts peaked through her hair. He licked his lips.

"I am not yet satisfied."

"You are never satisfied. I pity the girl you marry."

"I do not care to marry. Marriage is for men with a desire for monotony."

"You pretend, but with the wrong man," Dagr said. "I know you."

"If you knew me you would get dressed," Richard scanned Dagr's naked body, strength and purpose etched into the many scars he had gathered in battle.

Dagr smiled, and moving the girl, lay on his stomach, exquisite ass and powerful back on display. Richard was so easy to tease. "Forget it. You would not find pleasure in me," he said.

Richard returned Dagr's smile, accentuating his dark nature to perfection with a flash of straight, white teeth...a rarity, even among the wealthy.

"You are so much more pleasant when you smile," Dagr continued, peering at Richard through half closed eyes. "You would not frighten so many girls if you did. You are getting a reputation as the devil incarnate."

"I am not enjoying this game that you are playing Dagr, and you are testing my patience." Richard could look darker than night when provoked.

Dagr thought better of taunting Richard any further.

"Have it your way. I will get dressed."

Although Dagr enjoyed teasing his brother at arms, he had no intention of hurting his feelings. Richard was one of the fiercest men he knew, but had little tolerance for having his soft side exposed.

Dagr got up and searched for his scattered garments.

"Stay for a smoke, a drink?" Richard finally asked, voice gruff.

"I do not drink in the mornings. You really should give up that habit, Richard. But I will smoke with you if you wish." Dagr poured fresh water into the washing bowl, and splashed his face. "I will not see you for a while. I have business with the King."

"You will be safe? Promise me that." Richard said, a chill rising on his heart.

Dagr turned to him and shook his head at the ridiculous request. Any battle he attended held the promise of death. How he loved this rough, stunning, irrational man. "Promise me that you will send her home with provisions and will tend to her needs."

"I will...but you are too generous with her. She does not expect it. You are forever the knight."

"Not as a knight. I ask you as a man. Look at her. She served us obediently all night, gave everything you asked and never flinched once. She risks everything, and you nothing."

"She does serve eloquently, does she not? She is the bravest of them all."

"The bravest," Dagr agreed. "But you must be more careful. There has to be a limit to what you unleash on her. She is yet so young..." He brought the bowl of herb over to Richard who was now sitting in a chair by the fire, legs crossed and exuding his most privileged self. "She reminds me of someone."

"Who?" Richard was instantly curious. "Are you hiding a lover from me? What is she like?"

"Not a lover," Dagr said, smoke curling from his mouth. "Just a maiden."

Richard waved his hand in the direction of the bed. "Would she serve like her?"

Dagr stared out the window at the pretty, frost covered garden below. "She is not for you, Richard. She is too fragile for the kind of games you like to play. I have no chance with her. She is already betrothed..."

Richard guffawed. "What does that matter? We have not worried ourselves with such details before!"

"I love her," Dagr confessed. And because he had his back to Richard, he did not see the flash of pain that crossed the devil's eyes.

"Well that is news," Richard choked out in not so well-disguised surprise. "But what would you want with a girl that could not possibly give you what you need? Surely, there are others more suitable."

Dagr turned around and glowered at Richard. "I like you better when you are not jealous." He picked up his cloak and sword. "And do not sit there looking so demonic. If the King did not expect me this afternoon, I would enjoy sparring with you. Somehow, you have managed to raise my ire."

Richard inhaled some herb, staring menacingly in Dagr's direction. "I have always thought that you were a slave to your emotions. It does not become a man of your reputation."

Dagr opened the chamber door. "Farewell, Richard." He turned his back to leave. "I sail for France tomorrow." The door shut quietly.

Richard stared at the massive slab of wood studded with iron, suddenly sorry to have been such an ass. He had forgotten that when Dagr loved, he loved with the force of a hurricane. France. That meant a year or more...if Dagr came back at all. He looked out the window to where Dagr was sitting on his tall black stallion. What a frightful figure he was on his mount! Even Richard, a skilled warrior, would not want to face such vehemence on the battle field.

"My lord," a soft voice rose from the bed and interrupted his thoughts.

Richard turned and faced the girl, sitting up on her knees, breasts jutting out in perfect, round mounds of tender succulence.

"Will Lord Bretel be coming back?"

Richard stripped his shirt and approached with the stealth of a lion. "No, my sweet, it will be just you and I."

"How would you like me, my lord?" She slipped into a submissive pose on the bed with the grace of a gazelle.

Richard pulled her to the edge of the bed, and, falling to his knees on the rush mat that covered the stone floor, splayed her open.

"I will serve you, maiden." Richard bowed his head to her tender, pink sex.

"My lord?" Her hand slid down protectively, covering the wet-

136

ness that now flowed freely. She was frightened. Richard on his knees could not bode well, but fear was an aphrodisiac. She gripped the linens with determined fists. Richard's breath on her inner thigh was the very beginning of well-calculated torture.

CHAPTER 25

They were now part of the Awoken.

Inasmuch as Richard and Aiden had been born to a task given only to certain incarnates, they had taken a long time to arrive at their awareness. But that was not to be blamed on them, as time is of no concern to those who are as old as the hills. Everything was unfolding as it should.

Pan waited patiently for the men to recalibrate their senses. Of course, they would remember everything, each nuance of every second spent back in time. It had been easier to just have them relive their experiences than for them to spend the whole night discussing their memories. And surprising them with the time travel was, in Pan's estimation, better than having to argue with Aiden about Richard's readiness. Because Aiden would have argued, out of his age old protectiveness of Richard, as his friend and his knight, even though consciously he would not have understood why.

Richard was the first to open his eyes and sit up. Pan faded into the shadows.

Aiden came-to after. He opened his eyes to see Richard contemplating him quietly, a grim look on his face. Pan was nowhere that Aiden could determine. He nodded, acknowledging Richard's discomfort.

"I had no idea. I certainly did not plan it," Aiden rose and added to the fire. He looked at the clock. An hour had passed. He poured them both some water.

Richard scowled. "Did I imagine that cloven hoofed creature before everything shifted? Pan, if I remember my mythology correctly?"

Pan reappeared, the scent of pine strong and musky.

Aiden smiled as Richard stood suddenly and stared at the large apparition before him, his emotions displayed clearly on his face.

"What?" Pan asked as Aiden gestured at him.

"How about a smaller version of you?" Aiden said. "Just until Richard gets used to your energy."

"Of course." Pan scaled down to the size of an average sized man. "I don't even look like this...I could appear as my normal self. Would a pillar of energy work better?"

"This is what we understand you to look like, Pan. It's fine. Sit down. I know...you don't need to sit." Aiden found his chair and let out a sigh. "What's going on? I didn't expect you, and you might have given Richard some time to get used to me before you sent us back."

"This was easier," Pan said.

They all sat in silence for a while. Richard thought about Iona, and how she had used the same trick as Pan, allowing him to experience the past when she'd connected him to Dagr. It was clever. No words could convey feelings like this, and now there was no question of his connection to Aiden or Brigida. Apparently, he had sought the company of men in that lifetime. It was all very bizarre. Finally, Richard spoke.

"This might be normal for you," he said to Aiden, "but in my world, even with Iona as a partner, I am not privy to experiences like this. I've been on the periphery of magic."

"It's true, this will be your first lifetime to join the Work," Pan said, ignoring Aiden's stare.

"The Work? What the hell might that be?" Richard barked.

"To bring humans in harmony with the natural world. Iona and Sahara have been doing it for centuries, Aiden too...you're new, but have contracted to join them."

"I don't remember anything of the sort," Richard began pacing the floor.

"There are some things you don't remember yet from the end of your lifetime with Dagr. But soon, things will become clear," Pan replied.

"Couldn't you just enlighten me now? I'm getting tired of being rationed information. I'll ask Iona if you won't."

"Humans are impatient creatures. I've never understood the hurry. Iona won't tell you, in any case."

"I have ways of making her talk. I'm sure she will," Richard growled, increasingly annoyed.

"I'm sure she won't, Richard," Pan answered evenly. "She answers to someone more influential than you, my friend. There is a code of conduct and even she, a sorceress invited to places others are not allowed, is bound to it. Well, I have done my work here. You have been introduced sufficiently, I believe. The rest is up to you. Try not to worry...another useless human endeavor. But there is no mistake here, you were chosen along with the others for your courage."

"Courage? What will I need courage for? To work with nature? Seems pretty benign work to me," Richard said angrily.

"Not all energies are in favor of nature returning to her throne...don't underestimate the darkness. This planet hosts all manner of forces."

And with that, Pan disappeared.

"More coffee?" Aiden asked, watching Richard as he stood staring by the window.

"All I fucking wanted was to hire a builder," Richard muttered. "Sure, why not? It's not like I'll be getting any sleep tonight."

And with a new awareness, a heightened intuition, Aiden once more saw the dark force of the Earl Richard Dumont.

CHAPTER 26

My path is not born of destiny, but my own making.
I follow no man but walk to the beat of the music I make when my
feet touch the earth.
The Goddess feeds my heart and the moon illuminates my soul.
My shadow side is where my dreams are born.
I am Stardust Woman. Walk with me.

Aiden waited his turn at the counter while Holly served her customers. She was beaming, unable to contain her excitement at seeing him. Her face was flushed, eyes cast down. Aiden smiled at the shyness she still felt in his presence. Dressed in jeans and a merino wool sweater, Aiden was the picture of delicious manliness, eyes fastened firmly on the girl who now rushed to his side.

"Aiden!"

They leaned in for a kiss that although modest in expression, promised much more.

"You've been well?" Aiden asked as he held her hands, ignoring the stares of curiosity.

"Yes, but I'm even better now. Coffee? You must have left very early this morning to get here by breakfast time."

"I couldn't wait to see you. And yes, I'm hungry and dying for a coffee." He felt the rush of energy that came with knowing that she would be his later.

"I'll be right back. I have something new on the menu for breakfast. Do you want me to let Sahara know you're here? I've got her slaving in the back," Holly smiled, her love for Sahara openly evident.

Aiden winked. "She knows."

"Right. Forgot how you two do that. Ok, wait here, I'll get your breakfast."

"I wouldn't dream of leaving."

Holly leaned in once more. She whispered in his ear. "Vous êtes un rêve dans un rêve, mon amour."

Aiden's sudden grip on Holly's wrist left her weak and wet. Her heart got lost in the depths of his love. Then, leaving his overwhelming presence, she hurried to the kitchen and hid in Sahara's arms.

"Alright?" Sahara held Holly tight, their bodies pressed together.

"He's larger than life. He's...I don't know...incomparable."

"I know. I know. Too big for the room he's in. He's always been this way." Sahara kissed Holly's forehead. "Love you. Want a break from people? I can go serve for a while."

"No. I'm ok. Just needed your grounding." Holly felt her cheeks. "Am I still blushing?"

"I'm afraid so," Sahara laughed.

"You two are killing me."

Sahara returned to her work, suddenly pensive. Holly slid her arms around her.

"I love you."

Sahara nodded. She waited until Holly left the kitchen and then allowed herself the tears that had gathered with Holly's words. Aiden. She ached to run out and hold him, but also wanted to afford Holly these precious moments alone. If she was honest with herself she would admit to needing him more than she thought wise. His was a love that could not be circumvented. Was it a mistake, allowing him to consume her so completely? Oh, whom was she kidding? Being in love with Aiden was something that even centuries couldn't erase.

Sahara's tears, so seldom overwhelming, threatened to drown her in the fullness of her emotions. But she should have known that Aiden would have felt her angst. He stood behind her, a large enveloping warmth.

"Sahara? What is it?" He turned her around and brought her chin up to look her in the eye. "Is something wrong? Can I make it better?" His mouth closed on hers and she melted into his embrace.

"There's nothing you can do, save leave me. I'm afraid of my love for you. I'm stronger when I'm alone." Sahara winced at the pain in Aiden's eyes. She lowered hers.

"Leave you? That's madness, Sahara. I've just found you." He kissed her deeply. "You're wrong," he said as she rubbed herself against him, trying to disappear beneath his skin. "My love can't make you weak. I don't ask anything of you. I'm drunk on you too...I feel lost to our connection. But I promise not to take anything that you can't give me."

"You've met Richard?" Sahara's words were muffled against his chest.

"I have."

Aiden moved Sahara out of the kitchen to the back hall and pinned her against the wall, his energy rising, her wrists in a tight grip over her head. She pushed back with her hips.

"Stop fighting me Sahara."

"You're angry."

"I'm not."

"I feel it."

"That's not anger."

"Please, Aiden, I don't know any other way."

He understood. She couldn't talk her feelings through until she'd been masterfully taken. She needed to expend that energy to be able to discuss a difficult subject. And he would give her anything she asked.

"If you want to be owned, I can give you that, my love."

"Yes!" Sahara closed her eyes and imagined the dominance Aiden was so good at.

"I have meetings until two. Shall I come fetch you after that? Will you be done here?"

"Yes."

"Do you want the terms now?"

Sahara, trembling, held onto the hardness of Aiden's arms. "Yes please."

His hand tightened around her neck just enough to send a rush of erotic pleasure through to her sex. He whispered in her ear. "Your house. No alcohol, no herb. I want you in that short black chemise you have, stockings, lay out the cuffs, crop, tickler, and wand. When I come upstairs, I want you on your belly, knees splayed open."

Sahara groaned. "Not one bit of wine?"

"No. I want you raw, with nothing to alter your senses." He let her go, watched her gather herself, and tidy her clothes. How he loved her petite frame, the way she moved in that cat-like manner. He turned to walk away.

"Sahara," he said over his shoulder.

"Yes?"

"I want the witch tonight. All the darkness."

"As you please, my lord." It was all Sahara could do to not fall at his feet in humble pose. In his hands, she knew that she was safe. There she found the freedom to be completely at ease with her kinks. In his hands, there was solace and abandon. She watched his back as he returned to Holly, and once again marvelled at his indisputably powerful walk, and the confidence that he wore like armor.

Holly set a plate before Aiden and smiled.

"This looks delicious!" Aiden's hunger had transcended the ridiculous.

"It's nothing fancy. Just some thinly sliced baguette, crisped with an herbed olive oil, pancetta, a bit of roasted tomato and slices of unripened buffalo mozzarella. Here I'll pour you some fresh coffee. The other got cold."

He took a bite. "Mmm. The basil makes this...and these olives! You've outdone yourself as usual."

Holly beamed. "I've got lots of new ideas for the menu. I was hoping you'd love this."

"I'm sure you do, and I'm going to try them all!" Aiden flashed a devastating smile. She stood rooted to the ground, staring at him.

"What?"

"I love that smile. I have a surprise for you...later. It's not what you think."

"You have no idea what I'm thinking right now."

"I do. And it's not that." She laughed heartily, as did Aiden, completely forgetting that the whole place could hear them and was listening very intently.

CHAPTER 27

*I seem to have loved you in numberless forms, numberless times, in
life after life, in age after age forever. ~ Rabindranath Tagore*

The cabin smelled as it always did - the smoky scent of the wood fire,
the headiness of incense and the comfort of beeswax candles. Here
lived a woman whose destiny was firmly in her hands.

A storm gathered outside. Winter wind howled around the sturdy
little cabin. The sky was dark with the coming snow, and even though
it was only three in the afternoon, the day seemed old.

Aiden greeted Ulfred. The pup was growing fast and already had
a sense of his position in Sahara's life. He was to protect and carry the
energy of the Wolf in her magic. There were more powerful totems
but the Wolf was exactly what Sahara needed. The solemn guidance of
his charge was imprinted upon Ulfred's loyal heart. He lay back down
by the door, where the scent of every entering spirit, physical or ethereal, was examined. Aiden he already understood as an integral part
of Sahara's pack and would listen to his commands, even though they
were equals on the astral plane. Ulfred was an old spirit.

Aiden took some time to prepare himself. He added to the fire,
listening to the sounds of nature outside and the crackling of the aspen wood as it burned. He'd made sure that Sahara had a more than
adequate supply of firewood. She wouldn't be cold this winter or any
winter if he had anything to do with it. He thought back to his time
travel. That hut that he'd been in, Arinn's and Dagr's dwelling...it had
the same energy as this place - lonesome, powerfully intimate and
seeped with magic.

He could feel her - waiting. Sahara. By any other name she would
still be the ancient being who tripped over centuries to make her mark
on the consciousness. She was up there, ready for whatever he wished
to exact upon her.

Aiden took it seriously, this work. He knew that what they did
was much beyond the erotic expression of their love. It was how Sahara maintained equilibrium, and how she processed the immensity of
her emotional being. He was honored to be the man whom she trusted
to master her in bed. And so he let her anticipate the sound of his
steps on the stairs. He let her gather her courage and her lust.

When the clock struck four, he made his way to the loft. His body hummed with desire and the anticipated sight of his lover in a compromising pose on the bed.

Just like every time he saw her beauty exposed, Aiden was almost felled to his knees with a desire for worship. How stunning she was, all in black except the lusciousness of her naked sex. Sahara lay trembling.

Aiden removed his shirt, and his belt. He laid them down silently by her side so she could adjust to his scent and presence. She was so beautiful, her breath heavy now, the smoothness of her tight little ass a tantalizing tease.

"Keep looking straight ahead. Take your ankles in your hands."

She reached back and lifting her feet brought her legs into the desired position. It opened her up a little more.

Aiden grasped her by the crook of her knees and pulled her roughly to the edge of the bed.

Ah, the scent of an aroused woman. Aiden willed himself to stay the course of his plan. How he wanted to lay down beside her and hold her close, leave a trail of kisses on her back, take her mouth with his.

Picking up the tickler, Aiden gently ran the feather over Sahara's back and along the soft flesh of her inner thighs. She sighed with contentment, lifting up a bit to entice him towards her bottom.

"Stay still," he warned. The soft touching continued until he found her suitably relaxed. Turning her over, he ignored her silent pleas for kisses and put cuffs on her wrists and ankles. Sahara's nipples pressed against the chemise, making a pointy statement about her excitement. Aiden imagined them on his tongue.

Sahara watched him pull the leather ties through the cuffs, muscles bristling, intense; his eyes so full of love that she had to breathe through the gathering tears.

He tied her legs so that her knees were drawn up, leaving her viscerally exposed. The ties continued to her wrist cuffs. Aiden tied these above her head to the headboard. Sahara let out a breath of deep satisfaction. She loved being this open with him and so utterly at his mercy. Whatever he would do, she would accept as his wise interpretation of her needs.

Bound to his satisfaction, Aiden feasted on the delicacy before him. His mouth ached to taste it. To the sound of plaintive, medieval music drifting through the cabin, Aiden proceeded to torture Sahara's pussy with the feather she had left out for him. Gently, with deliberate strokes, he teased her lips and clit to a throbbing fullness. Sahara

146

begged for release, but he only told her to mind her mouth.

When he knew that any more would break her, he slid his hands under her ass and licked her with that sinful tongue but stayed short of her clit, which she begged to have inside his mouth. Instead he picked up the crop and laid out a pattern of painful marks on her spread legs.

"Safe word? Anytime you're ready, Sahara," he teased, knowing full well that she was not going to admit defeat this early on in the game.

"Fuck you!" she said, her clit aching to be touched.

"Fuck me? No, my lady, it is you who is going to be fucked, and fucked well when I see fit."

Sahara growled at him and thrashed around on the bed. The wind picked up outside and set the shutters to banging.

"Storm's raging out there, Sahara. Is that you? How you feel inside? Do you want to show me your rage? You're afraid of loving me, you said. Want to stop this train we're on?"

"I want you to fuck me! Untie me."

"That's not what I want. I want you to tell me what's making you hurt."

Aiden picked up the wand and applied it almost imperceptibly to Sahara's swollen clit.

"Harder Goddammit! I want to come!"

Aiden's exquisite body hovered over Sahara as he leaned in to kiss her, his tongue a deep tease. "I want to lick your cunt, suck your clit; fuck you hard until you come on my cock. That's what *I* want. But first, I want to know what's making you talk about leaving...I'm never going to leave you. Never."

"I'm the worst thing that could have come between you and Holly," Sahara confessed. "I want out. I want to just live my life out in peace and not be part of anyone's pain."

"It's a little late for that, isn't it, Sahara? What do you think is going to happen to Holly if you suddenly tell her that it's over? Are you mad? It would kill her." The crop cut painfully into Sahara's skin.

"Aiden, please..."

"That's not your safe word." He sat down with the feather again. "Your pussy's so swollen, it's so pretty, your clit is throbbing. By the way, you're right, Richard *is* spectacular. If I were a jealous man, I would wring your neck for fucking him...sucking his cock. But I can't really blame you. He's elegant and dangerous." He picked up the wand again. Sahara groaned.

"Even I can see how a man that dark and savage looking could appeal to a whore like you. And I asked you to bring the witch to me today, not the woman who's afraid of my love. I know you have strength far beyond anything you've shown me. The witch, Sahara. That's who I want."

The wand made contact. Hard. Sahara screamed, reeling between memories of Richard inside her, a delicious pirate of a man, and Aiden's more refined beauty by her side.

"Come, my love. Come," Aiden whispered, as Sahara released and squirted with abandon. The energy rose between them. Aiden felt a surge of air like a tornado whip through. The shrill cry of a sorceress awoken filled the room, and Sahara broke the bonds of the cuffs. Free, Sahara's eyes shone triumphant.

She touched her soaking wet pussy. "Here. Spank here. Please Aiden."

"Tell me you're strong enough. Tell me you'll love Holly until she doesn't need you anymore." Aiden's eyes pierced Sahara's heart. She'd never seen him so passionately intent. He was the very image of Dagr on the battlefield...the ancient sorcerer was resurrected.

"Please...here, Aiden. Hurt me here."

"Promise, about Holly, I need your word. I know what your word means, Pan told me. You belong to an order whose word has been kept by blood spilled into a common bowl. There's an unbreakable bond between us. Promise!"

Sahara fumed that Pan had told her secret. Why would he have told?

"Because I am now part of the fold. I have added my blood to the bowl. Richard has too. He's been initiated. Yes, don't look so surprised. You made a contract, remember," Aiden read her frantic thoughts.

"...Our contract. But this only makes things more complicated!"

"Want me to spank that pretty cunt of yours still?" Aiden stripped his jeans and stood, magnificent, before her. "Promise."

Sahara splayed herself open further. She spoke the words.

"I promise." The candles hissed and sputtered and they were left in the dark except for the shadows from the downstairs fire.

Aiden positioned himself above her and spanked Sahara's wet pussy pink.

She offered her mouth, and he obliged, groaning as Sahara took him balls deep.

"How you do that...Oh, God Sahara..."

She sucked and licked and teased until Aiden, low on restraint, forced her onto her hands and knees.

"Hard. I need it hard."

"You're so fucking wet," Aiden said, his muscular belly soaked with Sahara's cum.

"I love you Aiden!" Sahara breathed as she came.

Aiden roared and came deep inside her, a satisfying orgasm washing over him in waves.

They collapsed onto the bed. Aiden pulled Sahara on top of him and hugged her tight.

"Mine," he whispered.

CHAPTER 28

Hey. Have you heard from Holly? Aiden sent a hurried text to Sahara. It was seven forty five and Holly was late. She was never late. She was punctual to a fault.

No.

Sahara's text only worried him more. *I thought you said she'd be there by seven.*

I know. I'm beginning to worry.

She may have gotten held up at the café.

She would have called. You know her. Aiden began pacing the living room floor. *She's not answering her phone.*

Sahara's silence was too long for comfort. *Are you picking anything up?*

I think we'd better go look.

Aiden's heart lurched as he read Sahara's words.

I'll go. I'll keep in touch.

He drove out into the night. The roads were slick, and visibility was poor. Christ! He should have picked her up. Anger felt better than fear, he decided.

Sahara's call came through on his Bluetooth.

"Aiden! Can you project to me where you are...let me feel your energy, I'll follow along."

"OK. I'll do my best."

"If I can feel you, I'll be able to pick up on the energy of your surroundings. Anything distressing will come up. Can you see much?"

"Not really. It's bad."

"I should have come with you." But Sahara knew why he had asked her to stay home. He wanted her where he knew she was safe. It was easier for him this way.

They drove in silence for a while.

It happened simultaneously - Aiden's startled voice rang out just as Sahara commanded him to stop. A large buck with a full rack stood in the middle of the road. Aiden thought he had hit him, the truck had absorbed the impact, but the buck stood firm and was seemingly unharmed.

"What was that noise?" Sahara asked, alarmed.

"A buck, I hit him. But he's just standing there...he's not leaving." Sahara recognized the resonance of shock in Aiden's voice.

150

"Aiden, get out of the truck! Do you have a flashlight?"

"Yes. I'm going to pull the truck off the road."

"Holly is somewhere to the right. Don't panic! I'm calling emergency services right now."

Aiden veered his truck around the curious creature in front of him. He turned on his hazards but doubted anyone would see him until they were much too close anyway. Scrambling down the bank beside the road, Aiden cursed the weather and all the reasons why he had wanted Holly to come to his house for the night.

His foot caught on something as he slid down, not knowing where he was headed, just that he desperately wanted to feel Holly safe in his arms. He soon came to the realization that he was standing over Holly's overturned car. With a sinking feeling, Aiden shone his light into the cabin of the Bug. Holly's tear stained face turned towards him. She let out a grateful cry.

Scrambling to the other side of the car, Aiden tried the door. Mercifully, it opened with some force applied. He pushed himself inside, scanning Holly's suspended body for signs of blood.

"I'm here, darling. It's ok now." He touched her face gently with his hand. She began to sob. Aiden thought he would die from the sound.

"I'm going to try the seat belt...do you hurt anywhere?" Why hadn't the airbags deployed? The seat belt wouldn't budge.

"No. I don't hurt. Aiden...I was so scared no one would find me."

"I know, babe, I know. I love you...here, put your arms around my neck, when I cut through the belt, just lean into me." Aiden prayed that he wasn't making a mistake. What if he hurt her! But no, he just had to get her out of here, she was shaking with cold. He took a large knife out of its sheath. Holly groaned as he pushed up against her body to cushion her from the release of the belt.

Grateful that he kept his knife razor sharp, Aiden made a quick, decisive slice and Holly's weight shifted onto him. "Alright? I've got you."

Slowly, he angled her out of the car until they were lying against the snowy bank.

Holly trembled in his arms. Aiden kissed her face a thousand times. His mind raced as he thought up possible ways to carry her up the deep ditch. He was strong enough to carry her but the bank was slippery and too steep to get a proper foothold. The last thing he wanted was to drop her. If only it wasn't so fucking dark!

"Do you think you can stand up, sweetie?" Holly's face nuzzled into his neck brought a deep sense of comfort to the man who could face any kind of his own pain, but was intolerant of anything that hurt Holly.

"Yes."

They scrambled up the bank, three steps up then sliding back down, then tried again, and again. The bank was simply too steep and icy to navigate.

"Look!" Holly pointed. A flash of lights lit up the road. Help had arrived, to their silent relief.

Holly held Aiden's hand. He sat beside her in the ambulance, his face a lie of peaceful composure. She knew that on the inside, he was torn by thoughts of what could have been.

"Aiden, I'm ok now."

He smiled in that way that she loved. "I know. I should have come to get you...I didn't realize how bad the roads were. I'm sorry," he kissed her hand.

"It's not your fault. And you can't keep me safe all the time." She was sorry she'd said it as the words left her mouth. In Aiden's mind, it was his honor to protect her.

"You know what?" she said, anxious to change the subject.

He shook his head, but gave her hand a squeeze.

"I must have gone unconscious for a bit, or fallen asleep. I dreamt that I saw a massive buck, with the most stunning rack I've ever seen! He stayed a while, he even talked to me... in my dream I mean. He told me about a raven. Like the one we sometimes see when we go for a walk in your woods? He said the raven would send a message to Sahara...to tell her where I was. Isn't that funny? Aiden? You look like you've seen a ghost."

Aiden's eyes filled with tears. He leaned over and kissed her sweetly, his mouth a tender, soothing balm.

"I saw him too, babe. He was standing in the middle of the road where you had your accident, waiting for me."

"Oh?" Holly's eyes rounded into surprise. "I guess he was real, then. I thought I'd imagined him. But..."

The paramedic motioned to Aiden. "We're here. The doctor will run a few tests and hopefully you'll be able to take your wife home tonight."

Holly smiled. Aiden did too. Neither of them bothered to correct the man.

CHAPTER 29

They fussed over her, laying by the fire at Aiden's. Sahara's herbals, arnica and rescue remedy had been employed as soon as Aiden had brought her home. Nothing broken, just bruised. Later, Holly languished in Aiden's large tub while he read her Whitman and washed her hair.

"I'm going to give you a warm oil massage," Sahara said.

"Oooh. But first, I have to eat something. What can I eat?"

"Aiden's making you something, right, Aiden?" Sahara looked over to the kitchen where he was preparing a tray. But Aiden was too lost in thought to hear.

"I think I scared him badly," Holly whispered. "You should have seen his face when he found me. And I don't think he scares that easily."

"No he doesn't," Sahara agreed. "Have you told him that you moved your things here; I don't think he's had a chance to go into that room yet. That'll cheer him up!"

"No. There's been no time. Has he told you about the deer and the raven?"

Sahara hoped that her face didn't give her away. "Yes. He did. What do you make of it?"

Holly smiled wisely. "I think it was your friend, Iona. She protected me. She sent the buck. You don't have to pretend, Sahara. I'm getting better at not feeling jealous about her. And she's helped me twice now. I know that she did it for you, and that's ok."

"Forgive me sweetie. I don't mean to hide things from you. I just don't want you to doubt my love. Iona's love for me should not be a worry to you. When you feel better, we can have a long talk and you can ask me anything you like." She meant it, she really did, but somewhere deep down Sahara hoped that Holly wouldn't ask too much.

"I'd like that," Holly smiled. "Sometimes I feel like a child that's being kept in the dark for her own good."

And once more Sahara marvelled at the strength and wisdom of one so newly incarnated.

Holly loved how the early morning light slowly revealed Aiden. He was lying on his stomach, his face turned towards her, hair messily grazing his shoulders, a pillow bunched up under one arm. She felt so small beside him, especially looking at the expanse of his back and the knotted beauty of his shoulders and arms. Even though she had never imagined that she'd ever love a man, she was terribly in love with this one.

She reached over to run lazy fingers over his back, but before she even touched him, he opened his eyes and fixed her with a smoldering stare. Holly smiled, a wave of nervous excitement overtaking her.

"Don't look at me like that," she said as her hand caressed his face, pushing his hair aside.

"Like what?" he asked dreamily.

"Like you're going to eat me alive."

Aiden turned over and gathered her up, pulling her against his warm body, arm holding her prisoner.

"I'm not going to eat you alive...today. But when you're feeling better..." he whispered in her ear, through the tumble of her long blond hair. "We're going to spend the whole day together. No work for you."

"I know. I guess I'll let you tell me what to do this time. I actually don't feel bad, maybe I can go in later in the after..."

"Don't even think about it," Aiden growled. "There's no way you're going anywhere today. Sahara and Lilith have it covered. You have a hard time sitting still, don't you?"

"Said the kettle to the pot."

"That's pot to the kettle."

"Whatever. Hey, what about my car?"

Aiden kissed her neck. "After breakfast, we'll talk about details. Not now. Your car is being towed." *And then I'm going to buy you one with working air bags,* he thought, but didn't dare tell her. He ran his hands over her lithe, curvy body. She moaned and stretched out under his touch, moving against his erection.

"I don't think you're going to be able to behave," she teased.

"Watch me. I will. Ignore him, he has a mind of his own. Today, it's going to be all massage, playing with your hair, catering to your every whim and platonic kisses."

Holly burst out laughing. "Platonic kisses? You have no clue what one of those even is, never mind being able to execute one."

"Oh no? Here, turn around. I'll show you one."

Holly turned into his arms. He grinned at her playfully. "Ready?"

"Aha," but she looked doubtful.

154

He began with her ears, her neck and her hands. Then he took her mouth, dropping light kisses on her closed lips, warning her not to try anything sneaky like letting him in. They rolled around, laughing, Aiden taking care not to touch her anywhere that she was bruised.

"There. You feel nothing, right? I feel nothing. Platonic kisses."

"I feel nothing." She wanted to spread her legs and ask for his hand, but this was too delicious, having to wait for such a handsome man.

"What's my surprise by the way?" Aiden pulled her close again, fighting the urge to ravage her with his tongue.

"Oh, it's nothing, really," Holly giggled.

"Tell me, wench, or you'll have to suffer my being a gentleman for days."

"Have you been downstairs, to your spare room?" Holly's eyes sparkled.

Aiden broke into a broad grin. "You didn't! You moved in?"

She nodded, delighted with his joy. "I did. A room of my own."

"*Come're.*" He pulled her into a tight bear hug. "I love you. Bad. Of course, I'll never allow you to sleep in there…it was all a trick."

"I love you, Aiden. Kiss me. Please. For real."

CHAPTER 30

"My business is changing," Aiden said while grinding some beans and putting the coffee on.

Holly was sitting at the kitchen island, wrapped in a blanket and watching him gather breakfast. Dressed in low slung workout pants and a t-shirt, Aiden was a delicious host. He padded over in bare feet to stir the fire once the coffee was brewing and eggs were on the boil. The house was warm and cozy, the lights low. Aiden had a skill for setting the mood. Right now he was in the mood for revealing his mind.

"I have had to make a decision about whether to grow exponentially or to keep things at the same level they are now. But I have a big build coming up this spring, and it's pressing me into these changes."

"How's it going to change things? Does it mean hiring more project managers?"

"Yes. But there's more to it." He poured them a coffee and motioned towards the nook under the stairs. Sitting opposite each other, feet hooked on the edges of each other's chairs, they were pleased to enjoy the stillness of the morning hours together.

"Every house I build takes on its own energy," Aiden explained. "It requires an intuitive knowledge of it, and in a way, the building and I begin to 'speak' to each other as soon as I make the commitment to create it. Something from nothing. One day it is a pile of separate elements - lumber, concrete, nails, etc. - and then it takes on life. It's the same in your work, I'm sure. One minute it's a bin of flour, eggs, and yeast and the next it's a delicious loaf of bread. That's creation...and we infuse the creativity with our own essence."

"As Sahara would say, it's alchemy," Holly replied. "And I know exactly what you mean, even though our businesses are something entirely different. The ingredients I choose, of the highest available quality, added to my skill and maybe most importantly, the love I put into my work, adds up to a croissant that offers something intangible to my customers. That's what you're talking about?"

Aiden smiled. "You have no idea how badly I've wanted this...to love a woman whose mind I could share and who understood my ramblings."

"Your mind was one of the things I was initially attracted

to...before I knew that other parts of you were equally to my taste," Holly grinned. "But let's stay on topic. You're getting that look on your face. So tell me more about these changes."

"You're very distracting! As I was saying, the business is expanding rapidly, and as you already know, the renos on your building have begun so that I can establish an office. I need someone to field calls for me and take over the books. Someone who will put up with my control issues and respect my commitment to clients. But the most challenging part will be to find crew foremen who care about building in the way I do. I have Drew, whom you've met, and he is the template. He understands how I work and what I need and when we disagree, he can communicate what the problem is."

"But you're managing more than what the building needs. You're also managing men who each have their own work ethic. It can't be easy."

"No, but so far I've been very lucky. For the most part, give or take a few guys who were just unmanageable, I have very loyal crews."

"That's because of how you treat them as well. I hear a lot of talk at the patisserie, and you're well respected."

"Say 'patisserie' again."

"*Patisserie.*"

Aiden got up to get take the eggs off the boil. He came back to kneel beside Holly and shoving her hair aside, gave her a nibble on the ear. She shoved him away. "Focus, Aiden," she said but gave his arms a caress.

"By springtime, I need to have four crews in place, the office running smoothly and still keep what's most important to me," Aiden sat back down, dwarfing the chair.

"And what would that be?" Holly teased.

"Work can't be my whole life anymore. I can let this thing grow into a monster or keep it at a level I can manage holistically. There has to be balance and already I feel that we have very little time together. Plus, you'll be expanding your business at the same time. Time is what I need more of now, rather than money."

"The way I look at it, we have this intensive growth period ahead of us, like a pregnancy, and then at some point we'll birth our babies and things will level out if we hire the right people and keep our eye on what's most important to us."

Aiden sighed with relief. "I'm glad you see it that way, because that's exactly what's happening. But I'd like to talk to you about something else," he offered a smile, and Holly felt a knot gathering in her chest.

"What? Is it about the big build you keep hinting about? Will you be away for longer stretches?"

Aiden's eyes gave away nothing. Richards' build. Another hurdle to jump.

"No. It's about your car. I'd like you to allow me to buy you a new one." He waited, apprehensive of her reply. It would be so much easier if she could succumb to his need to provide for her. But he was learning to respect her boundaries.

"But insurance will cover most of that cost. I can manage on my own, I think. Thank you for offering, though." Holly tread lightly. She too was learning, about love and relationships.

"I know that if left to your own devices, you can manage very well. But it would please me greatly and give me some piece of mind if you had a vehicle that was a bit sturdier and didn't place any further financial burden on you."

Holly wanted to kiss his face...run into his arms, for his constant concern for her; but she stayed put, because it was important to her to maintain her autonomy.

"But I love my Bug!"

"I know," Aiden proceeded cautiously. "But with the amount of weather we get and the possibility of hitting a deer on the back roads, I feel that a bigger car would be better. Remember, you didn't travel these roads in winter before we got together. All I'm saying is, let me cover what extra costs there are over the insurance payout. Your airbags were defective, so you should get a decent amount anyway."

She gave in. It was more important for her to know that he wasn't worrying about her than anything, because that was torture for her as well.

"Ok."

"Ok, what?"

"Ok, you may help me."

"You're not going to negotiate?"

"Nope."

Aiden grinned. "May I buy you a Volvo?"

"No! I'm a simple girl, I don't want anything too flashy."

"But it's the safest thing going...or something else all-wheel drive...a Subaru?"

"Well, we can look together. Let's do a little road trip to Denver."

Aiden opened his arms and Holly slipped onto his lap, burying her face in his neck.

"You need to take care of me...I know that. I've decided that I'm not going to fight you. If we can promise to always talk things over, I think we can find a way."

Aiden tangled his hands in Holly's hair. "I do need to. Thank you for understanding. And don't think that you don't take care of me. What you give me...it's invaluable. I give what I have to give and you give what you have. It's still us contributing to the relationship in our own way. It's just resources. Money is no different than any other resource as far as I can see. I use it to make your life easier and you feed my life by being you...and all that incredible food you prepare." He pulled her face to his. "I still can't believe you're here...are you really here?"

"I'm here." Holly's heart ached in the most beautiful way. Aiden's smile broke her to a million pieces.

"I know exactly where I can take you for overnight in Denver," Aiden mused. "Our first hotel stay together. I'd like to make it special."

"You're not going to believe this...I've never stayed in a hotel in the U.S. Only in Europe. So this will be a first."

Aiden growled. "Prepare to be spoiled."

"You know what else I've never done?" Holly teased, dropping sweet kisses.

"Nope."

"I've never had hotel sex." Holly struggled to get away from Aiden as his eyes turned dark.

"Oh no. You don't get to say that and then run off."

Holly slipped the top of her nightie from her shoulders, exposing tightly pursed nipples.

"Hi, I'm Holly," she said, "and I'm a raving slut!"

Aiden laughed, a deep sensual sound that tugged at Holly's sex.

"Sinful," he muttered.

Shattered by her dreams, Iona awoke to find herself embraced by the dark comfort of her room. It was sanctuary, this space. Her eyes roamed her surroundings. Every piece of furniture in the room was something she had picked out with a sensitivity towards its energy.

She loved large furniture, and her apartment, with its twelve foot ceilings and generous proportions, allowed for some very old and imposing pieces.

Her heart was still pounding hard after the encounter in the astral plane but ensconced as she was in her lavish bed, she was able to slow down her breathing and her racing mind.

She wished that Richard was here. In his arms, she knew no fear. But Richard had requested a few days of silence, as he processed his meeting with Aiden. He had been angry, and justifiably so, as she had not warned him of Aiden's identity. Still, she had no remorse. A good witch knew when to interfere and when to leave things be.

Richard had not seen it in the same way. He had always said that he could deal with Iona's secretive ways, but this time, he felt that she had gone too far. Still, she would bring him around. Richard no longer lived in a world that allowed for leaving her side. So she felt fairly safe...he would forgive her.

If he had been here, he would have woken her from her distressed murmurings. He would have gathered her up in his arms and sheltered her from the storm. He would have pressed his hard and chiselled body against hers and demanded her attention. She knew that his hand on the small of her back meant ownership of her body and her desires. He understood that she was nobody's slave but that her tightly controlled life made more sense if she could bow down to a trusted Master now and then.

He never asked her where she went in her sleep though she was welcome to share. But sometimes he did fix her with a demonic stare if her dreams meant that she woke up in tears. Richard knew that Iona in tears meant Iona crossing boundaries that were best left undisturbed.

She reached for her phone and stared longingly at his number. If she wanted to, she could command him to call her...make her energy so strong that he would be compelled by an angry need to dial her. But something in his voice when they'd talked last now reminded her to respect his wishes. Still her dream haunted her. The Aspen King, in full royal regalia upon his throne, demanding her cooperation. But what he asked for, even Iona could not justify. She had made herself available to his whims once, and it had ended all that she held dear.

Not this lifetime, she vowed. She would find a way. She would break the spell that she was under. Oh, yes, it would be a delight to indulge in what the King proposed. There would be pleasure in making his wishes come true. But it would be short lived, she knew. And forever after, she would regret her choices.

He had helped her to find Holly. He had been gracious and even, dare she hope, altruistic in his motives. After all, the Aspen King was a part of all that was good and noble on this earth. But even he had a weakness. And that weakness was golden haired and the epitome of kindness.

CHAPTER 31

He felt a familiar nudge at heart center while sleeping contentedly with his body wrapped around Holly's warmth. A feeling of urgency welled up and Aiden opened his eyes to the dark of his bedroom. He didn't feel any sense of danger, just simply a command to respond to something ancient.

The scent of forest filtered in through an open window. An early morning snow had begun to fall and with it accentuated the wet aroma of nature returning to its winter slumber.

Aiden looked over his shoulder to where Pan stood in a corner of the room, waiting for Aiden to rise. Their communication, telepathic and instant, assured him that Holly would stay unaware of his departure. He tucked her in and dropped a kiss on her forehead. His heart twisted a little. Aiden had recently began to nurture a fear seeped in the frailty of life, and every departure from Holly's side brought out an insecurity that he would, at one time, have scoffed at.

He dressed quickly, then stepped out into the cold with Pan at his side.

"Where are we going?"

"To see the Aspen King."

They trudged through a familiar section of forest towards a grove where Aiden burned winter fires...a place of great solitude. It was always dark here. Always powerfully lonely. It was here that Aiden found the greatest infilling of silence.

Pan stopped and touching his third eye to Aiden's, blessed him for his journey in a language that Aiden failed to recognize.

"You're not coming with me? Which direction will I take?" Aiden looked around him as the familiar became strange and unrecognizable.

"The way will be made clear. Just follow your heart." And with that, Pan disappeared into the shadows.

Aiden gathered himself and stepped out onto a path to his left. The trees were alive, all curiously watching as he chose his steps carefully over rustling roots that sprang up this way and that, threatening to trip him, along with vines that grew with lightning speed before him.

The sound of laughter, soft and mischievous, filled the air.

I have a feeling that my life will never be the same again Aiden thought wryly, his body responding to the urgency of creation around him. All senses on alert, Aiden found himself in a great hall with four walls of stone but open to the sky, draped with luxurious ivy and fern, crystal chandelier sconces lighting a path towards a massive throne upon which sat the resplendent Aspen King.

Aiden, surprised to see his shoulders hung with a scarlet and gold cloak, knelt respectfully, clutching a sword that felt as if it had been molded to his hand. Surrounding him, sat all manner of Fey. Gnomes and dwarves with flowing beards, pockets overflowing with sparkling gems; fire and water sprites; delicate maidens in translucent gowns; mermaids bathing in sea foam pools, tree spirits and flower devas...all silently awaiting the words of their King.

"Welcome, Son of Middle Earth. We have waited a long time for your return." The Aspen King's voice left all in his company trembling and touching their third eye to the sacred ground beneath their feet.

Surrendering his will to the King of the Fey, Aiden kissed the ground on which he knelt and offered his servitude.

Shaking the great stag's rack crowning his head, The Aspen King stood and extended his hand to Aiden. He stood ten feet tall, a broad and powerful figure, handsome of face and bright of eye, an auburn mane of hair spilling down his back. His energy filled the hall with such intensity that Aiden understood why the place was open to the sky.

He stood and approached the throne, steady and strong, as one who knew his place in such surroundings. The sword at his side grew warm, the cloak on his shoulders billowing as he walked, cognisant of the awed murmur among the Fey. They rarely saw such beauty and grace in human form, or one who walked with such quiet confidence.

Dropping to his knees once more, Aiden bowed his head and waited for further instruction.

But the Aspen King only motioned with his hand to his right, from where a pillar of light materialized into the form of a woman. Glowing with an ethereal light, adorned in a gown of finely spun flax, her golden hair crowned with daisies, cornflowers and ferns, stood a woman of such goodness and beauty that all in the hall dropped their eyes before her.

"Son of the Middle Earth, greet your lady mother."

Aiden looked up with surprise. His eyes filled with tears. Before him stood a woman with the ocean in her eyes, without age, holding the King under some kind of spell.

"Mother!" Aiden's voice broke, recognizing his Irish mother from centuries past. As Dagr, he had laid her to rest on a barge laden with all that she had loved on this earth, her magic tools, the treasures she had kept from the one man she had loved, and surrounded by all manner of greenery, he had pushed her out to sea, a sacred fire lit to consume her body.

He had wept then and he wept now, as she laid her hands on his shoulders and filled him with a love so poignant that he thought his heart might break. If only he could find his voice, and tell her how much he had missed her touch, the purity of her soul, the sound of her feet as they rustled along the hallways of the castle floor where they had once lived.

"Rise, my son." The Queen of the Fey spoke and gently lifted Aiden to his feet, where she embraced him and kissed his tears away.

"I am never gone from you. Remember that. Once I was fettered by a human body and I could only give you what humans have, but now, I am able to guide you from my place beside the King. I owe much to his love. When you begin your journey as an Earth Builder, once your gifts as an alchemist are awoken, you will need to listen to my voice."

"Mother, I will listen for your voice. I have missed you dearly, your wisdom, your teachings. I hope I can work as I did before, and honor my purpose. But how is it that you are here? Are you the Queen of the Fey? Because I remember another."

The Aspen King bristled with anger and sat unsettled on his throne but the Queen's hand laid gently on his shoulder quieted his discomfort.

"We must not hold on to things that once were, my son. We must accept that nothing is permanent. Those we love and know can become strangers to us, and we must move on to other loves, other connections. It does not seem fair on Earth, but here, we gently allow for the flow. But nothing is lost. The energy of the last Queen of the Fey is still dear to us, and we honor her work and her everlasting soul. She has moved on to other dimensions for important duties that only she can perform."

Aiden felt that he had just been told something that one day he would have to lean upon. It worried his heart, and his eyes reflected his fears. But the Queen smiled so brilliantly and sweetly that he was once more put at ease and kissed her hands, never wanting to let go.

"The King and I have something to give you. Understand that this gift comes with great love for the one you have chosen as your beloved." She held up her hand as Aiden began to explain that he loved more than one with his entire being. "Yes, we know, and we admire your choices, as both are integral to your purpose. But only one you will marry, in the traditional way, because the other is a spirit so free that no ceremony could bind her to you. She is no ordinary woman, and you need not doubt her love for you. But she is of great importance to us, and there can be no promises made. Again, I ask you to not be fearful. Try to understand that change is inevitable in your world."

Aiden nodded. What could this gift be?

The Queen brought forth a box tied with sweet grass and ivy. She handed it to Aiden who laying his sword aside, opened the tiny box with a wildly beating heart. Inside, a pillow of dried flowers, upon which lay a set of wedding rings so exquisite that Aiden could only hold his breath and admire their luminescence.

"These rings has been made by our finest craftsmen, from a quality of gold that will never be mined by men. The stone, a rare blue quartz cut to reflect your lover's heart, is of a quality whose value will never be appraised. It is for the maiden who has shown herself to be pure of heart and whose love for you will transcend anything that must happen as you continue your work. It is not only a ring that will be a symbol of your love for her, but also offers protection. You must know that your life's work is a dangerous road, my son, and dangerous for anyone who loves you. For this reason, we gift you these rings. They will be recognized by a certain few in Middle Earth...those who need know your identity."

"I am touched by this gift, and the protection you offer my beloved. Am I to assume that Sahara is offered protection in some other form? Can I not bring her something that will guide her work?" Aiden could not in any manner imagine gifting protection to one and not the other, and he hoped that his question was not seen as forward...too assumptive of his mother's love for him, or his importance here.

The Aspen King, who loved to shower his Queen with treasures to delight her, was won over by the romance and devotion of Aiden's heart. He was moved to reward his courage as well, for who, in their right mind, receives a gift and then asks for more?

"You are brave," said the Aspen King, "and pure of heart. I can see that as plain as I can see your resistance to understanding that

Sahara is one of us. Oh yes, she is only half human, and that is why you will never be allowed to tether her. But to reward your love for her and genuine concern for her safety, I will part with something that I have long admired."

He called to the dwarf upon whose neck hung a chain with a key. He instructed him to open a chest beside the throne amidst a great many oohs and aahs and craning necks, as the Fey tried to glimpse the contents of the well-guarded container.

The Aspen King lifted from the mass of jewels a delicate silver pendant, a dazzling oval citrine hanging from its length, with an energy so strong that all Fey were splayed flat on their bums, as the crystal commanded time and space around itself.

"It's not a guarantee of anything, mind you," The Aspen Kind said. "But it is an ally she will be able to trust."

"I am eternally grateful," Aiden dipped down on one knee and accepted the gift.

"If anyone asks, and many will, you must say that the jewels are from an old estate and that you lucked into them through a friend. This is as close to the truth as you can bring anyone. Now stand here. The initiation will begin, and then we will feast!"

"Feast?" Aiden couldn't contain his words. Just how much time could he be away before Holly would wake and wonder what had happened to him?

The laughter around him, from Fey, the King and even his mother who laughed as gaily as the rest, reminded him that in the Underworld, time was something no one really paid attention to.

He was initiated into the path of the warrior, but in this century, the sword would only be a symbol of his strength, for killing was not Aiden's way. Instead, he would use compassion and loving kindness as his tools for wearing down the enemy of the Middle Earth. Where greed and terror reigned now, his job would be to awaken the world to a renewed partnership with other dimensions. Although he did not know it yet, he was being initiated into the role of a leader, and even the Fey would heed his decisions upon Middle Earth. But as the Queen of the Fey advised her lover, the proud and powerful King, not all knowledge was necessary at once, for humans were limited in their view and easily misunderstood their own capabilities.

Aiden danced the night away, with maidens bright and fair, who all vied for his heart and tried to trick him into forgetting his beloved. He would be a delight to keep. But the Queen kept him safe from all bewitching. And besides, he was never more than two thoughts away from the one who waited for him in his bed.

Finally, when all the strawberry wine had been drunk and every morsel of food had been consumed, Aiden was released from the spell he was under and allowed to wander home.

And there Holly found him, when she awoke, sitting in a chair by the bed, watching her intently.

CHAPTER 32

"Like billowing clouds,
Like the incessant gurgle of the brook,
The longing of the spirit can never be stilled." ~ Hildegard of Bingen

"Have you been sitting there long? What time is it?" Holly just then noticed a box on the pillow beside her, glowing with an unusual light, almost as if it would levitate and disappear around a corner if she did not lay her hand upon it.

She looked toward Aiden again who appeared to have grown by a couple of feet, his eyes shining that startling blue, intense, like a lion about to surprise his prey.

"Open it...please." Aiden was almost at his wits end, anticipating he knew not what, a growing apprehension that Holly would never accept his explanations of the last few hours - but tell her he knew he must.

He watched her gently pick up the box, and with those long, slender fingers that he loved to hold, she opened it and gasped at the contents. An engagement ring with blue quartz matching Aiden's eyes shone brightly in greeting then receded its energy. Did she imagine that? Then there was the wedding band of the deepest burnished gold and crafted into a medieval braid of daisies, along with a band for Aiden of the same design but a heftier width. Aiden's ring was studded with tiny pieces of the same blue quartz. The two bands could have been a crown for a king and queen, their design was so artfully executed!

Aiden held out his hand and Holly slipped out of bed. Her eyes filled with tears when Aiden picked up the ring.

"I adore you, Holly. This ring cannot compare to your beauty and your heart. I've hoped for you for so long. Will you walk this lifetime with me, my love?" He slipped to his knees before her, a man lost to his emotions.

She could barely see through her tears, but she held out her hand and allowed him to place the ring on her finger, his powerful arms threatening to break her in half, he held her so tightly when she accepted the gift of his devotion.

They sat in the dark for some time, no words were spoken; they simply breathed each other in. She could hardly look him in the eye as he seemed so changed. There was a power that she was struck by, an energy of something other-worldly, her shyness returned and she remained curled against him.

He barely dared to talk, sure that if he spoke this moment would extinguish itself.

She was the stronger of the two of them - if only she knew. She braved the first question.

"Has something happened? You seem different...this ring. It's not an ordinary stone. Aiden, I have never seen anything like this."

"I have a story to tell you. Something happened while you were asleep. I don't expect you to believe it, but I must tell you - and where this ring came from.

And he told her the whole thing, while she listened wide eyed, the ring on her finger lighting up the space between them.

"And the most amazing thing, sweetness, is that where this quartz and gold were mined, is a place we here on earth, would never be allowed to find. The Fey protect parts of the planet from our greed. In essence, we will never be allowed to destroy this earth completely. There are many who work towards its protection, and when mines run dry, it is really when men are made blind to the riches beyond. Before we can do permanent damage to the earth, the Fey and some alchemists- magic workers - step in and make its destruction impossible."

"Oh Aiden, that is the best thing I've ever heard! And you and Iona and Sahara will be part of that protection of the earth! I'm just overwhelmed to be part of it, if only by association!" Holly clapped her hands and the ring exploded into rays of light.

"You mean to tell me that you believe everything I've told you and you're not going to run screaming?" Aiden blurted out.

Holly took his face in her hands. She sat very still. "Aiden, I never want to hear you say that you're worried about me running away. I love you. So much so that is cripples me at times, and I am overwhelmed by my feelings. But I do believe you, and always will. And everything that Sahara tells me. Maybe I am the most naïve person on earth, but if that means that the two of you will love me, then I will remain naïve and gullible and completely blind to what *normal* is. It hurts me when you think I will run from you...please don't say it anymore."

Aiden's sinful mouth broke into a rich smile and he kissed her vehemently. She wanted so very badly to slip out of her nightdress and lay herself before him, but he held her so tight that she could barely move.

"Are you sorry that I did it this way, in not so grand a fashion - ask you to be mine?" he finally said.

"No, my love, no. You know me well. I would be so nervous if you did something public and not knowing that it was coming had me at my most relaxed. I'm still afraid of you, Aiden Halloran. Do you know what kind of man you are?"

He shook his head.

"You're too handsome to make any woman feel anything but shaky, and you're intense and powerful in nature...altogether not the kind of man women have confidence around. I'm inexperienced and silly, I'm a girl...no, no, don't deny it. To know that you love me enough to want me for a lifetime is very heady business. And sometimes when you look at me, I get frightened and wonder how I will ever please you."

"Now it's my turn to say that I don't want you to doubt my love. You touch my heart in a million ways...and," Aiden smiled wickedly, "I can teach you anything you need to know, if you insist that you're a girl who knows nothing about men."

Holly blushed profusely. "Don't. You're a devil."

"I'm going to make love to you in a few minutes. The first time as my promised, and when I marry you, you will have to agree to a night of being ravaged in the most indecent ways."

"Oh Aiden, can you say that again...'when I marry you.'"

"When I marry you. You won't make me wait too long will you?"

"No...but I do have one more question. Please don't be angry. Was there anything from the Fey for Sahara? Surely they adore her. She is so like them, and so kind to the earth. Was there anything?"

That was the one part of the story that Aiden did omit, against his better judgement, just how much the Fey did adore Sahara and that she was part Fey. But he revealed the pedant that the Aspen King had gifted. Holly's pure heart was overjoyed for Sahara's sake.

"Oh, I just knew it! I just knew that they wouldn't forget her! Only she could wear this. It's like it has a life of its own."

The Aspen King sat up on his throne, his Queen long gone to tuck in the littlest of their brood, and allowed a smidgeon of his heart to open to Holly's joy. How pure was her love! It was something he was addicted to. He remembered someone from long ago, whose heart he had taken without thought. He called to his Queen. She understood. She would keep him from making those same mistakes. She was pure, purer than any of his previous beloved.

Aiden cradled Holly against his heart as he carried her downstairs to the low burning fire.

She slipped out of her nightdress and lay before him, a tender offering to a hungry wolf. Stretched out on the softness of the sheepskin rug, caressed by the warmth of the fire, Holly arched her back and held her breasts in her hands, her eyes wide and curious, waiting for her lover to pounce.

"You've got that look Aiden. Sometimes I think your passion will consume me," she writhed under his stare.

"I'm so very hungry for you. Open for me, sweet thing." Aiden slid his hands along Holly's legs.

She did so, trusting yet vulnerable, her hands opening her sacred place, as he requested, his eyes locked on hers, a virile, decadent man whose need overtook them both.

CHAPTER 33

"We'll have to tell our families," Aiden said as he fed Holly bits of breakfast. "Let's have your parents over for Thanksgiving and mine for Christmas."

Holly balked. "My parents will never understand. They'll be happy about you and me, but they won't understand about Sahara."

"Well, it's not kind to not tell them. We must. I promise I won't let them ambush you in private."

"It'll ruin our holiday...our first."

"It'll be bad for a day then they'll leave and we'll go back to our lives. We have to get past this. Please trust me on this."

"Ok. If you tell me that I have to then I will."

"I'm not your daddy. You don't have to listen to me."

"Well I'm not going to come up with anything brave, so I choose to be told what to do."

"Ok," Aiden smiled. "But I could get addicted to this submissive side of you. Or, if you'd prefer, we can have them up another time. It doesn't have to be a holiday weekend. But I'd like to have it over with before year-end, and I don't think that having them all up at once would be considerate of their feelings. Too much, perhaps, to have to deal with our lifestyle and also face each other."

"No, Thanksgiving's ok. On the Sunday."

"Sahara and I will cook. Shall I make my order now for the bread and coffee and pastries?"

Holly giggled. "It'll cost you."

Aiden laughed. "Write up the bill, little lady. I'll make sure payment is made in full."

Holly turned pensive. She blushed a little and began to play with her hair, a sign Aiden now recognised as something she did when she had something on her mind that she was shy to disclose.

"What is it?"

"Mmmm, I was thinking about when you're out there, in the world, you know, and how women are always staring at you, and secretly wishing they could find their way in? I see it at the café when you're sitting reading the paper, minding your own business. There's such an electric energy around you and it pulls women in."

"Yes. I know. There's nothing I can do about it. I don't mean anything to those women. I'm just something pretty to fawn over. It's not all that flattering anyway, to be an object." Aiden's face hardened as he spoke. "Does it worry you?"

"No. Not exactly. Before, when we were friends, I found it a bit amusing, but now, I feel protective - maybe jealous. I don't know. I don't want to be jealous."

"I don't know if you know this, but you attract men left, right and center. I'll admit to feeling murderous at times. We're human Holly. We feel things. As long as we're processing our emotions and being honest with each other, we're growing in our friendship. And above all, I want to be your friend. One that you can count on."

"I wasn't saying that I don't trust you around other women. I do. Implicitly. This is just new, feeling protective over you, wanting to shield you."

Aiden gathered Holly in his arms. "Let me tell you something I learned a very long time ago. When a warrior goes into battle with a trusted companion, they have to count on each other to not put the other person in danger. Now, many things are out of their control. But that is left to fate, and any time given to worry is considered danger-ous, because then they're not paying attention to what *is* in their con-trol...their skill and their interpretation of the situation. And so it is with us, my love. I cannot control who wants you nor who wants me, all I can do is love you and protect you to the best of my ability. Every-thing else is speculation and a dangerous slide into the unknown."

"That's what I was doing...sliding into distrust of other people's motives. That's not helpful is it?"

"No, but we've talked it over and our footing is even stronger now. Thank you for trusting me with your words. I want the hard stuff, Holly, not just the good. I want to experience it all with you, even the painful. I won't be a fair weather friend to you." He held her chin in his hand. "You've got me, heart, body and soul."

"I think you're going to come across as the big bad wolf to my parents, taking advantage of Sahara and me. But I know who you are. And I won't allow them to blame you."

"It's not going to be pleasant Holly for any of us. But if we see it from their perspective, and have compassion for their fears, we won't take any of it personally. I know who I am too, I don't need anyone's approval. But I will protect your honor as much as possible. Anyway, we can't change what other people think."

CHAPTER 34

I want you
From my darkness
From the ancient places in my soul
From my recollections of love once worn
Like a mist on the ocean, like sunshine on the hills
I want you, I've learned to say please and thank you and more
I can't see without your body on mine
I can't breathe without your words etched on my mind
I can't live without the naked need of your mouth
Play me. I'll be your willing song

He brought the wind with him.

Sahara stood at the side door of the cabin where she had just piled a few days' worth of firewood into the alcove. She looked up as Ulfred began to bark and lope towards the Aspen wood.

He was still a distant figure but unmistakeable in his walk. Sahara's heart skipped a beat and a rush of sexual energy rose up her spine. Aiden's aura surrounded him in expanding waves of faultless white and amethyst hues, the change in him poignant. A quiet murmur from the forest behind Sahara's cabin brought the news that her teacher was approaching, and that all portals were open to this lifetime's work.

It was an ancient response for Sahara to want to fall to her knees and accept Aiden's blessing upon her, as she would now walk until the end of their days as his student, and he would lead the group of Earth Builders. But she stood her ground. She would wait until she could read his eyes and sense his will.

He strode up to her, at once the tender soul and the powerful warrior. All veils were lifted and they were allowed a glimpse through the layers of time, where, as lovers and mystics, they had been beloved by the Fey. For one blessed moment, they were able to connect with their etheric bodies and slipping into each other's aura, become one.

Aiden's energy enfolded Sahara with a blanket of heat. He held her, as she threatened to collapse in his wake. Snug against his thundering heart, Sahara stared Aiden resolutely in the eye, even though she had never experienced such power or intelligence. It was not earthly, she knew that, and her body responded with a desire for surrender. There was nothing to do but allow for his leadership. It did not come arrogantly, but with an encompassing peace. It would be natural to follow such incarnated love.

"My lady," Aiden swept his lips softly along Sahara's. "I am your servant, inasmuch as you will never accept me as one now. Allow me to pledge myself to you."

Sahara's breath came short and labored, her whole being prisoner to Aiden's essence. How she wanted to learn from him. How she had waited for him to awaken and find his path. And now that he had, she could barely stand or think.

"My lord. I accept your love and your stewardship. I vow to be your constant student." She touched his face, marvelled at the intensity of his soul. "You have been to the Fey. Their mark is upon you."

Aiden's smile broke like sunshine on an overcast day. "I've met my lady mother and received her blessing."

Sahara's heart leapt. The Queen of the Fey! A greater endorsement from the Aspen King could not have been given. Only the most favored were allowed her tenderness. "I suppose you know of my association with the Fey now. There will be no more secrets between us, my love. We are bound by ties stronger than those of the heart."

The valley sank into a dark and stormy light. Snow began to fall around them, the cold penetrating and damp. Winter settled her heavy skirts upon the Aspen Wood.

Aiden led Sahara into the cabin, where he built up the fire and made a comfortable nest for them beside it.

"I have so much to tell you. And have even more questions. May I spend the night with you?"

"Yes! I've missed you in my space. We spend so much time at your place now. But I'd love it if we sometimes gathered here." Sahara fit her hands inside Aiden's.

"Of course, we'll be here anytime you want us. It'll take us some time to figure things out...you know that I love your home. This is where magic lives." He kissed her hands, leaving a trail of heat along her fingers. "I have something for you and something to tell you. Which would you like first?"

Sahara's eyes lit up like a child's. "Present first please!"

Aiden laughed. That laugh that unfurled all of Sahara's need. He produced a velvet pouch, and held it out to Sahara. "From the Aspen King...a token of his appreciation."

She looked him sharply in the eye. Maybe he didn't understand

175

gifts from the Aspen King as a mark of ownership. It was, after all, Aiden's first trip this lifetime to the Underworld. It would take him time to remember how the Fey did things.

The pouch took on life as soon as Sahara touched it. Gently, she dropped the pendant that slipped out of it into her hand. It recognised her instantly and became warm.

"Hello," Sahara murmured.

The stone responded with a gentle humming, while Aiden slipped the silver chain over Sahara's head. Yes, Sahara thought, the King is clever. A stone to activate the solar plexus, the seat of the will, to help her in her work but also to heighten intuition and the activity of the Third Eye. The King expected great things from her, and offered her his assistance - a close connection that he kept with the Feminine and those he liked to think his own. He had claimed her with this gift. Sahara opened her heart to the stone and was rewarded with a feeling of deep affection from her guard.

"I see that it is aligned with you already. It suits you to perfection."

"Yes - I love it. I've missed you, Aiden, these last few days. I've been buried in my own affairs, and am ready to reconnect with you. Holly will be coming over tomorrow; we'll be making plans for the winter. I'm teaching her about seasonal eating and we're creating recipes for the café to reflect winter's gifts."

"This is why I love you. All your witchy, earthy, sweet bits of you!"

Sahara snuggled deep into his arms. "I'm looking forward to a winter of hibernating with your and Holly's love."

"May I tell you my news now? Holly agreed that I could share."

"Tell me!"

"As you know, or gather, I had my initiation ceremony while in the Underworld. I'm beginning to remember things. I wouldn't say learning them, just remembering, from other lives."

Sahara nodded, Aiden's energy picking up. "That's how it is, we remember."

"Right. But also, I was given something for Holly...a ring."

"Yes? A ring. Oh! A ring!"

Aiden grinned. "A ring."

"Are you telling me that you'll be asking Holly to marry you?"

"I'm telling you that I did."

"Oh, darling! Of course she said yes! *Did* she say yes? It's all happening so quickly!"

176

Aiden kissed her as she laughed and cried. "She said yes. I'm afraid it was all very low-key and not terribly romantic in the usual sense. I just couldn't wait to ask her and wanted so badly to share that intimate moment with her while the day was breaking. Sahara, you're not in any way upset that we did it on our own?"

"Upset?! Are you mad? I am ecstatic! But you must, just must, allow me to throw you a little celebration? Just us three. Let's surprise her with it?"

"Well who else would we invite that would understand? Tomorrow night?" Aiden's heart could not have been fuller. "But I think you should go see her. She's probably dying to show you...It's a rather large blue quartz, for her protection as much as anything. My lady mother understood how I wish to keep Holly out of harm's way as I start out on this new path. I'm afraid I accepted my appointment without knowing any of the details."

Sahara stared at Aiden. "A blue quartz the color of your eyes? With a band of daisies and a delicately turned twig?"

"Yes! But how..."

Sahara bowed her head before an astonished Aiden.

"I don't think you understand what this all means...who you are in the scheme of things. You're not only the leader of an ancient group of fantastically brilliant alchemists. You have been gifted the mythical wedding set of Tristan and Isolde. Only a few people on the planet know it even exists. There is no higher honor given by the King of the Fey. But you must know that now Holly has been claimed as well," Sahara said, alarm sudden in her voice. "She will be recognized by that ring."

Aiden jumped to his feet. "I don't understand. What do you mean?"

"Oh Aiden. You have accepted the gift. It may seem like a trick to you, but truly, it is an honor that comes with great responsibility and it's just a continuation of your association with the Fey from before. You must have agreed to it when you reviewed your life chart before reincarnating. We are all claimed now, you, Holly, me, Iona and Richard. Our work will begin in earnest."

"But Holly has had no say." Aiden felt as if the whole world was spinning and he was about to fall off the edge.

"My love, but she has had. She must have. It is an Underworld rule that one must agree to belong to the Fey. Has she told you anything that would give you a clue to any dealings with them? I just can't imagine her initiating anything.

177

The realization of what must have happened hit them both at once.

"The accident!" they said in unison.

Aiden's anger rose instantly. Sahara tried desperately to calm him.

"This isn't tragic, Aiden. She'll be under their protection now, and must in some way be part of our work, or this wouldn't be happening."

"You don't believe a word of that, Sahara! You know as well as I do that she is altogether too naïve to be left in any kind of a relationship with the Fey. She'll believe every trick they throw at her."

"It's probably my fault, anyway, I asked Iona to help and she called on the Aspen King to keep her safe until you got there. She may have been unconscious. Hypothermia could easily have set in. We're truly lucky that nothing worse happened."

"But unconscious and vulnerable. I remember now that she said she had spoken to the stag who kept her company while she slept. She thought she was dreaming but obviously she was unconscious for a while. Christ! They can be so beguiling. She would never suspect any trickery." Aiden was pacing now.

Sahara was lost for words and solutions. She only wanted to calm the beast before her and settle his anxious heart.

"You have one way of finding out."

"What way?"

Sahara sat limply down on the sofa. "You can ask Iona. You've officially taken over her interim role as leader of the earth builders, and you can in fact demand her cooperation. She'll know by now that you've been appointed, and is no doubt waiting for your contact anyway. If anyone can explain this to you, she can."

"Why do I feel that I'm about to step into the fire?" Aiden's hardened, anxious face and tense, virile body could not have struck a more aching part of Sahara's heart. How beautiful he was, even like this. Iona would lay eternity on the line to reconnect with such masculinity. She sighed.

"Lie with me Aiden. I just want to close my eyes and forget about everything for a few hours." And into his willing embrace she fell, as she had done so many times, so many centuries ago.

There was a throng of people clustered around Holly when Sahara dropped in to see her the next morning.

She entered quietly and found a seat at the end of the counter. Holly's contented smile found her heart beating wildly. For the first time, she felt that her presence was going to put a sour wrinkle into the genuine well wishes from Holly's regulars. Naturally people would assume that Holly would now abandon her affair with Sahara. Society was weaned on 'normal'. And normal had nothing to do with polyamory.

Indeed, there was a curious hush when Holly greeted Sahara with a tight embrace and kiss on the mouth. It was too public a place to show Sahara the ring. It was too intimate a moment to share with veritable strangers. Sahara motioned Holly to the kitchen much to everyone's disappointment.

With tears flowing freely, Holly and Sahara embraced, the ring on a gold chain around Holly's neck warm with their emotion.

"Do you see, Sahara? It's magic...it reacts to my heart. From the Fey."

Holly's hushed and reverent tone reminded Sahara of Holly's purity, her willingness to accept the impossible.

"I see. It's beautiful, like you. It suits your and Aiden's love so well. I'm so happy for you, darling."

"I've never been happier. I never imagined that love could be this good, or that my life could be so full. I don't deserve it...shhhh...." Holly placed a finger on Sahara's lips. "It's true, I don't deserve such devotion; because I always doubted that I would find love. And yet, it found me."

Sahara nodded. "Aiden is over the moon. I think he's afraid you'll change your mind, because it happened so quickly and without much fanfare."

"Never!" Holly whispered. "Never. I don't even need a ring. I mean, I adore it, but more than that I adore how much he wanted to give it to me. That he loves me enough to ask me. I know that you won't agree, but I'm not in his league, not one bit. He's sophisticated, and brilliant and trouble, but somehow, he finds a home in me."

"Because you're all the things he's looking for, you silly goose!" Sahara kissed Holly soundly, warning her to keep quiet, their giddy laughter spilling into the café. "Ok, I'll pick you up later to bring you over for dinner. You still want to spend the night, right?"

"Nope." Holly laughed. "No, I'm done with you now that I've got my big ring." Sahara's nuzzle on her neck brought a low moan.

"I think that's what everyone's going to expect," Sahara nodded toward the buzzing café. The fire in Holly's eyes rose instantly.

"I'll never give you up. Not for anything or anyone. You're mine."

Hands clasped together, they walked out of the kitchen. Lilith was serving as fast as her legs would carry her.

"Hey boss!" she admonished. "I could use some help here." She came closer and whispered, "Your love life is a magnet for customers. We might have to hire another server."

Holly laughed. "Don't worry, help is on its way. I'm hiring an apprentice."

"You are? Who?"

"A young man. From France."

Lilith wrinkled her nose. "A boy?" She looked doubtful that a boy could be trained sufficiently to Holly's standards.

"Not a boy, Lilith. A man. My age. Don't worry. He comes highly recommended."

"Hmmf! I don't think we need any more men messing things up around here." She said it as Aiden walked in and took his seat next to Sahara. "I've never, in my whole life, seen such goings on," she added. But she served them both with a warm smile.

CHAPTER 35

Ulfred sat by the door watching Sahara string fairy lights along the beams in the kitchen.

"I should have done this long ago, Ulfred. Look how pretty this looks! Holly will love it. I'm going to weave some in on the mantle."

Ulfred barked and wagged his tail. Sahara smiled at her rapidly growing puppy. She wondered how she'd ever lived without him. Even Willow found him good company. Sahara often found them curled up together on the front porch, watching the wind play with the grass.

Supper in the cook stove oven, Sahara took her time making preparations for Holly and Aiden's engagement dinner. It was time to celebrate. She knew that the weeks ahead would bring many changes to their lives, not the least of which would be Aiden meeting Iona, and integrating the work of the Group into his and Holly's relationship.

It seemed to Sahara that as lifetimes went, this one had the potential for the most turbulence. Secretly, she planned to make this winter as smooth as she could for her lovers, let them adjust to their varied projects, act as an assistant to both. She enjoyed being the one in the background and letting others shine.

Aiden had taken on, in her opinion, too much, what with plans for expanding his home, creating office space, renovating the café, and preparing for Richard's build. Thank goodness he had Drew, who was now second in command with added responsibilities, and as trustworthy as they came. Hiring administrative help would also carve out some more time at home. Aiden hated being away from them more and more. He had confided that he was overwhelmed at times but that his creative juices were flowing. Although how he would work with Richard was in no way clear in his head, Aiden had never been more inspired by the plans for the mountain retreat Richard and Iona planned.

"It's bigger than anyone has any need for," Aiden had said. "But the design is waking up everything I love about architecture. It's in every aspect elegant and centered around principles of sacred geometry. The mind and spirit cannot help but react to it. It's inherently beautiful. Any old soul would recognise its magic. I resisted working with Richard, but I cannot not build it. It's a dream project for me."

"Does it remind you of castle life? When you weren't with me...Brigida...that time in the woods, you had a life of privilege. You lived well, and for some, that is something they crave in subsequent lives. Especially when the next life is more of a struggle."

"Well, I can't say that this lifetime is a struggle financially, but I was happy with a simple life in the woods, it seemed so natural. I suppose that that part of my past life surfaced early on for me, and I set to recreating that through my subconscious. But I noticed it with Richard. He is very much the nobleman still. It's in the way he carries himself. One has no doubt that he is a man of influence."

"But your love of sacred geometry as it pertains to building...that's something you carried over from the past. I wish we still built that way now. People are happier. They resonate love in buildings that incorporate those principles. I read about it once."

"Oh? Where?"

"The Prince of Wales. He wrote about it in a book called "Harmony." You'd like it.

"Really? Interesting. Are you...a monarchist?" Aiden had smiled his lazy smile, teasing her.

"Not in principle. Monarchy is outdated and in light of all the need in the world, can we really justify it? But because I once lived in a manor home, I have a certain fondness for it. And maybe I tend towards submissiveness because I was used to life under the social system of that era. Although, there was no lord as progressive as Dagr. Remember? He was fond of a fair community and farming in a way that protected the land for future generations."

"I remember," Aiden had touched her face gently and kissed her. "He was far ahead of his time. The more I discover about him, the more I want to go back and learn more. I feel that I am meant to bring something back from that time, some kind of understanding. We'll see."

"We still have to bridge that relationship - between you, me, Richard and Iona. And Holly of course."

"It's only you and Iona that I worry about, if I'm to be honest my love. Can either of you behave if left alone? I'm convinced that you love her, which I understand, considering your history. And Richard...well." Aiden shook his head.

"You don't trust me." Sahara wasn't surprised of course. But it did hurt. She coveted Aiden's trust.

"Not in that regard," he had said honestly. "In many ways, implicitly, yes. We must navigate this as best we can."

"For Holly."

"And for us. Our own love."

Sahara sat in front of the fire, fresh greenery scenting the room, the cabin dimly lit, remembering their conversation. If Aiden was any other man, she might not contemplate reigning in her blatant desire for lovers such as Iona and Richard. But because he was so honorable, she wanted very much to rise to his standard. But could she? Her instincts, if Sahara was to listen to them honestly, almost shouted her inability.

The smell of sourdough bread baking - a surprise for Holly - filled the room. It was peaceful here, rustic and reminiscent of life in the Oracle Wood. If she closed her eyes, Sahara could almost touch it, the simplicity of their previous existence. Even the loneliness and the drudgery of the work it took just to survive, was a pleasant recollection. Her fondness for solitude and wandering among the trees had not left her. Nor had her love for early music. The plaintive sound of the recorder on the stereo evoked wistful emotions. Oh it had been a magical time, even with innocence lost and the constant fear of being discovered by the king's men.

Sahara allowed herself to remember and feel - Dagr's inescapable strength. The knight who knew more war than any man should have had to endure, steadfastly living by a sacrosanct code of honor and dreams of a better world. She could access the way he smelled, the feel of his skin, and when Aiden kissed her, even the taste of his mouth. It was all so very complicated. Where were the boundaries between this world and that? It seemed that as they discovered more and more, it was easier to slip back in time...continue living as they once had. Some days she craved it with all her might.

In the moments just before waking some days, she could feel the fabric of her kirtle in her fingers, smell the smoke from the fire in the hearth; hear Dagr moving around the room banishing the damp of the night from their tiny dwelling. She strained to keep her eyes shut tight, and hold on to the memory for as long as she could...when it had been just her and him.

But that memory made little sense, as she had never lived alone with Dagr. Still, she grasped for moments in time when for some reason, they awoke alone together in a room she did not recognise. Where was Arinn, in these recollections? Sahara left the fire to get dressed before the memories brought her in danger of disappearing altogether. The familiar whistle of a text message returned her to the present moment.

I'm in town. I'll pick Holly up. No need to drive out again. Love.
Sahara sent a quick message back. *Desperate to hold you.*

If Aiden could feel her raised energy and sentimental heart, he didn't give it away. Instead, he quoted a snippet of Yeats. But his words only fed the nostalgia that Sahara was succumbing to, as she put on a black vintage gown that flowed freely to the ground. The mantle of the wise woman and centuries of experience lay upon her. She was changing, as Aiden was. She thought of Holly, the tenderest part of them. With shaking hands, she wrapped a gift for her, a set of light blue Celestine geodes that although separate, fit each other perfectly, just like Holly and Aiden's love. For Aiden, she wrapped one of her favorite books; a treasured edition of Thoreau's 'Walden Pond'. He had a copy, she knew that, but this one was filled with notes she had made, the ramblings of her heart. He would value this more than anything she could have bought him.

It was almost time. They would be here and she should try to be a little more grounded, a little less open to the enormity of the moment. There was time to cast a spell and find her center. She put on the pendant that Aiden had brought from the Fey. Yes, that was better.

***

"Oh! I thought Sahara was coming. Were you still in town?" Holly dropped a luscious kiss on Aiden's lips as he found her locking the café door. She was flustered but smiling brilliantly, having hastily slipped into a knit dress that accentuated every one of her curves.

"I love you in dresses," Aiden tried to hold on to her for another kiss, but she was busily looking through a bag of supplies she had put together for their dinner.

"You do? I probably shouldn't feed your appetite," she teased. "Wait, I think I forgot the olives."

Aiden caught her by the waist. "You needn't bring anything. And where's your coat, woman? It's winter you know."

She ran laughing to his truck. He couldn't help smiling at her girlish ways. He caught up with her, and demanded her house keys.

"I'm going to get your coat. Don't argue. You might be warm now, but you'll be sorry in the morning."

"Yes sir!" she saluted. She let his hand wander along her leg, to the edge of her stocking.

"Want me?" She looped her arms around his neck, on tiptoe.

Aiden stepped back, earnestly searching her face.

"What is it? I don't mean to tease you...I'm just playing." Sometimes the intensity of Aiden's blue eyes left her unsure of what she was doing.

"I'm just broken by you, sweetness. That's all." Aiden held her tight against the thunder in his chest. He couldn't tell her that he had seen a vision of her like this before, standing pressed against a tall black stallion, her heart on her sleeve. Or that he feared his love for her was like trying to hold a fleeting wind.

⁕

They held hands as Holly chattered about her day, and told him that she was looking forward to having dinner cooked for her. The ring on her finger was something neither of them were used to. They both caught themselves staring at it, and smiling about what it meant.

Holly unbuckled herself and turned towards Aiden, sitting on her knees to nip at his ear.

"I love you."

"Buckle up. I mean it." Aiden reached his arm across her, searching for the seat belt.

"Oh Aiden!" she protested, but she did it, because neither his voice nor his body language left her with any choice.

He took her hand again, and brought it to his lips.

"I'm sorry, I don't mean to be so abrupt. Winter roads..."

She nodded and squeezed his hand. "I know."

They rounded the corner into Sahara's long and winding driveway.

"I love this part." Holly sighed with happiness. "Knowing that in another moment the cabin will come into view. Seeing those lights in the distance, imagining Sahara inside."

"Me too. How the dark settles so tightly in the valley. I feel it here." Aiden pressed Holly's hand to his heart. "She's so good at making us feel at home. Wanted."

"We love her. But she's not really ours, is she? I know that. I don't know when I began to realize it, but I did."

Aiden was caught off guard by Holly's deeply intuitive truth, which she stated so calmly.

"What do you mean?" He parked the truck and turned to look at her.

Holly looked down. He was radiating a light that she hadn't seen before, a wholeness that enveloped the space around them. It warmed her, but left her grasping for words.

"I mean, she's not a love that you can own. She gives herself freely, but she cannot give her whole self. I understand, I think. She

185

has her work, with Iona, and she isn't truly of this world. I'm rambling, it makes no sense."

Aiden pulled her into his lap, one powerful hand across the small of her back, the other in her hair.

"You are making sense. That's the problem. She's not going to be like any love you or I have ever known."

"Well, I haven't known much," Holly interrupted, undone by his body against hers and the sure way he held her.

"But you know enough to know that although she loves us unconditionally, her life is her own."

"Yes," Holly nuzzled into Aiden's warmth. "I can't do without her - I love her as she is."

"You're incredible." He leaned her back, and left a trail of kisses down the front of her neckline, reaching for the warmth of her breast.

"I'm not scared, you know. I'm going to enjoy every minute of my life with her...*oh!* We have to go in...*Aiden.*"

Sahara opened the door to them, a dark, confident beauty. It took a moment, but Holly realized that something special was going on, what with Aiden's grinning and Sahara's stunning dress. She exclaimed about the fairy lights and how pretty everything looked bathed in candlelight.

Aiden opened a bottle of champagne, quietly watching his lovers embrace and whisper their hellos. There was such beauty in their devotion. He counted himself fortunate to be part of their world. Sahara's energy, the mood in the cabin and Holly's sparkling laughter created a vortex of memories. He wondered about the gifts on the table, laid with antique china and crystal stemware; two silver candlestick holders burning white tapers; the opulence of the table setting against the rustic background of the cabin so achingly familiar. Too familiar to be anything less than a peer into the past.

Nothing escaped Sahara's notice: the set of Aiden's jaw, the tight grip of his hand on the bottle, the way his body bristled against whatever he was fighting emotionally - raised a worrisome flag. She handed him a champagne flute.

He found respite in her eyes.

CHAPTER 36

The wild boar roast heating over the fire was almost too much for Arinn's senses. Dagr had set their simple board with what little crockery they owned, but in the middle stood a silver candlestick and the whitest taper Arinn had ever seen...a gift from Richard. How extravagant it looked next to their wooden utensils and plates.

There were other luxuries - a linen cloth and napkins, berry preserves to go along with the roasting roots, a loaf of fine white bread; onions and herbs scented the meat. A container of honey tempted Arinn's fingers. It had been a long time since they had tasted the essence of wild meadow flowers. She licked her lips.

Richard came in from tending to the horses, a chore he was not used to but gladly performed as he processed his emotions. Brigida was wrapped in furs by the fire, her color rising, Dagr holding a cup of mead to her lips. He was laughing as she made a face...too sweet! It was Richard's first chance to taste overwhelming jealousy. Never before had he cared whom Dagr loved or bedded. But now, faced with such a blatant look at how empty his life would be without Brigida, he fought feelings of desperation.

Before, when they had shared a woman, it had been by mutual consent. Now, he neither consented to nor relished the sight. Dagr's look spoke of ownership. It was painfully obvious that whatever moments he had left with Brigida would be shared with a man he loved but wished in the moment to be somewhere else. He had not forgotten what a tall and broad man Dagr was, but against the backdrop of the tiny hut, he seemed more so. Other men of that stature looked boorish but Dagr had a grace that softened him - accentuated his handsome features. If Richard had not personally seen him in battle, he would not believe that the softness he saw now in Dagr's eyes could turn to steel. Ah, but he would never get over his attraction to the fair haired knight, no matter what complications life threw at them.

He hung his cloak on the hook by the door and waited to be invited further. For the life of him, Richard could not find his equilibrium in this situation. Dagr looked up, his eyes merry. The joy of these precious moments with Brigida momentarily erased the gravity of the evening.

"Supper is laid, my lord." Arinn came forward and extended her hand. Richard took it, and allowed himself to be led to the table. She sat him next to Dagr's place. She had every intention of keeping Brigida by her side and the men opposite them where she could observe their energy.

"Sit, my lady," Dagr insisted, as Arinn stood waiting.

"Shall I not serve, my lord?" Arinn asked. She would never get used to his unconventional habits.

"Allow me."

Arinn sat and folded her hands in her lap. Brigida reached over and took one of them in hers. They smiled at each other, a tenuous attempt at comfort. The hut was too small for men like these. They took all the space with their warrior's bodies and intense love. Too much love. Too many questions.

Dagr poured the mead, and proposed a toast. "To friendship and a peaceful life," he said. They drank, Richard downing his in one gulp.

He watched Dagr serve with the manners that came so naturally to him. The women first, bending over them, his smile freely given. Arinn touched his arm gently, reassuring him of her love. It was obvious that they were in tune with each other. Where one ended the other started. Daring to look Brigida in the eye, he found her watching him intently. She could not speak, but her body screamed for his touch and her eyes begged his forgiveness. Confused, in love with two men, Brigida was the victim of life's follies and the whims of the powerful. Two great tears followed the curves of her face. Both men's hearts wrenched with sorrow at her pain.

Somehow, they managed to eat, making small talk and laughing at Arinn's voracious appetite. It did Dagr good to see her enjoy the meal. There had not been much to cheer their table these last months. Richard spoke of the inevitable first.

"Have you thought about where you might live? This forest can't hide you forever."

Brigida looked up sharply. It did not take one with the Sight to understand her sudden anxiety. Moving would mean leaving Richard for good. She motioned for more mead. Dagr obliged. Arinn nodded her consent for more as well.

"Not now, Richard," Dagr sighed, tired of having to think about how hard life was now.

Richard irritated, stood and began to pace.

"Surely you have talked about this before? It must be on all your minds."

"We have not. I...we...we were waiting for Brigida."

Brigida's shoulders shook with her tears.

Arinn took her gently in her arms.

"And now? Would you stay? It is dangerous, you know that. And this has only been possible while I was bringing supplies."

Dagr nodded. "I know. I thought of France."

"France? You are well known, and they have their own problems with heretics."

"You mean, their intolerances."

"You know my meaning, Dagr."

"Southern France then. I am hardly known there. Life would be easier. The weather is amiable."

"Forget it. With two wives? Even there, you have been feted by a few too many nobles," Richard produced a pouch of herb.

"May I speak, my lord?" Arinn put in, facing Dagr.

"You do not need my permission to speak, my lady," Dagr took the bowl of herb offered by Richard.

Arinn nodded. "You are fluent in French, my lord. In the south, we could make a small home, Brigida and I could grow much of our own food. You could hunt, as you do now, for game. I am tired of being cold and hungry."

This last statement hit its mark. Dagr's fist hit the table, upsetting everything on it.

"Have I not worked night and day to keep us as comfortable as possible? Did you not hear what Richard said? The French are not known for their tall, fair haired warriors. We will be an oddity from the start."

"I did hear, and still, I am tired of being hungry. This country does not want us. I am tired to the bone of being afraid. There must be a corner of that land where we can live in peace!" She stood now, a fiery wisp of a girl, unrelenting.

"And who shall we say Brigida is? Hmm? Should we put her in danger again?"

"Your wife? I could be Brigida's maid."

Richard almost choked on his herb. Dagr stared at Arinn.

"Pardon me, my lady, do you mean to say...?"

Arinn looked to Richard for help. He sat upright, his mind working, a glimmer of hope in his eyes.

"Yes. Does it matter now who is who? You are no longer a knight. Perhaps you could arrive as an obscure noble, and we could continue as we did before, one of us the lady's maid...I could serve Brigida easily."

Brigida shook her head. Richard took his chance to pull her into his embrace and held her as she desperately tried to make her thoughts known. All she could do was shake her finger in disagreement. She could never take on a position that she was neither born nor married into!

"This may be a good idea after all, Dagr," Richard said, his body relishing the feel of Brigida against him at last. She had curled into his warmth, giving up on being part of the conversation. "I can provide you with a hefty purse. Enough to buy a small chateau, some land. We can come up with an identity...perhaps this plan is not so outlandish after all."

Dagr looked at how Richard held Brigida, fierceness and tenderness wrapped into one. How could he separate them? He had never seen Richard in love before. It suited him...very well. Brigida was comfortable in the arms that once had known no allegiance to any woman.

"I suppose...some place by the sea. There was one village that I remember well. In the hills above the water. Good hunting and fishing. I would have to find a way to make a living. I will not have you supporting me for the rest of my life."

Richard spoke softly. "I would. You have earned that and much more."

"I know you would. But I could not," Dagr sat down and invited Arinn into his arms. "A lady's maid, my love? Your kindness is greater than even your beauty."

"It would be my honor," Arinn's eyes misted as Brigida signed her love. She looked pointedly at Richard. "You would find us safe passage, my lord?"

Richard bowed to Arinn's request. "I will find safe passage. You have my word."

Dagr and he exchanged knowing glances. Safe passage on horseback from the Oracle Wood to the sea would be near to impossible to arrange and take days and days of riding. Fresh horses would have to be found along the way. After that, an anonymous sail to Calais even more difficult. There was no one Richard could trust as an ally, and Dagr was not easily disguised. Richard knew that he could not join them for the trip. There would be no way to explain leaving for such a length of time without escort. He sighed. Later. He would think of it later.

They passed the herb, silently smoking and drinking the last of the mead. Arinn's eyes glowed brightly from the wine. But it was more than that. It was also seeing Brigida in Richard's arms, imagining this dark force of a man exacting what he needed from her beloved. The sexual tension in the room had risen dramatically as they all fell into the magic of the herb. There was no hiding the perk of her nipples through her worn kirtle, nor Dagr's notice of Richard's attention to them.

She could tell that Brigida felt it too, her cheeks flushed, eyes wide if hollowed...Arinn wondered if she had the strength to say goodbye to someone she clearly loved.

She felt wicked and strangely driven to pushing the limits of Dagr's love for her. The light was soft, the hut warm from the fire and their breath. Dagr had cleared the board, and rearranged the benches around the hearth. Richard's shirt was open at the neck, shirt sleeves rolled up to the elbow, revealing strong forearms and olive skin. The candle had long since burned away, so the only light in the room was cast by the fire. Dagr had never let her smoke as much as she had to-day. Spirits danced in the flames and whispers from the Underworld took her deeper into a frenzied desire. She sat on the floor, trying to ground herself, afraid of the feelings taking over her good senses.

Brigida slipped away from Richard, warm and full, and sat down beside her.

"What is happening?" she asked telepathically, hoping that Arinn would understand. Her time with Hannah had not been only a lesson in herbalism, she had been privy to the teachings of Dagr's mystic mother, as left in hidden notebooks behind a loose stone in the still room wall.

Arinn melted to Brigida's touch. "I wish we were lying in the long grass, like we used to before. I am being taken by the wicked spirits...I want you," she whispered into Brigida's ear.

Oblivious to Dagr's and Richard's stares, neither of whom dared move a muscle, Arinn turned into her lovers kiss.

CHAPTER 37

"Are you ready to see me yet?"

This was the third time that Iona had typed and then erased her text message to Richard.

She wanted to see him. Desperately. She wanted his touch, his smell, his voice. But he had remained aloof and cool, and barely responded to her attempts at contact. It wasn't like him. He was mannered like the Earl he had once been.

She paced her apartment. She *had* to see him.

Over the last three days she had journeyed to the Underworld and listened without surprise as the Aspen King laid out her new duties under Aiden's leadership of the Earth Builders.

The time had come and she was glad of it. She had no resentment at handing over her position. The group worked as one and although she was a natural leader and the most gifted alchemist of them all, she was ready to be guided by the one who had been talked of for so long.

But she couldn't find peace about the only problem with Aiden's succession, no matter how distracting the parties at the Fey court. Of course she was beloved, and the King spared no effort at entertaining her. His love of Iona was as real as the centuries that had passed since they had first met. She was one of them.

Iona had lingered at the feet of the Fairy Queen, playing with the children that followed her with awe, "*Mother, isn't she beautiful?*" they asked.

She was tender, the Queen, with great compassion in her eyes for the tortured Iona.

"I cannot bear to speak of it. It is unforgivable."

"Nothing is unforgivable." The Queen gently played with Iona's hair, where she sat with her head in the Queen's lap. "My dear, he understands the way of the Fey, and when you explain it, he will find room in his heart for you. Everything was arranged as a learning. Remember, he made his choices too."

"But when I explained it to him before, he didn't understand. He said he never would..."

"You are not his anymore," the Queen answered. "He has no reason to hold this against you. What is done is done."

Iona burst into bitter tears. "And cannot be undone. I shall pay for it forever."

"Are you not reunited with Richard? I think that out of the two of them, Richard is the man whom you are most suited to. You must let the idea of Aiden go. What is left of you and Dagr must stay in the past. Build what you have. Let go of the rest."

"But that is just it! Richard has already wondered at our connection...and Sahara as well. To explain it to them is to tell them what happened. I can't bear it. They will hate me. We had such perfect love. And now, I can never be part of that circle."

"Go home and face your path Iona. If anyone is allowed a peak into their past lives, it is to learn, and to let go. To live each life fully one must be willing to abandon all that went on before. You know that it is only in your world that time has any meaning. Here, we understand that what has happened and will happen is all part of the present moment. It's all happening at once, and to not learn from it is madness. Find your center, Iona! You are capable of so much. Try, my darling, to forgive yourself."

"How? I do not know how."

"Decide," the Queen sighed and moved Iona away gently. "Just decide."

"Will I know love like that again?"

"It is not for me to say."

Iona looked deep into the Fairy Queen's eyes. There was nothing but tenderness there. Once, she had been a distraction for the Aspen King, one that the Fairy Queen had chosen to understand. Choice. Was that it? One had to simply choose their state of mind and heart? Did she suffer because she refused to forgive herself? Of course, she knew it was true. Forgiving oneself meant discarding who one knew themselves to be, and facing the unknown.

If Aiden and Sahara wanted to, they could discover things for themselves. Iona was no longer the only awoken one. They didn't need her to travel back in time, remember their whole life together. But she wanted to be the one to tell. She needed to be the one to tell.

The vibration of her phone startled Iona as she sat daydreaming of that meeting with the Queen. Richard!

She stared at it, not understanding. *Aiden?* Not Richard. What was happening? She felt herself moved by a familiar emotion. A remembrance. Dagr's insistent voice as he stared into her eyes and demanded an explanation.

Hello Iona, it's Aiden. Sahara shared your number. I'd like to meet. Just the two of us.

She sat for a long time just looking at his words and running her

193

fingers over the face of her phone; touching his energy.

Finally, slowly, her fingers moved across the buttons.

Hello Aiden. Of course. She sent it.

Calm down! Calm down! Heart jumping somersaults in her chest, she typed again. *Denver or...? I can meet any day after 10 a.m. except Wednesday.*

I will come to you. Tuesday. Would you be comfortable with dinner?

She would make herself comfortable with whatever he wanted. Her fingers itched to write, *It's been so long. Hello, my love.* Instead, she wrote, *Yes. Where?*

At Le Poireau Ivre. Seven. I'll meet you in the lounge.

The Tipsy Leek. French. Of course. The stab of pain was expected. She wondered if he did it on purpose, or if he remembered yet? No matter. It was a bitter memory - her medicine to swallow.

I'll see you then.

They would meet somewhere where the atmosphere was quiet, reserved. Theatrics would be out of place. He'd chosen excellent cuisine, a dimly lit room, a renowned wine cellar. If she didn't know better, she would think it romantic. But she was certain he had chosen it because all the elements would keep her subdued and introspective, remind her of the manor home they had once shared. He knew her well, which meant that he remembered more than a little of their relationship.

Although she had waited six hundred years to sit at a table with him again, to feel his warrior's heart, she now thought that it had happened somewhat suddenly. One moment she was bleeding desire to hear his voice say her name, and the next his invitation sent shivers of apprehension up her spine.

They would have to work together, for as long as this lifetime would host them, but that was different. That work was sacred and secret. They were bound to it by old instincts. Dinner, however, was not about the magic that they would weave together, but about personal expectations.

What did he want from her? Apologies? She had made a hundred of those, in this life, the last and all the lives in between. Did he want to state his boundaries...yes, that must be it.

She'd have to tell Richard. She picked up her phone again.

I know you're not ready. But I have to speak with you. Please. The last word came with difficulty. She was not used to begging men for a place in their day.

I already know. Richard's text was immediate. *He asked me first. Always the gentleman, your Aiden.*

Iona bristled against the tone of the message. But she chose to stay civil. This was not the time to antagonise an already pissed off lover.

I'm sorry.

Please don't do that. You're not. You're sorry that I took it badly. I can take care of myself, but it was your decision to leave me vulnerable that I resent.

She felt the first crack in his resolve to punish her. *Come over?* She wouldn't add insult to injury by pretending he was wrong. It made her hot...his anger. Her phone rang.

"I want to go back in time Iona. Tonight. I have a question."

Savoring the sound of his throaty command, she agreed. "Ok. Do you want to eat first? Can you come now?" Breaking bread was, traditionally, a way they made peace after a disagreement.

"No. I have work at the gallery. I'll come later."

They were silent for a moment, each of them anxious to move past this barrier and be on solid ground again.

"I don't know how to stay angry with you. I should know better and love someone I understand."

"But you don't. You love me. We're not that different, Richard."

"We are. I'm not calculating to your detriment," he snapped.

"Let me explain, make it up to you?" Iona shifted in her chair. He remained silent. "Talk to me."

"I like him. He's familiar...elegant. He reminds me of things I didn't know I craved...a life that still resonates deeply," Richard sighed. "I keep thinking that I should be wary of him - because you love him. But I'm not. He's too excellent to resent. It's you I'm wary of."

Such honesty! It felled her.

"I understand," her voice, smooth as silk, beckoned his forgiveness. "We can work through this. What do you need from me?"

Richard's darkness came forth like an errant wave. "I need to understand why you decided to leave me unprepared for my meeting with Aiden. What purpose did it have? And I know that you let me experience him the last time we made love. I felt him. That was *your* doing."

"I will. I want to tell you everything. I need to touch you, please Richard." Iona's weakness for his hands almost drowned her in desire.

"Iona?"

"Yes, my love."

"I want to see you and him in the past. To help me understand what you're feeling. You owe me that much."

CHAPTER 38

I was always known as the mysterious one, and my mysteries
were woven and intertwined into the fabric of time.
I was serious, undefeated and brave.
This was a burdensome blessing as I was destined to be alone
with those gifts.
But I always wore those gifts ruthlessly and without apology
Nausicaa Twila

Night closed in on their unconventional circumstances. The Oracle Wood wasn't a place for wandering in the dark. They were sequestered without escape. Richard suspected that this night would color the rest of his life. A man of influence and might, he had to accept that the events unfolding before him were entirely out of his control.

Brigida would either be his one more time or she wouldn't. All he could count on was the desire that swept through him as Arinn and Brigida continued to kiss. He was experienced in all kinds of love play, and two women in his bed was nothing new. Sharing two women with Dagr was nothing new either. But he had never been in love before - save for with the man who stood at his side - staying any movement on his part with his hand, and he had never had to ask permission to join in. All of a sudden he faced sharing someone he adored, not someone who was there at his command.

Dagr was watching him closely. Curious. Richard wondered if this was in a way some kind of punishment. He looked him in the eye, resolute, in no position to make any demands.

What he saw in Dagr's look was nothing short of demonic. Behind that, compassion. Behind that...lust. He gritted his teeth.

The fire burned fragrantly with the wild apple branches that Dagr had thrown on. In the close quarters of the room, there was no escape from the heat. Arinn had laid Brigida in their bed, and with a consummate passion, left their kissing to slide her hands along Brigida's legs. Richard's breath caught. He was strangled with anticipation. He had taught Brigida what made him lose control, and she had had a chance to teach him about her needs too. Seeing her in the arms of Arinn brought out the voyeur in him. He would have many nights to remember this. Too many nights to remember this. And while he ached to watch, he felt the agony of knowing that it would be this one

197

time, and then forever...nothing.

Brigida, my love, my heart. The murderous look on his face, brought on by the pain he felt twisting in his chest should have caused Arinn alarm as she glanced his way, but instead, it gave her courage.

Without shame or even a look towards Dagr, she slipped off her kirtle. Richard could not help a low growl at the sight of her taut nipples, shrouded somewhat by her waist-length hair, yet protruding long and maiden pink. Her slender form awoke a rampant need to see more of that perfectly rounded bottom. His mouth watered and he licked his lips.

Naked, and helping Brigida slip off her clothes, Arinn led them all into deliberate sin. Was it the wind or a wicked spirit that stirred the flames in the hearth and howled its way out the chimney? Brigida kept her focus on the tender hands that exposed her neck to love bites, to lips that suckled her breasts, on the words that Arinn conveyed telepathically.

Do not be afraid. Let me...

I am not strong enough. He is not strong enough...this will break his heart

Brigida writhed under Arinn's weight, legs wrapped around her hips, holding on, holding on.

This is the only way, if you want us still. You must let Richard go.

I cannot. I know that I must.

Brigida hoped that strength would be hers. Her body, still healing, betrayed her. It wanted what it wanted, and she was powerless against it. Unfolding to it, Brigida called on the spirits that guided her and asked for endurance.

They found their pleasure in the way they had done when their love was new, eyes closed; legs scissored, rubbing rhythmically.

Arinn moaned out her orgasm. Maneuvering Brigida gently to the edge of the bed, she got on her knees before her.

Your turn, sweeting. No, do not be shy. Let him see. Let them see how much I love you.

Brigida lay back, her face flushed with color as Arinn spread her open and blew warm breath on her sex.

The first kiss met her just above her pubic bone and lingered on the soft flesh at the top of her legs. Then lower, deeper, where sex meets thighs, muscular from riding and wandering the hills. She arched her back as Arinn's tongue found her clit and tried to push her face away, close her legs. This was too much, more than she could bear...the emotions...Richards' rising energy. Oh yes, she could feel him from across the room, the lover who had taught her about what wild men want.

But Arinn insisted, her lips clasped around Brigida's clit, sucking, pulling, one finger inside the tight wetness of her pussy.

How she wished that she could talk, voice her needs like Richard had instructed her. She needed the words! But thoughts became jumbled as Arinn pushed her fingers inside her, thrusting, all of them in now, hand working its way in. She looked up and stared wickedly at the two impossibly gorgeous men scant feet away from her. Their lust only made her feel more like the wanton wench Richard had awoken in her. She spread a little wider and encouraged Arinn to keep going by thrusting her hips. Arinn's tiny hand slipped in and she pushed instinctively on that most sensitive spot. Brigida reached her hand to her clit and rubbed vigorously. Her voice echoed as she found her release, Arinn's arm soaked.

Dagr kept his hand on Richard's arm, waiting for a signal from Brigida that she was ready. Richard had stripped his shirt and Dagr had not missed Arinn's appreciative glances. Both men feasted on the eroticism before them, and to their surprise, had learned a thing or two about how women played.

Arinn held her hand out. "Come, my lord," her eyes pointed at Richard. Dagr sucked his breath in, chest tight, almost unable to bear the thought of what Arinn might mean. Richard, with one quick, searching glance at Dagr, went to her. All was fair in love and war, it seemed.

She stood on tiptoe and sniffed through his raven hair, holding his hands in hers. He smelled different than Dagr. The fierceness in his eye was almost enough to fill her with fear but she held strong. She wanted to know what Brigida knew...how he felt to the senses - his hands like iron, his skin tanned dark, his eyes impenetrable. He felt like the magic she experimented with when Dagr was not looking.

She lifted her lips to his, and allowed herself a brush against them, never letting her gaze wander toward Dagr. She knew that he was furious and that it would mean the fucking she desired. Had he really thought that she would not want a taste of the forbidden?

Her hand slipped down to Richard's leathers and ever so softly she cradled his manhood, closing her eyes. His energy was overwhelming, a dark cloud on the horizon of her lust.

"My lord," she whispered in his ear. "Might you prepare me for Dagr, in the way you taught Brigida to obey?"

He bent over her hand, lips barely touching skin, then turned her around. Dagr stepped a little closer, hands clenched in fists, leathers straining.

Touching her shoulder lightly, sliding his hand along her inner arm, he tugged on her hair. She lifted her head higher, breath suspended.

"Stand with your feet a little further apart. Wider. There." He crouched and drifted his hand along the inside of her leg, stopping just short of her sex. She could feel his breath warm on her bottom. Her knees buckled and she gave a whimper.

"Shhhh."

One hand slipped to the front of her body and he cupped her breast. She ached for him to fondle her nipple, pull it. But his hand left her and she found herself dripping down her legs.

"I can smell you...your sweet fragrance. He picked up some of her wet on his fingers and tasted, then slipped out of his leathers and stood naked behind her, a towering demon. She slipped to her knees, wanting to serve him but he yanked her up by her hair, hand on her throat.

"Not without my permission, my lady." But he turned her around to face him, and placed her hands behind her back. Pushing her hair aside he exposed her breasts and those tight, tempting nipples. He slid to his knees.

"Tell me, do you fuck like a lady or a whore?"

Arinn looked him in the eye, bold, taunting.

"Like a whore my lord."

Her left nipple disappeared in his fingers and he twirled it gently, his smile dangerous.

"And do you serve on your knees like a lady or a whore?"

"Like a whore, my lord."

Richard kissed along the underside of her breast. Finally, tortuous moments later, his mouth found her nipples and he sucked hard. His lips travelled toward her belly. She shook as he stopped at her cleft. Standing suddenly, he led her to the bed, and thrust her across his knees. In that moment he noticed Brigida in Dagr's arms, her legs wrapped around his waist. He was kissing her, chest bared as she clung to his shoulders.

For a moment, Richard felt the urge to rip them apart. She had looked at him like that, starkly hungry for his love. But then he remembered that she was stolen and had never truly belonged to him. He watched them, Dagr's beautiful body straining, Brigida crying.

Arinn stirred in his lap. He looked down at the delicious curve of her ass and began to caress her back with care. She lay with her hands still clasped behind her back. He noticed that her knuckles were white with anticipation. She tried raising her hips, to urge him on. Although he wanted to badly, he refrained from striking her. Tenderness was always a great aphrodisiac. He wanted to anoint her with oil, the way he had Brigida on so many nights in his chamber. To rub fragrant oils into her skin and work the knots from her shoulders and back. He wished that they were in the comfort of his bed, on piles of linens and furs, so he could tie her hands then torture her with hours of pain dipped pleasure. If only he could erase the shadows of the hardships she had endured living in the woods. Because Dagr loved her, he loved her also, and because her eyes were filled with ancient wisdom. He could tell that she wove magic like Dagr did. She smelled of it, and of a sexual hunger that he recognized well.

"I want you on your hands and knees. Here, on the bed. Face away from me."

"Yes, my lord."

She complied, curious at her own eagerness to show him everything. She hoped that he would take his time to explore.

She arched her back, opening. He was on his knees again, face close, pulling her right to the edge of the bed, so that he could access her easily. She was pink, her coloring different than Brigida's, lips furling like a lily, clit swollen, and dripping wet.

"Reach back and spread open for me."

Her fingers teased along shamelessly, allowing him full view.

"More."

She showed him more. Spreading her bottom, hearing the rumble in his chest, pulling on her clit, her lips. Still he did not touch her and she was dying for his hands. Did he want her to ask for it?

"Will you punish me my lord?" she chanced the question.

"For what, my lady? Do tell."

"For my dripping cunt. For wanting what I felt in your leathers. For wanting your tongue deep inside me."

She trembled, imagining Dagr's reaction, but she wanted to bring him to an unrelenting desire. Because she had already become addicted to the warrior. Some part of her needed to experience his brutality. She did not understand why, but she needed it. It had started the day of the massacre. Dagr's darkness was her drug. And Richard was just the man to evoke Dagr's rage.

Richard growled. She was the first woman who had not needed to be instructed into whoredom, who knew how to ask for the sharp sting of a hand on her ass. He would acquiesce. But first, he would taste her. He closed his eyes as his tongue found her. He was rough, demanding, unashamed as he probed every inch of her. Her tenderness and willingness was, as he imagined, Dagr's opium. A few sharp swats on her bottom brought moans of pleasure. She bucked against him, begging for more. But he left her, shaking, her legs slick from her juices, and pulled Brigida from Dagr's arms.

Brigida yelped at his roughness and searched Dagr's eyes, whose love spilled overwhelming and complete. She turned into Richard's kiss.

Dagr went to Arinn, and kissing her back, whispered along her skin. "If we sin, we sin all together."

"I do not believe in sin," she bit back, panting now.

"I do not care what you believe," his fingers found her swollen clit.

"Please, my lord, please."

His hand closed on her throat. "Hand or whip?"

"I hate when you make me choose."

"I do not think so, your cunt is dripping wet," Dagr's hoarse voice grated.

"I want Richard's whip, in your hand."

"Would that please you? To have me take another man's whip to your hide?"

She turned to look at him and was shocked at the blatant pain in his eyes. "Just this once, my lord. I want to feel what Brigida felt. His whip. Do you understand?"

He nodded. Richard had Brigida in his lap, on the bench by the fire, as she sat impaled upon him, hips undulating. Dagr had to admit it. They were stunning together. Richard turned his way, that familiar question in his eyes. Maybe this once, he would grant him that one unanswered request. Because his lust was raging despite his agony, because Arinn watched him with baited breath, because Brigida was tensing into orgasm, he crossed the room and taking a fistful of Richard's hair in his hand, he kissed him, a long and decadent kiss that saw Richard explode deep inside his lover.

Dagr picked up Richard's whip hanging by the door. Arinn presented. He would have her, submitted to his will, ass lightly blushed by the whip, cunt swollen and ready for his cock.

Although she begged for more, he had not the heart to hurt her. He teased her with a light touch of the whip, and the end of it brushing her opening. She was his, and his she would remain. Poignantly aware of Richard's and Brigida's quiet observation of them, as they sat in a tight embrace, Dagr took Arinn with the skill he had honed on many before her. Every breath and every kiss spoke of his love. Every kiss of her breasts and every tease of his mouth on her nipples was to seal her to him forever. He doted on all the tender places; where her hairline met her neck, where her breasts met her flank, where her hips met her thighs, behind her knees, and teasing her clit with an experienced tongue.

She moaned and molded herself to his hands, opening to his manhood when he pressed into her; she looked like a child next to him, but she loved him like a woman and provided everything he asked for. He understood her body as much as he understood her soul. She luxuriated at the opportunity to be salacious under Richard's gaze. And Dagr gave her that, this one chance to act out her desires. She was completely awoken to her sexuality, unashamed and relishing Richard's stare.

She clung to Dagr as he held her aloft in his arms and fucked her hard. Her teeth bit into his neck, his hands on her ass, legs wrapped around him. She came down his legs, uttering ancient words, a witch awoken.

Fervently, she kissed him, arms circling his neck.

"I love you. I love you. My lord! Thank you."

He could not tear his eyes away from her, sparkling under her newly found sexual openness. She was in her fullness.

"For what do you thank me, my lady?" Dagr cradled her against his heart, a satisfied smile on his face.

"For this," she shook her head, not even understanding it herself. Her awakening was profound. In Dagr's arms she had been safe to act as wild as she wanted to. There was no need to question her authority over her own body, to not answer the call of her lust. Here she was as free as any man had ever been to admit that the body wanted what it wanted, and that it was not shameful.

Dagr knew that she would never be the same again, the shy, quiet girl whom he had gently broken into loving a man's touch. She would never again wonder about her power over him or anyone else for that matter. She had found her inner guidance. Her magic would be stronger now, because she was free and wild and uninhibited.

"Is there anything else I can give you, my lady?" He knew her. She was still vibrating with need. He was sure he would regret it, but he could not help himself.

Richard sat spellbound as Arinn supplicated on the floor before Dagr, in complete submission. Brigida had spent many an hour in this pose before him...waiting.

"I would serve Lord Dumont, on my knees, if he so desires," Arinn said. She waited quietly, Dagr's breath uneven. She had no need of asking Brigida, they were one, in desire and thought.

"As you wish, my lady," Dagr whispered, hardly aware of anything around him. She shook him to the core, this irreverent witch. They would be leaving, anyway, so this one time he could be generous. Dagr knew how addictive Richard could be to a woman of fire.

She rose to her knees, and beckoned Brigida, making room on the fur that lined the floor underneath her.

Richard, exchanging a meaningful look with his knight, grasped the immensity of Dagr and Arinn's love.

It was beyond any physical connection, even any emotional connection. He had never seen such devotion or totality of passion. For as long as he lived he would not forget the feel of Dagr's mouth on his, or regret revealing his weakness for him. He would also never forget his debt to the woman who called Dagr her own...if there was any chance of Dagr hurting her with that kiss, he would not have done it. Richard knew that. Arinn's trust in their love had paved the way.

He saw that Dagr touched her with reverence even when he was being rough. His hands begged her compliance and his body elicited ecstatic responses, but his mind and emotions focused on her connection to him. She melted to his mouth and hands with complete trust and devotion to his pleasure. Perhaps out of their loneliness for other people these last two years, they had found such intimate bliss, but it was more than that. Richard knew the measure and depth of Dagr's honor, generosity, chivalry and courtesy - all the parts of what made him an exemplary knight- permeated his love.

The two women on their knees before him lowered their eyes. Dagr knelt behind them, and bound their hands gently with rope. Richard's stare burned hot. They had not done this for a long while, and certainly not with women that they loved. Dagr would remain behind them, his fingers at their service as they pleased the dashing Earl with their mouths.

Take care, my friend. Dagr's eyes spoke clearly as they swept along Richard's long and sculpted core, where he knew Brigida had worshipped. *We will do this, but it is me you must obey this time. They're mine.*

Richard, consumed by a furious passion, laid a deceivingly gentle hand on Arinn's golden head. *Oh to be under the command of his favored knight when war stained his eyes!*

<hr/>

All she could see in the dark of the room was the shadow of him in his chair by the fire, and the glow of the joint when he inhaled. He had been silent for a long time.

She knelt at his feet, her long kimono open, naked underneath.

"Richard?" He held out his hand and she curled up in his lap.

"One question keeps rolling through my head, over and over." He offered her a drag.

"What is it?" She took a little, tensing when he slipped his hand inside the silk robe towards her belly. It had been a long night of regressing and she was wrung out from waiting for his touch. She had made herself half-crazy thinking he would never do it again.

"How I can compete with that kind of love? He didn't just love you, erm...her, he possessed her in every way possible. No wonder you can't forget," he scowled.

"It's not a competition," she purred, as his hand slipped lower, insistent. She spread her legs a little and laid her head against his chest.

"I know how you love me, and it's your love that will sustain me for a lifetime. But you can understand how that kind of thing doesn't disappear, no matter how much time goes by? I can't help loving him...but I know that it hurts you, darling." She wondered if he saw the irony of it all. He offered absolutely no apology for having feelings for Sahara.

"Which brings me to the next question," he rasped out, as his fingers found her wetness.

She had been afraid of that. One day, the question would surface and she would have to explain.

"If you and I had that one night to connect; if Richard had one chance to taste Arinn, why have we always talked about a lifetime together? Somehow, I felt that I had loved you for years, and you've never said otherwise. In fact, I *know* that it was a lifetime. I feel it." His curious eyes held her prisoner while his fingers tapped relentlessly against her clit. "Was there a lifetime in between?"

"Don't, please," Iona slid to the floor and he covered her, his hot, dangerous, hard body against her softness; leaving no room for lies. "In time, when it's time, the four of us will find our way back, and everything will make sense. But for now, please trust me."

He spread her legs with his knees, his breath against her ear. He meant to own her, his muscled, tattooed body such a delicious tease.

"I'm finished with trusting you, Iona." He thrust inside her, as she raised her hips towards him. She closed her eyes, listening to the rhythm of his movements. He filled her without compromise, all his attention on her ecstasy. "I think it's time we all got together. I *will* know what secrets you've been keeping!"

She opened her eyes. "Harder, my lord."

"I need you, Iona. To be mine." His hand closed on her throat.

"And her...do you still need her?"

"I do. Somehow, she's never left me. I'm sorry." He repositioned, pushing her legs up over her head, opening her indecently to his gaze. She blushed, and caught the look of surprise in his eyes. And then he understood. "You're thinking of him." His thumbs opened her, he slipped down, his mouth hovering over her clit.

"If it takes a lifetime, I'm going to make you forget," he whispered as his tongue took its first delicate swipe.

She moaned. "Make me forget, Richard. Please, make me forget!"

CHAPTER 39

Sahara sat with Aiden's list in her lap. He'd left this morning for work, and at her request, handed over the plans for his office renovation.

She loved his handwriting. It had captured her from the first time she'd seen it, on the note he'd left on her cabin door the day she'd moved in. It said a lot about his personality. Smooth, elegant, and decidedly masculine. She ran her fingers over the paper. His energy lingered still.

Pick up permits at town office.

Call Sam and arrange to drop off plans/paint chips/permits

Choose furniture, bathroom fixtures/lighting (have fun!)

Call staffing agency for names of applicants - I can do interviews next week

Love you, thank you...this helps a lot. Take care of each other.

He'd insisted on hiring her as his assistant. She had said she didn't need the money. She'd do it for fun and for love. But he had it his way in the end, explaining that it was a lot of work taken off his plate and he wasn't going to take advantage of her love.

She knew that handing over the design aspect made him crazy. He liked creating inviting spaces. But since time was of the essence, he had had no choice. Opening her laptop, she clicked on her favorite home décor store. He'd allowed a generous budget but said that she had to stick to it. She planned on surprising him with some savvy shopping. Considering that he was also going to add on to his house and pay for the café renos, she wanted to be careful with his money.

Holly would be coming over early afternoon. Sahara had a platter of appetizers ready, and Prosecco chilling in the pantry. They'd have all the rest of the day and night to enjoy each other's company and talk over Holly's vision for the café. So much change to come before Winter Solstice, Sahara's favorite Pagan holiday.

Holly had messaged her early this morning, as soon as she had set the bread to proof.

Aiden's going to take a look at cars for me this week - then we're going to Denver to get one. Do you think we should stop by Iona's store and meet her, or would you like to have her over, so we can all be together? I haven't asked Aiden yet what he wants

There was no mistaking Holly's nervousness. She wasn't sure of the protocol. After all, this was no ordinary meeting. Iona represented so much in their lives.

Immediately after, Sahara had messaged Aiden.

Are you looking at cars in Denver this week?

He answered honestly, understanding her meaning. *Yes. I've asked Iona to meet with me. I need to test the water, as it were. I just can't imagine meeting her for the first time in a group setting. There are too many variables. You can trust me*

What does that mean? She shot back without taking a moment to think.

It means that you can trust me. Don't read anything into it. I've spoken to Richard. But not to Holly. I will though.

Before or after?

I haven't decided. I want to do it before, but I'm worried that she'll be anxious

She trusts you. Wholeheartedly

I know, Sahara. She sensed that he was becoming annoyed. It killed him to not be forthright. *But she's said on a few occasions how beautiful Iona is, and I think it makes her feel vulnerable*

Sahara sent a heart emoji. *I'm sorry, I don't need to interrogate you. I guess I'm feeling vulnerable too. Iona is more than beautiful. You'll see. She has a power that is hard to resist*

You know who I am

I know

And they'd left it at that. But Sahara had her doubts, based mainly on the fact that she hadn't been trustworthy when she'd met Richard.

———————✵———————

"Do you know that my apprentice is coming next week?" Holly took another bite of the fried halloumi. "This is the best cheese, ever! We're going to get fat eating like this."

"Nobody who has as much sex as we do gets fat," Sahara quipped. "And thank goodness he's coming, I have no idea how you managed Thanksgiving and Christmas without one last year."

"It was hell, to be honest. I was in tears every night. But with you and him, it'll be ok. He's already apprenticed with a bread maker, so I won't have much training to do there. And you've become so good at the pastries, I'll be sad when you have to go away on book things." Holly leaned over to kiss Sahara. "Mmmm. You taste like my favorite olives."

208

"Does he speak English, your boy?"

"Why do you and Aiden call him 'my boy'?

"Just teasin', sweetie. More Prosecco?"

Holly nodded, looking around the cabin.

"Every time I come here, this place looks more and more witchy. It's so cozy and I love your altar. It's like a cave or hobbit's house. A magical nest. I feel so at peace here."

They moved to sit by the fire.

"I'm looking forward to Solstice. It's the best holiday. I love the colors, the smells, the rituals, the decorations. Will you help me get ready?" Sahara snuggled into Holly's arms.

"Of course. As long as you teach me about the meanings of your work, and let me be part of your magic? I'm so curious about it all." She began to play with Sahara's hair. "Sweetie?"

"Yes?"

"When you and Iona and Aiden do your work, the things that Aiden told me about, do you actually meet or is it all done in the spirit realm?" Her fingers pulled and teased with loving care.

Sahara sat up and looked at her.

"What are you worried about? Tell me."

Holly blushed, embarrassed at her fears.

"I'm worried that the three of you will remember what it was like to be together before and..."

"And that we'll forget you and start our own love affair?"

Holly nodded.

"There will be times when we'll have to get together, but mostly we work remotely, in meditation or astral travel. Once a year we travel to a secret place, and perform high magic. But sweetie, you know Aiden. He's devoted to you!"

"I know, I know. But he's such a passionate person, I wouldn't even blame him...I mean, who could resist Iona?" And then, quietly, "Can you?"

Sahara took a careful sip of her wine. Surely, truth would be easier than a festering lie?

"We're friends."

Holly accepted the vague reply, with a kiss from Sahara's perfect mouth.

<hr />

She wore velvet. A long green gown with an almost indecent neckline, allowing her breasts a tender peak at the world. A gold chain with an unpolished diamond hung between them. The sleeves tapered elegantly over her delicate hands. It made her look slimmer than she already was. Her titian hair hung free. She had slippers on, black with gold embroidery. A plaited sash wound itself possessively around her waist. Any other woman would have looked overdressed, or even costumed. But on Iona it looked simply seductive.

He'd seen her in something like this once, when she'd been his wife.

He stood when she entered the lounge of the restaurant. There was no mistaking her identity. He had imagined that he would be immune to her beauty but his throat was suddenly dry and his chest tightened with a rush of recognition. She drifted towards him, Arinn's essence clearly visible through those opaque, cat-like eyes.

They stared at each other for a few moments, caught in the potency of remembering. Aiden finally recovered his manners and taking her hand, kissed it lightly.

Seeing him bent over her hand like that took her spinning back to the day when he had professed his love for her and taken the first taste of her lips. Her eyes filled with tears. The intensity of Aiden's energy left her emotional and weak. He motioned to the comfortable leather chairs in a corner of the bar.

Iona watched as he folded himself elegantly into the chair, and crossed his long legs. The black slacks and slate, form-fitting merino wool sweater he wore draped his body perfectly, accentuating slim hips and broad shoulders. The server appeared immediately.

"What may I get you, Iona? Wine?"

"Yes please. I prefer red."

He ordered a bottle of Chilean Pinot Noir.

"It's been a long time, Aiden. A very long time."

He nodded, pensive, as the young man poured their wine. He handed her the goblet. Their hands brushed, Aiden looked up and held Iona's gaze.

"I wondered if I would remember, or if we'd be strangers. We both look different.

"You don't look much different. You're still the tall, broad, fair warrior. It's in your hands too, Dagr's strength. And your eyes. The same intensity and honor. I'd know you anywhere, in any century. I can't forget.

"But it's not the same lifetime, and we can't resume where we left off," Aiden cautioned.

"Do you remember where we left off?"

"I've been as far as when you assisted me in the time travel. Thank you. I'm in your debt for that day."

"No debt. This isn't Medieval England. What I did, I did because I...for Sahara and Holly," Iona lied. But her eyes spoke the truth. She sat up straighter, adjusting her legs, one slipper peeking seductively from underneath her dress.

Aiden made no pretense of noticing how her breasts moved with her, nipples pushing against the soft of the velvet. It was instinctual for him to want to part the neckline and liberate them. He took a drink, as did she.

"I wanted to welcome you into your work, Aiden. We've been waiting for you for a long time. I can help you...if you wish. The others will expect you to know the protocol and are eager to make your acquaintance. As far as I know, I'm the only one who remembers you from a previous lifetime."

"And Richard."

"And Richard. But he's an auxiliary member. He won't be involved in the magic work. He's with us because he has certain connections in the business world and can open doorways for those in the group who infiltrate the Illuminati. We have planted several businessmen already who although seemingly worldly, are alchemists; experts in developing sacred economies."

Aiden listened appreciatively. A smart woman...his weakness.

"I've been receiving instructions already, through Sahara and Pan. It's amazing how quickly one remembers. It's like an imprint."

He leaned in and she thought that he might touch her, but he only moved around the candle that sat between them. "But I'm not here to talk about that, Iona. I want to talk about you and me."

"Are we going to eat, Aiden?" Iona asked, stalling.

He grinned and she gripped her goblet tighter. The charm in his smile and devilish flash of white teeth was almost too much.

"Yes, we're going to eat!" He stood and offered his hand. She took it and rose, suddenly very close to him. He smelled good, like Dagr had...pine and musk. Her mouth watered.

"Hungry, my lady?" He couldn't help it. She brought out the distant century. Probably on purpose, he surmised. He didn't trust her or her magic. But he had to trust himself. That much he knew.

They shared a charcuterie board and lingered over it. Iona drank in every movement of his forearm muscles as he served her, the way he leaned back and watched her, wine in hand, and the lazy smile that she had loved for so long.

"I need you to promise me something."

Anything, my lord. Let me fall at your feet and offer my devotion. Let me be once more under your command. "What should I promise you?" Her eyes flashed.

"To stop invading my privacy. Your raven disguise doesn't fool me. I don't care what agreement you have with Sahara, if she permits it. But when I'm with Holly...you must leave us be."

She saw by the set of his jaw that he meant it. He wouldn't be trifled with. The massive surge of his energy made it impossible to do anything but agree. She lowered her eyes, and gave her promise.

Satisfied, he sat back and offered a conciliatory smile. "I don't mean to control you, but this is one thing I won't tolerate." Something nagged at the back of his mind, something that made him feel anxious, almost frightened, but he couldn't place his finger on it. Still, he knew that Holly needed his protection.

Neither of them could eat any more. Aiden's emotions were raw with resisting the sorceress; so beguiling as she caressed her wine goblet, her smile deceptively innocent. He knew that she was working her magic on him, unremorseful, shameless in her need of him.

She, in turn, almost flew out of her body in a tempestuous rage. He was strong, impenetrable. But something inside her bade her to desist...to honor his love for Holly. She had known that consummate love once.

"You love her. Very much."

"I do. Impossibly." *Like I once loved you.*

His thought showed. They shared a long, heartbreaking stare.

"Let's walk," he stood abruptly, towering over her.

"To where? It's freezing out."

"Your place. There are things we must do."

She stared up at him, surprised. He took her hand and pulled her up. "Come!"

She followed him, shaken, as he led the way out, placing her cloak around her shoulders, and handing over her soft, kid gloves. His face bore no sign of what he meant to do at her home, and he was silent as they walked. Was he aware of how her legs trembled, how his firm hand on hers created a wicked heat in her heart, how his long and purposeful stride had her almost running to keep up? She thought of Richard, and wondered what he was doing...if he was smoldering with anger or jealousy? He had allowed this meeting, and had trusted that she would keep their love promises. Oh how her heart pounded.

"Aiden, slow down please!"

"I'm sorry," he apologised, lost in thought.

"What's wrong? Why are you dragging me home?" To be honest, being dragged by him only stoked her passion. He was the warrior she remembered, focused and determined. They had arrived at her doorstep. She opened the door, almost weeping with the frantic energy that enveloped them.

"This is what's wrong." He pushed her inside the dark hallway and imprisoned her against the brick wall.

"Once." And with that his mouth took hers, hard, bruising, his tongue deliciously warm and still tasting of blood red wine. She could feel his hardness, the blatant sex that seeped from his pores, the way he held himself in check from ripping her dress apart.

She did it for him - parted her neckline and showed him.

He bit her neck and she cried out. His hands soft on her breasts, fingers punishing on her nipples. And then, he tore himself away, and walked ahead of her up the stairs.

They ended up in her kitchen, where she lit candles and incense. Aiden looked like he had just walked through the gates of hell. She noticed that his hard-on was still there, and recalled the feel of its magnitude against her. He walked into her living room, towards her altar.

"Set up your altar for ceremony," he commanded.

"What kind of ceremony?" She hoped against hope that it wasn't what she thought it would be.

"We're going to cut emotional cords," he answered, tortured.

She crumpled at his feet. "Not that! Aiden, please! I'll stay away from you, I promise."

He looked at her, sad and defeated.

"I refuse to take the chance of not being able I to stay away from you. I remember, and in time, this will destroy what I have with Holly. I will not hurt her, Iona, I won't! You and I have had our time. And it's over, forever." His eyes filled with tears. "I'm going to have a family with Holly, and I can't afford to meddle with anything that would put that in jeopardy. I love her so much."

"But we still have to work together. This will change things!"

Aiden felt sorry for the stricken look on Iona's face.

"You know as well as I that the only reason you're resisting this is because you know it will keep me from wanting you. And you don't want to let go of what we had."

"But if it was only you and Sahara? Would it be different?"

He sighed. "You can't wish Holly away, Iona. She's my life. Sahara and I are committed to her - her happiness. It's a cruel twist of fate that she resembles you so closely from before. I don't know the purpose of it, honestly."

Iona wept. "I can't do it."

He picked her up off the floor and held her, tender now.

"We must. There's no other way. Here, I'll start a fire. You prepare the altar."

"Aiden, please."

"I've already dishonored Holly and Richard tonight. It's taking all of my strength to not bed you right here and now. Please, Iona. I cannot do this for the rest of my life. I'm going to be working with you, *and* Richard. Our lives will be interwoven and you will at some point be sitting across the table from Holly. She loves you already and is loyal to you. There *is* no other way."

"You don't want this either do you? Tell me that you wish there was some way?" Iona begged.

Frustrated, he conceded. "I'll tell you this once, and it will have to last you a lifetime. Yes, I do feel love for you, I want you, I remember now. But hear this, sweet lady, Holly means more to me." The flash of pain in Iona's eyes almost felled him. He remembered too well, the power of their love and lust. "You're forcing me to say things I know will hurt you. Holly and I will be married and all of my devotion, except for what we share with Sahara, is for her. I am hers. Wholly." He stood and turned to the fireplace, silently arranging the wood.

All her strength having left her, Iona went to prepare the magic. One kiss, was all that had been granted her. But it had been exquisite, like their love once. She approached him one more time, begged his hands upon her. The fire was blazing, and the room was charged with electricity.

Although he wanted to slip his hands towards her sex, to feel the wetness he knew had gathered there, to taste her, he pushed her way with a look of unbearable need in those clear, blue eyes.

"It's time," he said.

She changed into her mystic's gown, black, with lace at her wrists. She was resplendent, covered in an undeniable power. She led them in the incantations that awoke the spirits who would guide them, tears flowing freely down her elfin face. Her fingers were adorned with garnet rings, a smoky ruby graced her neck. Aiden repeated after her, both of them slipping into the ancient language they had long ago learned. It was like no time had passed at all, the sorcerer and his witch, comfortable with the energy they raised, invoking the four directions, calling upon the Great Goddess, in soulful unison. How he had missed this!

The fire stirred high, a surging heat in the room; Aiden stripped to his waist. All the air seemed to be sucked out of the apartment, and Iona threw the windows open to a mischievous wind. The curtains blew toward the street, in danger of being torn from their hooks. Her eyes glowed green, raking Aiden's half naked body. He stood resolute, the warrior re-awoken, and she envisioned him suddenly with sword in hand, preparing for battle - the battle with his own past.

There was no more reason for delay; Aiden picked up the length of silk sash Iona had chosen for the cord cutting ceremony. She held the scissors in her hands.

"With these scissors, we cut the energetic bonds of love and desire between us."

He covered her hands with his, and with one last look of remembering, pushed them together over the scissors. They threw the cord into the fire, where it burned quickly and silently.

"So mote it be," Aiden uttered, his eyes closed, missing the look of defiance on Iona's face.

CHAPTER 40

A week passed before Sahara heard his knock at her door.

She opened it to the howling winter wind and swirling gusts of snow, Ulfred barking excitedly as Aiden walked in, a large parcel in his hands.

"What's this?" she asked, stealing a kiss as he bent towards her, a grin in his face.

"I'm so happy to see you," he handed her the parcel. "But maybe you should put that down, so I can hug you properly."

Sahara laughed and fell into his arms. "I've missed you! How was work?" She avoided the other question.

He shook the snow from his hair, settling on the stool at the kitchen counter. "Work away is done with until the New Year."

Sahara clapped her hands. "Yes!"

"I know! I just have the ones near town to finish. I'm looking forward to the dark days of December with my lovers." He waited until Sahara finished grinding coffee beans, looking around at the winter décor she had set out. It was like the forest, comforting.

"You know what I miss?"

"More than me?"

"How am I supposed to answer that?" he winked. "Anyway, I miss making things from wood. I touch it every day, installing beams and custom carpentry, but I miss just having my knife in my hand and cradling a branch, whittling it into something. Or making stools like I made these for you. I'm going to take some time this winter to wander the forest and find fallen wood that speaks to me." He nodded when Sahara pointed to some crusty bread and the wire basket of eggs on the counter. "I worked magic this week Sahara...I know now what was missing in my life. I've always been content, but now my life is so much more abundant."

"Sometimes you don't know what you don't know," Sahara said, passing him a plate and cutlery. "So what's in the box?"

"Presents for Solstice. From Iona."

Sahara poured the hot water into the bodum and the fragrance of coffee rose on the air. They were silent for a few moments.

"So you saw her. Was it what you had expected?"

He shook his head and decided to get right to the heart of things. "No. I didn't expect to remember loving her, if that's what you're asking."

"Oh Aiden!" Sahara said, gripping the edge of the counter. "You remember, then, what she meant to you."

"Yes, the moment she walked into the restaurant, I was fully awake to the love Arinn and Dagr had shared. It was immediate."

"What did she wear?"

Aiden smiled. A typically female question. "A long green velvet gown. She's clever, she knew that it would stir up memories. But I suppose that it had to happen."

"Do you understand now how difficult it was for me to resist her and Richard after our regression? It was like being there. You can tell me, Aiden, whatever happened. I know how it is with her."

He sipped his coffee and stabbed at his food. "I kissed her. Once." He looked up, remorseful.

Sahara reached across the counter and touched his arm gently. "I didn't really think you'd get away without wanting to. Aiden, it's just a part of our journey. It doesn't hurt me at all. As long as you come home to me."

She came around and wedged herself between his legs, against his chest, surrendering to his arms.

He kissed the top of her head. "I tried so hard not to, but there needed to be a moment of completion. To taste her and remember, then move on. We did a cord cutting ceremony."

Sahara looked up, surprised. "She agreed to that?"

"Not exactly. She tried to dissuade me. I wanted to give in. She asked me if it had been only the four of us, would it be different."

"Oh dear! What did you say?"

"I told her plainly that she couldn't wish Holly away. I also told her she had to stop showing up as a raven when Holly and I were together, spying on us. Of course I didn't tell her what she could do with you. That's your business to organise." He held his cup out for more coffee.

"How did the cord cutting go? I've always loved working magic with Iona. She's so visceral in her execution."

"It was wild. Satisfying even though she resisted at first. I felt entirely in my element."

Sahara picked at the croissant crumbs on Aiden's plate. He put his arm around her and held her, amused at the way she snuggled in. She was like a kitten curling into his warmth.

"What happened after?"

"Well, it didn't settle right away. I felt more at peace. I'm not sure if Iona did. I didn't feel the need to ravage her afterward. I was in a totally different head space after that. I mean, she was still as stunning as before, of course. Iona seemed less distraught...I'm not sure, though. She can look very innocent. I don't know her well enough to tell if that can be trusted."

"I see. Yeah, she can be tricky. But so lovely..." Sahara mused. "And then?"

"Then we had coffee, and she served me some exquisite walnut torte. All you women ply me with sweets." They smiled at each other. "We sat by the fire for a while. I think we spent more time just looking at each other than anything else. I felt like she was eating me alive at times. She's so hungry for what we used to have. I hurt her, Sahara. I told her that there was no hope at all. In the end, she asked me to stay."

Sahara sighed. She kissed his jaw. He was warm and safe, back in her arms.

"*Did* you stay over?" she asked, trying to appear nonplussed.

"Of course not. I'd already crossed a line. It would have been taking too many liberties with Richard and Holly's expectations of me. But we did do one thing..."

So there was more. Sahara nodded, urging him on.

"I couldn't just leave her like that. It was all so sudden and raw. Even for me, it wasn't enough time to understand the energy between us. I did eventually leave, after a few hours, but before that, we sat by the fire watching the flames in silence, remembering. I played with her hair, held her hand - comforted her. It was so familiar, to have her that close, but innocent. She's like a child at times, ancient in other moments. I think that if she could have sunk beneath my skin, she would have."

"Skin?"

Aiden faced Sahara's questioning eyes squarely. "I had my shirt off - well, it was already off from when we were cutting cords, we whipped up some pretty strong energy. She was dressed, but that gown had a very liberal neckline. Not much left to the imagination."

"Ayayay. You're stronger than me."

"We're good then, my love?" Aiden kissed her gently.

"We're good. Always."

"I'll tell Holly everything later today. I'm going over to pick up some of her things to bring to my house. French boy is coming soon." He sighed. "Do you think she'll forgive me?"

"She will. We had a great chat one night this week. She's too good to keep a grudge. She even told me that she wouldn't blame you if you were attracted to Iona. And she's very loyal to her. So I doubt this will come between you. She's learning fast, what life with witches entails."

"Are you going to tell her anything about you and Iona and Richard?" Aiden asked.

"I almost did..."

"And?"

"And then I just couldn't.

"Maybe you should cut cords with them as well?" Aiden suggested.

Sahara looked away.

"I should..."

"I asked Sahara to meet us later at your place." Holly handed Aiden a box. They were piling her personal things by the door, and a few favorite bits of furniture. The rest would stay in the apartment for the apprentice.

"Will she be? I was there this morning. She's done a great job of arranging my business affairs - that list I left her with, remember? Until today, I hadn't realized what a relief it would be to have an assistant. I must have been crazy to keep doing it all myself."

"Not so crazy. I know what it's like to have to give up some control. It's not easy. And yes, she'll join us. You know what I love about her?"

"Nope." Aiden grabbed Holly's hand as she passed by and pulled her in for a hug.

"I love that witchy thing she does...you know...puttering around in the cabin, hanging herbs to dry, making her potions, casting spells. The cabin seems to be getting more and more mystical, like its grown roots into the ground - and come alive."

"Mmm. You smell good."

"Are you even listening?"

"Yes. I heard everything you said, witchy things, herbs, spells...but you still smell good."

"Don't Aiden," Holly melted into Aiden's arms. "I can't think when you do that. We've got to go!"

"There's nowhere to go," he whispered, sitting her down on the kitchen chair. Holly looked up at him and groaned as he unbuttoned his shirt.

"I'm getting that feeling again, Aiden."

"What feeling?" He let her undo his belt.

"When my pussy gets all tight and achy."

"Tell me!" he commanded.

They lay in bed, Aiden twirling Holly's hair in his fingers. She had her eyes closed, listening to his breath. The sound of the phone jolted them.

Holly looked at her text messages, laughing as Aiden tickled her while she hung over the end of the bed to where her phone lay on the floor.

"Stop it!" she kicked her feet. "Look what you've done. Sahara's on her way to your place, and we're not even there! C'mon!" She pulled her clothes on. Aiden remained stretched out, watching her rush around.

"Pass me your phone."

"You're going to blame this on me, aren't you?" she threw his clothes at him. "Don't even try to get away with lying, Aiden Halloran."

Something in his eyes stopped her mid-step. "What is it, babe. You alright?"

"I have something to tell you."

CHAPTER 41

"Hi Dad."

"Holly! What a lovely surprise. Here, I'll call your mom to the phone too."

"No! Dad, wait. Can I just talk to you alone?"

"Of course. What's going on?"

Holly sat on Aiden's front porch, wrapped in a wool blanket, sipping a steaming cup of peppermint tea.

"Are the two of you doing anything for Thanksgiving?"

"Noooo. Did you want to come home?"

Holly shuddered, an involuntary reaction to the thought of being in her small town and having to visit her old life.

"I thought you and Mom might want to come here?" She waited as her dad adjusted to the surprise of her invitation. She could tell, because he didn't answer right away.

"Well, I'd love to, Holly. I'll have to talk it over with your mother."

You mean you'll have to ask her if she has forgiven me for leaving her. Holly gathered her courage. "I'm with someone. I'd like you to meet him."

"Oh! Well that's wonderful. Is it serious?"

"We're engaged...I'm very happy."

"Then I'm happy too. I'm sure your mother will be as well. Who is he?"

"A builder. Aiden Halloran. You'll really like him Dad. He's...he's like you. Warm heart, kind."

"If you love him, he must be something. I'm sure we'll get along, sweetheart. Don't worry about anything."

"There's more Dad," Holly looked through the window to where Aiden and Sahara were standing in the kitchen, watching her. She gave them a thumbs up, but was shaking with nerves.

"Is it what I think it is?"

"No. I'm not pregna..."

"Because I would be ok with it if you were, Holly...I don't care about any of that tradition bullshit. I just want you to be safe and happy."

"I know, and that's why I want to talk to you alone. I know you'll understand." Holly's hands began to shake. Aiden came out of the house and knelt at her feet. That thumbs up hadn't fooled him one bit. He held her legs firmly in his big hands and she began to relax, allowing herself to find courage in his touch.

"I'm also in love with someone else."

"Hmmm? I don't understand."

Staring into Aiden's blue eyes, Holly gave up her secret.

"I'm bisexual, dad. I'm in a polyamorous relationship. With Aiden and a woman...Sahara.

The bit of silence suddenly seemed less uncomfortable than she's expected it to be. She heard her dad shuffling around, then take a drag of his cigarette.

"I thought you quit smoking?"

"It's not a cigarette."

"Oh!" Holly smiled into the phone. "Well?"

"Well. I know that you're not hetero, Holly. I didn't know *exactly* which way you flew, but I knew it wasn't hetero."

"Really? How long have you known? Does Mom know?" Holly sat up straight, giving Aiden a surprised look.

"I've not talked about it with your mother. I don't think she knows. I've known for a long time. There were a lot of clues if one paid attention. It doesn't matter to me. Like I said, as long as you're in a good place."

Holly began to cry. "Dad. I love you."

"We'll come out, sweet pea, and no need to worry. I'm glad you called me. But I can't be the one to tell your mother. I'll support you but it has to come from you. You know how she is about these things."

"I know. It's against her beliefs. I couldn't stay Dad. I just wouldn't have been accepted in our community. And there was no one there for me...to love."

"I understand completely. There's nothing to apologize for. Just text me the address. I'm looking forward to meeting your Aiden, and Sahara. Would it help if I told you a secret?"

Holly laughed, relief in her voice.

"Sure, Dad. Although I doubt that you could have done anything too bad with the eyes of the congregation on you all these years?"

"It's not about me. But yeah, I hear you. It's about your grandma Devon. She was gay."

"What? I don't believe it! But she was the most religiously devout person I knew. How did she get away with it?"

"She didn't tell anyone, except me - because I read one of her letters one time when I was being a stupid teenager and rummaging

222

through her dresser looking for money."

"Dad!"

"I know. Anyway, she had a letter from this woman who loved her. They had had an affair. Your grandmother died never living her truth, because she was afraid of what would happen if everyone found out. She was furious that I had discovered the letter. But I didn't care, and told her so. My mother married a man and lived unhappily to please others. It was our great secret. I was the only one who ever knew. I loved her more after that. It opened my eyes to a lot of things, that letter."

"Dad, are you crying?"

"Never mind. Holly, I'm so proud of you."

"I'm sorry that I hurt you and Mom by leaving so suddenly and not keeping in touch."

"Love you, sweet pea."

"See you soon!"

Aiden took the cup from Holly's hand. "Come inside, my love. You're shaking, and I've made you a nest by the fire."

"You always make me feel so welcome. Thank you."

"This is *our* home now, Holly. Everything I have is yours."

CHAPTER 42

When ideas formed in Sahara's mind, they seldom disappeared. Instead, they found root and grew steadfastly until she gave in to their whims.

One such idea popped out of her mouth as she lay in Aiden's arms in the great bed that faced the forest.

Drifting her hand across the expanse of his chest, and admiring his proud profile, she whispered, "I'm going to go see Iona, darling. There is some magic we need to tend to, and I need a day in Denver before Solstice."

He opened his eyes and for a moment seemed to be searching the ceiling for an appropriate response. His hand lay across the hard of his stomach, and Sahara took it in hers. Finally, he turned to look at her.

"Dare I ask what this magic is about?"

"I'm thinking of raising protective energy over Holly around her mom's visit. We've got some other business as well. And I still have some shopping to do. Are you decided on what to get Holly for her Solstice gift?"

Aiden lay on his side. "I've already bought her a pass to the spa up on the mountain. She can use the hot springs and saunas as much as she likes. You can too...it's a family pass." He grinned. "And I opened an account for massage, for whenever she wants one. I also bought her a beautiful cookbook, 'A Kitchen in France'. I've hidden a box full of other things. You'll have to wait to see. I'm afraid I won't be able to keep from spoiling her. I know she doesn't care about things, but I want to give her so much."

"Me too. I have some things I want to pick up for her in Denver. You won't mind if I buy her lingerie, will you?"

Aiden laughed. "No! Is it really for her?" He pulled Sahara on top of him, hands on her bottom. "I love how much you love her."

Sahara heard a note of warning in his voice.

"I won't do anything to jeopardise us, darling." She folded her arms under her chin and looked him in the eye.

"You won't be surprised if I don't believe you?" Aiden said.

Sahara slid her legs on either side of his hips. Her warmth found his.

"I'm going to stay away from Iona...in that way."

"How?"

"I don't know, really," Sahara admitted. "But I'm determined."

"I know now what lives between you. I don't think you can, Sahara. I really think that cords have to be cut, to make it easier. When I was with her...I wanted so badly to just go back to the past."

Sahara sat up and slid onto him. He thrust up, hitting her cervix with practiced precision.

"Oh!" She fell into his eyes.

"What we have, babe, this connection that allows you to orgasm with your whole body...you have it with Iona too, and I don't think you can walk away from it. Please cut the cords. Your magic is powerful, it will end our torture." Aiden's hips moved towards Sahara's pleasure.

She hung her head, closed her eyes.

"Please, Aiden, don't ask me for this...not yet. I'm just not ready."

"Are we going to keep lying to Holly?" One more thrust and Sahara collapsed into his arms, face buried in his hair, against the shoulders that bore all of their guilt.

"It's my lie, not yours. Oh darling!" She shook with her release. Aiden gripped her as he came hot inside her.

"No. It's ours. I have to keep your lies. You have to find the courage to let Iona go in that way."

"I can't," Sahara breathed, overcome with the essence of their souls mingling. "It would be letting go of Dagr too, and I can't...not yet."

They lay quietly, absorbing each other's energy. When they fell asleep, it was with nothing resolved.

Iona opened her door, a sweet smile on her face. "I was so hoping to see you before the Solstice!"

Sahara let herself be embraced, the feel of one so familiar, so dangerously delicious. She placed her travelling bag on the floor.

"Will you stay with me, Sahara?" Iona asked.

"I will. But we must stay in separate rooms. I've promised Aiden to be good." She laughed and wagged her finger. "You must try too!"

Iona took her hand and held it to her heart. "I don't have a spare room," she purred.

"Sure you do...it's...oh." Sahara suddenly understood. It didn't take a psychic to figure out what Iona would use the other room for.

"I'll sleep on the sofa. No matter."

"You can have my bed. I'll take the sofa. What kind of hostess do you think I am?" Iona challenged.

"Hmff!" Sahara retorted. "The kind that can't be trusted."

They giggled and walked hand in hand to the living room, with its roaring fire and generous proportions.

"Did you come to town to see me or..."

"I have some shopping to do. And yes, to see you."

"Do Holly and Aiden know where you are?"

"Yes. I'm not forbidden to see you!" Sahara said defensively.

"I'll assume then that Holly approves of our friendship?"

"Yes. Friendship. I want to talk to you about Aiden," Sahara blurted out, suddenly feeling very nervous.

"Won't you come any closer?" Iona asked, all honey and innocence.

Sahara, who was aching to be held, slipped gratefully into Iona's arms.

"Be good darling. I beg you. I can't resist your arms, but you must behave."

"Aaah, but you feel right in my arms. I miss you. So much. I promise to be good."

They snuggled in, staring at the fire for a time; remembering.

"Was it torture?" Sahara whispered after a while.

"Yes."

"Did he feel the same to you?"

"In some way - his presence. Because he's so tall and broad, with that same intensity in his eyes. His body evokes that honor bound energy. But Aiden is tempered by the forest and peace while Dagr was tempered by magic and war. Aiden will unfold now...we made magic together, as I'm sure he told you. That part has not wavered, his integrity. Sahara, he is a powerful man. When he steps fully into it, he will bring much to this realm."

"I know. I think that in some ways I will lose him to it, the way I am lost to the stories I write. It's his purpose."

Iona kept her hands to herself but could not keep from nuzzling in against Sahara's neck.

"He's so beautiful. I saw how everyone looks at him, women *and* men. He commands space, like Dagr did. It's not just his face, although that was enough to melt me, but his skin, his hair; the way he holds himself. All I could think of was *service*. He inspires service.

"For you and me, perhaps, because we're daughters of another century, and because we desire men from that perspective. But from Holly, he gets something else...she's not a natural submissive. She offers him a spirited resistance when he becomes too traditional. He loves that about her." Iona's pained face almost made her stop, but she had to keep going. "I love her. Madly. What's past is past, Iona, no matter how much we might crave to recapture what we once had."

"I can't bear it."

"What is it that has us so entangled? I don't understand why we cannot remember without there being a feeling of despair. Did we all die tragically?"

Iona shook her head and Sahara knew that she wouldn't tell. And yet, she was reticent to discover on her own. They would discover together, all of them, come heaven or hell.

"Have you told Richard what happened...that kiss? Aiden confessed to Holly."

Iona sat bolt upright. "He did? Whatever for? Surely she wouldn't have welcomed it?"

"Because he cannot *not* tell her! He's marrying her, Iona. And planning to make her pregnant as soon as she gives him the word. She wasn't....Iona, for the love of God, what's wrong?" The stricken look on Iona's face was alarming.

"Pregnant?"

"Yes! Pregnant. Aiden is ready for a family. It can't be that surprising, can it?"

"I just never thought..." Iona wrung her hands.

"Darling, is it because you want children? You know *I* can't have any. I would love to. It's just never happened. Have you and Richard talked about having a family?" Sahara was beside herself trying to placate Iona whose eyes wore all signs of hysteria. She embraced her until the trembling stopped and she felt her surrender to the warmth between them.

"I'm sorry. I don't know what got into me."

"I wish I could help you. I'm sure it's because of your recent time with him. I should admit, while we're at it, that being around Richard isn't easy for me either. I could easily fall into what we once had. But I've promised myself to learn from Aiden's integrity."

Iona unwrapped herself from Sahara's arms and stood, once again in control of her emotions. "I'm going to make us dinner. Do you mind if I ask Richard to join us?"

"Noooo, I don't mind." Sahara replied, a little surprised at Iona's sudden recovery. "I'm just not sure that it's wise, considering. I'm not made of steel."

"It'll be fine!" Iona snapped, then apologized. "I haven't seen Richard in while, to be honest. He's been avoiding me. But I don't think he can resist seeing you."

"Right." Sahara absentmindedly began to light the candles in their wall sconces, muttering under her breath. Maybe having Richard around would have a stabilizing effect on them both.

CHAPTER 43

"He was now in that state of fire that she loved. She wanted to be burnt." ~ Anaïs Nin

He knocked and she answered, wondering why he didn't use his key. Surely he must have one?

They stared at each other, Sahara's eyes raking his athletic body, and the way his teeth flashed into a roguish smile. He extended his hand and taking hers, kissed it. He smelled faintly of something expensive, looking up at her with a curious gaze as his lips met her skin.

Sahara remembered. The essence of centuries past clung to him like the mist over the rugged moors they had once trod. The warmth of his touch spread along her spine and threatened to tempt her resolve. Richard let go just as her hips began to respond.

"It's been a while," he said. "How are you, my dear?"

He waited patiently as she processed all of her emotions, his body close to hers. Iona hung back, watching their auras begin their familiar dance.

"I am well," Sahara replied, wrenching herself away from his stare. Dropping her eyes, she smoothed herself like a sparrow ruffled from a strong headwind. "And you?"

Richard gave a little laugh. "As well as can be expected, considering recent events," he said and moved past her to embrace his lover.

"You return, like Saturn, with all your mysterious rings pulling us into your orbit," Iona melted into Richard's arms gratefully, for she had truly not known what to expect from him this time.

"I return to claim what is mine." Richard's voice bore no question of needing to be obeyed. He kissed Iona soundly, with Sahara's eyes drilling into his back. Sensual and stealthy as a black jaguar, Richard commanded the room with unrelenting intent.

Sahara slipped away to sit by the fire, and allow them a few moments alone. Her legs barely carried her, as desire overwhelmed her. Aiden's words rang in her head, and she sensed his closeness. The awoken magician now, Aiden was covering her with his protection. But she wished him here, among them.

"May I pour you a drink, Sahara?" Richard stood by her side, a bottle of wine and two glasses in his hand.

"Yes please," she replied, grateful for the escape alcohol would provide. She reached up to take the goblet.

He sat down opposite her and observed her quietly. She knew that he was exercising great control, because his eyes couldn't lie. He wanted her, naked, begging and surrendered. Sahara shook involuntarily. She met his eyes and answering his desire in the only way she felt that she was allowed.

"I'll be honest," Richard said. "I liked it better when we didn't know much about our past. It was easier."

She stayed silent.

"Drink," he prompted. She took a sip, closing her eyes as the warmth of the wine slid down her throat. She wanted him to hold her, and be free to feel his lips on hers. Once...it had been no sin to think this way.

She heard Iona working in the kitchen and a vision of Arinn rose, cooking over the outdoor fire, smoke scenting the air as the fat dripped from the meat she was roasting. Arinn had always made their meals, prepared their tonics, and cared for their well-being. Sahara's brow furrowed. The word tonic spread caution across her subconscious.

"What is it?" Richard asked.

"I don't know, I thought I remembered something...but it's gone."

I love you still

Her eyes shot to his as she heard his thoughts. It wasn't helpful, being able to read his mind. Just more perfectly timed torture.

Her cheeks burned under his attention. She couldn't help it - to stare at him, the way he sat in his chair, the cut of his clothes, his raven hair - nor remember that she had once been his to command. She couldn't help feeling that strange pull of his personality, arrogance tempered by his kind heart, nor the sharp intelligence that marked him irresistible. Time could not chase their connection away. But she had to walk away! She had to keep to the good.

"How's everyone at home?" Was that a hint of anger that she heard in his voice?

"They're fine," and then, "Richard, was it surreal meeting Aiden? I know you were unprepared, but surely you must have had a hint of fondness for him, once you knew?" She longed so much for them to be friends now that their lives were inescapably intertwined.

He measured his words before he spilled them. Sitting forward, and gesturing for her to join him in his chair, he bared his heart.

"I do like him. I admire the way he's built his reputation. I like his integrity. Ironically, I also hate that about him at the present moment, since it doesn't suit me." He gave a wry smile, and made room for her in his lap. "We're still arguing over the same women it seems."

"Was it hard, to remember your relationship with him? To remember what we'd been through? I'm still making sense of things. He's the best of all of us. Like Dagr was."

"It was strange to see myself in love with a man, because I just don't desire that at all now, and finding the reason why I go this tattoo." He tensed as Sahara ran her fingers over it. "Actually, once we'd spent a few hours together, he felt like a long lost brother. It was familiar. He tried to convince me that working together would be a bad idea. But I couldn't let go of it. I know that he's meant to build my home. He's the only one who can." Richard took Sahara's glass and put it down on the side table.

"I don't want to share Iona with him, but I want him to share you. How's that for a double standard?"

"Why do you think you feel that way?" Why she asked she did not know. She could easily guess his answer.

"Because she loves him, and that's dangerous. But you don't love me, so he has no reason to worry about you leaving him."

"Half of that is true," Sahara whispered back, her hands in his, his lips pressing to her forehead. "I won't leave him...ever again. But you're wrong about the other. I do love you...and Iona. It's still dangerous for him to share me, and he doesn't want to, if it can be helped. He will protect Holly to the ends of the earth. I don't want to mess with that." She wished he would let his lips wander.

"I remembered something after I met Aiden. A night you and I shared long ago. You've always been his, we loved each other but you were his. You'll always be his. But the time we had together was the only time I was truly a good man back then. You made me good - Aiden told me that he kissed Iona. He didn't exactly apologise, but he did tell me. I can't even be pissed at him because he makes it impossible and it would be terribly hypocritical of me in any case."

"I want you to meet Holly," Sahara slid to the floor at his feet. Being in his arms was too damn hard.

"I will. I want to meet her. Half out of curiosity, to see what has him so enamored, and also because you love her. I want to know everything about you." He shrugged in that French way. Europe had left its mark on him.

"It'll be a shock, Richard."

"Oh? Why's that? I've met plenty of beautiful women."

Sahara shook her head. "Because she's the exact image of Arinn."

Richard looked perplexed. "Truly? How is that possible? I can't imagine...!"

"You won't need to imagine. She's as beautiful and as innocent as Arinn was in the early days."

"Now, why do you say early days? Did something change? I'm still grappling with Iona to tell me about our relationship. I sense years together but we've only uncovered that one night."

Sahara laid her head in his lap. He stroked her hair gently. Sahara longed to ask him to pull it, to lay her on the carpet and cover her.

"I don't know either," she moaned. Unbearable, this game of pretending they could stay away from each other. "I want to know."

Iona appeared, a tray of appetizers in her hand. She put them down on the coffee table, and folded her long, gazelle legs beneath her as she sat beside Sahara. The energy shifted as it always did when she was in the room. She smiled.

"Planning anything without me?" she asked.

"No," Sahara answered, taking a tiny asparagus tart from the tray. She stared at it for a moment, then put it down.

"Something wrong with it, my love?" Iona purred.

"No. I don't think so...I'm just not hungry anymore." Sahara shook her head, trying to shed the sense of dread she's had over the last hour. Strange.

<hr />

They teetered on the brink of madness all evening; through dinner while Richard and Iona caught up amiably, setting aside more serious discussions for another day, and while Sahara picked at her food, trying to catch a memory by the tail.

Iona watched her closely, and always the perfect hostess, tended to her every need. Richard's expansive energy kept her magnetised to him, every now and then touching her hand. It would be so easy to slip into their arms, to allow them to lead her into naughty games, perhaps let her see that wicked, wicked room! She was wet with imagining what they did in there, and wishing she could be their slave. But her love for Aiden and Holly kept pushing away the instinct of allowing herself to be seduced.

Richard's voice broke in on her thoughts. "What do you think, Sahara?"

"Hmm? About what?"

"Iona says that dominance by seduction is the best way to a woman's heart."

Sahara blushed, as if they had caught her in her illicit thoughts.

"I think that I know better than to be caught up in a conversation like that."

"Don't tease her," Iona laughed, clearing the table.

Richard stood at the back of Sahara's chair. "Go sit down, both of you, I'll do this." And he shooed them away.

"What's wrong?" Iona leaned her back against a chair, sitting on the floor by the fire. Sahara lay across her legs, clit vibrating, mind in a terrible tangle.

"I can't be here with the two of you. I can't help what my body is feeling. I want you to undress me and lay me out for the taking. I want Richard's mouth on mine and your..." she broke off, miserable.

Iona's fingers gripped in Sahara's hair. Her voice resonant with need, she said, "I want to see you begging for my whip!"

Sahara groaned and curled into a ball. "Please don't. I can't say no to you."

"Don't say no."

"You promised."

"I lied. I want you. So badly that it hurts my heart. I want you in my bed, and in my life like before."

"I'm going to get a hotel room. I'll break my promise to Aiden if I don't." She let Iona's hand caress her face and travel ever so slowly towards the neckline of her shirt.

"I don't want you to go. You must stay. Please, Sahara. We have so little time together, and I know that you want this! I want to see Richard with you...one more time?"

"There will never be only one more time!" Iona's hand found her breast. "There will always be another time and another, and then we'll end up in each other's life like before. I love Holly, Iona. She's my beloved, and there is nothing that can change that. You have to accept it!"

The sudden pain of Iona's fingers pinching Sahara's nipple ripped like lighting through to her groin. She sat up, eyes blazing. "You have no intention of letting me go, do you? You don't care who I love or even honoring what this lifetime is meant for!"

Iona, with a demonic look on her face, ripped Sahara's shirt from

233

her shoulders, staring hungrily at her erect nipples. "No! I don't care! I love you and nothing can make me change my mind. I have waited six hundred years for this; a chance to be your lover, to be your beloved!"

Richard stood in the doorway, a dish cloth gripped tight in his hands, his jaw tense, devouring the scene before him.

"For Aiden, then." Sahara pleaded. "For him. Can you not do it for him?"

Iona collapsed to the floor, weeping. Sahara went to her, broken, a shamble of emotions and need. The mood around them softened as Richard turned out all the lights and put on some music to soothe their souls. He brought a packet of herb, and settled Iona on the chair.

"Come, my love. It is high time we found out what this is all about. I am tired of being put off. Pull yourself together." His voice was loving but terse. He would not to be trifled with.

Sahara let him rearrange her shirt, obediently standing while he gently tended to her, his desire raw and blatant.

"I think we should smoke a joint. Then we can talk over all the things." Richard sat down and began to roll their herb, quietly, in thought. He was especially seductive like this, a man with his mind engaged, and his heart seeking truth.

"You know," he began, "if we were just any other four people, this would be easy to navigate. We would either agree to be polyamorous or we would not, but at least we would have all the information at hand that we needed to make that decision. But this situation is far from ordinary." He placed the three joints in a crystal ashtray and stood to pour their drinks. "We are prisoners of our past lives and that has to end. We can pretend that we can stay away from each other, but let's face it, at least two of us are incapable of trustworthiness." He raised his hand to stay their protests. "Don't even bother. I know you, Iona, and Sahara, you have been honest about your feelings."

Iona shot him a venomous look. "Are you saying you *can* be trusted? I doubt it!"

"I'm not saying I don't want what the two of you want, of course I do. But here's the thing, I know that I won't initiate it, while you would. That doesn't exactly make me a saint, but if anyone in this room can behave, it's me." He passed Iona a lit joint, and then one to Sahara, then took a slow drag of his own. Inhaling deeply, he pointed at Iona. "Oh, this is good. I don't know where you get this stuff, my love, but it's always the best there is.

"I don't mess around with my spiritual journeys. It's the same as

234

I always get. Organic, bio-dynamic, incubated in a pyramid container, surrounded by a crystal grid, and spoken over. You won't find any better."

Sahara took a small drag and allowed herself to be infused with the sacred energy of the herb. A few more drags and she was fully open to spirit, floating between here and there.

"This is better," her nerves untangled, she thanked the plant deva for her wisdom.

They sat without talking, in the soft light of the room, the fire making shadows on the walls. Richard served their drinks and sat behind Iona on the floor, cradling her close, once in a while dropping tender kisses on her head.

"Are you feeling better now, darling?" he asked, as Iona lifted her lips to his.

"I am, thank you."

Her voice was soft, yet tinged with a hint of rebellion. "It took us so long to find our way back. So long, and I waited so patiently for our lives to return to what they once were."

Sahara watched them kiss, and marvelled at just how arresting they were together. He, so debonair and she so fragile in her beauty. Life was strange, and cruel, and beautiful all at once. Richard's hand strayed to Iona's neck, and instantly, she was alive to her passion. Fascinated, Sahara stared at how hungry their kisses became. She lowered her eyes when Richard caught her licking her lips.

"I'm too tired to talk now," she said, unable to face Iona's stubborn longings for the past. "I think I'll just close my eyes. No need for you to move." She curled herself up on the sofa, pulling the blanket over herself.

"Will you truly be comfortable here?" Richard asked, tucking her in. But she was already fast asleep, having begged her guides to anoint her with slumber. It was the only way out from the desire that smote her being.

What awoke her, she never discovered, but she sat bolt upright, and surrounded by darkness, followed the sound of some mysteriously beguiling music down the long hallway.

Padding quietly on her bare feet, clothed still, she found herself facing the doorway of Iona's spare chamber. It was ajar by centimeters. Sahara crouched to the floor, pulse quickening. Her eyes adjusted slowly to the dim light inside the room. She trained her ear to discern the voices, which undulated between Iona's breathless pleas and Richard's commanding baritone. She could barely make out a bed, high and with four posters, Iona's figure standing at one of them, arms tied behind her, a long gown open to the waist, breasts bound by rope; the scent of incense perfuming the air.

Sahara's palms began to moisten. She should turn away, but the scene before her was mesmerising. Richard, shirtless, in jodhpurs and riding boots, stood before Iona, a whip in his hand, the end of it just under Iona's chin, forcing her to raise her head high.

"Look at me, my lady," Richard commanded.

"I can't," Iona replied, voice acerbic, "with your whip in my face."

"Careful!" Richard warned. You forget that I own you and can whip you for your sharp tongue. Look at me!"

Iona turned her head, then spat on the floor. Sahara gasped, a little too loudly. What century was this? She rubbed her eyes, then sprawled back on the floor as the door opened abruptly.

"What in Christ's name are you doing here?" Richard stood over her, a scowl on his face.

She looked up at him, along the length of his muscular legs, accentuated in their riding pants, the shine of his boots, the belt at his waist, his defined core, the lust in his eyes.

"I...I don't know...I heard music." She cowered but not from fear. It was a learned, expected response.

"Get in here!" Richard held the door open wider, a sardonic grin on his face.

"I can't. I'm going," Sahara turned, but was caught by her hair in Richard's solid grip.

"You must, my lady. I won't take no for an answer."

"But Aiden...!" She heard herself pleading, even as her sex grew wet and she trembled from desire at being handled with force.

"Aiden, Aiden, Aiden! I am sick of hearing what Aiden wants!" Richard bent down and with ease picked Sahara up and cradled her to his chest. She felt the pounding of his heart. She sensed the melting of his soul. She looked him in the eye and was surprised to see tears.

"What is it, my lord? How can I please you?" This was madness! Was she so easily turned away from loyalty towards her beloved?

As if reading her thoughts, Richard spoke. "You aren't to worry about your beloved Aiden. I have instructions from him, and there's nothing to be concerned about."

Spoken to him? Was she their chattel? Were they deciding what she could or could not do?

"And what does my beloved say?" she asked, still in his arms, aching for the feel of his mouth, so close to hers as he answered.

"That should you find yourself here, unable to flee your desire, I should take you. He may not have given you permission, but he gave me mine."

"Impossible! He would never!" She moaned as Richard's teeth found her neck, while one hand pulled her head back to expose it.

"Oh, but he did. And do you know why?"

"No. I don't know." She was slipping into oblivion.

"Because you have always been the good one. The one who tried to make everything right when things went wrong. The one who forgave the unforgivable, the one who tried to keep us all together, to be a lady when your soul screamed whore. You don't need to always be good. He loves you that much."

"What are you talking about, keeping us together; forgiving the unforgivable? What do you know?"

"I'm not in the mood for talking, Sahara. And anyway, he's only sent this much information, I am as much in the dark as you. I imagine that sooner or later, our lovers will grace us with what they know." He pointed toward Iona. "But for now, you may serve me by tending to my lady's needs." And he placed her at Iona's feet.

CHAPTER 44

Holly sat with pen and paper on the kitchen stool, wearing pyjama shorts and a cami, her golden hair in a ponytail, staring into space.

"For the life of me I cannot remember what my mother's favourite dessert is!"

Aiden looked up from the pile of house plans on his desk. "You're agonizing over nothing. Everything you bake is exquisite. She'll love whatever it is."

Holly swung around to face him. "I suppose so. Still...hey! Are you trying to sneak a peek?"

"Not trying, doing. But you're not showing much."

Holly blushed, and Aiden grinned.

"You always blush when you're thinking about doing something naughty."

"Hmm, not good. You're beginning to figure me out. Soon, I'll lose all my mystery."

"I doubt that, little girl." He waited.

Holly spread her legs a little and pulled her shorts aside. "Stay," she warned. "Want this?" She spread a little wider. "No! Stay, I said."

"How about a compromise? I'm ready for a break. Come sit on the sofa with me."

"Ok," Holly agreed. "But this better not be some kind of a trick." She wrapped herself in a blanket and watched Aiden add to the fire. "I've been thinking about Sahara. I wanted to talk to you about something."

Aiden's intuition told him that things had suddenly turned serious, and he was sorry for it. There had been too much worry lately, and all he wanted was to relax in Holly's arms and forget the inevitable. But ignoring Holly's need to talk was not his way.

"Of course. What is it darling?"

"I know that Iona and Sahara are lovers...still."

He hadn't expected *that*. Sitting beside her, Aiden took Holly's feet in his hands and began to rub. He was careful not to let all his breath out in a rush, or alarm her by the sudden tension he felt. "Pardon me?"

"I *know*. I asked Sahara about it once, and she told me they'd *been* lovers. But every time she goes away to Denver, I sense something. You know too - don't you?" She left it at that.

In the silence that followed, Aiden learned that Holly's eyes spoke only of understanding, and that the heat between them rose as they faced something unknown. He steadied his heart.

"Oh, Holly." Aiden swallowed his sorrow.

"I'm not angry, sweetie, I'm not. I understand it."

"What do you understand?" his voice bitter, unsettled the gentle Holly.

"Well," she began slowly, "I understand that she, and we, are part of something that is not easily managed. It's not her fault, or yours, or mine or anyone's for that matter...that we incarnated into this. I don't know what it's all about, but I know that Sahara loves me and that I matter to her, very much - but she can't be expected to just drop what was before." She reached for Aiden's hand. "I just needed to talk about it."

Aiden sighed.

Her hand in his was hot, and her cheeks were burning with embarrassment. He was still so much more man than she was comfortable with.

"I want you to know that you can say anything to me. I don't want you to feel embarrassed to share anything. There's nothing that I don't want to hear about your thoughts. Ok?"

"Ok."

"I must ask your forgiveness. I didn't feel that it was my responsibility to share what I knew with you. It is Sahara's to tell. Still, I lied to you." He shook his head. "This is terrible no matter how we slice it."

"But I'm not upset about it. I think we need to talk about it honestly, but if I was in her position, I wouldn't know what to do, I'm sure. I don't know anything about what you and she are going through, but I know that it must be killing you both to keep it from me."

"You're so trusting and we don't deserve that."

"So, now that you know I know, I need to tell you something about me. You think that I'm so innocent, and you try to protect me from everything, but I'm not everything that you think I am."

"What are you talking about? You're nothing if not perfectly good." Aiden scowled, thinking about how much this breach in trust must be costing their relationship, even if Holly didn't admit it.

"Aiden! You've put me on this pedestal, and I don't want you to do that. I'm about to fall off, and that hurts more than if you'd never thought of me as perfect."

The look in Aiden's eyes struck her silent for a moment. How she hated that hurt shadow.

"I didn't realize...I'm sorry. I want us to be real with each other."

"So let me be real. You'll be the first person I've told this, and if you don't want me after that..."

Aiden grabbed her by the wrists and pulled her into his arms. "Don't. I don't care what this is. You can't scare me away."

Holly extracted herself from his embrace so she could look him in the eye. "I've killed someone. In France."

Aiden showed no emotion while his heart pounded, as did hers, and they spent one candid moment just absorbing each other's fear. Holly's tears poured onto his lap, where they remained, a watershed of long-held emotions.

"What are you talking about...killed someone? Figuratively speaking?"

"No. For real. I was driving home from a late date with Julie one night, and got lost. I was scared because I didn't recognize anything about where I was, and I was just crawling along the street, hoping to see a street sign. And all of a sudden I was surrounded by a group of young men. They just came out of nowhere! And I stopped instead of going on. I was so nervous I couldn't get my windows up and they were reaching in, and laughing at me, saying I needed a fuck or I wouldn't have come down there. I panicked, and stepped on the gas, and just as I did, one of them stepped in front of the car...and I hit him...straight on."

Holly let herself break down into sobs of regret.

"My God, Holly!" Aiden cradled her face in his hands. "No one would blame you for that. It was a matter of safety, surely you know that!" Aiden's mind raced with all the ways he wanted to fix this for her, to erase it from her life.

"But I didn't stop! I hit him and kept going! It was one thing to react in panic another to leave him there." Holly's tear stained face wore all the horror of that night.

"Ok. Slow down. Let's think this through. Do you know for a fact that you killed him? Perhaps the others took him to the hospital? Wouldn't they have reported your licence plate?" But even as he said it, Aiden knew the truth.

"No," Holly said miserably. "There was a report in the paper about a fight among local gangs, and that one had been killed in a hit and run." She hung her head.

Aiden placed his hand under her chin and looked her in the eye.

"Sweetheart, it was an accident. You don't have one bad bone in your body. If it had been safe for you to stop, you would have."

"But I should have admitted to it. You would have."

"You don't know what I would have done."

"Yes I do. You would have done the right thing. Which makes it worse. I have recurring dreams of turning myself in."

"Are you mad? I'd rather turn myself in."

"That would be kinda impossible since you have no passport to prove you were there then. No, this is my burden, not yours."

"Ok. We'll figure this out. I'm so sorry this happened." Aiden held her close.

"I am too. More than I could ever express. So you see, I have no right to ask for perfection. I'm far from it."

"You have a right to ask for honesty from us. That shouldn't be a negotiation."

"But I do have empathy for what Sahara must be facing. By some twist of fate, I came into a relationship that would have evolved between the three of you sooner or later. She's with Iona tonight, isn't she?"

"Yes," Aiden replied quietly, thinking of Richard, the fourth that Holly didn't take into account.

"One time, I had to confess to Sahara about kissing you, when we were new and I had to admit to her that I liked you even though I knew that she liked you. It was hard, to face losing her trust."

Aiden looked up into Holly's knowing eyes. She was talking about his kiss with Iona.

"We'll get through this, Aiden. For whatever reason, we have been born into this mystery. I would be jealous if I thought this was some kind of game you were playing, and hurt enough to leave you both. But this...this is not something I can fight against, so I've decided to accept it."

"It was one kiss. I'm not making an excuse. I could have avoided it. But I wanted to know what the past felt like. I knew that I was betraying you, and yet..."

"No Aiden. Not betraying me, staying true to your journey."

"I don't deserve you."

"Make love to me. Softly. Show me that our love is stronger than our circumstances."

Aiden's possessive hand at the back of her neck and his sinful mouth on hers was like a healing balm spread onto festering wounds. She opened as his body sought hers. No matter what, they were one.

She was sure that her heart had room for it all, and until it told her otherwise, she would bask in the love she craved every minute of the day. When Sahara came back she would spare her the need to confess. Her love for the free-spirited witch had grown into an indescribable ache that haunted her day and night. She would tell Sahara that she knew and offer her space to keep her honor. As far as Holly was concerned, if Sahara loved Iona then she would too, and seek her friendship. Iona had proven herself compassionate and loyal when she'd rescued Aiden, and for that Holly would never be able to repay her.

With these thoughts and Aiden's talented hands heightening her mood, Holly placed all the pieces of their love puzzle into carefully organized compartments of her soul, and gave in to their heat.

Aiden listened to her breathing, following the rise and fall of her belly, paying attention to each movement of her hips. He left nothing to chance, as he had a goal in mind and this was the perfect moment for taking Holly into a spiritual experience of his love. His regret at leaving things unsaid fueled his passion, and Holly shied away from his eyes, bright with that light she had seen when he had returned from the Aspen King. It was a side of him that she didn't truly understand.

He left none of her secret places unexplored, kissing all her erogenous zones, ears, neck, nipples, inner thighs, armpits and the soft of her soles lovingly and with tortuously slow detail. Her moans were met with Aiden's words of encouragement, easing her into naked vulnerability.

"I'm so wet...I don't know what's happening, I feel like I'm half here and half somewhere else." Holly eased herself onto Aiden's leg and undulating her hips, succumbed to the pleasures of a clitoral orgasm. Aiden held firm and accepted her deep kisses and the moans that she left in his mouth.

"Ride it out, sweetie, take as long as you need."

"I'm dying for you inside me."

Aiden growled and grabbing a pile of Holly's hair in his fist, bit along her neck. She writhed like a snake, arching her back. Her breasts were lost in his large hands, nipples bruising against his palm.

"I love your tits, your ass, you cunt, everything."

"I want your cock. In my mouth."

"Please."

"Oh Aiden! Say please again. Beg me for my mouth."

"I want your mouth, sweet thing, I want your tongue wrapped around my cock. Eat me like ice cream."

"I want you to come in my mouth, Aiden."

"Yes, please."

She climbed on top of him and turned around. Pussy facing his hungry mouth, Holly swallowed Aiden as far as she could. But it was difficult to concentrate while he massaged her with patient strokes, each one just shy of entering her. She'd never been more wet, or more ready for entry. This time, he stopped her just as his pleasure rose up, and flipping her onto her back, he took her clit into his mouth and rolling it with his tongue, brought her to another riotous climax.

"I can't. I can't do anymore." She was shaking, eyes shut, hands balled into fists, all her bits sensitive.

"Just one more, babe. Aiden placed her legs on his shoulders and moved a pillow under her hips. He took her hands in his, and told her to open her eyes.

"We're going to do this together. Keep your eyes open. Look at me when we come."

"Ok." Hair spread around her, lips red from sucking, Holly looked the lustful woman that she was. Aiden was smitten all over again.

"I love you."

She nodded. Words were unavailable and unnecessary.

Aiden eased himself in and waited out Holly's initial reaction to his energy deep inside her. When she began to move her hips, signalling her readiness, Aiden thrust against her cervix, one, two three, stop. One, two, three, harder than before, stop; again - a rising crescendo. Then, fucking hard, finding that sacred spot, he took her to the top, screaming, gushing, her hands gripping her nipples. Holly came as he filled her with hot cum, mouth open, eyes rolled back, body shuddering, a river of sensations flooding through her body and brain.

He held her while she trembled in his arms. It would take her a while to come down.

"It felt as if you were right under my skin. I'm so open, my heart....vulnerable."

"Surrendered."

"Yes! What is this? The top of my head feels as if it's open to the sky."

"The energy of your orgasm travelled all your chakras, and released through your crown."

"How do you do that? I thought I had felt it all when you made me squirt that first time we were together, remember?"

"I remember," Aiden grinned. "That was good, but this is better, yes?"

"I feel you inside me, in my soul, deep, like we became one."

"I entered you through your cervix, to your heart. We made love with everything we had, our bodies and our energy fields. Our souls."

"Tell me."

"For a woman," Aiden said, caressing along her spine, "the cervix is the place of the emotional heart. It is the spiritual gateway to her soul. When you became thoroughly aroused, you allowed me into that part of yourself, emotionally. And as I touched your cervix, you released into a whole body orgasm. It's as much a spiritual union as a physical one. The sensations can last for days."

She absorbed his wisdom and his love. She had never imagined that a man could find her soul this way. She was humming with emotions and a love that left her shattered.

"I just can't even verbalise how I feel right now. I feel so close to you." The word 'close' triggered a realization. "Aiden!"

"What is it, my love?"

"We didn't use a condom!" She sat upright, and stared into Aiden's brilliant blue eyes.

"No," he smiled.

Holly placed her hands over her heart. "Maybe we'll be pregnant!" Then, "You said you would wait for me to signal you...did I?"

"I felt it from you. Are you happy, darling? Or did I misinterpret your cues?"

"You didn't! I've been thinking about it, but thought you'd say I had too much on my plate already."

"You do. And I do. But I thought about what I said to you before and realized that we'll always be busy...there is no perfect time. If it happens, I'll be the happiest man on earth."

"Oh sweetie! A little man like you. Imagine!"

And Aiden did, from long lost memories, he remembered the child he had once mourned.

CHAPTER 45

It is at the edges of ourselves that we find our true magic

This was the best time of year for witches, Sahara decided, when there was so much opportunity for drawing within oneself. She busied herself around the yard, sweeping her porch, picking up sticks blown in by the wind, and wrestling with linens hanging on the line.

The darker days, the rain, the trees made naked by weather, all made her long for a deeper solitude, a descent into the Underworld with thoughts and prayers and soul yearnings.

The air was crisp and lightly scented by wild apples, the last of the wormy ones rotting on the ground and becoming fodder for future soil. Nature created everything with a slow hand when it came to what was underfoot. The aspen leaves shone brilliantly when the sun came out from behind the indigo clouds, lighting their quickly fleeting glory. She looked around and smoothed her skirts. It was cold, and the shawl she had wrapped around her shoulders was hardly warm enough, but she didn't care; she was in her element, a child of the Goddess, communing with the mystical while tending to mundane chores.

There was a sacredness to a life of simplicity. This she had craved for years, and now, with several books behind her, the ones that she had been born to write, she could foster a peaceful existence, in love and intoxicated by future adventures.

She was on fire. What she had experienced with Iona and Richard recently fed her to the core. The days ahead were full of promise. She longed to make magic with Aiden, witness the skills that were awoken in him, and to teach Holly about the life of a mystic. Holly had asked for it after all, and Sahara adored teaching an eager student. Together, the three of them would live the impossible; love so stretched by new borders that it could only evolve into a spiritual awakening.

She had decided, in the nights that she had been back, that she would confess all to Holly and let everything unfold as it would. It had been folly to think that she could escape the life she had mapped out before incarnating. She was ready to accept herself as she was. There was no way but through honesty, no matter how fearful she may be of it.

It had been three days since she'd returned and asked for space to integrate. Aiden and Holly had agreed and left her alone, but there was no way of avoiding the energy that flowed from the Aspen Wood to her cabin...from whatever sorcery Aiden was brewing. He would be practicing his art now.

But today they would all meet, break bread, and speak what was on their hearts. Holly was busy receiving the new apprentice, and breaking him into the rhythm of the bakery. Aiden was overseeing the progress on his new offices and gutting the space into which the bakery would expand. Their lives were full but joyous. Sahara had had little contact with her lovers since she'd returned, her responsibilities to the Society had been pressing. As Winter Solstice approached, every member tended to their individual tasks and added to the collective effort of joining the Fey in their work of preserving the planet.

Looking around, Sahara planned the site for housing chickens, just over there attached to the side of the tool shed. They would have their own eggs, vegetables and several fruit trees. Wild berries were in abundance, as were roots to cure for plant ally powders. She would bake bread in the cook stove oven and make preserves as Holly had wanted. Mushrooms would be dried, herbs jarred for teas, tinctures made for medicine, and stars consulted for wisdom. It was a lovely thought to imagine Aiden in the background of their domesticity, their anchor and grounding as the Sacred Masculine. It was, in reality, a return to the life she had always loved, before everything had gone awry.

Heart quickening, Sahara turned towards the Aspen Wood and the figure approaching along the well-trod path. Aiden. She shielded her eyes from the sun, and watched as he walked toward her, his strong gait interrupted only by the moment he took to stop and observe her from afar. His strength preceded him as always. She could almost taste him on her tongue, the honor of his character, his power.

Ulfred appeared from behind the house and standing at her side, gave Sahara a questioning look.

"Go to him, Ulfred. Go!"

Ulfred poised himself as his wolf predecessors had done, and let out a plaintive howl in greeting. Then, loping quickly, he disappeared into the tall grass. He was used to living with them both now, they shared his care and his protection. There was still that pang of bitter acknowledgement of what Ulfred replaced; a child of their own. Sahara longed for the patter of little feet, but now was certain that she would never have any of her own. No matter how many times she and

Aiden made love, no seed was ever planted, no life quickened from their togetherness.

Her lover approaching, Sahara prepared her heart space. He came to her with that lazy smile, his eyes twinkling, eager to hold her. He swept her up in his arms and laughed as her kisses landed on his eyes, his lips, his cheeks. Putting her down, he appraised her clothes.

"I like this witch's garb. You look downright medieval. Will you be wearing this to town?"

"Would you mind?"

"No! I would love to see the stir you caused in this. But you're used to making waves."

"Why are you still talking?"

"What else would I be doing?" Aiden grinned as she twirled around him. "You're so playful today. You're making my heart light. Thank you."

"You know what I've been thinking out here?"

"Do tell!"

"About our life. Simple. Chickens, a garden, lying under the stars."

Sahara frowned as Aiden's face turned serious. "What?"

"I want that so much. A simple life."

"We can have it. Whatever we imagine."

"But we're not simple people, like I used to think we could be, tucked away in this lonely corner. Now we're five travellers on a dangerous path."

"Not yet, Aiden. Let's talk about this later. Right now I want to dream."

He led her to the back porch, where they sat on the stoop, and stared at the mountains before them.

"What are you thinking?" Sahara played with Aiden's hand in hers, stroking his fingers, drawing spirals on his palm.

"That this is real. What is before us. Nature. You. Me. Holly. Each moment we have together. Nothing else matters."

"We can work out all those other things, darling. I had an epiphany while I was away."

Aiden raised an eyebrow. "Just an epiphany?"

"Aiden please, let me finish. I was thinking that we have to accept the life we are here to live. We've been fighting against it, trying to change what has to be. We know our destiny. We asked for this. It is for good, this journey, trying to find the places beyond jealousy and ownership. I'm going to ask Holly's forgiveness and tell her everything."

She already knows." Aiden kissed Sahara's small hand tenderly.

"What do you mean...did you tell her?"

"No, she's as intuitive as you and I. And she understands more about our lives than we do. I am in awe of her wisdom."

Sahara wiped away a tear. "I suppose I shouldn't be surprised. The moment you gave her the ring, she was opened to our world."

"Even before that. She was born wise."

"Is she angry?"

"No. She's devoted to you. You can do no wrong."

"You called Richard. Why?"

"Because I love you like she does. And I also decided something about our journey. We'll live honestly or not at all."

"My lord!" Sahara cried. She knelt before him. "You are my teacher. My guide. I will live by your mantra: honestly or not at all."

"I want to know what he does to you. What you look like in his arms. I am so full of desire to taste the past, that it's haunting my days and nights. There's something we must uncover, and until we do, we will have no understanding of our further journey."

"Aiden!" Sahara's passion broke open. "Soon, Iona promised, before Solstice; we'll travel back, the four of us. The time is drawing near."

He nodded and stood. "Here. On the ground, Sahara. Lie down, and lift your skirts."

She did as she was told; bared herself before his burning eyes.

"My lady. You are ever so compliant, ever the willing lover." Aiden took her in the cold, wet grass, her breasts peaking from the blouse that he ripped from her shoulders, and then turning her, urgently from behind, while her hands tore at the earth and her cries greeted the thundering sky.

"I will fuck you like this until my dying day," he promised. "I will love you like this until we disappear, and then I will look for you among the stars. You are mine, and mine you shall remain."

CHAPTER 46

"Like this, Francois. Test the oven with your hand, you'll find that it will be a better judge of the temperature than the thermometer." Holly brushed past her new apprentice, with whom she was well pleased. He came highly recommended and took great care to listen carefully to her instructions.

"Tomorrow we'll go over the bread recipes and next week I'll let you have a chance to run the routine. You'll find it easy after a few days. We bake the same three types except at Easter and Christmas, when we add in traditional French staples. The desserts rotate, but I have a chart so there aren't any surprises."

Francois nodded. "Is it just the three of us in the patisserie?" He was a charming lad of twenty four, wiry and fit, with a shock of black hair and a proud Gallic nose.

"Yes, usually, except for extra servers on busy days and my partner Sahara will be helping us over the winter, as needed."

"Your partner?" Francois questioned in his heavily accented English. "She is a girl?"

"Yes." Holly laughed. "You'll meet her tomorrow. Sooo, how do you like your apartment? Do you think you'll have everything you need? I admit it's a bit feminine in décor, but you can change things around as you please."

"Ah non! It is perfect. I've been living with my parents - I know, embarrassing - so a whole apartment is very luxurious."

"Well, just let me know if you need anything."

In that moment, Aiden poked his head into the kitchen. He was covered in dust, hair in a top knot, and motioned Holly to the doorway.

"Come here and give me a kiss, woman. Then I'll need you to come to the back room to go over the design again."

Holly stood on her tiptoes and placed a tender kiss on Aiden's lips. "I'll be there in a minute. Aiden, this is Francois. I wanted to introduce you to him yesterday but you kept disappearing."

Aiden extended his hand. "Hello Francois. Welcome. I'm sure you'll enjoy working here. Holly's not too much of a tyrant." And with that he gave Holly's bum a light pinch, and laughing, left the kitchen.

Francois gave Holly a puzzled look. "That is your...brother?"

"No. My partner."

Francois's eyebrows shot up. "Your partner? But, you said..."

"I know. They're both my partners." Holly smiled as Francois scratched his head.

"I see. It is very liberal, in this town?"

"Not really," Holly replied. "Well, not at all."

"I've ordered extra dishes to add to Aiden's set, so we have enough of everything. And a white linen tablecloth." Sahara and Holly walked hand in hand along the stream, their cheeks rosy from the cold.

"I know. You already told me."

"Are you nervous? We'll be right there. We won't leave you alone if you don't want. Have you spoken to your mom?"

"No. Just my dad. He's trying very hard to be supportive. He had his own wild days, you know? It was the time of free love and all."

"But your mom was more conservative?"

"I guess. I mean, she's done stuff, but somehow she's forgotten what that was like."

"All you have to do is present yourself as you are. Own it and the rest is up to them. I know it's easy for me to say. I don't have anyone to please."

Holly squeezed Sahara's hand. "You say that so nonchalantly, but I know that you think about your parents."

"It's been so long, I sometimes forget I had any.

"Oh sweetie! I'm sorry."

"I'm really excited about Francois," Sahara said, changing the subject. "You'll have time now to enjoy life a little more. And maybe we can take a trip somewhere in the spring?"

"Really?! Where?"

"Wherever you want to go," Sahara smiled at Holly's joy.

"We'll ask Aiden."

"No, I mean just you and me. You'll have Aiden taking you on a honeymoon somewhere, and I want to take you somewhere on my own."

"A honeymoon?"

"Yes, you silly goose! There's going to be a honeymoon."

"But you're not coming?!"

"Absolutely not! Aiden wouldn't want it anyway. He'll want you all to himself."

"Well we'll see," Holly blushed.

250

"We'll see what?" Sahara stopped. "What will we see? You're going on a honeymoon, I can guarantee that if I know Aiden at all."

"We'll see...if I can even waddle around by then."

"You're talking in riddles. Holly, you're not...?"

"I'm waiting to see. When you were away, we didn't use any protection, and I'm hoping!"

"Darling! That's so exciting! He didn't say anything at all. I thought you'd agreed that you would try when you were more settled with the café?"

"Yes, but then we just did it. I'll tell you about that night later. Anyway, something very special happened."

Sahara walked in silence, adjusting to the news. There was still the matter of telling Holly about Iona. She sighed.

"Sweetie? You know that I want this for all of us, right? He'll be ours, the baby. Yours as much as mine." Holly took Sahara in her arms. "Don't cry. It wasn't very sensitive of me to just blurt it out."

"I'm so sorry Holly. I don't mean to cry. I'm overjoyed for you. It's just that I thought I was over wanting children, and lately, I've been craving one so much."

"I know, I know. Holly suddenly had an idea that broke into a broad smile. "Sahara, you know what? I could carry your and Aiden's child! Why haven't we thought of this before? Yes! I can. I want to! Think about it...hey, what's wrong? Are you ok...what's wrong?" Holly had never seen Sahara look at her with such pain in her eyes, almost as if she was recoiling from her.

"I remember!" Sahara let go of Holly's hand, ashen, and collapsed in a heap to the ground.

Holly looked desperately around her; the day was turning to night, and they were far away from the cabin, Aiden in town still, and her phone in her purse at Sahara's.

"Goddammit, Sahara. What! What's going on?" The wind suddenly felt colder, the sky more menacing. She had no choice but to leave her there on the cold ground and run to the cabin. Ulfred refused to budge from Sahara's side. He curled himself up beside her, offering his warmth and began to howl. Holly ran as fast as she could, her lungs expanding with new found strength, mind racing. What could possibly have made Sahara look so horrified? They had walked so far...

In his truck driving home, Aiden felt a tug at his heart and a surge of fear as Ulfred's call reached his subconscious. Sahara! He pressed on the gas pedal and headed for the fork in the road towards

251

her cabin. All manner of questions entered his mind. He was grateful for the plowing service Sahara had hired to clear her road, and that at least today, there hadn't been any fresh snow. There were still patches of ground visible here and there, in protected corners. He trained his intuitive ear towards Ulfred's howls. Past the cabin, where a few lights burned, along the riverbed. Where had she gotten to? It would be pitch black soon. In the misty distance, he saw a lone figure approaching. Holly, running and waving her arms. He swallowed hard.

Coming to a skidding halt, Aiden reached for the passenger door. "Get in, get in!"

He took Holly's hand in his, she was trembling and pointing frantically in the direction she had come from.

"That way!"

They drove on, Holly stammering out what had happened, Aiden trying to calm her.

"I just didn't know that she would react that way. I'm so sorry, I should have known that it would be a sensitive subject." Aiden squeezed her hand hard. "I'm sure that wasn't it, babe, don't blame yourself..."

"Then what?" Holly cried. "She said, 'I remember.' I triggered something!"

"We're here!" Aiden slammed on the brake and jumped out to where Ulfred stood guard. "Get in the back seat, Holly. Now!" he commanded as Holly stood questioningly over Sahara.

She scrambled in. Aiden placed Sahara across her lap, and threw his coat over her.

"Should we go to the hospital?"

"No. She's fainted. She'll be ok. We'll take her home and take care of her there."

"But..."

"It's ok babe. I know what I'm doing. This is something that should have been addressed sooner." He cursed under his breath. "Darling, don't worry. It's going to be ok." He gave Holly a reassuring glance. "I love you. We're together. It's alright."

"Ok." Holly was grateful for Aiden's confidence because she had none in the moment. Was love always this hard? This ache for your beloveds? This constant wonder if one would lose the people they loved most?

She glanced over her shoulder at Ulfred sitting in the back of the pick-up, his nose to the wind. "Good boy," she whispered.

252

Aiden threw directions around like wildfire. "Bring blankets. Let's cover her up. There, in the kitchen cupboard, is a small wooden box. Yes, that one. And a glass of water please."

Holly peered into the box with its orderly rows of tiny vials, a feather, a mortar and pestle, bundled sage, a notebook, and some things she didn't recognise. Aiden stirred some powder from one bottle into the water. Setting it down, he opened another, and lifting Sahara's head gently, he waved the vial under her nose. She awakened sputtering. Immediately, he offered her the drink, which she took obediently, observing him with strangely shadowed eyes.

"It's alright now," Aiden whispered. "We're both here. You fainted."

Sahara continued to look at him with that curious gaze.

"Thank you, my lord."

Aiden's breath quickened. Something wasn't right here. He motioned for Holly to come closer. "Holly's running you a warm bath."

Holly sat down beside Sahara and took her hand. But Sahara wrenched it away and turned her head. "No!"

"Sahara!" Holly pleaded. "What is it? Are you so angry with me?"

But Sahara remained silent, with tears rolling down her face.

"Aiden, I can't bear it!" Holly wept.

Aiden's growl sent Holly jumping.

"Come away. She doesn't recognise you. She thinks you're someone else."

"Who?"

"Arinn."

"Arinn? But they loved each other! What's this about?"

"I don't know, Holly. But I'm going to find out." He reached for his phone. "Darling, can you make us something to eat please?"

"What are you going to do?"

"I'm calling Iona and Richard."

"Is Sahara in danger?" Holly paled.

"No. But we need to get the others here to find out what memory has surfaced. Can you take the night off?"

"Not really, I mean, I can get things set up and come back."

"Ok. You can use my truck, but I want you to go before the snow starts tonight."

"I don't want to leave her."

Aiden took her in his arms. "I don't want to make this worse for you than it already is, but your presence is making her upset right now, and until she comes out of the memory, we should probably keep her confusion as minimal as possible."

"I understand," Holly sank her head against Aiden's chest. How hard and unforgiving a place it was and yet so safe. "Will you tell me everything that's happened?"

"Of course. Every word," He looked at her hand, where her ring, awoken, shone brightly. "Keep this on my love. Promise."

"I'll keep it on."

"Promise."

"I do, promise."

"That's my girl," Aiden whispered into her hair, hugging her close. "I'm so hungry suddenly. Ravenous."

"I'll make us something. You stay with Sahara. Aiden. I need you to make sure she'll be alright...not slip off to somewhere where we can't reach her."

"She'll be alright. I've cast a spell, and she has allies."

"I wish I understood your world more."

Aiden kissed her. Roughly. A sorcerer's kiss.

CHAPTER 47

A witch ought never be frightened in the darkest forest...
Because she should be sure in her soul that the most terrifying thing
in the forest was her ~ Terry Pratchett

They had driven through the night, and answered his call with never a question. They were all near exhaustion, Richard grim, Iona - shoulders squared, but with haunted eyes, Aiden standing in the doorway, ushering them in as snow blew into the kitchen.

He peered past Richard at the Mercedes SUV covered with snow and ice. If the weather forecast was correct, nobody would be getting out today. He'd already told Holly to wait for his call and not attempt the drive.

Richard looked around the cabin, leaving Iona to sit by Sahara. Although he wanted badly to join her and take Sahara in his arms to offer comfort, he knew that this was not his place and it wouldn't be welcomed. Once again, he was at a disadvantage with Aiden. He hated this position. It seemed that centuries erased nothing of their dynamic. The energy of the room was very familiar, and he knew why. Here he felt Sahara's true nature. It was not like Iona's whose strength rose from somewhere dark, as befitting one so sought out for her alchemical skills. Sahara's home spoke of her adherence to the light. There was mystery, but it was clear and unfettered. So this was what it was like to be in her orbit. He envied Aiden immensely.

Aiden's deep voice broke in on his thoughts.

"I'll make some coffee. Would you like breakfast?" He smiled as warmly as he could, considering the circumstances. He felt a fondness for Richard, it couldn't be denied. The tension in the room was so much more than about Sahara's need of them. It was to be determined how they would act around each other: as lovers and friends, navigating the boundaries of their comfort levels. Aiden could very well feel Richard's desire to hold Sahara in safety. He viewed it with curiosity, and an openness that he hadn't expected. Iona had yet to come and greet him physically, making herself busy at Sahara's side, but her energy pounded at Aiden's heart center - wild, uncontrolled, desperate.

"I'd kill for a coffee," Richard replied gratefully.

They lost themselves to a few moments of watching Sahara cradled in Iona's arms. She was awake and alert, curious as to why they were here, asking for Holly. She had forgotten everything of the previous evening. Aiden's magic was nothing if not thorough. Both of them found the two women's embrace warming their hearts. It was so easy after all, to remember the wonder of their previous lives.

Aiden excused himself to answer a text from Holly.

What's happening? How's Sahara?

Awake. She remembers nothing. I'll have to explain to her why everyone's here. She's been asking for you

Oh, thank God! The weather is terrible. I'm already wondering when I'll be able to see you

This will take a while...I don't know. But I promise I'll call you as soon as I'm able. I'm not going to keep anything from you. You have my word

I love you. Kiss Sahara for me

I will. Don't drive in this bad weather, please. Talk soon my love

He ground the coffee beans and warmed the oven. Richard stood by the fire, contemplative. He was exquisite, Aiden thought, once more aware of the excellence that he had previously admired in him. In any case, he felt so familiar here, as if he'd always been part of the scenery. The recollection of Sahara's recent tryst with Richard tugged at Aiden's heart. Sharing her should feel worse, but somehow he trusted this man who should by all rights be his enemy.

Sahara came to his side. She searched his face for explanations. Taking his hands, she waited.

"While you were out walking with Holly last evening, she told you something that triggered a memory from our previous life and you fainted away. Sahara, please promise me that when you go somewhere far from the cabin by foot, you'll leave a note and take your phone."

"Yes, ok...the phone doesn't work out there anyway."

"I know, but please do as I say. I insist. And yes, to answer the question on your mind, I erased the triggered memory. For your safety, only. Holly was scared out of her wits."

"Oh no! What did she tell me?" Sahara pretended to be calm, while her heart raced, imagining what they faced, if she was right as to why Richard and Iona were here.

"She told you that I didn't use any protection the other night...that she was hoping to be pregnant." Aiden's grip tightened.

"Yes. I remember that now. That shouldn't have made me upset. I knew you were going to try sooner or later."

"I want to talk to you some more about it, the being ready for a baby...when we're done here. I love you so much, darling." Aiden pressed her close, dropping kisses on her hair. "I called Iona and Richard because it's time to discover why this caused you such alarm and what memory came up. There's no more point in delaying. We were going to do this anyway. I think the right time has presented itself to us."

"I can't disagree. Give me a bit of time to gather myself? I'm going to take a bath. I'd love some coffee too, and could you make me some food?"

Aiden laughed. "Of course."

He was acutely aware of Iona's sadness as she sat embraced by Richard in front of the fire. If this wasn't complicated, he didn't know what was. His heart ached for them all. There was history here, so strong that it was palpable in the air. Sahara gave Richard a quick hug and kiss on the cheek as she passed him. There was no use in pretending that they weren't intimately acquainted.

Aiden poured the coffee and brought the cups fireside. His hand brushed Iona's as she reached for hers. Their eyes met, under the intense stare of Richard.

"Croissants are in the oven, Holly's specialty. I've put eggs on the boil, and Sahara has some homemade blackberry preserve."

Richard nodded. Iona sipped her coffee, her delicate hands wrapped around the mug, unfolding her energy, letting it fill the room.

"Here's how I would like to proceed," Aiden suggested. "Let's take some time to eat and get used to this sudden gathering. Then, we'll walk over to my place to get integrated into the energy of the land. I think that's important. Seeing my home will be another portal to my energy and our connection. The more we understand each other, the easier it will be to find balance on our journey. But I'd like to do the regression here, for two reasons. One is that Sahara will be most comfortable here."

They all understood that he cared little at this point about everyone else's comfort. This was to be a journey for Sahara's healing.

"Also," Aiden continued, "this cabin is most resembling the one that we were at in the past, in the Oracle Wood. Making the journey back will be strengthened by the energy here."

"Hey, where's my coffee, mister?" Sahara called from the bath. She was making light of things, but her voice carried an edge of anxiety.

"Excuse me." Aiden stood. They watched him bring her coffee and a robe from upstairs. He served the croissants and tended to the fire. He was in charge, from beginning to end.

"Will Holly be joining us?" Richard ventured into unknown territory. The quick swipe of Aiden's energy through his surprised him.

"Not for the regression. Not unless the storm ends. Not unless I feel it is of benefit to her." Aiden softened. Perhaps he was being too abrupt. "Having said that, I promised to tell her everything. If the storm has abated by the time we're done, then yes, I will fetch her."

"I've explained to Richard already about it possibly being a shock seeing Holly," Sahara came down the stairs, dressed in her ceremonial black gown, Aiden's pendant at her throat. Richard drew in his breath at the sight of her in witch's attire, and stood, as was his custom when a woman approached him. He made room for her on the sofa beside Iona and chose a chair nearby.

"Yes," Aiden agreed. That's another thing. But we'll cross that bridge when we come to it."

They settled into each other, the two men in the chairs flanking the fire, each of them attentive to their lovers. Aiden worked his magic, secret spells for peace among them. They kept the conversation light, and to anyone looking in, it would seem like any four friends visiting over breakfast on a stormy morning. The only thing was, the air was laced with sexual tension and an anticipation of the hours to come. No one knew what those hours would look like, or how long they would be gone, or how they would feel when they got back. The past was no place for lingering; it was just somewhere to find understanding. It couldn't be an excuse for the present nor could it be ignored. They had all loved each other once, in that murky medieval existence. They had battled the politics of the land, known riches, tasted poverty, run from ignorance, and drank from each other's cups. They had laid themselves bare and found satisfaction in each other's arms. They had shared in licentiousness, and paid the price for it. They had been in love.

But finally it was time to carry on, and Sahara found her warm things. "We must be on our way," she said. "I have extra scarves..." Pulling on her heavy cloak and tall boots, Sahara looked every bit the mystic, wrapped against the cold. She held the door open for them, and they walked into the storm.

With Ulfred leading the way, they trudged towards the Aspen Wood, breath misty on the air. Without him, they would have had to rely on their intuition as to the path, as it had disappeared under the snow. But he barked and herded, keeping them in single file, the women in the middle. It was all Iona could do to not shapeshift and fly ahead. To Aiden's! Her heart leapt with joy at the thought as much as she feared the day ahead. Surely, after this they would abandon her for her wretched secrets. A twig caught her foot and she fell, on all fours into the white powder beneath her. Aiden turned quickly and caught her up. Their bodies burned as contact was made. Richard resisted taking her from Aiden's arms. Instead he took Sahara's hand. And in this fashion, now paired, they found Aiden's home surrounded by the sacred grove of trees.

"It'll be warm enough," Aiden said, as he unlocked the door. Sahara asked about fire, seeing that the hearth was prepared. She loved that particular quirk of his; always ready for the next time he'd need warmth.

"Sure, why not. We can take our time here," Aiden agreed.

Richard handed over his coat, eyes roaming the living space appreciatively.

"Alright?" Aiden asked. "I know it's barely noon, but if you'd like a scotch, I have your preference."

"I would, thank you." And then, "Did you build this? Of course you did, I see you in every detail."

"I did. I'll take you through in a bit."

"This is why I want you to build my home. You understand the connection between the owner and the building itself."

"Come sit down, we can talk about this later."

"You still have reservations, don't you, about building for me?"

"Richard. Stop pushing. After today...we'll make decisions." Aiden steered him into the great room.

Iona wandered into the alcove, and perused Aiden's books. His magic tools were tucked in a dark corner, behind a chair. She dared not touch them, understanding how important it was for a magic worker to protect their practice...but she wanted to...to feel his power. Sahara joined her.

"Iona, are you frightened?"

"No," Iona lied and Sahara gripped her hands.

"You're the most experienced of us here. You can take us through this journey without any worries. I know this."

"It's not the journey, beloved. It's the secrets I must confess."

"But surely it can't be too bad. Whatever has happened to us is behind us."

"Not entirely. You're being naïve, as usual."

"Iona!"

"I'm sorry."

"I promise that it won't matter. We'll get through it."

"We'll see." Iona looked around. "I was barred once," she mused, "from entering Dagr's home."

"Never! He never would have barred you. You were his first love, his most cherished."

"Once. But not always."

"Let's join them." Sahara nodded at Aiden and Richard, in deep conversation over their drinks. "This can't be easy for them."

"Easier for Aiden than Richard. He's very possessive of me...with men."

"Well."

"Well, what?" Iona snapped, nerves raw.

"Well, I don't think he has to worry about it. Aiden has Holly to consider."

"So you keep saying."

He took them around, and ignored the tiny gasp from Iona when she saw the bed in Holly's room. What kind of trick of fate was this? Their beds were identical! Richard threw Aiden a quizzical look. The other man shrugged and moved on.

They wandered upstairs into the master's quarters, with its expansive view of the forest and a bed big enough for four. Nobody spoke of the sins committed within the confines of these walls. It was difficult enough to keep from imagining them. Iona felt as if her heart was being ripped open.

Sahara thought of the first time she'd shared this bed with Aiden, when Dagr's name had surfaced, and how their lives had evolved after that. So much had happened in such short a time. It was surreal that so much life had been lived before they'd met and now, a few months later, the past had exploded through a portal none of them could have imagined.

And in the midst of it all, Holly, the purest expression of what the past had been: open, trusting, loving, a reflection of Arinn's being so many hundreds of years ago.

It was the Universe expressing itself through the experience of their love.

It was love experiencing itself through their willingness to explore its boundaries.

Pushing society's borders of what was sacred, what was sin?

They were of this world and of spirit, of Fey and of magic.

They were seekers, diviners, adventurers, peacekeepers and warriors.

Together, they had broken the rules when rule breaking was punishable by death.

Together, they would continue to test the waters of the sensual and forbidden. For love like theirs had no beginning and no end. It was bound by rules made by men and ignored by angels.

Sahara cherished their bravery. She wanted more. More of the strength she found in Aiden's arms, more of the darkness she fell into in Iona's kiss, more of Holly's vulnerability and trust, more of the wickedness that Richard was expert at delivering.

Should. A word that found itself between them all. Should they? Could they? Would they?

Was fear of the unknown, of failing at it, of feeling emotional pain, enough to keep them from each other?

Or should they just swim, naked, in the river of their desire.

"It's time," Aiden's voice and hand on her back made Sahara turn and fall into his loving blue eyes. She followed him and the others down the stairs, where they bundled up once more and headed into the winter storm.

Why was it always storming when life became complicated? Why was her heart racing and thudding like a base drum? Was it Aiden's heat beside her? He was in warrior mode, his face fierce, his body hardened against the cold and the hours ahead.

And so it was that the hour had come for them to taste history at its most raw. When war was de rigueur, when witches were burned, when sex was evil and womankind was viewed as the downfall of man.

"Everything I did, I did out of love. I cannot erase it, I can only seek your forgiveness." Tears streamed down Iona's face as they sat at the table, hands held, candles lit and fire blazing.

They had smudged, drunk of a honey wine, eaten enough to keep up their energy and covered the cabin in a spell for protection. Pan's wisdom had been evoked, and the aroma of the forest permeated their senses.

"We are bound by love and by the oaths we made to each other six hundred years ago," Aiden said. "We go into the past as friends, and return as friends. Nothing from there can hurt us now, and we go knowing that the past has no power over us except what we allow. We will find the answers we need for the purpose of soul growth and learning. So it has been spoken, so mote it be. Let us journey."

CHAPTER 48

"Come away, O human child!
To the waters and the wild
With a faery, hand in hand,
For the world's more full of weeping than you can understand."
~ W. B. Yeats

Each day rose and fell the same way, with Brigida looking towards the shadows of the trees, mourning the leaving of Richard.

They resumed their life, knowing that each sunrise meant a day closer to when they would leave their life in hiding and start anew in a strange land.

Every evening Arinn and Brigida asked for stories of France. How were the people? Was it warm? What were the forests like? Were there verdant fields and rabbits to eat?

Of all the things he told them, they loved the stories of the ocean best. It was warm...yes warm enough to get into! He told them of the afternoon light, like none he had seen anywhere else. The gardens thrived well into the autumn months, and the forests were full of game. Dagr had decided on the south of France, where protected from his usual liaisons in the North, he could carve out a life for them, relatively unnoticed.

Richard had gone on ahead, to purchase property, and to make connections with a trusted friend of Dagr's, the elderly Compt de Beauchene.

"I beg you," Dagr had admonished Richard, "do not come back to tell me that you have acquired a large estate. Our needs are simple. What's most important is land that can be used for gardens and good hunting grounds."

"I may be in need of a chateau myself. You could be left to run it. Money would not be an issue, I would pay for its upkeep."

Dagr shrugged. "You'll do as you want, I can see. Be practical. We may have to move on. Beauchene can be trusted. But he's not a favorite at the French court, so in that sense I must still be careful. I have no intention of throwing my presence around. Nothing too ostentatious. Promise."

Richard had agreed, but rode away making plans for something befitting a knight of Dagr's excellence. Oh how sorry he was that life

262

had changed so much that their days together were coming to an end. He could not imagine the years ahead without Dagr, or Brigida; and to assuage his grief, he made busy with a passage of the channel, and visions of a home they would be comfortable in. No one could stop him from stocking the stable with sturdy horses, or the bedchambers with the best linens, or hiring a cook who would see skillfully to their meals. If it killed him, he would not see them in squalor among a pack of curious or unwelcoming villagers. No. He would make a 'home away' for himself, of which a distant 'cousin' would be left in charge. That was the plan. He had some lands he could sell here, they meant nothing to him. Richard had made himself especially useful to the King over the years. He had been duly rewarded. But that reward belonged to Dagr, as dirty as it was with spilled blood. No matter. The only thing that was important now, was making the people he loved, his only family, safe. He would seek reasons to visit France as often as possible. Yes! He could bear their parting only by imagining their reunions.

Dagr waited for word that a passage for three had been purchased, along with a disguise for them all. He spent countless hours teaching Arinn the right inflections of the French language, repeating useful phrases for everyday life. But their lessons fell apart as the women found his speech seductive, even when he was making mundane conversation. And they laughed until they cried when he said that what they had found so sultry was how to bargain for eels.

"Will we ever come back here?" Arinn asked. She loved these woods, how the English rains made everything vibrantly green, and the smells of a familiar landscape.

"I think not, my lady," Dagr held her hand as they walked the path towards a favorite clearing. Brigida trailed behind, singing. Except that it wasn't really singing, more of an out-of-tune howling, the only thing she could verbalise, as her voice had never returned. But she tried to make sounds, to find a way to speak to them without practicing telepathy. She missed using her mouth for speaking.

"I have a wonderful idea, my lord." Arinn looked up at her towering lover. He was ever so handsome, tanned from days in the saddle hunting to provide for their table.

"Yes? And what might that be?" Dagr turned and beckoned for Brigida to catch up.

"It came to me in a dream. I could go to the Dark Pool and ask the Fey for a healing for Brigida! I wish I had thought of it sooner. We have wasted so much time."

263

Dagr's hard grip on her hand caused Arinn to yelp in pain.

"No! I forbid it. Arinn, your dream came from the Fey. I must warn you...a favor from the Fey comes at a price. You will not."

"I can decide for myself if it is a price I can pay. Let go my hand! You are hurting me."

Brigida came hurrying alongside of them, curious about their conversation and Arinn's confrontational stance. "What is the matter?" she asked, signing crudely.

"Nothing," Dagr barked and walked off in anger.

Their outing was ruined, nobody was talking, and in the evening, Dagr stayed out chopping firewood.

"You need not look at me that way, Brigida. He is being stubborn."

But Brigida only looked more distressed. She was not so skilled at projecting her thoughts that she could make herself plain. Damn her feeble head. She hit her open palm against her forehead. It only made Arinn more determined to heed her dream.

"Do you think I have not thought of approaching the Fey?" Dagr whispered to her, once they were sure Brigida was asleep.

"I suppose not! Or you might have mentioned it," Arinn's eyes flashed.

"You are impossible! Of course I have. You must listen to me, I understand their ways," he hissed. But he knew that often she did not listen. She was strong of mind and will. And it made him afraid.

She decided to leave it unspoken for a week. When Dagr appeared to have forgotten her intention, she called upon the Fey and asked for a favor which was granted with much excitement. Finally, a chance to play with the golden haired maiden, so favored by their King. He had noticed her once, as she had lingered by the brook behind the hut where they drew their water. After that, he had come often to visit her in the woods, unnoticed.

That night, Dagr and Brigida lay in each other's arms, as Arinn sat mending their clothes by the fire.

"I have never been so tired in my life," Dagr mumbled, his hand falling away from playing with Brigida's hair. Brigida was already nodding off. He looked at Arinn apologetically. "I meant to still bank the fire for the night..." Arinn looked up, eyes guarded. In that instant, the shadow of realization passed across his face. A low, desperate growl escaped his lips and he fell asleep, forgetting everything.

Arinn rode hard into the night, led by a stream of light, the phosphorescent presence of fairies. She rode without fear, they had promised her safety. By morning, she had arrived. The Dark Pool lay undisturbed in the forest glen. She had been abandoned by her companions, and stood shaking with excitement. Dagr would be angry at first, but when he realized that Brigida was returned to her former self, he would surely forgive her. She stepped closer, and peered into the depths. Nothing. The pool was impenetrable by sight alone. The waters were like a black non-reflective mirror as she hung herself over the edge of a large, flat rock trying to spy any life down below.

Not understanding where the inclination came from, Arinn decided that the best thing to do would be to slip into the pool. She dipped one toe in the water, expecting it to be frigidly cold. But to her surprise, it was pleasantly warm. It was as if the water beckoned her. Taking off her other shoe, she slid from the rock she was on, and let herself be swallowed into the unknown.

Instead of sinking down to the bottom and entering some kind of portal as she had expected, Arinn found herself sitting at the edge of another pool, this one in a sun-dappled forest, the water sparkling blue, edged with ivy and fern. It was simply the most beautiful place she had ever seen. There was not one iota of anything that could make a human being uncomfortable here. Not the temperature, not the essence of the place, not the light or the sounds surrounding her. For all about her, were all manner of Fey, playing games or dancing, singing and laughing. She could only sit and watch for a very long time, so long in fact that she became quite sleepy and lay her head down on the moss and closed her eyes.

She dreamt of Dagr and Brigida, and their life before the troubles. She dreamt of how she had been awoken to love by the girl who had come to mean everything to her. She dreamt of Dagr's constant devotion, how he had met her a child in need of protection, and with a patient heart had acquainted her with the love of a man. She dreamt of their losses, and how she missed her life at the manor. How much Dagr had suffered in losing his child, and now the struggles Brigida faced having to sign her precious thoughts. It was not that they could not communicate, because Dagr had taught them about connecting telepathically, and as the days wore on they were all getting better at it. Arinn dreamt of the magic Dagr had instructed her in and that it was he who had told her that the Fey were their allies, and could be called on for help, as much as they also needed humankind for their purposes.

Dagr had learned a lot from his mystic mother and the Fey, but he could not heal Brigida could he? He knew every herb and root that was useful in medicine, but he could not make one tincture to loosen Brigida's tongue! It was for them, that she had come here. Because her love for them was bigger than any concern she had for herself. No matter what Dagr said, no sacrifice was too big for her beloveds, and she would keep her wits about her, not let the Fey trick her. Besides, how could anyone so helpful be unkind? Surely they would never meddle in the love that the three of them shared.

Arinn woke up convinced of her mission and with complete well-meaning naiveté, set down a long road winding past the pool. She didn't know what she was looking for, but she would know it when she saw it. Even if Arinn had happened upon someone along the road who could have warned her about not trusting as she did in the good will of the Fey, she would not have listened because she was in fact, naïve, and open-hearted, even after everything that had happened to her. She wanted to remain this way. It was her gift, being this optimistic about the intentions of others. And if she were any wiser, she might have known that nothing was free, because every coin has two sides and that there was no light without shadow. The Fey always asked for a service in kind. If they gave, you gave. That was the rule. It was not that they were being unkind - oh but they were tricky to be sure - it was just that they had a way of operating that was different from human ways, and when they had a lesson to teach, they made sure it was well learned. Centuries meant nothing to them, and if it took Arinn a lifetime or two, then so be it.

Arinn realized after a time that she was now being followed by a long gaggle of fairies, pixies and the like. They trailed behind her in a happy swarm, sometimes running ahead, and beckoning her further. She wondered how long she would be gone, because a part of her was already missing the warm kiss Dagr bestowed upon her every morning and the soft touch of Brigida's cheek against hers.

Just as she had that thought, she stood facing a large doorway, so tall that she had to crane her neck, hanging with ivy and a dainty flower she did not recognise, emitting a heavenly scent. Encouraged by the smiling faces around her, she opened the heavy, creaking door and stepped through. As soon as she did so, she was transformed, now wearing a resplendent gown that accentuated her winsome, womanly beauty. Her hair had been brushed out to flowing gold, and on her head a delicately woven crown of holly. Taking her hand, a few Fey maidens led her down a carpet of moss toward a throne upon which sat the King of the Fey.

Arinn fell to her knees, awestruck by his splendor, and - but how could it be - his resemblance to Dagr? She was sure it was a trick of the eye, but nonetheless, she felt comfortable in his energy, which was so great, it filled every inch of space around her.

"Welcome!" he thundered, and stood up off his dais and walked toward her, hand extended. He was so beautiful a man that Arinn could not look him in the eye, and she was glad that she was not wearing the clothing she had started out in. His masculinity was astounding. But it felt familiar. Richard and Dagr were, after all, men who also commanded space without effort.

He led her to his throne and left her sitting at his feet, his smile making a fool of her heart.

"What may I help you with my dear?" He was young, and virile, yet somehow old in spirit.

Arinn's heart stopped its wild beating and quite calmly, she explained Brigida's dilemma. The Fairy King seemed to know a lot about her lover, and indeed, would be able to help. But enough of serious talk, he announced, and whispering into the ear of a waiting elf, set about organising a lavish meal in her honor.

"Oh, but I do not have time for that! I must get back home. You see..."

"Do not fret," he smiled, "you have all the time in the world." She relented.

It was only after the feast and a hundred dances in his arms that he asked her to join him on a pile of pillows by that very same pool she had entered through.

"My dear, I am ready to help you with your request."

"I will be eternally in your debt," Arinn uttered.

Aside from the flash of knowing in his eyes as she said that, Arinn saw no reason for worry. Dagr had been overprotective of her, she thought satisfactorily.

"When you get home, you will find Brigida restored to her whole self, and there is only one small price for the favor I grant you." He was so close as he whispered his words, that he could have easily kissed her ear. Every bit of womanly desire was awoken in Arinn, and she vowed that she would willingly pay the price. What was it?

"It is the price of jealousy," he said matter of factly, as if he asked this very thing every day.

Arin laughed so heartily, that soon the King joined her. Tears of relief flowed down Arinn's face. He wiped them away with a tender hand, his eyes boring into hers. They were so blue.

"What, my fair lady, is so amusing?"

"You said the price is jealousy. Well, I will take that price, because I have never been jealous one day of my life. I never will be. It is not in my nature. And besides, I have nothing to be jealous of. We all love each other as one. So you see, it is such a small price as to be no price at all."

"I see," hummed the seductive voice of the King. "Well, if you are sure of yourself...it is the only price I require."

"I am sure. But I am curious, why would you require jealousy as the price? Would it not be unkind?"

The fairy king flashed his expansive smile. "Not unkind, my dear. Simply a lesson in finding one's equilibrium. Humankind is still finding the boundaries of love. And there is no lesson more pure than love at its most challenging. For us, jealousy serves no purpose, but in your world, jealousy is a way of gaining control in love. And for some reason, jealousy is often required as a symbol of one's devotion."

Arinn heard every word he said but did not understand that the Fey chose only the strongest to teach the rest of the world through their mistakes. And Arinn, so pure of heart, was also of an iron will, and she would live life after life until she had unravelled the puzzle handed her by her teacher. And once she had passed through the fire, a portal would be opened for the rest of humankind. And so it would be, because now Arinn was leaving, a little sadly, with the king's kiss on her hand, and his assurance that he would be at her side, should she need him, or wish to return. He wanted her to return.

In an instant, Arinn was at the edge of the Dark Pool, in her old clothes, and in a desperate hurry to get home. She had no idea how long she had been gone, but she was sure that it was long enough for Dagr to be awake and plenty angry with her disobedience.

His great horse stood where she had left him, chewing the soft grass under the birch trees. He whinnied upon her approach and tossed his head.

"Home!" she commanded. They went swiftly, but still it took a day and Arinn began to worry about Dagr's reaction to her absence. When she got home, however, it seemed as if nothing had changed since she had left. Her sewing still in its basket by the fire, and Brigida lay in Dagr's arms, both of them fast asleep. She sat down quietly and picked up her sewing. Everything would have been fine if a branch had not fallen from the trees above and made a terrible racket on the roof.

"Who goes there?" Dagr sat up abruptly, hand on his knife, arm tightening around Brigida.

268

"Go back to sleep, my lord," Arinn soothed. "It is only a branch falling.

Dagr lay back down. "Will you not come to bed soon, my love?" He searched her face for an answer, but instead found the one thing that gave her away. He was at her side in an instant.

"What is this?" he asked, his voice dangerous, taking the precariously positioned crown from her head.

Arinn swallowed her fear.

"Holly."

"Holly, yes, I see that. Where did you get this?"

She could not lie. There was no point. "I went to the Dark Pool." She stood, and dropped her sewing.

Dagr crushed the crown in his mighty hand. "Holly is the sacred tree of the Fey. It is meant for protection from their wiles."

"You see. They themselves offered protection!" Arinn pleaded. Wake Brigida up. You will find her healed."

"No! It is a trick. This crown only shows their humor. They are laughing at you. It offers nothing!" He threw it into the fire.

"We must not burn holly without permission!" Arinn shouted, horrified, as the fire surged into great flames, throwing so much heat that they were forced to stand back.

Brigida woke up as Dagr roared, his hands around Arinn's shoulders, shaking her in his fury.

"I have never whipped you, my lady, when it did not involve play, but today, I will punish you. You have disobeyed me one time too many."

"Beat me. I do not care. I will welcome your whip. There is nothing that I would not risk to bring Brigida her voice."

"My lord! Please. What has angered you so?" Brigida's voice rang sweet in their ears, as clear as the day she was born.

Everything came to a standstill. All the shouting, their anger and Dagr's fear.

Brigida placed her hands over her mouth. Tears rolled down her face.

"I can speak! Oh, my loves, I can speak!"

They fell upon her, and for an instant, all their worries and disagreements were forgotten. Brigida laughed and recited a recipe for calendula balm, shouting at the end, her arms outstretched, jubilant. She wanted to know all about Arinn's adventure and vowed her undying loyalty for the risks she had taken. She strictly forbid Dagr from whipping her beloved. He was made to promise.

"You are both forgetting one thing," he said, in a last attempt at making his point about the Fey. "What was the price for this? You still have not said."

"Now you will see that all your fears are unfounded, my lord," Arinn announced, pleased with herself. "They asked for something that will never happen. It is not possible!"

"What is it?" Dagr's voice was low, the hair standing on his forearms, expecting the worst.

"Jealousy! You see, it is nothing! I will never be jealous. I have never been before."

Brigida looked stricken, she lost all her color, sitting down abruptly.

Arinn looked at her, confused. "You do not believe it can happen?"

Dagr turned on his heel and strode to the door. "You are a child. A stupid, willful child. And I *will* whip you!" And he left with a bang of the door.

Arinn collapsed to the floor. All she had hoped for, their joy, was now ground underfoot by anger and misunderstanding. Brigida picked her up and took her to bed.

"Rest, my love," she said, quietly, still marvelling at the sound of her voice. "It will be alright. You will see. Nothing can come between us." She watched the holly burning as if it could not be destroyed. Strange, it was such a delicate thing, but created such heat. She closed her eyes and listened to Arinn's sobbing. Surely such a pure heart could never know jealousy.

CHAPTER 49

Word came that Richard had bought a modest chateau in the Perigord region. It was hidden from view, built on a hill but shrouded by a great oak and pine forest. The house that Richard chose was crafted from the honey colored limestone abundant in the plains below. It was a handsome estate, with established gardens and forests ripe with game; a demesne run poorly by its former owner, but that under the right hand, could prove quite productive. They could travel by river from the Atlantic to the hills where they would live.

"I thought we talked about settling by the Great Sea," Dagr queried Richard.

"Too far. I would never be able to visit you there."

"I see." Dagr scowled. "I promised them the warm ocean."

"You will like this just as well," Richard was a bit ruffled by Dagr's displeasure. "In fact, it reminds me of England. Green, but warmer, more dry, with several villages not too far off for supplies. No one will wander up those hills. It is private, as you wanted. And you can go to the Great Sea here and there. It is not an impossible journey."

Dagr looked at the sky, quiet. They had met at the edge of the Oracle Wood. Dagr missed the open moors.

"What is on your mind, my lord?" Richard asked.

Dagr sighed. "I will tell you." And he recalled the whole story about how Arinn had gone to the Dark Pool, and the price of the healing.

"Brigida can speak!" Richard clapped Dagr on the back. He longed to hear her voice once more. "You found her at the Dark Pool, remember?"

"I know. I have thought about the irony of it all."

"Arinn does not strike me as the jealous type, and after all you have been through. Why so angry?"

"Because nothing that the Fey say can be treated lightly. If they ask for something, they mean to get it."

"If it has not happened yet, it will not." Richard decided on optimism.

"You are a fool, like her. It has been the only time I have ever thought of beating a woman."

Richard guffawed. "You would never."

They sat in silence while they shared a portion of cold, roasted venison.

"I brought you some provisions." Richard pulled a sack from his horse. "Soon, you will be a man of your own again, growing your own food and hunting game. It will be good, your life there."

"I miss having work, not war...a demesne to manage."

"I meant to speak to you about that," Richard said. "I have some interests that I run along the river. I will need a trustworthy man to carry it out. And the estate will need care...there are tenant farmers running their pigs in the forest, and further into the valley, productive fields...even a vineyard. There will be plenty to do."

"Just how much land comes with this 'modest' chateau?"

"Plenty. But nothing that you cannot manage. Your estate was the most well run in my earldom. The house is not grand - solid, well proportioned."

"This work. On the river?" Dagr doubted that it was within the boundaries of the law. "Will it mean time away from home?"

"Some. Here, drink. We will make plans later." And then, "I would kill to hear Brigida's voice again."

Dagr grinned. "I expected as much. I suppose it will do no harm."

"My lord," Richard bowed. "You are a true friend."

They rode into the opening later, to shouts from both Arinn and Brigida. Even though Richard presented a complication to Brigida's heart, they had no visitors, and a chance to share a meal with someone other than themselves was highly welcome.

Richard insisted on having Brigida talk all evening, which brought uproarious laughter when after a few drinks of mead, she began to slur her words. He followed her into the woods when she went to fetch more water, and catching her by her hand, kissed her soundly, rejoicing in how her body responded to his.

Arinn came around the corner of the hut as they were leaning against a tree. Brigida was speaking in her softly lilting voice.

"Richard! I have a secret," she blushed.

"You do, my love? Pray tell!" He lifted her chin, and kissed her forehead.

"I am with child once more. I have not yet told anyone. I will tell tonight!"

Richard began some frantic calculations in his head, from the time he had seen her last, when they had been reunited to now. It was possible. She was not yet showing.

"My lady, I am overwhelmed with this news! Dagr will be pleased to hear it." They both thought of the child that had been lost. Richard felt a deep remorse, but she was interrupting his thoughts.

"I cannot be sure..."

"Yes? Speak freely my lady."

Brigida raised her violet eyes to his midnight black, she touched her belly gently.

"Do you mean to tell me that this child could be ours?"

"I do not know. I just do not know."

Arinn slipped away, an odd ache in her heart. She rubbed at it, trying to erase it. What was it? Sadness? Fear? Was she worried for Dagr's sake? Should Brigida not have told Dagr and her first? She must forget about it, wait until Brigida was ready to tell them. Then she would be better able to understand the thing twisting in her emotions.

Richard knew Dagr well enough to understand his quickly averted glance when Brigida, full of happy tears, shared her news.

With a quiet smile and a fervent embrace, Dagr went on to toast the health of mother and child. But Richard knew that Dagr had the same question burning. Whose child was it? On all of their minds, was a reverent recollection of the one they had all mourned. Richard vowed to himself that he would send Brigida every comfort possible. But no one spoke of what the trip to France could mean, with hours on horseback, and then facing an often turbulent sea.

Unable to rest, both men sat up most of the night, staring into the fire and watching the women they loved sleep, curled up in each other's arms.

"I will return with some supplies that you will need for the journey. Warmer garments."

Dagr nodded, his jaw working. Richard kicked a stray coal into the fire.

"What are you thinking?" Richard could no longer keep from asking about the inevitable.

"Nothing. I want this time to be peaceful for her. I cannot forgive myself for the...other."

Richard leaned in and whispered. "I ask you again, what are you thinking?"

Dagr hissed back, "Leave it! There is no sense in talking about it now. We will be far away. It will not matter."

"But surely, if the child is..."

"No!" Dagr's eyes flashed danger and Richard sat back, duly warned. "Whatever happens, she remains with me."

"I see. For her sake, I hope that he is fair of hair."

"And for mine?"

"As you said, she will remain with you. I obviously have no right to her, or the child, even if it..."

"Even if the child is yours, Richard," Dagr's voice softened. "Her world is with me and Arinn. We did what we did, out of our love for each other. But there it ends."

"I know it. But you will not deny me a place in her life altogether?"

"How can I? Do you not know who I am? I love her, and you. Besides, you own us now."

Richard paled, hurt beyond measure. "My lord! That is cruelty not worthy of your character. I do not own you. The chateau is a gift. It is the least I can do." He stood, making for the door.

"Sit down, Richard. It is too dark to ride this wood at night."

"You will never forgive me, will you?"

"I have forgotten it. All that matters now is their safety and peace of mind."

"I love her still."

"I know."

"Maybe I should take a wife. Forget about all this."

Dagr looked up with a wry grin. "And torture the poor woman with your traitorous heart? No, Richard, that would be worse than what we face now. You would be cruel to her in the end."

"Then what is left for me?"

"All that is left is what you see before you. Two women dependent on our honor. Richard, we have to put aside everything that seems ordinary. I was never meant for this world that we live in. We have made our own rules. We have to live by them."

"So you will not leave me out? You will let me know the child?"

"No matter whose child this is, Richard, you will know it. By my love for you, I swear it."

Richard, fierce, a warrior of great bravery, knelt before Dagr and bowed his head.

"Once again, my lord, I am in your debt."

"And I in yours," Dagr replied. "If this child is yours, then you have put this joy in her heart. And if it is not, it has been your care for her while we were separated that kept her from going mad. She has told me - of all the walks you took her on while all she could do was weep, and all the risks you took to keep her clothed and warm, fed from your own gilded plate. And even how you tended to her body."

Richard looked up, surprised. He supposed though that Dagr would have figured things out.

"I would be a fool to think that you were not being watched. And you probably still are. Sooner or later if we did not leave here, we would be facing another danger, and this time, you would be taken in for questioning."

"How do you know this?" Richard looked horrified.

"Because I have traced the tracks of a horse that does not belong to either of us. You are being followed, my friend. How soon is our passage?"

"I have it arranged for two months from now."

"Good. They must travel as men. Too late and the disguise would be impossible."

Richard's face turned dark and menacing. "I will kill anyone who gets in our way! Why did you not tell me of this follower?"

"Kill anyone else, and *you* will need passage to France. And I did not tell you because you act before you think. Besides, I was hoping to apprehend them myself."

"I mean what I say, my lord!"

"I am afraid of that," Dagr replied, and threw more wood on the fire.

CHAPTER 50

It was in those last months when they barely lived each moment without thinking about the future, that Arinn noticed a change in Dagr.

He seemed to pay less attention to her, and dote entirely on Brigida. Of course, she was just as careful to give her beloved the best cut of rabbit, the first cup of herbal brew, but Dagr seemed entirely obsessed. True, he was as loving as she had ever known him to be, as devoted to their life together, but was she imagining that his love for her was waning? Everything he did, he did with the babe in mind. Arinn began to wish that she was pregnant, or that Brigida was not.

She approached him one day as he sat by the fire outside, sharpening their knives and making ready for travel. His muscles worked with each stroke of the knife against the whetstone, his hair now to his waist. She licked her lips, hungry for his skin against hers.

Dagr smiled and setting his tools down, pulled her in, setting his lips to her neck.

"I have missed laying with you, my lady. We must make time for each other. You have been keeping to yourself."

"Nonsense, my lord! It is you who have been too busy tending to my lady to have time for me," Arinn pouted.

"Arinn, that is not so. I have been as in your service and at your side as ever. What is this about?" Dagr kept calm outwardly, but inside, he felt a twinge of knowing.

"Oh, I understand, of course. She is with child. I knew that you would be worried. But I still need you. I need your love."

Arinn, come back to me! Dagr whispered deep in his soul. For in Arinn's eyes he saw a change so subtle that another man may have missed it. But not he, who loved Arinn's sweetness with desperation. She had always been his light, his beacon of what was most good on this earth.

"My love for you is great, my lady. What can I do to prove it to you? Please, do not doubt me."

Arinn turned away from the pain in his eyes. To see this much power succumb to fear made her nauseous. What was wrong with her? It was almost as if she was not herself. Neither of them wanted to say it aloud. *If they did not, it would go away.* Arinn's eyes filled with tears.

"My lord, I ask your forgiveness. I must not be feeling well."

"May I make you some tonic, or perhaps you would like lie down for a spell?"

"I think I will sit by you. Watch you work. That has always been my pleasure."

He made her comfortable on an old stump, and began to work on his sword. It flashed before her eyes, back and forth, back and forth. How beautiful were his movements, the tension in his chest. Her eyes fell to the slim of his hips and she remembered the night of the massacre, and how he had fucked her, a wounded animal. She licked her lips. He noticed and lay down his weapon.

"My lady?"

"Please, my lord."

He did not have to say anything to Brigida, who touched his arm gently as she left the cabin. She had felt Arinn's sadness lately. This would do her good, an afternoon in bed with Dagr. She should be more careful to not seem so needy. But in the last week, she had felt an anxiety that would not leave her. Perhaps she would ask Arinn for a tonic. Some roots to heal melancholy. Maybe it was the trip ahead that worried her. Arinn would know the cure.

Time was running out and Richard never did come back with the warmer garments he had promised. Dagr made several trips to the edge of the wood to search for any signs of strange hoof prints. He knew the imprint of Richard's horse like he knew that of his own great beast, but he did not discover anything amiss. So many questions arose; was Richard staying close to home because he had uncovered a spy, or was he perhaps already being questioned about trips away without reason or escort. It made Dagr nervous, but he kept all his thoughts to himself.

It was during one of the days he was away that it occurred to him to make his own request at the Dark Pool. He would trade Arinn's cost to the Fey with one of his own. There had been nothing until now that they had refused him. Bolstered by this thought, he found himself by the edge of the water, when Pan appeared from the thick forest mist.

Their friendship warm in Dagr's eyes, he accepted Pan's greeting.

"I have been waiting for you," Pan stabbed at the moss underfoot with his hoof, nostrils flaring, eyes the color of amber.

"Waiting for me? I suppose you knew that I would come."

"You are denied entry into the Dark Pool, my friend. What is done is done. This is not your journey, it is hers."

Dagr bristled and his anger rose. "How can it be counted as fair, a maiden so naïve, so unable to discern what serves her and what does not?"

"This is a far greater matter than what you see immediately before you. This time you cannot interfere. She is wiser than you think. What she is embarking on is for many lifetimes, an unravelling of conditioning placed on human kind."

"Rubbish! She has no knowledge of this great work you charge her with. She only saw reason to help her beloved and paid any price to get it. It is the most unfair act of the Fey I have seen you defend!"

"Be that as it may, you see it one way, we see it another. For the greater good, this must be. She has agreed. She is brave."

"She is a child!"

"Exactly the reason what you love about her, her innocence, and also the reason why she is perfect for carrying this out." And with that Pan was gone, only his snorting through the woods could be heard.

"A sacrifice. That is what she is," Dagr growled out loud. "A God-damned sacrifice." He blamed himself, and rode home, as defeated as he had ever been. He ached for Arinn's arms, her tender care, the smell of her hair, the love in her eyes. He longed for the days when she had been no man's, when he had first touched her lips with his, before he had meddled with her future and introduced her to the wise woman in the woods. This was surely his doing, this madness.

But all of Dagr's longing was dashed the minute he rode into the clearing, as a great wailing reached his ears, and Brigida came stumbling from the hut, hands and skirts covered in blood.

He was off his mount in an instant, and ran to her, where they fell to the ground in mourning once again. Brigida's cry was raw in his ears. His heart pounding, he begged for an explanation, although the truth rang in his soul, and he averted his gaze from Arinn, who was collapsed with a heavy thud in the doorway of their home, reeling from shock.

Brigida turned when she heard the noise. She struggled to get up. "Dagr, help her! Help her please!" She began to crawl on her hands and knees to Arinn's side.

Warrior instinct kicked in. Stepping over Arinn, he sat Brigida by the fire. Lifting Arinn from the floor, he laid her in the bed and set to heating water in the cauldron over the fire. Selecting some herbs from the medicinal cupboard that the women kept well stocked, Dagr prepared a wash for Brigida. She was trembling horribly, ashen of face and unable to stop the tears from flowing.

He would think later. Arinn, he estimated, would come out of her faint soon enough. He pushed aside his fears and the bile that rose to his mouth. There were some things that even he could not stomach, and betrayal was at the top of the list. Throwing his cloak to the floor atop his travelling blanket, he lowered the now greatly weakened Brigida to the floor. Here, directly by the fire was where he had to leave her, the alcove was too cold. He apologised softly as he undressed her, and threw the garments aside, not daring to look at their contents. Tenderly, he washed away the blood from her legs, and, when it was sufficiently infused, offered her a tumbler full of yarrow and agrimony tisane.

"You will stop bleeding soon enough, my darling," He wrapped her warmly in her cloak and held her in his arms. She continued to cry, great sobs interspersed with words of sorrow.

"I was not careful, Dagr, please forgive me!"

"Ssshhh," he admonished. "This is not your doing. Oh my love!" He covered her face with kisses, wiped at her tears and runny nose, now and then checking to the bleeding by pressing a clean cloth to her sex.

"Tell me what happened," he finally found the courage to ask her the question again.

Brigida fought exhaustion to tell him how they had spent the day before wandering the woods to press them into their memory. Both of them had succumbed to melancholy, and she had suggested a tonic be brewed to lift their spirits, and ease the anxiety of the coming departure. Arinn had supervised the mixing of the herbs. They drank of their concoction before bed, and then, this morning...

"So you both made the brew, did you?"

"Yes. My lord, what do you suggest?"

Dagr's eyes betrayed him.

"Never! She would not!" Brigida recoiled in horror. "You are distraught, my lord. I will forget your suspicions."

He bowed his head, perplexed and sorry for having upset her further. "It is only because of the healing. Remember, the price to the Fey."

"No," Brigida whispered, closing her eyes. "I will not believe it."

He observed her as she slept finally, still in his embrace. His dark beauty, ever faithful to her first love. Her lips so red, her eyelashes like coal against her paled cheeks. Her hair had grown again, and he ran it through his fingers. How often had they made love with her hair clenched in his fist, how often had they spoken of the children that they would have; free spirits running the forest. Now that hoped for laughter was once again splattered against her skirts. He could not help the tears from coming, or his love for her from catching his breath, which is how Arinn found him when she awoke.

She lay quietly until he noticed her. Her heart threatened to betray her fear, it thundered so wildly within her chest. She stepped barefoot onto the cold floor, and sat down at his feet. He looked at her with compassion but it was mixed with his own fear and accusation.

"How is my lady?"

"She will heal, as before," he whispered, but could not keep a cold edge from his voice. "Tell me everything, Arinn, I beg you. I will not be angry, I give my word, but I need the truth."

"No," Arinn shook her head. "It was just the way of nature."

Dagr was always able to trust the knowing in his heart. Always. Today it said one thing, Arinn said another. He wanted to believe *her*.

"Do you swear darling? Promise me that you tell the truth. I cannot bear a lie." He took her hand in his. It was cold. "You're so cold. Here, warm yourself by me." Arinn's closeness reminded him of their encompassing love. "If I accuse you wrongly, my lady, I beg your forgiveness. It is only because of your promise to the Fey. You can understand that I would worry."

"I promise." Arinn laid her head to his chest and traced her finger along Brigida's face. "Things will be better when we go to France. All of this will be behind us, and we can try to have a child again."

"We? Are you craving a child, Arinn, or are you speaking of Brigida?" Dagr asked, surprised. She had always said that it was not for her. He would give her one, if she were only to ask and set aside the herbs that kept her barren. The thought brought a spark of hope.

"I may, my lord. Once we are settled. Perhaps it would not be so terrible, the birthing?"

"My lady," Dagr shook his head in disbelief. "You cannot imagine my hope." Perhaps his knowing was based in fear. Arinn's body against his was enough for now, to keep him from thinking overly much. Yes, in France, it would be better.

Brigida healed quickly under their combined care. Arinn returned to high spirits, singing as she worked, laundering, packing up the few things they could take with them; their medicines most importantly. She looked to all their meals, leaving Brigida to rest. Now that the time was near, they all looked forward to saying goodbye to difficult memories. No one talked about how much they would miss fair England, with her bewitching landscapes, and her turbulent sea.

On the last day, Dagr rose well before dawn to make his last farewells to his beloved country. Padding softly across the floor so as not to wake his lovers, he groped among the cloaks by the door, looking for his. This one was obviously not his, he thought, as his hand found a tiny packet sewn into the lining near the hood. He would have moved on but curiosity got the better of him. He loosed the packet from the seam and stepped out into the moist night air. Wrapping himself against the cold - or was it fear - he sniffed inside the leather pouch. He rubbed the herb that fell out of it between his fingers. He tasted it with his tongue. Pennyroyal! Overcome by a cold sweat, Dagr shoved the herb into his leathers, and walked purposefully into the woods. By a great oak where he had often sought the wisdom of his departed mother, Dagr sat in sheer dismay. His sobs and breaking heart were invisibly witnessed by the Fey, who came to sit by his side.

"Lady Mother, guide me. I can no longer trust my own wisdom," he prayed.

She came to him, robed in the shimmering dress of the Fairy Queen, and as he looked up at her, astonished, she laid her hand upon his brow.

"My son, I give you strength for the journey ahead. Go with courage. Go with love in your heart. There are trying days ahead, but you are always the son of my heart, remember that. You can always call on me."

"Lady Mother. Tell me what the road ahead is. I am bewildered by my own thoughts."

"It is for you to discover. You will make the right choice. Have faith in your own decisions."

He watched as she faded away, then made his way back resolutely to the hut where Arinn and Brigida were waking. His faced unreadable, Dagr stirred up the fire for one last time.

CHAPTER 51

Of all the dangers I've encountered, you have been the most loved

The fire had died down completely in Sahara's hearth. As the temperature change registered on their skin, summoning them back, the door to the cabin flew open, and in it stood a snow covered and breathless Holly. She was wrapped in a large, ice encrusted shawl, a tree branch in her hand for a walking stick, and a cumbersome bag slung over her shoulders. To the four at the table, she looked like an apparition from another century, startled as they were out of their journey to the past.

Aiden stood abruptly and sent his chair flying. Sahara ran to the door, ushering Holly in, taking her bag. Iona, a shattered look on her face, wrapped her arms about herself to keep warm. Richard sat in irrepressible shock as he watched Holly emerge from her wrap and coat, standing there like a beacon of his tortured past, devastating every imagined meeting he had had of her. His heart pounded so loudly that he was afraid everyone could hear it. Iona took his hand, sending a cold shiver along his spine.

"Sweetness!" Aiden stared past Holly into the impossible dark. How did you get here? Where is the truck? And what is in that bag?"

"At the end of the drive. I walked in. I brought coffee and other things...clothes." Holly sat down at the table, breathless, wiping the ice from her face, and accepted Sahara's offer of scotch, grimacing as it sped heatedly down her throat. She glanced at Richard and Iona, attempting to stand. Aiden pressed her back down.

"Walked? You could have easily been lost in the blizzard; frozen to death! He knelt at her feet, taking off her boots. "I thought you were going to wait for me to call you?" He rubbed her feet briskly and motioned for Sahara to put the kettle on.

They were all reeling from their memories, in need of time to integrate back, to talk about the thing that had Iona weeping silently. And what had happened after Dagr found the pennyroyal? They had come out of it too soon. Only Iona knew what had happened next.

"The power is out everywhere. Check your lights. You're out too. I sent Francois home with Lilith until the blizzard is over. They have fireplaces. He would have frozen at my place. I didn't want to call, in case you were all still...busy." Holly stared up at Richard, thrown by his strikingly handsome face. He had finally stood and extended his hand.

"My lady," he muttered, then faltered backward.

"Richard, you've got to sit down," Aiden ordered, and directed him to the sofa by the fire. "I'll get you a drink."

They walked around Holly like shadows, this way and that, organising themselves into the reality of what their journey had revealed and the presence of such an undisguised reminder. Nobody spoke for a long time, except for Aiden as he made them comfortable, Holly near Richard by the fire, until her bath was drawn, Sahara now and again in Aiden's arms, offering her comfort for the realization she must have had about her inability to have children, Iona gently wrapped in a blanket with a goblet of blood red wine in her hand. He had kissed Iona's forehead with tenderness, and whispered something in her ear. Holly took it all in. As much as she was glad that her terrifying ordeal through the blizzard was over, she was equally as nervous to be in their midst. Here was an energy that she was completely unfamiliar with. It was shadowed, and unavailable to her sensitivities.

But one thing did move her emotions, the lingering touch of Richard's hand, and the haunted look in his eyes. How strange, she had been baking for his gallery for the last two years without knowing the man behind the orders. And now that she had met him, she was touched profoundly by his essence. He was like Aiden, strength and intensity. But where velvet would describe Aiden, silk would describe Richard. They were like two sensual sides of a luxurious throw. She had expected someone completely different, but who that was she could not recall. Gratefully, she slid into the bath, so as to silence her fluttering heart. She needed to calm down from the overwhelming fear she had stuffed down while fighting her way to the cabin, which she herself didn't know how she'd managed. Taking off her ring, she laid it glowing in Sahara's hand, then closed her eyes.

Sahara smoothed Holly's hair, and rubbed some scented soap into a washcloth. "Let me."

Holly nodded, and then clasped Sahara's hand to her heart.

"I came at the wrong time didn't I? I interrupted."

"Nonsense," Sahara comforted. "It's alright. We'll get back to it."

"Richard. He looked so shaken when he saw me. I really shouldn't be here."

"It's alright! Everything is as it should be. We'll talk it over later." Sahara passed the washcloth over Holly's body, repetitive strokes, singing quietly under her breath. Holly pulled her in for a kiss.

"You're not alright, though, are you, my love?"

Sahara shook her head, eyes cast down.

"I can wait until you're ready to tell me. Can I make it better?"

"You *are* making it better, by being here."

"I'm not making it worse by being a reminder of the past?"

Sahara looked up, astonished at Holly's astuteness. "No," she lied. She wouldn't burden Holly with the fact that her sudden appearance at the door had made the memory of Brigida's miscarriages so very real, so very impossible to process.

"I wonder what the Universe was plotting, having me incarnate resembling Arinn so," Holly mused. "It seems so unkind."

"Life is not always kind, sweetie. But it is always exactly the mystery we are seeking. Don't worry about me, this will all pass. Everything does."

"I can go upstairs if the four of you need to keep going. I'm sorry..."

"No," Sahara admonished. "We're in this together, darling. No more secrets. You're one of us." And then, suddenly, "I've slept with Richard. Recently."

Holly gasped. She stopped Sahara's hand, squeezing so hard that Sahara gave a cry of pain.

"But Aiden!"

Sahara had no way out but to continue telling the truth. "He knows. He understands. I don't know how to convey how sorry I am that I kept this from you, or that we are in this mess."

Holly stood, splashing water onto the floor. "I don't know what to say. Aiden never told me. I thought..."

"You thought that you could trust us. Go ahead, say it. We deserve it."

Holly dropped the towel to the floor and stood shivering once more, even though a moment before she had been submerged in steaming water.

"I'm the fifth wheel... I...," she stammered, shaken. "I'm trying hard to be open, to understand that what we've got isn't regular, but I don't know...how can I be part of this, if the four of you still have so much to figure out? I should walk away."

"No!" Sahara pleaded, afraid now that Holly looked so hurt. "No! For Aiden, if not for me. Please Holly! You're not the fifth wheel, God, no! You're our beloved. The past has to be worked out, but we both love you desperately. We need you. Remember, you told me before, that I couldn't scare you away no matter what had gone on? Tell me that you still feel that way!"

Holly melted at the sight of Sahara's tears. She pulled her into a tight embrace. Sahara undone was more than she could bear. "It's ok. It's ok. I love you so much Sahara. So much. I'm nothing without your and Aiden's love. Nothing."

But Sahara knew that Holly was the strongest of them all. Her heart was pure. Her love was devoid of jealousy. And maybe she was what they all needed, to remind them of the purity of love. She was humbled by Holly's substance and resilience. Together they walked hand in hand into the living room, having vowed to stay by each other's side, through whatever trials were ahead.

Aiden took one look at them and knew that Sahara had told it all. He faced Holly's stare directly, and held out his hands to her. She welcomed the regret in his eyes with a compassionate smile.

"We're in this together, for good," she whispered as she stood on tiptoe for his kiss.

"You're incredible. Thank you," he said, a grateful sigh on his breath. This was only the beginning, of a complicated love.

"I want to discover everything about you, Aiden. What makes your heart beat, what lies in your past, your mind, your soul? I want to know it all, and cherish it."

She thought that Aiden's arms would crush her, if her love for him did not. "Everything that you are, darling, that's what my life's journey will be," he vowed fervently.

CHAPTER 52

The storm raged on for four days and four nights, within and without.

They were dark days, without sun, only the buffeting winds and the snow, swirling about the valley. Sahara cranked the emergency radio to catch news here and there about the worst blizzard in years, everything was shut down; the snow plows were either helping people out of their homes or stuck themselves.

Inside the cabin, a cozy fire burned and there was no shortage of supplies. Sahara had laid by a whole winter's store, half by instinct and half by Aiden's urging. They had squash, carrots and onions for a curried bake, potatoes roasted in their skins in the cook stove oven. There were caramelized parsnips for a hearty soup, chickens for stuffing, apples and frozen berries for crumble, and bread made by Holly to be eaten with homemade preserves. They ran out of butter but there was plenty of olive and coconut oil. Even the eggs lasted. Sahara had had the foresight to whisk and freeze several dozen, enough for omelettes spiced with dried herbs and finely chopped sundried tomatoes. The only thing they had to ration was the cream for coffee. Aiden offered to traipse to his house for more, but was shouted down by the others, it was too much of a risk to send him out. They could have tea made from the bundles of wild mint hanging from the kitchen ceiling or the tins of herbs inside the cupboard. What raw sprouts Sahara had in the fridge were reverently divided among them and jars of lacto-fermented vegetables were opened to share.

Early in the morning, when everyone was asleep, Holly would rise and quietly proof the bread for the day. Aiden and Sahara traded sleeping on the sofa so she could have the bed each night. She loved those early morning hours of working by candlelight. She thanked the powers that be for the cook stove and the fireplace. With them they were safe and warm and well fed. The hot water heater didn't work after they had drained it for her last bath, but the well water could be heated on the stove, enough for their washing needs.

It was very, very quiet. The snow made an insulating blanket so thick that no sound from the outside world could be heard. It was like in the past, Holly thought, making do with what you had put by, the fragile life of humans embroidered onto the tapestry of the world. She enjoyed the solitude while everyone slept, the first wisp of light over the horizon, and playing with Ulfred in the snow. Sahara's truck and

Richard's SUV were almost buried in snowdrifts. As far as the eye could see, which most days was barely a few feet, there was only white. White snow on grey sky, against shrouded mountains, in silent woods. She had never felt this peaceful in her entire life. Even though they were sequestered and barely knew how to be with each other, it was still a time of joy, and laughter, a time of discovery and deepening friendships.

They discovered that Iona sang a lot, haunting melodies full of ancient words, and that her voice rang more true than a silver bell, calling up the very sweetness of her soul.

They found that Holly was an effervescent cascade of laughter and enchanting smiles, always with a compliment or uplifting thought to share, equally attentive to all, considerate in all things.

They were astounded by the wealth of stories remembered by Sahara, with interesting anecdotes about life through the ages, and her love for weaving magic into their day.

They became quickly aware of Aiden's desire for work and tending to their comfort, carrying wood and stoking the fires, heating water and shovelling a path to the shed for supplies. More than anything, Richard and Iona saw his devotion to Sahara and Holly, the way his every breath was attuned to their love. But that only made them long for the past again.

Richard proved to be impressively good at reading aloud, his voice steady and deep, and leading them in intelligent conversation. He was a leader by birth and by that long gone incarnation. His curiosity about Holly was too evident to hide, and although he never said it, it was plain that he ached to be near her to experience her energy.

Careening between mixed up emotions about who belonged to whom, they distracted each other with snow fights to release their sexual energy. In the evenings they laid by the fire staring at the flames and smoking a little herb, tumblers of scotch shared by the men and thimblefuls of wine shared by the women. Nobody wanted to drink too much or enter any kind of state of heightened emotions.

Holly told them all about her upbringing, drawing whoops of laughter as she performed little skits about life in the Midwest. She was glorious, incandescent, a golden maiden that pulled them all toward her. It was no surprise to Aiden when she told him quite innocently in bed that Richard was only the second man in her life whom she'd been curious about. She blushed profusely and pulled the covers over her head.

"Oh, so you *are* interested in him!" Aiden poked her ribs, making light of this revelation.

"Well not like I'm interested in *you*! Just like, you know, he's handsome and smart. I like *that*. You know that I never look at men, anyway."

Aiden was sure that he would prefer her to look at a hundred men over this particular one.

Holly ventured further. "Has Sahara told you what he's like...you know?" More blushing and giggling.

Aiden sat up on his elbow and stared down at her. "Yes. He's rough."

Holly hid her face in her hands. He peeled them back. "Do you like the idea of that?

"Yes," Holly whispered. "The part of me that's inexperienced, curious. I'm just new to this, so everything is exciting."

"I love your natural love for sex, and that you don't feel guilty about your desires. It's inspiring to see a woman really owing her eroticism."

"Aren't you jealous at all, Aiden? Just a little?"

"Sometimes, when I look at him, and wonder if she would like him more than me. Jealousy is really about fear...fear that she'd leave me, or not want me anymore. I'd be more prone to it if I thought he wanted to manipulate her from me, which he doesn't. I'd be worried about someone who for their own egoic reasons, would try to wedge her away from me. But he's not insecure like that. Knowing who Sahara is, and what she went through in her previous relationship and why it failed, gives me a clear picture of her needs. If I want to be with her and respect her I have to accept her authenticity, or walk away. We both have our boundaries. We've both tested them." Aiden shrugged his shoulders. "I can't imagine her changing. I don't want her to. Are *you* jealous?"

"No. I thought I would be, but more than anything I don't want to be the one who's in the way of how you want to live your life. And I want to matter."

"Madness! Your words are madness, woman!"

"Am I a woman? I feel like a child next to Iona and Sahara."

Aiden grinned. "You're all woman. I'll prove it to you."

"No! It'll be too loud!"

"Do you think Richard and Iona are abstaining? Do you think Sahara and I have been?"

"What? And here I've been fairly humming with horniness!"

"I can fix that," Aiden removed his t-shirt and laughed as Holly hid under the covers once more.

· · · ✦ · · ·

Awakened by Holly's accidental clatter of baking pans, Sahara wandered into the kitchen, exclaiming that it was the fourth day of the blizzard. Would it ever end? Holly offered tea, and as they stood poking through the cupboard making a decision about which one to have, Iona surprised them at the counter.

"Good morning." Sahara, forgetting herself, did what was most natural for her, and took Iona in her arms, dropping a kiss on her surprised lips. It was moments before Sahara realized what she was doing, and in alarm, looked over at Holly.

But Holly was neither upset nor surprised, instead she moved closer, and without any qualms, also dropped a kiss on Iona's mouth. Tender and quick, the kiss moved on to Sahara, and there it lingered.

A connection had been made and trust built, and finally the time was right to reveal their past life journey.

That day, after smudging and calling in her guides, Iona shared with Holly the whole of their regression. She felt that it was hers to share, the terrible things she'd done to betray everyone's love. She didn't make any excuses about it, not once, just shouldered the cost to Brigida, and pondered the cost to Sahara.

"But you had no choice in the matter!" Holly protested in Iona's defense even though her heart hurt for Brigida, and now Sahara, who sat clearly upset by the recollection. "Your motives were pure when you went to the Fey," Holly continued, "and you had no choice about the price."

"Well, I did, my dear, I did," Iona sighed. "There's always a choice, and Dagr had warned me, but..."

"But you disobeyed out of your love for Brigida!"

Richard and Aiden exchanged glances. 'Disobeyed' was a curious word. It warmed their blood.

"Yes, but even so," Iona said, "when jealousy came, I made more wrong choices. I hurt the ones I loved out of choice, and those choices are affecting this lifetime." Everyone understood that she was speaking of Sahara's empty womb, but only Holly didn't know that Iona touched on her unrelenting desire for Aiden.

"But they forgave you. I know they did! From everything I've learned of Brigida and Dagr so far, they loved you so much that with time, I'm sure it was forgiven."

"I can't forgive myself," Iona said, glum, her expression forbidding anyone from offering their embrace. She just couldn't bear it. She didn't want to talk about how much being here with Aiden made her misery deeper than the price of the Dark Pool, how much she longed for a chance to be his beloved, and that if given half an opportunity, she would move heaven and earth, perform any magic, to taste him once more. If someone had offered her a release right now from the haunting past, she would refuse it. Even as painful as it was, it was a pain she relished. She wanted it all, the past, the present, to have the foursome reunited. She would make it better. This time she would stay as pure as the driven snow that had thrown them all together.

It didn't seem to be the right time for the four of them to discuss their deepest feelings about the shock of Arinn's betrayal, or how much the past now felt so real it was almost within grasp. They didn't dare sink into the love that once had been so strong between them. Not with Holly's heart at stake. But perhaps this was better. Her presence was forcing them into introspection. Words could be left for later.

Richard was increasingly aware of how much Dagr had meant to him then, and he saw Aiden with new eyes, measuring him against the man he had once been and finding that there was not much difference. This man was as principled and as demonically in love with love as before.

Aiden had intense dreams about the castle he had once lived in with his parents, Richard's father's castle, and woke up each morning craving to put his hands to the building of Richard's estate. His days were spent in agony wanting to return to Brigida, and comfort her for her loss. Every time he looked at Sahara, the memory became fresh. He was tenderer with her than he had ever been, attentive and sweet, and even when he lay with her at night, he took her reverently; speaking spells over her womb. His kisses there were as dew on a rose, and indeed, had her lifting her hips towards his lips. He would take this pain from her if he could.

Holly felt the precariousness of the situation but determined that there really was nothing to fear. She was loved, and Iona, sweet Iona, was a victim of events that would have made anyone trip over their decisions. She wasn't blind, she saw the connection between Iona and Sahara. She felt the electricity between Richard and her beloved. But soon, they would all go their separate ways, and then there would be time to work out new boundaries. What was done was done. She had no intention of being petty or pretend to understand the intricacies of lives as complicated theirs.

Only Sahara saw everything as if the sun was shining through the roof, like a spotlight would on a dark street corner, revealing the truths underfoot. They were still bound together, with history, with love, with desire. They had much to transcend, because obviously there had been no closure in the past, or else, why would the sight of Richard's back as he stood at the fire make her tremble and ache for him to turn with love in his eyes? Why was this not gone and forgotten? Why could Iona's touch, no matter how untrustworthy she still was, drop her to her knees? Why were the nights full of nightmares, as if her heart was being wrenched from her body by some cruel, invisible force? What were the whispered words that broke sweat onto her brow? She heard them as she tossed and turned, but they were never clear.

The morning that the storm broke, they all felt as if they had been on a journey of a thousand miles. Iona, subdued, was making everyone nervous. Her unleashed power bubbled beneath the surface of her being. It was unnatural, everyone but Holly decided.

"I'm going to walk to my place, and get the snowmobile," Aiden said after shovelling the front porch and re-stocking the firewood in the alcove by the side door. I'll bring my snowshoes back as well." He waved his cell phone. "There's still no reception. Richard, you and I can go out to the road later and see if the snow plows are anywhere near. We might get this lane cleared. Otherwise, you're stuck here, I'm afraid."

"I'll come with you. Are you expecting tree damage at your place?"

"I don't know. Possibly, with the winds we've had. I'm more worried about pipes bursting. Are you sure you want to come? The snow will be thigh deep. You haven't the right boots or pants."

Richard laughed. "Don't worry, I'll deal. I haven't had a workout in 5 days. This'll be just what I need."

Aiden looked doubtful. By the time they got there, Richard's pants would be soaked and his boots full of snow and ice. "OK. As you will." He turned to Sahara. "You've got everything you need in case anything comes up and we get back later than I anticipate? I'm thinking 4 hours at most, to get there, dig out the door to the garage and get the sled out. I have to heat up the house."

Sahara nodded. "We'll be fine. Be safe." Should anything go amiss, Iona would be on the wing anyway. Between them, they had all the resources they needed. "Wait, I'll pour you a thermos of tea to take."

Richard and Aiden burst out laughing. "A flask of scotch would be nice too," Aiden said, reading Richard's thoughts.

They set out with the three women arm in arm watching their struggle and uproarious laughter. It would be quite the physical endeavor, to cut the trail through all that snow, but they took it like men used to battle.

"Come Ulfred," Holly said, as she turned into the cabin. "Let's make ourselves busy."

"What are you planning to do?" Sahara asked, as Iona picked up the broom and began to sweep the porch of drifting snow. Willow came out and sniffed the air, then turned back in.

"I had an idea," Holly whispered to Sahara.

"Yes? Why are we whispering?"

"I thought that since the men will be gone for a while, we could air out the house and all that...you know...male energy, and do something nice for Iona. She's looking so drawn and pale. Why don't we make her a hot bath? And I saw you have some coconut and chocolate, I'll make a little treat for her. That might take the edge off?"

"Oh Holly! You're amazing. She'll love it. I know, she's hurting."

"K! I'll start heating the water on the stove!"

"What's going on here?" Iona came in, alert to their whispering.

"You're having a bath!" Holly grinned.

"What? No! It'll take forever to heat all the water. Too much work." Iona waved them away, as they came to hug her.

"Not too much work. You're silly," Holly said. "And you can do something for me, too."

"Anything," Iona purred.

"After the bath, would the two of you make some magic? I'm dying to learn something, anything! Even if we just light some candles and incense and lay out some crystals? I have the two of you here. It would be so nice to watch you." Holly looked hopeful.

A spark returned to Iona's eye. "What do you think, shall we make some magic for our little apprentice, Sahara?"

"Oooh! Will I be an apprentice?"

"Well, you did tell me several times that you wanted to learn," Sahara laughed. "Iona, if you're game, I'm dying to make some sister magic."

"What's sister magic?" Holly asked, intrigued.

"It's when sisters - women who are dedicated to each other's safety, growth and well-being, gather to make magic. It's very powerful. If you'd like to learn the craft as you've suggested, it's good to

292

learn in a loving sister circle. Trust is very important," Sahara didn't need to look at Iona for her to know that the last statement was meant for her.

"Are men not invited to this kind of magic, male witches, then?" Holly began to fill pots of water to heat on the wood stove.

"Mmm, sometimes," Sahara replied, wondering if she should reveal Aiden's experiences. She decided that it would do no harm.

"Aiden has been to some. Not as a witch, he wasn't awake to that yet at the time, but as a representative of the Divine Masculine. He'll tell you about it. But in general, sister magic is special time for women only. Not because we want to exclude male energy, but because we wish to bond as Shakti's daughters."

"Wow. I have so much to learn. Who's Shakti?"

"It's Hindi for Power - she's a goddess, universal energy. Don't worry, I have books you can read."

"Have you done ceremony with Aiden, since he's become more aware of his path?"

"A little bit. Iona more."

"Oh," Holly said, surprised. "What kind? Is it ok for me to ask?"

"Of course!" Iona said. "It's was for our work with the Society of Earth Builders. He's our leader now."

"I'd be afraid, I'm still finding my equilibrium with his energy."

Iona and Sahara exchanged glances. Holly had Aiden wrapped around her finger, and they all knew it. Not by anything she had done to manipulate him, but just by being her own, sweet self. And that was pure magic, to inspire a man's heart through clarity of soul.

"Well, I'm sure he would be delighted to teach you anything you'd like to know," Sahara grinned.

Holly blushed, glancing coyly at Iona. "What she really means is that Aiden taught me about loving a man."

"Ah, yes," Iona smiled wistfully. She remembered when Dagr had taught Arinn about men, and how intoxicating that had been. "I'm going to get changed into my robe," she added and padded off to her room, tears blinding her eyes.

Aiden glanced back at Richard. He was covered in sweat under his own clothes, trailblazing without snowshoes was damn hard work. His legs were burning with the effort.

"We have to keep on. You'll cool down too quickly if we stop."

"Don't worry about me, old man!" Richard yelled over the wind that had picked up once more. He was exhausted, but they were almost there...he hoped.

"Old man? You're older than me, and I'm not the one lagging behind."

"How do you know how old I am?" Richard laughed.

"I had you checked out."

"What? Whatever for?'

"You were sleeping with my lover. I'm strange like that."

"Oh, that. Right," Richard grimaced.

They carried on in silence. When the house came into view, Aiden was relieved to see that no trees had fallen down against it but plenty in the clearing were broken from the heavy ice. He greeted the tree spirits and offered his assistance. The forest came alive with a strong gust of blustery wind. He had been missed.

"Must you?" Richard asked. "Your sorcery hasn't left you, I see."

"Neither has your appetite for the women I love."

CHAPTER 53

"I haven't had this much time off since before I started the café. And that seems like forever ago." Holly lay stretched out on the carpet in front of the fire, Sahara and Iona lying on either side of her. They had spent the afternoon in communion with the spirits, inviting Holly into sacred space, teaching her about the tools of magic, meditating and chanting ancient songs that drifted over Holly's subconscious like mist over the sea. She had let herself fall into their wisdom and carefully crafted rituals.

Iona took her hand. "Has this been nice? Do you like the feel of magic?"

Holly turned towards her. She touched her face, and was surprised by the energy emanating from the witch. She pulled back, overwhelmed. "I do."

"It's ok," Iona reached for Holly's hand again. "I won't bite. I'm just heightened from the things we did."

"You feel different from Sahara," Holly let her hand drift through Iona's hair.

"We all do, that's the beauty of energy." Sahara wrapped herself around Holly's back. She smiled at Iona. This felt so good, right, like they had always been together.

"I never imagined that one day I'd have friends who inspired me like this. I like the conversations we've been having. Real. This is beautiful. Thank you."

Sahara hugged in a little more. "You're the gift. Don't ever doubt that. We've been gifted with your loveliness."

Holly's hand tightened in Iona's hair. Iona's eyes flew open.

Come to me my darling! Iona invited Holly further, expanding her energy to enfold her.

Holly pushed back with her bum into Sahara, who responded with a little nudge. Permission had been given.

"May I kiss you?" Holly whispered to Iona. Her eyes were doe soft, her lips a crimson red.

Closer sweetness

Their lips met, eyes open. Holly moaned at the softness and fullness of Iona's mouth, breath suspended, Sahara's body heat urging her on.

"Mmmm. More," she opened her mouth, letting Iona in.

Iona's lingering kisses left Holly's lips and met Sahara's.

Holly watched them, fascinated. They knew each other well, what purpose each little bite served, what response each little kiss elicited.

Holly's body began to move with a wicked rhythm, under the hand of Iona, who had unbuttoned her shirt.

"Aiden won't mind, will he?" she asked, shaking as her breasts fell voluptuously from her bra and Iona twisted her nipples into peaks.

"He won't mind, sweetness. Ssshhhh." Sahara slipped out of her shirt, and sat up on her knees. She closed her eyes as Iona's tongue wound itself around her tight, dark tips.

"Show me yours," Holly begged of Iona. She was floating, clit hard and throbbing. This was heaven.

Iona parted her sweater. Holly gasped. Her mouth watered. Iona was wearing a peek-a-boo bra, a delicious shred of pink lace.

Iona wiggled her breasts, and pulled Holly's face closer. "Yours. Kiss them, naughty girl." She growled as Holly said *please.*

They played like nymphs, free of rules, downy skin on skin, lips like velvet, hands kneading.

They explored; as fingers pulled and teased. But they didn't go any further than this, the erotic display of their passion and curiosity was greater knowing that this was all there was.

"I love your titties," Iona said as she dressed Holly again, adjusting her shirt. She bit Holly's neck.

"I love yours," Holly's hand reached to the back of Iona's neck. She pulled her in for another kiss. "You're delicious."

If I can't have him, I'll have you

Sahara gazed dreamily at the two women who occupied her heart. She should know better, she thought. Still, the look on Holly's face was worth a little venture into the unknown. She was glowing. Passion looked good on her. She deserved this, after so many years of longing for a woman's touch. Sahara was happy to indulge her. In fact, it was her goal to give Holly every experience she craved.

They were primed for love, eagerly awaiting their men's return. The room was heady with pheromones, and unrealized release.

"Here, these should fit," Aiden handed Richard dry clothes. "We can put your boots by the fire once it gets going." He glanced at Richard's rock hard physique, the tattoo on his back. *Damn,* he thought. That body had taken years of dedication.

"What's going on with the pipes?" Richard wondered.

"The snow acted as an insulator. It's not that cold in here, relatively speaking. The pipes are ok."

"That's good. I have to find a way of contacting the office. I told my assistant that I was going in this direction for a couple of days, but she'll be worried by now."

"She?"

"Yes, she. Not my type, in case you're wondering."

"I'm not. Just curious, what any assistant you hired would look like."

"Like a very competent woman. I'm faithful to Iona. Well...you know."

"Uh-huh."

"I am. What does *your* assistant look like?"

"Like I've never had one. Just hired my first. She's also very competent."

"What?" Richard contemplated his reflection in the mirror, not entirely satisfied. "Do you mean to tell me that you've been doing it all by yourself all this time? How terribly inefficient."

"Yeah, control issues."

"Well, you'll need help once you start my build. I require a great deal of attention on my projects."

"Sahara will be taking over some things here as she has time, along with the new assistant, and I have two good foremen to handle my other projects."

"So you've truly decided to do it...build my house?"

"Do I have any choice?"

"Don't be ridiculous. I know that you can't be talked into anything you don't want to do," Richard laid his wet things by the fire. He turned to look at Aiden. "Do you want to talk about what happened back then? I know it's in the past, but it's rather ghastly. I suppose in the end they didn't know whose child it was..."

"I can't. Not yet. I just never expected that. Arinn was Dagr's great hope for humanity. She was without fault, as far as he could see. It was so much more than the miscarriage for him. He was never truly a medieval thinker. He was ahead of his time, and Arinn was a symbol of the world he craved."

"That's how you view Holly...as a great hope."

Aiden shot Richard a warning glance. "That's none of your business!"

"I can see it, the repeating of histo..."

"Leave it! Leave Holly out of it."

"How can we? It's clear that she's part of whatever we have to overcome."

"Richard, I'm going to say this once. I don't care what mess the four of us get into, Holly is outside of that. She looks like Arinn, I get that. It makes no sense, and I can see that you can't help reacting to her. I'm sorry for whatever pain it causes you, but I will protect her to my dying day, and as much as I have shared Sahara, I won't share Holly or sacrifice her to our past. Understand?"

"You're a fool. How can you protect her from what she was born to?"

"Back off!" Aiden thundered. "And you can stop calling me a fool. One lifetime of that was more than enough."

Well you are *a fool, and Holly is much more than a coincidence,* Richard thought.

"I heard that. Don't be an idiot. I know she's not a coincidence. I just don't want to see her hurt."

"The whole thing is impossible," Richard said, allowing the emotions of the last few days to sweep over him. "I know what she means to you. I remember that feeling. But I don't understand, how Arinn managed to get under my skin so. It was Brigida I was in love with."

Aiden shook his head. "I don't know either. It's a bloody mystery. But she was the kind of woman men lost their minds over, because she never fit the mold. She was an enigma, untameable. That's all I can make out of it."

"I can feel it returning," Richard said quietly.

"What?"

"Our friendship. This look into the past took away the last of my reservations about you."

"Why should you have reservations about me? You can trust me."

"Because Iona's in love with you. More than she can handle."

Aiden noticed the pain in Richard's eyes. He was surprised to see it actually. He had thought Richard more aloof in love. "I know. But I'm not encouraging it. I have feelings...because of the past, but I can keep it in perspective."

"She can't."

"She loves you, Richard. I see the way she looks at you. You're her master in all the ways that that manifests."

"Yes. But for a reason that only she knows; she wants to return to what you had before and it's bigger than her love for me. I'm patient, and will give her all kinds of room, but this has me unsettled."

"You don't trust her." Aiden looked away. It would be hard for Richard to admit about the woman he adored.

"No. I don't. I try, but she has never really *allowed* full trust."

"She's the most powerful woman I know and the most broken."

"If anyone else had said that I would be angry. But yes, you're right. And it makes her dangerous."

They both pondered that until it was time to go back. And when they got there, they found that the energy have shifted profoundly between the women. Holly had taken on a light, Sahara's smile was content and Iona had found her power again.

"Dare we ask what's been going on here while we've been away?" Aiden asked, dropping a bag of supplies in the kitchen. His skin prickled with the sexually charged air around him.

"Magic!" Holly offered. "We've been making magic!"

"I'll start dinner," Sahara said, and giggled mischievously.

Iona sniffed Richard's clothes as she hugged him. Aiden's scent! Richard bestowed a dark and dangerous look upon her. She rose to the occasion and returned his stare. "We've just been getting to know each other better. All quite innocent."

He would punish her, without a doubt, for always pushing the boundaries. But how they would muffle the sound of his hand against her upturned bottom, she didn't know. He would instruct her in how to bring herself to almost complete release but forbid her to come. He would make her wait, laying her out for his visual pleasure, and promise fingers, cock, tongue and filthy words, but she would be dripping wet and achingly swollen before his promises would arrive like much awaited parcels in the mail; to be ripped into - her hair in his hands, while his fingers dipped and retreated, hand soaked with her lust, commanding she come like a whore. And that was why she needed him, loved him, because he understood her better than anyone, and never, ever, disappointed her sexual addictions.

Aiden observed them from a distance, cradling Sahara as she worked at the counter. He wanted to be alone now with Holly and Sahara, to strip them naked and employ his tongue to their pleasure, both bent over the edge of the bed, their backs arched to reveal pink lips. He was hungry. After days of muted lovemaking, he wanted to hear their screams as he plundered with his tongue, to acquiesce to their needs, patiently extracting the trembling of flesh. He wanted to fuck, not make love. His artful teasing, his careful massaging of inner thighs, and squeezing of outer lips, the sashaying of a flogger, never hurting just hinting at pain, would prepare them for the stiffness of his cock. He wanted Holly to lose herself, as she was so good at doing, when she watched him demand obedience from Sahara, plug in place, nipples bound by those tight gold rings, spread as wide as she could be, blindfolded, repeating the words he insisted she say.

There had been no plow to be found. They would spend another night, maybe two. Aiden doubted that Richard and Iona would be able to resist the madness they enjoyed. Sahara had told him, about the room in Denver: the implements, Richard's prowess as a most masterful Dom.

His eyes roved over Holly, who between the two couples, alone in her lust, made herself busy setting the table. She refused to meet his eyes, and he knew why. She wanted it all. To see it all. To be the sacrifice. They had talked about it more than once; she wanted to be used. She had confessed all her fantasies, and there were many, but at the top of the list, was being used. She dreamt of being taken once then again, then used by another, then prepared for the next.

She had asked if this was wrong, if such needs were an aberration of normal sexuality, but he had assured her that she had to honor her truest thoughts, and that all her words were safe with him. Safety, yes, such things were embarked upon with people one trusted. Honesty, certainly. In the arena of full disclosure, why not? She had always imagined it with a group of women, but now, he could see that Richard whetted her appetite. He was dark and foreboding, like the storm they had just weathered. She couldn't hide it as she glanced at them now and then, in their own world, by the fire, hand in hand.

Aiden raked his hand through his hair, eyebrow arched. In other circumstances, if he trusted the situation, he would already have opened to the possibilities.

As he watched her, he saw the opportunity that she was aware of, and if she asked, he would deny her. Because trust was not present. Even though his loins were on fire to see her arranged on an altar for them to provide her pleasure - and there was an equal desire among them all, that was obvious - he would not have her exposed to Iona's wiles. Already, she had Holly blinded to her tricks. No, as much as he wanted to give Holly everything she wanted, this he could not do. Of course she could do as she pleased without his agreement, but he knew that she wouldn't because she trusted his wisdom, and that humbled him immensely.

She finally did look him in the eye. Her lust was palpable. Seismic. She questioned silently. He forbade. She obeyed immediately.

But he was crushed. To say no to anything she wanted always made his heart hurt.

Later, she would present on the bed, on hands and knees, and offer herself to Sahara and him, requesting slave-dom. Her cries of release would force a delicious tempest in the lower bedroom. Richard could only bear so much. It took all of his determination to not take the stairs two by two, and demand permission to view the taking of the innocent. Instead, he found Iona a most willing devotee of his erotic skills.

Nobody cared anymore about who heard what. And two days later, when the road was finally cleared, they parted with a certain understanding. What happened between them and among them was sacred and exceptional. They parted as soul companions, Holly part of the fold.

CHAPTER 54

"If a man is to live, he must be all alive, body, soul, mind, heart, spirit."
~ Thomas Merton

Holly wiped the bead of sweat from her brow, and stood back from her work. She had done as much as she could to prepare for the Thanksgiving/Christmas rush at the patisserie. How had she managed last year, with only two part time servers? Now it took those two, plus the apprentice and Sahara here almost every day.

Aiden was having a quick coffee in-between errands, preparing for the arrival of her parents the next day. He was, as always, surrounded by several women who vied for his attention. Was it her, or did they all seem to laugh too loudly and preen like guinea hens? Aiden caught her eye and smiled. Holly's breath left in a rush. He was the biggest surprise of her life.

The women caught the look between them and frowned. Aiden excused himself and joined Holly at the counter.

"All set?"

"Yes. I'm sorry you have to keep carting me around. We really must go get my new car. This is crazy."

"I've already taken care of it. I've asked to have it delivered here. There's no time to go and pick it up, we've all got too much on our plate."

"Oh, Aiden! You're too good. Thank you." She stood on tiptoe and kissed him.

"Whatever you need, little girl," he growled in her ear.

Holly melted against him. "Take me home."

"I'll warm the truck. Wait here."

He left, and she wondered how she had lived without him. She almost couldn't remember that girl because that was what she had been. His love had made room for her growth into the woman she was now. She loved him for it. Fiercely. And that, she hoped, would provide the courage she needed to face her mother. For how could she explain the love she had to someone who saw only what society had served up for centuries? But it was time for change, and she was a part of it.

They drove with few words between them. His hand had hers captured, and now and again, she would retrieve it to pass her fingers through his hair, or trace the strong line of his jaw. She adored the profile of his lips, the light in his blue eyes, the hard of his long legs, and the muscles that defined his arms.

"I'm so happy," she said, a deep contentment in her voice.

He glanced at her. "Are you darling? That's all I want."

"I'm scared of tomorrow though."

He squeezed her hand. "I know." He didn't try to talk her out of it. She had a right to her emotions.

"But you'll both be there to support me. That gives me courage."

"You can count on that," he said, voice husky.

"You know what?"

"No."

"I love our life. All of it. Everything that's easy and everything that's hard. I love that you and Sahara trust me with your world and...your friends. I could never go back to the world I inhabited before."

"You'll never have to," Aiden vowed.

"I want to ask you something. Do you think that my ring was the reason I found my way to the cabin the night of the blizzard? Because there was really no way for me to see anything. I was so scared."

Aiden shifted in his seat. That memory made him afraid, even now that she was perfectly safe.

"Yes, I know that that's how you found your way. That's why you have to promise to always wear it. And that you'll stop doing things that put you in danger. Sometimes, you and Sahara...it makes me crazy."

"Maybe we like life on the edge," Holly laughed.

"Maybe you're both impossible."

"Maybe we love you desperately."

"Maybe nothing makes sense without the two of you." He parked the truck, noticing that Sahara was already there, candles burning on the dining table. Home.

"Aiden?"

"Yes, my love?"

"I can't get used to you. I have such a feeling in the pit of my stomach when you touch me. It's almost torture, like a twisting that makes me ache inside."

He looked at her, Arinn incarnate. She didn't know that so often she echoed words from the past. He leaned toward her, and pulled her face closer. His eyes swallowed hers, his soul naked. "May I kiss you, my lady?"

She nodded, anticipating the moment when his lips touched hers. His scent cocooned her, warm, patchouli and forest notes. She closed her eyes.

"I can't do it!" Holly woke in a panic. She rolled over onto her belly and buried her face in her pillow.

Sahara put her arm around her, cooing in her ear. "Too much thinking, sweetie." She looked over at Aiden, sitting in the chair by the window, book in hand. "How long have you been up?"

"Hours," he mused. "I have an idea for this morning."

"It better be something to calm our lady love with, otherwise we might never get her out of bed."

"There's still so much to do!" Holly moaned.

"There's nothing to do, silly. The room downstairs is made up for your parents, I did a lot of the food prep yesterday; house is clean...what is there to do?" Sahara ran her fingers down Holly's back.

"I don't know. I think this was all a bad idea."

"Yeah, better to call your parents when you're pregnant and tell them then...that should be easier."

"Hey! You're mean!" Holly laughed. "Ok, I know. We have to do this. Let's tell them when they're full of turkey and in a food coma."

"I think you two should stop chattering and listen to my idea."

"Ok, what?" Holly sat up, breasts bouncing as she found her position at the foot of the bed.

"I can't really remember now..." Aiden grinned.

Sahara threw a pillow at him. "You're a boy!"

"Right. I may have taken the liberty of making us appointments at the spa. How does massage and sauna sound? If you don't want it, no big deal, but I thought it would take the edge off. Wait!" He held up his hand as they clamored over to him and drowned him in kisses. "First breakfast, a walk in the woods to ground ourselves, then to the spa. They'll serve us a light lunch. We'll be back in plenty of time to finish the meal."

"What do you mean, finish?" Sahara queried.

"I have the turkey dressed and in the oven on low already."

"What? What do you know about dressing a turkey?" Holly poked him in the ribs, her naked body cradled in his big hands.

"I had a mother and a sister who made sure that I spent plenty of time in the kitchen, learning how to feed myself," Aiden looked wistful.

"I miss my sister. She taught me much about how to treat girls. She didn't put up with my buffoonery."

"Will you invite her to Christmas? Say you will!" Holly kissed Aiden's fingers. She loved his hard working hands. "You've never spoken of her."

"She's passed away," Aiden teared up, and a great sigh escaped his lungs.

Sahara and Holly stared at him, dumbfounded.

"Aiden, darling," Sahara knelt at his feet. "Why have you never told us? We assumed..."

"I don't know. I don't like to think about her being gone, I still feel her so close that sometimes I choose to forget. And sometimes I think she will just show up here...that all I'd have to do was call her on the phone."

"What happened? Do you want to tell us now?" Holly wiped at the tears rolling down her face. This was so much worse than anything she had to face today.

"We were in the forest. I would take her with me when her friends weren't around. That's something my mother always insisted on, that I was considerate of her. You know, she made me learn how to braid my sister's hair. I adored everything about her since the day she was born."

Sahara covered Holly with a blanket. She was shivering.

"Anyway, we went out during hunting season, and I had my bow and arrow, and I was going to teach her how to use it. She wanted to please me even though I knew that she hated hunting. But it came so naturally to me, to provide food...which now we know why. She'd packed a picnic, and we drove out into the hills. After a while I could see that she was in it just for me, and I didn't care anymore about the hunt. She ran down a path, a deer path. I called for to her to come back immediately, but it was too late. A hunter mistook her for game."

"Oh my God, Aiden!" Sahara and Holly were both sobbing now.

"She died with the sweetest smile on her face, you know. She held my hand and stared right through to my soul. There was nothing I could do, except watch her slip away. It was as if she was filled with the greatest peace. She said, 'I love you Eedie' - it's what she called me when she was a baby. 'Tell mama I love her'. I was crying so hard I could barely see her. And she kept trying to console *me!* She kept saying 'My sweet Eedie'." Aiden broke down, and covered his face, crying so desperately that they could hear nothing but his pain.

They let him cry until he was spent, their beautiful man, overcome with grief. Finally, he was able to continue.

"I never did find the hunters. I screamed so loud and so long, I thought they would have come, but no. I carried her down to the truck and brought her home. There was so much blood. It all began again when my mother stood up from her work in the garden and saw us. She fainted to the ground. She told me it wasn't my fault, but it was, of course. My father never talks about it. I spent a lot of time in that forest looking for her, even though I knew I wouldn't find her. And I don't know why I brought her home, instead of going to the hospital. I was out of my mind with grief. God, I miss her!"

They held him until his breathing came back to normal, and he was able to smile a little. "I'm so sorry, I don't know why this all came out today. Forgive me."

"There's nothing to forgive," Sahara said. "Darling, we'll do a healing ritual after this weekend, sort this out. It *wasn't* your fault; you know that deep down. Thank you for telling us...for trusting us."

Holly nodded and hugged Aiden as tight as she could. "Let's have something to eat. Ground all this grief. I love you, I love you, I love you."

"Yes," he agreed. "Let's have something to eat and get some fresh air. Thank you. I needed to talk about it."

"You never did say her name." Holly ventured.

Aiden looked at Sahara, sure that she would guess, his blue eyes shining with the light of the Fey. "Lorelei."

But it was Holly who whispered..."Lorelei, Lara. Dagr's mother. Do you think...?"

"Yes," Aiden answered. "She was with me once more. For a little while." And he succumbed to fresh tears.

CHAPTER 55

He had to go out to find Holly's parents. They'd gotten lost, turning into Sahara's lane. He got out of his truck and greeted them heartily through the open car window.

"Just follow me. It's not far now. We have a nice big fire going for you to sit by." He smiled at the woman peering at him with great curiosity. She was nodding and said that she'd been in the car for so long that her legs had gone numb.

Aiden wondered by what happenstance Holly had managed to come from a woman she did not resemble one bit. There was a sparse familial connection in her father's face. Otherwise, he would have thought her adopted.

They spilled into the house with a bag of gifts and the perfunctory bottle of wine. Daniel and Simone Emory looked about them, he, warm and appreciative of what he saw, she, reserved, with tiny little pats for everyone's back.

"Well, Holly, it's good to finally see where you've landed!" Simone said, as she hugged her daughter.

"Hello Mother," Holly embraced her tightly. "I'm glad you're here. We're going to have the best time."

Simone cocked her head to one side like a bewildered chicken. "Well, we'll see," she clucked.

Aiden took everyone's coats and introduced Sahara. "Daniel, Simone, this is our Sahara. She lives just down that lane you turned into.

Sahara shook Daniel's hand and gave him a little wink. He returned it with a knowing smile. They liked each other immediately.

"Oh, a neighbor. I thought we were having a family dinner," Simone stuck her foot in her mouth without delay. Holly was about to retort when Simone caught her by the hand and exclaimed about the size of her ring.

"Well! Isn't that something, Daniel! You must have had to mortgage the house, Aiden. What kind of stone is that anyway?"

Aiden laughed. This truly could not be Holly's mother! "It's blue quartz."

Daniel took his wife by the elbow and sat her down by the fire. "Just rest here, Simmy, I'll pour you a glass of wine."

He has a genuine affection for her, Aiden thought, and gave Holly an encouraging nod. She was now running around straightening things that didn't need straightening at all.

Daniel brought his wife some wine and seeing that she was nicely occupied by Sahara, left for the kitchen again.

"Daniel, what would you like? We have white or red, a variety of liquor, or beer. Holly tells me that you like craft brew, I have some for you to choose from."

"Well, that's right kind of you, Aiden." Daniel clapped him on the back. "I do appreciate you making the effort."

Aiden poured the beer into a glass and handed it over. "I'm glad we have the chance to meet."

"Me too. You know, Holly's always been the apple of my eye." Holly came over just then. Daniel grinned broadly.

"I can see that." It was pretty clear that these two had something special. Holly trusted her father.

Daniel nodded his head towards Simone. "She's been kinda lonely without her baby."

"Oh Dad!" Holly nudged him with her hip. He nudged back. They laughed and hugged.

Simone looked over. "Your neighbor here has been telling me all about how popular your bakery is, Holly. Are you making those popovers I taught you when you were little?"

Daniel caught the steely look in Aiden's eye. He pulled him aside. "You'd better tell her before dinner. I know her. It'll be worse if we eat then tell."

"Of course, Daniel. Whatever you think is best," Aiden replied respectfully. He really could not bear to hear Sahara called 'your neighbor here' another time.

He took Holly by the hand and led her towards the fire. Her palms were cold. He recognised the sign of energy withdrawn; fear. He squeezed but she was too distracted to respond.

"Mom," Holly began, "I really must tell you something." She sat down beside her mother, and smoothing her hair, took a deep breath in.

Simone looked at her husband.

"Well? I thought as much..."

Holly reacted first with confusion then understanding. "No. I'm not pregnant! Truly!"

"What else could it be? I can tell that you're agitated," Simone shot back, annoyed.

"I want to tell you about my relationship with Aiden and Sahara,"

308

she stopped, letting that sink in.

Simone sat up straight as a poker. "What do you mean, Aiden *and* Sahara?"

"I mean, I am in a committed relationship with Aiden *and* Sahara. The three of us. Sahara is not only our neighbor, she's our life partner." Holly found new courage in Sahara's presence. Aiden's warrior energy poured over her.

"Do you mean in some kind of perverted polygamy?" Simone's eyes shot daggers at Aiden. "Is this the kind of man you are? Collecting women? I had a feeling that this was too good to be true. Why, you're a dirty, dirty beast! How dare you engage my daughter in this kind of sick thing! Well!" she sputtered, turning red in the face, her hands in enraged fists.

"Mother! Take that back. He's nothing of the sort. He's the best man I have ever met, aside of Father. And he's not collecting women! I'm bisexual Mother. Sahara's my lover too. And it's polyamory, not polygamy." There. It was out. But the tears were hot on Holly's face.

"You are not!" Simone screamed. "You're not! I gave birth to a perfectly normal child. Don't tell me this garbage. You're normal!" Simone's wounded ego rose violently. She stood. "I won't hear of this."

"Well you *are* hearing it. This is who you gave birth to. You can accept it or leave it. Dad has given his blessing," Holly turned pale, realizing that she had put her father in a terrible position. "I'm sorry Dad. I'm so sorry."

Daniel put up his hands. "It's ok, sweetie. It's ok."

Simone spun on him. "You knew? How could you Daniel? How could you not tell me, prepare me?"

"It wasn't for me to say. This is Holly's news and it's right that she tell you herself."

"No! Your loyalty is to me first, not to her."

Everyone drew in their breath. Sahara laid a calming hand on Aiden's arm.

"My loyalty, Simone," Daniel said ever so quietly, "is to our child when she's in need. I shouldn't have to choose. But in this case, I did, because I knew that you wouldn't support her."

"I'll never forgive you!" Simone hissed.

"Mother! You're overreacting. Being bisexual isn't wrong. Why can't you just love me as I am?"

"Because you're confused. It's sinful. God never intended it this way. Oh!"

"I don't believe in your God, Mother. I believe in something much more inclusive."

"That's convenient. What's next? Witchcraft? Rituals that sacrifice virgins? You're all a pack of sinners!" Simone looked disdainfully at Sahara. "You. You're disgusting. Stay away from my daughter."

It all happened quite quickly. Aiden's rising anger, Sahara's whispered spell, the crashing of a raven into the darkened window. Simone sat down abruptly, and although she was moving her lips, no sound came out.

"She's in shock," Daniel said. "Aiden, is there somewhere I can lie her down?"

"Yes, here." Aiden opened the door to Holly's room. "You can lay her down here. I'll bring water." He pulled Sahara aside. "What the hell is going on? You cast a spell!"

"I had to. Iona was outside. You saw the raven. When she's in protect mode, she's... Well, I cast my spell first."

"I see," Aiden said, grim. "Protecting whom, was she?"

"Always, you and me. But Holly now too. I didn't expect it, actually."

He nodded. "We'll talk about this later. Can you bring the water? I'll pour Daniel a drink."

"Of course. Aiden?"

"Yes?"

"You have to allow Holly to feel all of this. Be there for her when she needs you but give her space to experience this."

"I know. I'm learning. Thank you darling. Are you ok?"

"I am. I'm immune to such words. There is no truth to them and I know who I am."

"My tiny wisp of a woman, with the courage of a lioness."

"It's going to be fine. We'll get through this."

When Simone came out of her room later that evening, supper had been eaten. The conversation was muted around the fire, the scent of herb on the air. Daniel held out his hand to her, drawing her into his embrace.

"Feeling better?"

"I don't know," Simone looked around suspiciously. "Are you smoking pot?"

"Yes. Would you like some?" Daniel decided on humor.

"Don't be ridiculous, Daniel. I'm hungry."

"I'll make you a plate, Mother," Holly stood, her eyes puffy from crying.

"Thank you, dear," Simone said contritely, her own eyes red and swollen.

310

It was not acceptance, but it was the very first tentative step towards reconciliation. In the morning, Daniel and Simone left for the hotel that Aiden had arranged for them until they could fly back. Holly was sad that it was so, but Daniel thought it best. Her parents visited the patisserie before they left for home, and while Daniel inspected every corner with pride and genuine interest, Simone spent the time pretending to read the labels on all the preserves.

"She'll come around," Daniel said to his daughter who was tearful in his arms as they hugged good-bye.

"I miss you Dad."

"I'm going to come out again soon. And you just call me if you need anything. Although, I see that you're in good hands."

"I am. I've never been happier."

"It shows. And don't you worry about your mom. We've been talking some. She'll get past this."

"I think she's stopped loving me..."

"Oh no!" Daniel replied emphatically. "She definitely loves you. Fiercely. It's herself that she doesn't love."

CHAPTER 56

It was madness. They were like children, making preparations for Solstice. It had been decided that Richard and Iona would arrive a few days before, Richard having booked a suite at the mountain hotel, with a spectacular view towards the West. He adored mountain sunsets. They reminded him of the light across the hills in Northern England. They would gather at Aiden's for Solstice dinner and a midnight mystic ceremony.

Holly and Sahara hung lights and decorations on a fir tree outside Aiden's door. They made a garland from fresh boughs for the mantel, studded with red apples, oranges and pomegranates and strung through with fairy lights. There was a stunning wreath for the front door sent ahead by Richard. The house smelled of fresh baking and gently simmering chutneys. Iona had sent an array of bird feeders that were covered now in hungry nuthatches and titmice, chickadees and wood-warblers, mourning doves and woodpeckers. Grouse came out of the woods to feast on acorns fallen from the oak nearby. The Aspen wood was alive with rabbits and deer. Even nature was caught up in the excitement of the coming Winter Solstice.

Aiden surprised Holly and Sahara with a spruce tree planted in a bucket. He refused to cut anything down. He acclimatized it slowly to the house, and when they were asleep, decorated it with lights and pine cones, silver ribbon and hand-crafted feathery owls. There were strings of tiny knitted mittens too. He lit the tree and waited for them to come downstairs in the early morning, with only the fire in the hearth and a few candles strewn about to make for a cozy ambiance.

"Ooooh!" Holly whispered.

"Owls!" Sahara cried.

Aiden grinned as they rounded the corner and spied him sitting on the sofa.

"It's sooooo beautiful!" Holly sighed.

Sahara touched the little owls. "The house smells divine. Mmmm, there's nothing like having the forest inside."

"I can't wait for tonight!" Holly said.

"What's tonight?" Aiden asked.

"We put the presents under the tree!"

"Oh, were there supposed to be presents? Damn!" Aiden teased as Holly climbed on top of him and swatted him with a pillow.

"I haven't had presents for years!" Holly said.

"Pardon?" Aiden sat her down, trying to ignore the breast that was peeking out her nightie. She was wearing long, over the knee socks, and her hair was tousled from sleep. She was irresistibly sexy.

"My parents have always sent me money for the holidays."

"Really?" Aiden thought of the overstuffed stockings he'd hidden in the shed. Didn't they send you a stocking?"

"Pfft! Stocking! I'm too old!"

"You know that your hungry little breast is peeking out?" He couldn't stand it anymore, he wanted to touch it.

"Oh, it is?" Holly revealed the other, twisting her raspberry tips. "I'm also not wearing any undies." She pulled up her nightie, legs spread as she straddled him. Her clit sat jauntily exposed to the air.

Aiden growled. "I think I'll win if you're going to play cat and mouse with me." His hand drifted softly along her thigh, careful not to touch her sex. He smiled, all charm and seduction.

She pushed his hand away, and brought it to her lips. "Want to play?"

"Yes, but you'll wait."

"Why should I wait?" She kissed the tender of his palm.

"Because we're going to town."

"For what? We have everything we need."

"I'm taking you two for that massage we never did get. I'll lay you out for my pleasure later tonight."

"On an altar, like a virgin sacrificed?" Holly laughed at the memory of her mother's words.

"If you like." Aiden's look promised satisfaction, and made her heart beat faster.

"I would like. To be taken."

"To be ravaged and played with as we wish?"

"Mmm, Aiden!"

"I agree on these conditions."

Holly cocked an eyebrow in question.

"That you won't be allowed to reciprocate, no matter how much you beg. Receiving only. That you spend the day thinking about what we might do to you. I want you wet and fully ready for our attention, or you'll be punished. That you wear this all day and meditate on how you belong to me." He reached into his pocket and pulled out a dainty silver anklet, with tiny bells attached. "Wherever you go, you'll hear this anklet, and remember that you're mine and that when it pleases me, I can take you." He took the offered ankle and placed the gift upon it.

"Ooh. I like this game!" Holly pressed her legs together, fully aroused. She looked over at Sahara, who was devouring the scene from where she was sitting by the hearth.

"Ok. Get dressed." Aiden stood and took his shirt off. Ripped to the bone, he was all animal instinct and need. "Get up!" he motioned to Sahara, who followed him up the stairs, stumbling in the wake of his sexual magnetism.

They left Holly anticipating the day ahead.

CHAPTER 57

Surrendered I reach fullness. Vulnerable I reach sacredness. Naked I find integrity. Exposed I am transformed. This is the madness of love

"What is it?" Sahara held the package in her hands. It was square and flat.

"Take a look." Aiden kissed Sahara's flushed cheek. She and Holly had opened all his presents but this one. He had spoiled them, and it had delighted him to do so, each gift meaningfully chosen.

There were piles of books, elegant lingerie and the most delicious candles and soaps. There was the membership to the spa, and tickets to the opera in Denver. There were stockings full of magic supplies for Sahara and exotic ingredients for Holly; Spanish saffron and the best French lavender, Madagascar vanilla beans and Honduran nutmeg. And now this one last box that had been hidden behind all the other things under the tree.

'Open it!" Holly echoed.

She obeyed. From the box emerged a hand carved sign to hang outside her front door. It was made of Aspen wood, and lovingly polished with Tung oil. On its face, the words *Hidden Hollow*; below them, a simple mark - XX.

"Do you like it, darling?"

She nodded, a lump of emotion in her throat.

"Is it the right gift - is it the right time, my love?"

"It is...I'm...overwhelmed."

"What does it mean?" Holly asked, aware that something special was happening. The energy between her lovers was suddenly deep and serious.

"It means so much." Sahara stared into Aiden's eyes. "The X is a rune symbol. Gebo. It means gift, and speaks of a mystical union, a sacred exchange of sexual energy...and...marriage. Two XX's are the secret mark for the dwelling of a witch, a covenstead. You made this..." Sahara fell into Aiden's arms.

"I did. I love you so very much. I would marry you in the traditional way if I thought you wanted it, but I know that you don't, and especially not a ring. This is my commitment to you...a symbol of our journey together."

315

Sahara buried her head in his chest. She allowed herself to feel all of what he was saying with this gift. He was thoughtful, greatly sensitive to her nature and beliefs. He was giving her all that he could without overstepping her boundaries. She loved him for the intelligent and intense man that he was, always looking to her hearts longings.

"It is the perfect gift. I accept. I wish to be yours. So it has been spoken, so mote it be." She lifted feather soft lips to his.

Aiden's embrace and tear-softened eyes spoke his emotions. He couldn't bring words to the moment, just holding each other was enough.

"Does this mean what I think it means?" Holly whispered.

Aiden and Sahara burst into joyful laughter and pulled her into their embrace.

"Yes, sweetness! It does. Come kiss me!" Sahara beamed.

"Darlings! I'm so happy, SO happy! Aiden, you beautiful, beautiful man! What a surprise!" She kissed them both, and asked if it was too early in the day for champagne.

"A wee bottle of Prosecco will have to do," Sahara said, producing it. "Later, we can do more celebrating."

They drank to each other's happiness, to life, to love, to marriage - however unconventional - and to the coming years together.

CHAPTER 58

Sahara had Aiden install the sign right away.

They walked over to her place, hand in hand, falling in the snow, racing with Ulfred as he ran ahead, tail held high.

Aiden hung it to the left of her door, close to the kitchen window. Whenever he came in and out, he would see the symbol of their love. It was surreal, this new reality. He was a married man. He liked how it felt on his heart. He knew now how long he had waited for this moment. The only thing that could improve this feeling would be the day he would marry Holly. He smiled to himself, thinking about how his dreams had unfolded, and how fortunate he was to have found love with two incredible, strong women, each of them unique and great teachers. He was grateful beyond measure.

Lost in thought, he stood quietly contemplating the sign.

"Shall we go inside?" Sahara's eyes twinkled mischievously.

He laughed and caught her up in his arms. Sahara wound her hands around his neck. Holly opened the door, and Aiden carried his bride over the threshold.

"You are a properly wedded woman now, my love...or as properly as you'll allow," he kissed her soundly.

"And you're a proper rogue, not giving me a chance to put flowers in my hair or any naughty lace things underneath!"

"There'll be time for lace later," Aiden promised.

They filled Willow's dishes, and gave him his Solstice treats. Aiden checked the electric baseboard heaters and the thermostat, making sure there was enough warmth to keep the plumbing safe.

"Why don't we bring Willow to my place?"

"No, he wouldn't like it. And we better head back, or we won't be having dinner until midnight!"

"At midnight we're doing ceremony," Aiden reminded.

"Do you think Iona will let me participate?" Holly asked, as they began tying their scarves and putting on their boots.

"It's not up to Iona," Aiden replied.

"Tell me more about Solstice?" Holly took his hand as they started out towards the aspens. The sky was grey with clouds of indigo, the trees in the distance stark against the winter canvas. They breathed in icy cold air.

"It's when the sun is born again, on the shortest and darkest day of the year. It's symbolic of when light first came into the world, and is spoken of by many spiritual teachings, each one having their own interpretation of it. You're probably most familiar with the Christian version, but the Persians, the Egyptians and many others had their own 'births of the sun, or 'son' as it were, and they were all born of a virgin. Really, it's about man's awakening, about our own self-realization as spiritual beings, not only as humans in a physical world. It's what Jesus talked about when he mentioned being born again. And we are all born of a star in the Milky Way, did you know that? Next time we're out for a midnight walk, we can look. It's quite profound, the time of Solstice." Aiden looked down at Holly, wide-eyed and rosy cheeked.

"I'm looking forward to being part of it tonight!"

"Me too. It's going to be very special, and powerful, with Sahara in the lead."

"Oh, you aren't going to lead? But I thought you were..."

"No. In our work, yes. But tonight, I want Sahara to guide us. I admire her wisdom, I'd like her to take us to whatever regions of magic she desires."

He turned around, looking for his bride, and urged her along. "Come, my lady! This is no time for daydreaming!"

But she loved to walk behind them, to see them hand in hand. She loved the sexiness of Aiden's broad back, it reminded her of that first day when she'd watched him return to his homestead, and replayed their meeting in her mind's eye. He was all the things she had imagined him to be and so much more. He was a man in every sense, dependable, a gentleman, honest and true. She was proud of the way he adored their shared beloved and that he was capable of such romance. She loved his hands, accustomed to hard work. She loved his body, and how he owned hers. She loved the scent of his hair, and how it lay against his muscular shoulders - how he raked his fingers thought it, and often wore that pensive expression.

There was nothing she could find true fault with. He wasn't perfect, but what he was still honing, was simply his evolving humanity. It made her happy to see Holly's hand in his, because it belonged there and because it was safe there as well.

Tonight, they would break bread as friends and family even though their togetherness was complicated and still dangerous. But what could they do except forge ahead into the life they had chosen? Was there any point in avoiding courage, in entertaining fear? No. They were born to the road less travelled.

318

CHAPTER 59

"What're you doing?" Holly wiped her eyes. Cutting onions was the worst!

"Putting away the spoils. The two of you spent far too much," Aiden grinned, with an armful of gifts ready to head upstairs.

"Want to return anything? Ingrate!" Holly laughed.

"Well, nooo." Between books and music and cufflinks and stunningly tailored shirts, he had been showered with their good taste.

"I have one more thing for you, anyway," Holly said.

"No! Darling, really." He kissed her ear. "I have everything I want right here."

"There's no point in protesting...as soon as I'm done with making myself cry, I'm going to give it to you."

"Why don't I make us some coffee, and we can take a proper afternoon coffee and cake break."

"Like proper Europeans, even though we're not."

"Although I was, once," Aiden mused.

"Yes. Do you find it strange, that one lifetime you lived in France, or so the last regression insinuates, and that I lived in France? And Richard has a place in France. All these synchronicities."

"I'm no longer surprised by any of it," Aiden said. "It's a tangled web, and we're all caught in it."

"Iona and Richard will be here soon...is anybody watching the time?" Sahara chimed in. "Why don't I make that plate of cakes, and the two of you do whatever it is you have up your sleeve."

"Do you know what it is?" Aiden wondered.

"Nope. She doesn't tell me anything," Sahara joked.

"Wench!" Holly took her apron off, and washed her hands, squeezing lemon onto them to cut the smell of onions. "Ok, give me a minute to get it."

They met again in their favorite spot, under the stairs, cocooned in books and artful leaded glass cupboards, wall sconces with beeswax candles and the smell of leather and herb.

Aiden waited patiently, dressed in blue slacks tailored to fit his slim hips and long legs; and a crisp shirt, rolled up at the wrists. His hair was tied with ribbon matching his pants. He could have easily fit in this century or that. Sahara wondered if he had any business looking this disarming - she could have spent the afternoon just staring at him.

Holly handed him a small box, and kissed his forehead, at the third eye. "You've given me so much. This didn't cost a fortune, so don't even bother lecturing me about how I shouldn't have. It's just a little something to reciprocate my ring from you...not that anything could."

He took it from her, and waited a moment before opening it. The energy of whatever was in the box was immense.

"Thank you sweet thing," he kissed her hand.

"Open it! I can't wait any longer!"

"Ok."

He lifted the lid. Sahara leaned in. An antique silver bracelet lay cushioned in the box. It was clear that it was very old, a medieval design of a foxtail chain with hammered capping and clasp.

"Oh, Holly!" Sahara gasped. "It's stunning!"

Aiden could barely get his words out. "Where did you find this? Darling, this is incredibly unusual. This kind of design is rare. The craftsmanship is exquisite."

Holly put the bracelet on his wrist. It was a perfect fit. Aiden absorbed the energy, there was no doubt in his mind that Holly had stumbled on something that had belonged to a man who knew magic.

"I found it in Claire's antique store. She said she got in at an estate auction in New England, on her last trip east...Massachusetts, I think. Probably European she said, handmade. It reminded me of you immediately. Rugged and yet somehow refined. And in a way, it made me think of Dagr. I wanted to give you something that would remind us of our engagement, and suit your magic."

"Massachusetts, you say?" Aiden mumbled.

"I think so. You can ask her."

Aiden gathered Holly in. "I don't even have any words. Thank you, darling." His mouth surrendered to her happy kisses. "What a magnificent gift. I'm just amazed at its energy. Sahara, touch it, you can literally feel its breath."

Sahara smoothed the chain on Aiden's wrist. "I feel it! Incredible." *A sorcerer's ally...Massachusetts...Salem, I'm sure of it* was her telepathic thought. Aiden gave a small nod of agreement.

The sound of tires on crisp snow brought them out of their intimate moment. Aiden took Holly's hand and vowed, "Yours. Thank you, I will cherish it."

The strangeness of seeing Richard in Aiden's home struck Sahara poignantly. He was, in his usual manner, brisk yet warm, animal and gentleman. She grew warm under his stare as he raked her over with an appreciative glance. He was shameless. Dressed impeccably, Richard had an immediate effect on Holly as well. Sahara could tell.

For there Holly stood, in her very short, body hugging woollen dress, all bare legs and high heels. Her hair was piled messily on top of her head, and she wore the chandelier earrings she had chosen for their first dinner and ménage a trois. Irresistible to everyone in the room. She was shy, her cheeks in a blush. Sahara pretended not to notice how Holly almost curtsied before Richard as he bent over her hand.

Sahara turned to Iona and took her cape, standing on tiptoe to kiss her lightly tinted lips.

"Solstice blessings, my dear."

"And to you," Iona purred. "This dress!"

Sahara lowered her eyes. *I knew you'd like it.* She had chosen it with care. Usually preferring black, this time she wore a classic cocktail dress in pale lavender, a low scooped neck perfectly accentuating her small breasts scandalously pushed up by a black lace bra, which peeked just so from underneath. The bra and panties were a gift from Aiden, and she felt quite delicious in them. Her tiny frame in black heels made a seductive picture. Iona licked her lips and gave Sahara one more kiss, this one lingering for a breathless second.

"And you..." Sahara admired Iona's choice of a long, slim, black skirt, designed to emphasize her perfect round bottom, and an ivory cashmere sweater with two tiny black buttons on each three-quarter length sleeve, breasts untethered, a low v front exposing velvety suppleness. Sahara fought a fantasy of those pert-as-an-eraser-top nipples in her mouth. She turned just in time to see Aiden noticing those same temptations.

He came forward to greet their guests. *He looks immense beside Iona's winsome slimness. He could crush her with his weight,* Sahara thought, and immediately became wet imagining Iona at Aiden's mercy. *Oh my.* Her cheeks burned red. She left them at the door where Iona was admiring Aiden's bracelet with great interest.

"What have the two of you been up to this week?" Richard asked, taking the glass of wine poured by Holly. His hand brushed hers and she blushed once more.

"The usual. A half-dozen spells before breakfast, slay a dragon by noon and return home for supper." Sahara quipped, and accepted his kiss on her cheek. She winked at Holly, whose luscious mouth turned up into a smile. Flirting was her game. And she was in the mood for naughtiness. They were safe here, with Aiden to keep order among the rabble.

"I brought something for the two of you," Richard reached into his shirt pocket, and pulled out four pearls in a tiny silk pouch. "You can have these set for earrings, if you like. They're real, no need to bite them," he joked. "It's just a little thing, for Solstice."

They were perfect and obviously dear, but he made light of it. "Don't worry, I have something for Aiden too, I would have bought him pearls but I don't think he'd look good in them." He rolled up his sleeves, getting comfortable. They both stared at those tattooed forearms. It was quite obvious that Holly needed a drink. Sahara poured them each a glass as Holly threw an impetuous hug around Richard's neck, whispering 'thank you'. She quickly pulled back, avoiding his amused expression, and took the wine from Sahara.

"Stop being a brat, Richard," Sahara said. "You're making Holly blush."

"I'm sure that I don't know what you're talking about," Richard grinned.

"Pull back that rogue energy. It's all over us."

"Ah, that. Not sure that I can among such beautiful women."

Aiden and Iona joined them, and once everyone had a drink, they gathered by the fire and toasted to the season.

Iona was next with gifts. She had a mystic card set and essential oils for Holly, sacred sage and crystals for Sahara, a leather-bound journal for Aiden. "For your grimoire," she said. "And for the long winter, please accept this gift of herb. It's my very own blend. You must keep it in this pyramid container," she added, and produced one from her bag.

The biggest surprise was Richard's gift to Aiden. After that the evening took a decided turn, for no one including Holly could keep from anticipating the magic to be woven; such was the impact of the rolled up canvas in a gallery tube that Richard fetched from his car.

"Now Aiden, if you don't like it, I'm not going to be upset. I picked this painting up in France the last time I was there, and even though I'm not a witch like the three of you, I have excellent intuition when it comes to art. I think this belongs to you. I thought of you the instant I saw it. It's very old. The gallery owner I bought if from had no inkling of its worth. Iona hasn't seen it yet."

Aiden took the offered gift and sat with it in his hands for a few minutes.

"If you don't see it the way I do, and can't imagine hanging it, I..."

"I know. Thank you." Their eyes met. Richard's wore the mark of excitement. Art, and finding perfect owners for it was one of the things he lived for. He was sure that he wasn't wrong, because even he had recognized what was in the painting. Aiden felt a deep longing, but he knew not for what. There was no point in delaying. He unrolled the canvas with great care.

"Was I right, does this belong to you?" Richard asked.

Aiden could only nod his head. He passed the canvas to Sahara.

Iona and Holly came around to see. Iona walked away, and stood by the window, staring into the night.

"What is this place?" Holly wanted to know, the scene in the painting of a stately home on a wooded hill quite evocative.

"I don't know if it is *the* place," Aiden said, "but it's bringing back a strong feeling of where Dagr settled in France. The color of the stone would have been like this, and a chateau on a hill, as we discovered in the last regression. Remember Iona?" He called her over, to take another look.

They were all surprised at how much Iona had paled.

Richard stood and gently steered her to sit by him. "Are you alright sweetheart? Can I get you anything?" He took her hand and peered with some worry into her face.

"It's just a bit of a shock, seeing this. I'm being silly, it's nothing."

But neither Richard nor Sahara nor Aiden believed her. They had still not spoken about the revelations of the last regression, and that she would naturally be feeling sensitive about Arinn's part in the miscarriage.

Holly set to making Iona a cup of hot herbal tea.

"We should eat. There's still so much ahead of us tonight," Sahara noted, standing up, and lingering a passing hand over Aiden's shoulders. Richard had been right, the image in the painting was part of their past in some way. It had cast a new light on their evening. She had had an idea.

They sat by candlelight, Aiden having set up an altar in the middle of the living room. At each of their places, sat a small bundle of red-berried holly and ivy, denoting the season, and a tumbler full of mead. They had engaged the wisdom of the herb, asking for direction and finding calm within its heady aroma.

Sahara offered Holly a supportive glance. Tonight she would become a true part of their circle, as they shared their ceremony with her, calling upon the Sun God, embracing their own darkness and making way for the light that would slowly begin to lengthen the days once more.

She cast the circle. She invoked the Four Directions. She led them through a greeting of Odin, Thor and Freya. She chanted in an ancient tongue. The others sat in awe of her beauty, her dedication to her craft, to the energy that she raised as they tumbled towards the spells she had told them she would cast. They trusted her. She was the wise priestess. Richard and Aiden could barely tear their eyes away from her. They shared a silent moment acknowledging their love of this spectacular woman. It was too difficult to hide.

Holly, placed between Richard and Aiden, absorbed everything and with great pride in her beloved. Sahara was the gift she had been handed by the Universe and she couldn't imagine her life without her.

At the end of her ceremony and spell casting, Sahara asked that they share a kiss to seal their intentions for the coming season. It seemed so natural, to end this way. They had entered into magic together and the meeting of the spiritual with the mundane could be sealed with kisses, depending on the group present and intended outcomes.

The herb had prepared them for soulfulness. Sahara began, as the leader. She turned towards Richard, and taking his hands in hers, lifted her mouth to his, kissing him sweetly, his mouth opening to hers when it became clear that this would be more than a light touching of lips. They were stunning together. With the plaintive music in the background, everyone else came to the slow realization of what would happen next. No one dared break the circle. Holly waited, unsure, a little delirious with expectation. Richard turned toward her.

Cupping her chin lightly, with eyes open, he took his first, delicate taste of her lips. He pulled back to give her a chance to find safety in the moment. Aware of Aiden, who had let go of Holly so she could turn towards the kiss, he explored her mouth, willing her to open her eyes also. She did, and fell into his. He hadn't expected her to be so skilled with her tongue, and it was his turn to feel the surge of sexual energy that she had already succumbed to. They separated with Holly's hand running gently over his face. Richard accepted Iona's slight nod of the head. He had her blessing.

Next, Holly turned to Aiden, and welcomed his embrace. They

held for a long time, the music soothing. *My darling, I love you so.*

Aiden took her kisses, and returned them with passion. Sahara began to hum, a haunting melody, one that evoked the warrior from Aiden's past. When he let go of Holly, she was shaken, broken open by the two men who flanked her. In this moment, she was ready to open to a new knowing. She was flying on the wings of discovery. There was no sin in this kind of sharing. It was like the flight of a butterfly, freedom, innocence, love. She could let go of 'should we', because in this circle, there was safety, there was lust, there was love and there was sacredness.

If there was a most dangerous moment, it was when Aiden turned towards Iona. There was so much to consider. How would Richard react? This would be his first truly visceral encounter with Iona's need for another man. Even in this setting, his reaction was unpredictable. Aiden sought Iona's mouth fully aware of his beloved beside him, of the anticipation in Iona's eyes, and his honest realization that he wanted it to happen. He had wanted it after that time in Iona's stairwell. Once, after all, was not enough. It had only made him curious. Oh, he could keep from submitting to his desires. He had character, strong will and honesty to spare. But given permission, he was a willing participant.

He stepped closer, then let her come the rest of the way to him. She stood on tip toe. She grazed her cheek across his. She sniffed in his hair, and looked truthfully into his eyes. *My lord.* With a low growl, he met her lips. He felt Richard's move towards them energetically, then recede. He sensed Holly's pounding heart, her curiosity. He basked in Sahara's strength and wisdom. She had orchestrated it, this safe space for them to explore, knowing that all of them were guilty of lascivious thoughts. She had given them room in her magic to be authentic. Iona returned Aiden's kiss as he had expected, with the finesse of a skilled lover and the intensity of a sorceress. But more than all that, he felt her sadness.

The perfect finale to this surreptitious drama, was the kiss between Iona and Sahara. The others could only witness it with joy and wonderment. For they were as ethereal beings, joined together in loveliness, the light of the Fey shining upon them, goddesses - mystics, in sweet seduction.

There was an audible release of breath when Sahara finally turned to them and announced that now she intended to return them to that morning so long ago, when Dagr and his lovers left the Oracle Wood for good. They mustn't worry, she said, because she had asked

Pan to join them. And as she said it, he appeared, greatly diminished in size so as not to frighten Holly, but causing her to exclaim her surprise regardless.

"I'm so very tired," she proclaimed, and curled up at Aiden's feet, fast asleep.

"All is ready for our journey back. We leave as friends and return as friends. We must know what became of us, and one of us has already uncovered the truth. It is time for us all to be on the same footing. If we are to be magic workers together, we must trust each other and there must be only truth between us. Ready?" She held out her hands and they joined in their circle once more.

CHAPTER 60

"If light is in your heart, you will find your way home." - Rumi

He would miss this mist. As much as it was cold, it was also a reminder of the heavens. The feeling of clouds settling like so many blankets on fields and hills and forests was eerily comforting.

Dagr led his horse down the root gnarled path, Arinn and Brigida on the back of the great beast. The few possessions that they were taking—a few extra garments and the most precious of dried roots and remedies, their magic tools—were bundled in a blanket and tied behind Brigida.

He noticed that Brigida had her head laid sadly against Arinn's back, her arms wound around her lover's waist, humming quietly to herself.

She's afraid. Sad. I did this to her. There were many times when Dagr questioned his wisdom in living his beliefs.

Arinn sat straight and alert to the forest sounds. She gripped Brigida's hands close to her, keeping her as warm as she could, offering comfort. Now and again she would look towards Dagr and try to extract a smile. But he couldn't smile, and he couldn't look her in the eye. His own sadness over what he had discovered was so overwhelming, that he couldn't even imagine how he would ever be able to tell her that he knew. To even voice her betrayal seemed vile.

When they reached a smoother path, he jumped on the horse and urged him into a canter. They had to reach their meeting point before the dawn. Dagr thanked the gods for his large and capable steed. Richard would bring another, and their disguises. The days ahead were dangerous at best. A few days ride to the coast meant the inevitable wear on the body, cold, wet and the possibility of assailants. He knew that none of them were looking forward to any of it. But soon, they would have a saner life. It was his one comforting thought.

At least while riding, he didn't have to speak to Arinn, or look in her eyes. His heart broke all over again as he felt her warmth behind him, and the sure way she held onto his waist. His love for her beat in one direction and his disappointment in another. How could he reconcile the two?

Coming out of the woods and into the clearing, Dagr squinted to see two horsemen coming upon them at great speed. His hands tightened on the reigns. Hopefully, that was Richard and the manservant who was bringing the extra horse. To make sure, he led them back into the trees, and prepared his sword.

Richard's familiar whistle brought them out.

They embraced quickly, neither of them ready for goodbyes.

"Who's your man?" Dagr nodded towards the aging servant on horseback.

"He's safe...deaf. His speech is unintelligible. Hannah produced him."

"Oh. Hannah," Dagr said sadly. "I should have liked to have seen her again."

"Don't think now. Just get yourself to the coast. Here are the papers for the passage, and a purse of gold. For the love of God, stay safe." Richard looked at Brigida, who was sobbing uncontrollably at seeing him.

Dagr lifted her from the horse and briefly held her. "Say your goodbyes," he whispered in her ear. He made room for Richard to embrace her. He lifted Arinn off next, her hands on his shoulders warm and trusting.

"Do you wish for us to ride together, Brigida and me?" Arinn asked Dagr, still worried at his coolness.

"No, my lady."

"What is your plan?" Richard asked, feeling their tension.

Dagr had made up his mind in the split of a second, knowing deep down that this was the only way. He braced himself against the pain that was about to sear his soul.

"Arinn is going back with you, Richard." The words were incredulous to his ears, almost as if someone else had spoken them.

In the bedlam that followed, the cries of confusion, the tears, the questions, all that Dagr heard was the tearing of hearts.

"What in Christ's name are you talking about? Have you finally taken leave of all your senses?" Richard barked.

Dagr could only answer in one way. He pulled the packet of pennyroyal from his cloak. Shoving it towards Arinn, he demanded an answer.

She buckled to her knees. Brigida fainted in Richard's arms.

"Will somebody explain to me what is going on?" Richard roared, grappling to keep Brigida upright.

"This!" Dagr cried, tears blinding him. "I found pennyroyal sewn into Arinn's cloak. Brigida has lost her child once more."

"No!" Richard cried. "Why?" He stared fiercely at Arinn, angered beyond comprehension.

She shrank back. "I did not wish it so...I grew jealous...the fairies told me that I would, but I did not believe it. Dagr you must know that I *would not*, if I could have helped it! Please...do not separate us! Please, my lord, I beg you!" Arinn's tears fell bitter and raw. She held onto his boots, desperately splayed on the wet, cold ground before him.

He lifted her, reeling from the shock of his own words, and limp as she was now, thrust her towards Richard once more. "There is no time to explain the whole of it, Richard. Take her! I beseech you, care for her well." When Richard shook his head in disbelief, he added, "I vowed to protect Brigida and I will. I must."

"Is your damned vow more important than our love? Dagr! Look at me! Surely you can trust me. I promise you, my lord!" Arinn shouted, overwhelmed by the coming loneliness of her heart. She could not, would not, be away from them.

"I do not trust you, my lady, and our love is only as good as our trust." Dagr turned away, terrified of the hurt in her eyes. He loved her, oh, he loved her so much that he would rather die than inflict this impossibility on her. But he had to, for Brigida's safety.

"Dagr, think!" Richard pleaded. Brigida was coming to. He could not imagine her distress. "This will kill her."

"Richard, I must do this and you must trust me. As your brother in arms, I ask you to stand by my side."

Richard looked to the rising sun. Time was of the essence. Perhaps he could bring Arinn out later...when Dagr had calmed down. Yes! He could get him to see reason later. After they were settled, this mess could be worked out. "God damn you Dagr!" In one swift move, he lifted Arinn to his horse's back. She fought him, screaming, pleading; twisting back down to the ground.

Brigida came to, and remembering what happened, clambered into Arinn's embrace.

"Forgive me! My lady, forgive me," Arinn pleaded, wild eyed, the horror of their parting unbearable.

Brigida cradled her, forgave her. She understood. It was the price Arinn had agreed to pay for her healing. It was unfair, sickening, that her voice would cost this much. She wept hot tears upon the woman whose every breath had been her solace. She kissed her fervently, hanging on with sharp nails that cut into Arinn's skin. Then standing, with one last distraught look at the fierce man whose arms held Arinn prisoner, she turned to Dagr, and offered her hand.

329

"We must be on our way, my lord."

Shaken, and with blinding tears hot on his face, Dagr placed Brigida on the back of his great war horse and leapt on behind her. Circling Richard, he took one last look at his beloved, then galloped away, to the gut wrenching screams that would haunt his ears forever.

Coming soon...

The Wilderness Years

Awoken to his magic, Aiden remembers his talent for mysticism. Falling easily into his memories of medieval life and Holly's desire to be schooled in alchemy, he becomes the irresistible teacher once more.

While cauldrons bubble, friendships deepen between five fated friends - but what will become of their lust and their love remains to be seen. Sahara's consummate need for an authentic life is the magic that steers their journey.

ABOUT THE AUTHOR

photoworks by Sara Deyell

Monika Carless is an incurable writer and a solitary practitioner of the Wise Woman Tradition. She is a lover of the natural world and the mystery of life. Mother to two free-range daughters and partner to a magical man, Monika is happiest sharing from the heart and inspiring authenticity. Born in Poland and now living in Canada, this free-spirited rebel is interested in challenging social norms and dispelling taboos. Monika has been published in a range of magazines on a variety of topics including *relationships, intimacy, spirituality, self-empowerment,* and *environment.*

Follow Monika's writing:
www.elephantjournal.com (Featured Author)
Blog: Simply Solitary @ https://simplysolitary.wordpress.com/
Instagram: @monikacarless,
FB: https://www.facebook.com/MonikaCarlessAuthor/

42116794R00192

Made in the USA
Middletown, DE
01 April 2017